GLOR

RUINS

GLORIOUS RUINS

A Novel

JUDITHE LITTLE

LAKE UNION
PUBLISHING

Text copyright © 2025 by Judithe Little
All rights reserved.

Published by Lake Union Publishing, Seattle

www.apub.com

Amazon, the Amazon logo, and Lake Union Publishing are trademarks of Amazon.com, Inc., or its affiliates.

EU product safety contact:
Amazon Media EU S. à r.l.
38, avenue John F. Kennedy, L-1855 Luxembourg
amazonpublishing-gpsr@amazon.com

ISBN-13: 9781662528125 (paperback)
ISBN-13: 9781662528132 (digital)

Cover design by Kathleen Lynch/Black Kat Design
Cover images: © suteishi, © FrankvandenBergh / Getty; © Laura Ranftler / ArcAngel

Printed in the United States of America

To Misia, for the recognition you deserve

Chapter One

Sometimes, the most momentous events of one's life slip in unexpectedly. A gift from the gods when you are at your lowest and certain all is lost. That was what happened to me.

I was Marie Sophie Olga Zénaïde Godebska Natanson Edwards. In France, they called me the Queen of Paris. Proust called me a Monument of History. Those who knew me well called me Misia.

For more than a decade, I had presided over the Parisian art world. I was known for my salons, gatherings in my home where I assembled, nurtured, and inspired a coterie of then-unknown artists, names taken for granted now. Toulouse-Lautrec. Renoir. Bonnard. Vuillard. I sat as their muse and their confidante while they painted me at my piano, in my garden, or lounging on a chair in deep thought— thinking, usually, of how to solve their financial and artistic problems. They were struggling then, poor and tormented with self-doubt. I encouraged, insisting they not listen when critics scoffed at Renoir's works, said Bonnard's landscapes were hung upside down, and called Vuillard's interiors too flat. I saw brilliance when no one else did. Once, I purchased 150 of Van Gogh's paintings to aid his brother's widow because no one else wanted them.

My father was a famed sculptor. I had been born with his eye. But that was all I got of worth from him.

While my instincts for discerning quality art were exceptional, my instincts for discerning quality husbands were not. I was in the midst of catastrophe. My husband had gone mad for a young, beguiling actress. Even I found her ravishing. I had a photograph of her that I kept at my dressing table. I spent hours trying to look like her, fixing my hair as she did, even wearing the same clothes. He would go to her, then come back to me, promising to stay, then go back again. In the end, after months of drama and scandal—the newspapers reported on my travails as if they were weekly installments of the latest melodrama—he discarded me for her. It was my second divorce. I was thirty-six years old, at an age I'd always presumed I'd be certain of my future. Instead, I was lost.

It was in the face of this new reality that the unexpected arrived: a man at my doorstep wearing an enormous sombrero, a white suit, and a Spanish cape. He had come with a mutual friend, Jean-Louis Forain.

I couldn't help but laugh at the man's ensemble, but not in a mocking way. I relished eccentricity. Walking over my threshold, he laughed as well, his voice deep and full of bass. He presented himself as José María Sert. "Senora," he said with a bow, his arm making a courtly sweep.

I knew of him. He was a muralist, a few years younger than I, a Spaniard of growing renown for his opulent, baroque-styled visions of biblical, historical, and mythical themes he painted on giant-size panels. A few days before, Forain had suggested we meet.

I ushered the two men into my drawing room, where my maid, Aimée, took Sert's hat and cape. I sat on the divan and gestured for them to sit as well.

"Senora," Sert said, taking a chair. He leaned forward, his gaze on mine, not looking about. "You surprise me. Will you find it pompous if I say that, seeing you in person, I realize the genius of Renoir has fallen short?"

"I think most would find it pompous," I said. "But I'm curious to know what you mean."

"Usually, the subjects of famed works don't live up to the portrait," he went on, a Catalonian accent enlivening his French. "For you, senora, the portraits are exquisite, but the opposite is true. They don't live up to you. You have an essence to you, something *especial* that can't be captured in the limited confines of a canvas."

I was always able to judge false flattery. Instinct told me that was not what this was. And I appreciated the observation. From an artistic perspective, the portraits were sublime. But from my perspective, I found my jaw too square, my nose too straight, my cheeks too plump. I was known as an unconventional beauty, but did I truly look like that? I too had felt—or hoped—I could not be adequately captured in the two-dimensional.

Forain backed up instinct. "Sert," he said, "does not give false compliments."

"Good," I said, ready to take the focus off me. "Neither do I. Monsieur Sert, I saw your exhibition of the Vic Cathedral panels at the Grand Palais. I had heard about you, that you are not a canvas painter but create colossal murals swirling with characters and creatures of all kinds. I found your exhibition very brave."

"Brave?" he said, tilting his head with a curious smile.

"To display such immense panels in a place known for presenting small paintings. It's not something most would do."

"Senora, I follow my own guide. I am not a sheep."

"It appears you are not. Most artists wouldn't have the nerve to take on the wall decoration of an entire building, and a cathedral at that. A place of God. Most would find it too intimidating."

"I am not most, senora. But alas, the critics were scathing. Did you read the reviews? They called the colors 'heavy and vulgar.' They said the panels were not 'attractive.'"

I waved a hand. "Critics. They're used to seeing tortured renderings of bowls of fruit. They couldn't imagine the full effect of your frescoes in a vast space like a cathedral. And I dare say, attractive is not the goal.

Breathtaking, inspiring, humbling. That is the goal, and I found them to be so."

He put a hand to his heart. "Senora," he said. "You understand."

With much energy and enthusiasm, he told me of his inspiration. The Great Italian Masters, he said, were his teachers. He called them his *maestros*.

On Veronese: "Do you know, senora, that his paintings usually include a parrot? Yes! He considered it his signature."

On Tiepolo: "A depicter of optimism and allegories, of light and air and the most subtle, voluptuous shades of pink."

On Tintoretto: "He painted so rapidly, so boldly, they called him *Il Furioso*."

This man. He talked so much. At first, I found it irritating. But as he went on, I found it charming. I was amused by the theater of him. It had been a long while since I had been amused by anything. I was perfectly happy to sit back and listen.

As a young art student, he continued, he'd explored every corner of Italy, every important gallery, church, palazzo. "One time, in Calabria, I hadn't been paying attention and ran out of money. My horse was starving. I had to give it the straw hat off my head." His tone was serious, but the twinkle in his eye left me questioning the truth of this tale. I suspected that was what he wanted.

I played along. "Well, if it was as large as the one you brought with you this afternoon, he must have had quite a supper."

"He did, senora. You see, it's useful to wear a sombrero such as mine. You never know when you might come upon a starving animal."

I laughed, and he said, "Did you know, senora, that technically I have the right to keep my hat on in the presence of the King of Spain and to enter a church on horseback?"

I had no idea how to respond. I didn't need to. He kept talking.

He said he came from an ancient family of textile merchants in Catalonia, that these were privileges once earned in medieval times and passed down through the generations. He asked me if I'd been to his native Barcelona, the *motherland*, he called it. Had I visited Gaudi's cathedral? What did I think? He watched me closely as if the question was a test.

"Magnificent," I said. "Transcendent. It made me weep. But with hope, not with sadness. It touched a place in me I didn't know existed."

"Yes," he said, excited. "Yes. There is no other proper reaction."

"It is a place that makes you *feel*," I said. "As if sprung from nature and man. A mystical collaboration."

He leaned in as if telling me a secret. "I believe it is alive. A living creature, with tentacles!"

For all these months, I'd been imprisoned by my own thoughts of doom and despair, but now it felt like a new window had opened onto the world of José María Sert, part fantasy, part reality, entirely new and intriguing. I had Aimée bring out champagne for refreshment; this was a time to celebrate. He took his coupe with gusto, breathing it in, then swallowing it at once. The man was mesmerizing, mischievous. Though he was short in stature and going bald, he had the confidence of a gladiator. The wicked smile of a pirate. Everything about him was animated and alive. I felt in him a deep sensuality. A robust and wonderful sense of curiosity. And his eyes. Beneath expressive, teasing brows, I could see in them a steadiness and intelligence.

I'd forgotten all about Forain. He must have slipped out.

We spoke of our favorite places in Paris. He wanted to know if I'd been to the new Pathé cinema. Maravilloso, he called it.

"The screen is massive," I said. "I read it's the largest in the world."

"A mural that moves," he said. "That speaks! It's almost a miracle!"

We found we had mutual friends. The author Colette and the young Jean Cocteau who aspired to be a poet.

"The problem with Jean," I said, "is that he wants everyone to love him. He doesn't want to be controversial."

"The point of true art is to be in some way controversial."

"Exactly," I said. "Not to be—"

And then we both said, at the same time, "attractive."

We looked at each other, delighted.

"Senora," he said, "we are aligned."

He nodded to my piano. "What a privilege it would be if you would play for me."

My piano and its surrounds were in a state of chaos. During the uncertain periods of my life, I turned to music. Playing had always been my comfort, and I'd been spending hours at the keys, pouring sadness out of myself, hoping to expunge it. Now, there were musical sheets spread out in haphazard stacks.

I wouldn't ruin the mood of this visit by playing something dark. I was feeling optimistic, as if I were made of light and air and shades of Tiepolo's pink. I thought of Beethoven's cheerful *Turkish March*. A short but lively piece. Much like Monsieur Sert himself.

As I played, I glanced at him. He was not looking at his pocket watch. He was not yawning. He didn't seem distracted or to be thinking of other things. Instead, his eyes were closed as he listened intently, a smile on his face, his head bobbing to the cheerful rhythm. When I finished, he jumped to his feet and clapped. "Brava!" he said. "Brava!" He asked me to play it again, and I did. He came to the piano. "You are a marvel! Magnificent! Maravilloso!" He took my hand to help me rise from the seat. A frisson of desire ran through me. I had been studying his hands all during the visit. Expressive hands. The hands of an artist. Hands that could create. Even his thumbs attracted me. "Will you play for me again sometime?"

"I will," I said.

He told me he had a two-week trip scheduled to Rome the next day, that he needed to return home to prepare. "Senora, you should come. Will you? Meet me in Rome."

The proposition took me aback. It was a roguish proposal. Yet his daring excited me. I was surprised to find that every part of me desired to go with this unusual and exuberant man whom I had just met, to leave Paris, to go on an adventure.

Yet I resisted. Could I trust him? I'd been hurt by men enough in my life.

I said no.

The next day, he sent me the largest floral arrangement I'd ever seen, accompanied by a note apologizing for making such an indecent proposition. Most men would not have bothered. It told me his intentions were honest. That was when I knew I would go.

◆ ◆ ◆

E pericoloso sporgersi.

It is dangerous to lean out.

This was the warning on small plaques beneath each window on the Italian trains. All the way to Rome, I was sure it was a message for me. I was living again. I was leaning out, the wind in my hair, reckless, alive.

That's what I told myself. Deep inside, I was a jangle of nerves, wondering if I should get off at the next stop and turn back. I could be setting myself up for grave disappointment and heartache. Sert said he was not a sheep. Instead, could he be a wolf?

What if he wasn't there at all?

But as the train pulled into the station in Rome, I spotted him standing on the platform, smiling wide, dressed all in white and waving his gigantic sombrero. I was instantly at ease. When I disembarked, he greeted me with a wink.

"I had to make sure you recognized me," he said.

Never in my life had someone emanated being so happy to see me. He gazed at me with warmth tinged with unabashed desire. It was exhilarating to feel wanted again.

That first day, we strolled along the Piazza Colonna. We dined at Fagiano's. Our conversation never faltered. Instead, it rushed on in swoops and flourishes. About art and music and mutual friends. How was it we knew so many of the same people? And that we shared the same opinions of all of them? We were in that wonderful stage of discovery. I relished his wit. He seemed to relish mine. Most of all, we had fun. When the clock struck midnight, instead of retiring to our rooms, he took me to the Colosseum.

He said, "You know, senora"—it would be a few days yet before he called me *Toscha* and I called him *Jojo*—"the ruins can only truly be seen in the moonlight. That's when the ghosts of the gladiators and the lions come together and make their peace, the vestal virgins officiating. Can you feel it in the air?"

There was something in the air, that was certain. A magnetic pull between the two of us.

Rome was always a wonder, but with Jojo I saw it with new eyes. As the days progressed, we visited Raphael's *Cupid and Psyche*, Caravaggio's paintings of Matthew the Apostle, and Cavallini's mosaics. I thought I'd seen them before, but I hadn't, not properly. Jojo taught me to study the masterpieces from a new perspective, explaining why certain works were beautiful or true in ways I hadn't realized. He weaved connections between the scenes and history, literature, and gossip. Throughout our conversations, he wanted my opinion. I listened to him, but he also listened to me. My taste was more contemporary, and I told him of up-and-coming artists like Modigliani and Apollinaire, explaining to him the value I saw in their vision. I said I often visited his fellow Catalan, Picasso. I was one of the few he allowed to critique his works in progress. Intellectually, Jojo treated me as an equal, and he ensured everyone else did as well. He told docents to stand at attention.

"Senora," he told them, "is a trusted adviser to Renoir. She discovered Van Gogh. She is known as the Queen of Paris. Even Picasso listens to her, and he listens to no one."

We visited small churches Jojo knew, rustic on the outside but with the most magnificent ancient frescoes and sculptures inside. We dug through small, back-alley antique shops, competing to find the most amusing trinkets and treasures. We dined at restaurants where Jojo was greeted like a family member. We were served dish after dish of the most delectable food I'd ever tasted. Instead of devouring his meal, he fed me bites from his fork, holding a hand under my chin, watching my reaction closely.

"What do you think, senora?"

All I could do was sigh with ecstasy. "Everything is divine."

And the wines. Each was a new experience. He had me taste different vintages, wanting to know which I preferred as he elaborated on their flavors and textures. To Jojo, wine was history, soil, birth, death, battles won and lost, the blood of Christ and man, empires rising and falling. In everything, he saw the landscapes of time. With him, one didn't see merely a hill. One saw the centuries and what had passed on it.

"Food, wine, sex," he would say, "that is life!"

Sex. It seemed a crude term. Yet from him, it wasn't. To him, it was natural. Not something to be shushed away but something to be acknowledged and enjoyed. And I was no vestal virgin. There was no need to be coy. It wasn't long before my rooms at the Grand Hotel were occupied only by Aimée and my luggage. That Jojo appealed to women was obvious. He appreciated all the intricacies of the female form. He knew what he was doing. We made love as I never had before. His approach to sensuality and pleasure was methodical. There was no fumbling about. Thadée, my first husband, had been more of a friend than a lover. With Edwards, my second husband, we were conqueror and the vanquished.

Jojo was an explorer. He introduced me to the art of the siesta. In the afternoons and when we retired to his bed in the evenings, he broke the physical down to its simple parts. Taste. Smell. Sound. Sight. I'd never met anyone so sensory. So generous. Intent on pleasing me and appreciating how I pleased him. I had never been with a man so tender and openly vulnerable, and in turn, I was as well.

Toward the end of the trip, I told him about the plaque in the train window. We vowed that was how we would live our lives, leaning out, seeking adventure, embracing the unknown as we embraced each other. Not long after we returned to Paris, I presented him with a pendant neck chain I'd had made at Cartier with the words, our words, engraved on a silver charm. He wore it every day beneath his shirt, the pendant falling close to his heart.

E pericoloso sporgersi.

It is dangerous to lean out.

◆ ◆ ◆

Life had become bountiful again. Somehow, at middle age, while I thought I had been living all along, my life had actually just begun. I had Jojo, and thanks to him, another new force of a man entered my life soon after.

In Italy, Jojo and I discovered a shared passion for opera. When Jojo began calling me *Toscha*, I asked him why.

"Why? Isn't it obvious? Because she is a woman passionate for love and art and nothing else. She is you, mi amor."

I realized he was speaking of Tosca, the heroine of the Italian opera of the same name. As usual, I found his Catalan accent both humorous and endearing. But that he saw me as Tosca meant he understood me.

We were both eager to see Serge Diaghilev's opera *Boris Godunov*. On our return to Paris, it was one of the first things we did together. I, who'd seen all the major performances, was stirred as I'd never been before by the sumptuousness of the music and the majesty of the performers. Every Slavic fiber of my being tingled as if I'd been called home. Though I considered myself French, I was born in Russia. I lived the first two years of my life in Saint Petersburg while my father, who was Polish, finished a commission for the tsar's palace. I even had Russian blood of my own, thanks to my grandmother on my mother's side.

With *Boris Godunov*, I became obsessed. Jojo and I didn't miss a single performance. But to our surprise, the theater was never full. We determined that the ear of Paris wasn't ready for the brilliance of Russian music. I couldn't bear the sight of empty seats. For each performance, I bought out all unsold tickets. I filled the seats with everyone I knew and even those I didn't. I wanted Diaghilev, this genius I had never met, to have the illusion of financial success. He was a mastermind, and I felt a strong artistic connection to him.

Then one evening, Jojo and I went to dine at Prunier's. Everyone went on Friday nights for the Portuguese oysters. As we ate, in walked a tall, elegant, impeccably dressed man with sensitive eyes and a delicious white streak swooping through his dark, brushed-back hair. He had a young man in tow, Vaslav Nijinsky, one of a long string of principal dancers who would become his lovers.

"There's Diaghilev," Jojo whispered to me with a nudge.

Jojo had made Diaghilev's acquaintance during the exhibition of his Vic Cathedral panels at the Grand Palais. In a different room, Diaghilev, on a mission to introduce Russian arts to Europe, had organized a stunning exhibition of Russian paintings.

At Prunier's, Jojo rose. He invited Diaghilev and his companion to join us. To my delight, they did. Jojo introduced me. "Madame Edwards"—unfortunately, that was still my legal name—"is an accomplished pianist," Jojo said. "A virtuosa in her own right."

Diaghilev seemed uninterested. I found him to be aloof. Nevertheless, praise for *Boris Godunov* instantaneously poured out of me. I spoke from my heart of the magnificence of the singing voices and the music, the exceptional quality of the cast, the luxuriousness of the set and costumes. Slowly, before my eyes, this initially guarded man softened, sharing details with me of the trials of the production, the endless choices and compromises he had to make, and how miraculously it came together.

"And how it did come together," I said.

Diaghilev swallowed the last of his second bottle of wine. "Madame, your taste is impeccable. Flawless. Unimpeachable. It's exactly like mine. You may be the only woman I could ever imagine marrying. Sert, I beg you to let me have her."

"We'll duel," Jojo said with a wink, "at dawn."

It was that evening Diaghilev and I discovered we were soulmates of the platonic kind, brother and sister in the arts, the same taste, the same instincts, brought into the world on parallel paths, each of us finding our calling in promoting those who deserved to be promoted. We had both come from musical backgrounds. We were born just a day apart in Russia. Neither of us had known our mothers. Omens, we decided. We stayed at the restaurant talking until five in the morning. He came to see me the next day at my apartment to continue a conversation that had yet to end.

Diaghilev described himself as a charmer and a swindler and a man with no scruples. He said he had no artistic talent of his own except that he knew how art should be. He knew talent. And he could see the future. "I was born to be a patron of the arts," he said. "Alas, I was born with no money."

I, by virtue of an arrangement with my former husband, Edwards, was flush with money.

And I could see the future too. "Have you ever considered," I said to him, "using the passion you have for *Boris Godunov* to bring the Russian ballet to Paris?"

Those next few years, my drawing room was the center of the new Ballets Russes. Diaghilev and I assembled the best painters for set decor, the best choreographers, dancers, composers, and musicians. I worked with Stravinsky and Debussy and Ravel at my piano to perfect their scores. I was raised in a musical household. I learned to play piano before I could read. I had played Beethoven's *Bagatelle in C Flat* on Liszt's knee as a child. I had been Fauré's favorite pupil, disappointing him when I chose to marry Thadée rather than perform. I had heard all the music in the world worth hearing so far. To find something new and innovative, appropriate for the Ballets Russes, was a difficult task.

But when I knew, I knew.

Jojo added his touch to the productions, helping design sets and costumes. I strung together donations for funds. I was at rehearsals every day, sitting in the empty audience, soothing Diaghilev's anxieties, and helping him resolve the endless questions that came up before any production.

What do you think of this dancer, Misia? I'm not certain he's the one.

What do you think of this part of the score? Something is off.

With each performance, Paris was stunned by this new mix of theater and visual arts, by compositions and choreography that weren't borrowed from the old but were completely new. We watched from my box on high. Me, Jojo, Diaghilev, Cocteau, and other friends, leaning over the railing. At the end, there was no polite applause. Parisians either stormed the stage to congratulate the dancers or were in an uproar when the boundaries of traditional ballet were pushed too far. As Diaghilev said, he knew what audiences wanted to see before they did. It could take months or even years before a new production was appreciated by the public. The Ballets Russes was a rebellion against all that was stale and dull, and Paris wanted to be a part of it, whether to cheer or to heckle. Season after season, all of Paris was transfixed by the Ballets Russes' brand of ballet: athletic, bold, exotic, fierce.

I had never been happier. I was loved and in love. I was not just a muse as I had been with Thadée, or a wealthy patron as I had been with Edwards.

I was one of the creators.

For the five-year anniversary of the Ballets Russes, Jojo and I presided together in the foyer of the theater as we did before every opening. We were there, before the performance of Stravinsky's *The Rite of Spring*—a masterpiece I'd had to convince Diaghilev to accept—when Jojo put an arm around my waist and pulled me in.

"Marry me, Toscha," Jojo said. "There's no reason to wait anymore."

Edwards was dead of influenza. Despite our troubles, the news had saddened me. Practically, my allowance had ended. But it wasn't that. Jojo was a man of wealth. My lifestyle and ability to contribute to the Ballets Russes wouldn't be affected. The truth was, I was afraid.

"Jojo. Marriages don't end well for me."

"But this is different. You'll be married to me."

During the performance of *The Rite of Spring*, a riot broke out in the theater. The audience found the music startling and Nijinsky's choreography too primitive. It was so loud, Nijinsky had to shout stage directions to the dancers. Diaghilev worked the lights, flashing them in an attempt to quiet the hecklers. In the throes of the bedlam, Jojo and I watched from my box, high above it all. The Ballets Russes had always been controversial. But there was something different about this. There was an edge to the crowd that night. Something more raw than a reaction to a ballet that would later become known for its genius.

When war came, the Ballets Russes was put on pause. The world was put on pause. Jojo and I directed our attention to helping France and put our wedding plans on hold.

Chapter Two

"It's too frivolous at a time like this," I said. "Not far from here, men are living in trenches. They're dying. Husbands, sons, brothers." I glanced at Jean. *Lovers.*

While Jojo was at his studio, Jean Cocteau had come to our apartment with the composer Erik Satie. They had an idea for a new kind of ballet. As the gatekeeper for Diaghilev, they knew they had to come through me.

But this war was no time for a ballet.

For two years, Paris had been dark and shuttered, its citizens hungry and cold, almost a million French soldiers killed with no end in sight. Jean was on leave from a medical division at the front. He was still elegant, impeccable, lean, a bloom in his buttonhole, his dark hair swooping up from his forehead like a halo, though Jean was no angel. "What people need," he said, "is a way to go on. A way to interpret this new world we live in."

Satie nodded. He was attired in his usual bowler hat and one of multiple identical velvet suits, his goatee wiry and gray, an umbrella always nearby. "And madame," he said, "we've dedicated it to you."

Don't they all when they want something, I thought. I wasn't going to fall for that.

Satie was best known as the cabaret pianist from Le Chat Noir. Though Satie's attempts at more elegant compositions had always moved me, Diaghilev was thus far unimpressed. He felt the same about Jean. So many ideas for ballets. Diaghilev dismissed them all. Come back, he would say to Jean, when you can astonish me.

"Madame," Satie said, moving toward my piano. "May I?"

"Of course." I was always willing to listen.

I sat back in my chaise longue and closed my eyes. Soon, I realized I had never heard a composition like this, not from Satie, not from anyone. It was at times lyrical, hypnotizing, joyous. Once I even laughed out loud when I recognized the unmistakable sound of American ragtime. Ragtime in a ballet? The juxtaposition was strange, yet somehow compelling, refreshing in a world where everything had become so serious. The last note faded off into the silence of my drawing room, and I realized Satie had done it, the old rascal. Despite his daily bottle of brandy, he had created something astonishing. Almost.

It needed tinkering. There was work to be done. In places, it was repetitive. It lacked a sense of form. And Satie, like all artists, was sensitive. Would he be willing to accept constructive criticism?

I wasn't sure.

"The score has potential," I said, "but a ballet is more than the score."

Jean leaped to his feet. Just twenty-seven, he was ambitious, untiring, certain he was destined for importance. "The concept, dear Misia, is an allegory for our time. Desperation hidden behind the facade of the whimsical." He sprang like a bird atop an armchair as if he were onstage. "The theme is the fairground parade! Imagine, if you will, a set that replicates the scene just outside the main tent. Here, a select few perform excerpts of their acts to entice the audience to buy tickets for the evening show."

He hopped down from the chair and bounced about my drawing room, deftly avoiding Jojo's collections of antiques and large crystals, acting out parts. He was a Chinese magician producing an invisible egg from his sleeve and pretending to eat it. He was a lively American girl miming Charlie Chaplin, cowboys, Indians, typing, cranking a car. He was an acrobat, balancing on a tight rope. There would be no pirouettes or pas de deux, he said. Instead, the movements would be common.

"It will be the first ballet in the history of history based on the everyday," he continued. "Derived from the popular entertainment of the masses. The circus. The music hall. Nothing classic. Nothing boring or expected. No princes or princesses or swans, no, no, no . . . out with the old, as the saying goes!"

It was absurd, light, yet with a dark side. According to Jean, the Chinese magician was secretly a torturer. The American girl was destined to go down with the *Titanic*. The acrobat was severely depressed by the "sadness of gravity." I wondered if Jean's hair that sprung loftily from his head—hair that knew no gravity—was an electric reaction to his imagination.

"And listen to this, Misia. Picasso has agreed to do the stage decor."

I gave him a skeptical look. Was this really true? Picasso had never done a set.

"You know he loves the circus," Jean said. "All those clowns and harlequins he paints. The set and costumes will be designed using principles of Cubism, as he says, an expression of our distorted, fractured time, not for the sake of beauty."

Jean continued to expound as I absorbed his ideas. I'd met him years ago, drawn to his exuberance, and brought him into my salon to meet my friends, hoping to channel his talent.

When he was called to war, he sent me letters from the front. His sensitive mind coped with the horror by imagining war as a performance, uniforms as costumes, wounds as stage makeup, artillery and cannons the orchestra, death a character actor. In the midst of destruction, he ached to create. He would die, he'd written, if he could not.

But as of yet, he was taken seriously by only a small circle. He deserved recognition. Satie did too.

"The idea is tempting," I said. "The score . . . it's remarkable. And set decor by Picasso is intriguing . . ."

Satie nodded. "His name alone will bring an audience." And the assurance of an audience would appeal to Diaghilev, who was always short of funds.

One thing was clear. This ballet, *Parade*, Jean called it, would be a spectacle. Bold. Unusual. Provocative. Avant-garde. It was the very definition of the Ballets Russes.

In the lead-up to any production, passions always ran high. The "dogfights of great art," Jean called it. I spent the next year resolving quarrels and artistic differences between Jean and Satie, dancers and choreographers, set designers and costume makers. I worked with Diaghilev to refine their ideas as the show gradually came together.

Often, I was blamed for meddling.

But I was born with a vision and an ear, and I could sense it: the raw rumblings of genius. I always had. And when I found it, I nurtured and guided. I didn't let go.

The day of the premiere, I chose an exquisite navy gown of beaded silk that showed off my arms and décolletage, an old Poiret because there was nothing new now. Poiret was off fighting the war. I put on one of my best diamond necklaces, a gift from Jojo. The fact that it was an afternoon opening because of the blackout was no reason not to wear a tiara. I had Aimée fix a silver one around the bun in my hair. Jojo and I arrived early to the Châtelet, taking our place in the theater's foyer. And as with *The Rite of Spring*, we were still unmarried. I had finally agreed, but war came before we had a chance. A wedding didn't seem appropriate. We'd lived together so long anyway. We decided to wait until after.

In our box before the lights went down, Diaghilev, after checking on costumes, backdrops, musicians, and dancers, rushed up, out of breath. I surveyed the crowd through my opera glasses. The house was full with the cream of Paris society and the best of the artistic world. The Comtesse de Chevigné. The Comtesse Greffulhe. The Princess de Polignac. Auric. Poulenc. Apollinaire. Miro. Proust. All had come to see a performance that had taken root in my drawing room. But my name wasn't in the program. The credit would go to Diaghilev. To Cocteau. Satie. Massine, the choreographer. To Picasso.

I didn't mind. I preferred it that way. All I truly cared about, even more than the art itself, were the people who created it. I loved them, their pleasures, their work, their troubles, their joy in life. I wanted to live all of that with them. I wasn't one to collect pictures to hang on the wall. A portrait mounted over the mantelpiece was like a cadaver to me. I didn't read many poems or books. I had stacks of unopened letters from Proust. So dense! There was no time for that.

It was the process I loved, even the "dogfights." The intangible. I was awed by the artists' noble endurance, their unrelenting attempt to put themselves in the position of a god in the hope of making sense of the human condition. The struggle to arrange brushstrokes, or notes, or words to capture a glimpse of the origin of our souls was my obsession.

What sort of glimpse would *Parade* provide? I had yet to see it performed in its entirety.

At last, the lights went down. A few opening strands of Satie's music and Picasso's curtain, an old-fashioned circus tableau, lifted, giving way, like the nineteenth century. Behind it, a Cubist backdrop of tall, slanting buildings with windows suggestive of black ghosts, a haunting effect. I watched the audience shift forward in their seats.

Then the "circus" commenced. The Chinese magician with his imaginary egg. The little American girl turning the crank of a car. Picasso's two-faced carnival barkers with front and profile views. Strains of ragtime mixed with the sounds Cocteau had insisted on to represent the mechanization of modern life: a gunshot, a foghorn, a typewriter. There were a few whistles and boos from the seats. I wasn't surprised. *Parade* was bold. Many in the crowd anticipated the usual classic movements, costumes, and music, the typical gravitas.

But by the time the acrobats took the stage, the catcalls were louder and more disruptive. This was countered by others who applauded, defending Picasso, Satie, Cocteau, and Massine. In the orchestra seats, at least one fistfight broke out. The ballerina playing the little American girl fled the stage in tears. The police were called in. In the melee, Diaghilev hurried backstage. Jean rushed up to my box, his eyes wild, his collar uncharacteristically loose. A woman, he said, had tried to stab him with her hatpin.

He clutched my arm, looking out over the gallery below. "What is happening, Misia? Why is everyone so upset?"

"Isn't it wonderful?" I said. "You've done it. *Parade* is a success. You've created a scandal. A succès de scandale! Everyone will be talking about it—about you—for weeks, months. It's what you wanted."

"Is it?" Jean said.

"Why must you always want people to like you?" I said. "You would do better as an artist if you were more concerned with making people not like you."

He dropped my arm. "Misia, don't be obtuse. Not now when my life is in danger."

I looked behind him. There was no one there. Jojo, irritated by Jean's tendency to exaggerate, ignored him. "History is not made with polite applause," I said. "*The Rite of Spring* was just three years ago. Now it's considered a masterpiece. Stravinsky a genius. You can ask Picasso too. A sign of great art is controversy. Think of *Les Demoiselles d'Avignon.*"

Here Jojo chimed in. "Caravaggio's *Death of the Virgin.* Michelangelo's *The Last Judgment.* Despised by all when they were first revealed."

He put a hand on the small of my back to guide me toward the exit as the fracas went on. It was time to bow out while we could. I had no interest in being caught in the fray.

"True art, real art," I said to Jean as we left, "is like an earthquake, a volcanic eruption. People don't like change. They have to be shaken out of it."

◆　◆　◆

We met afterward at the Café de la Paix, where we always convened after a premiere to celebrate or cry or both, my generous Jojo hosting and calling for bottle after bottle, plate after plate. Everyone was quickly drunk, especially Satie. "Jackasses, all of them," he kept shouting.

Next to me at the table, Diaghilev, who loved food, feasted like a starved animal. He kept a proprietary, monocled eye on Massine on his other side. They were partners in more than just choreography.

Massine, annoyed with Diaghilev over something, argued with him in Russian.

The ballerina who played the little American girl was still crying.

Jean, still vacillating between exhilaration and panic, reenacted for all his escape from the woman with the hatpin.

Now, everyone was laughing, even the little American girl.

Except Picasso. Oblivious to all else, he whispered sweet nothings in a tall, blonde ballerina's ear, stretching to reach it.

I looked from person to person with deep happiness. This was the great exhalation after a performance, after the soul has been laid bare, emptied out, for better or worse, a wineskin that needs to be refilled. This was what I lived for. To be surrounded by my imperfect gods, by my art, living and breathing.

◆　◆　◆

The day after a premiere, I always woke, unwillingly, before dawn.

The morning after *Parade* was no exception.

I, who prided myself on sleeping past noon, rose before the sun, before Jojo went to his studio, before the rustling of my maid. Even the colorful fish in Jojo's aquariums floated about in a drowsy trance. I put on the first dress I could find, pulling a cloak of Jojo's over it, glancing at the mass under the covers to see if I'd disturbed him. I hadn't. Beneath the canopy of his bed, Jojo slept as he lived—deeply.

I was too restless for that. After *Parade*, the same question plagued me that always had when the figurative curtain on my latest achievement had come down: What would I do next? What if there was no next?

Outside, in the typical Parisian gray, the slate of the sky blended into the roofs and the buildings so the world looked like a smudge. On the street corner, the news kiosk was still closed up, its metal shutters pulled down. Later, when it opened, Aimée would fetch the papers and journals. I would sit in my chaise longue with my tea, Mezzo, Jojo's Pomeranian, asleep on my lap. I would spend the rest of the day devouring *Parade*'s reviews, which were sure to be fiery. That, for me, was part of the fun, a sign that we'd truly *done something*. In my drawing room, visitors would come in and out, and it would be my job to remind Jean and the rest that today's controversy was tomorrow's masterpiece. Genius, to those not sensitive to it, needed time to be absorbed.

Glancing again at the news kiosk, I was glad, for now, it was closed. The shutters offered a temporary reprieve from the day's headlines, which were sure to be the same as they'd been for weeks. More Frenchmen killed at Verdun.

Jojo and I were right to postpone our marriage. In the summer of 1914, when the war first started, troops were mobilized and so was I. The military governor of Paris was a friend. There was an immediate need for ambulances. I went to the great Parisian couturiers.

"They owe a great debt to you, Toscha," Jojo said.

When I wore a gown by Poiret or Paquin or Worth, the ladies of society, of the theater, wanted one too. But now no gowns would be made. The couturiers' delivery vans would sit idle. I had fourteen of them converted into ambulances. I recruited volunteers, an assortment of friends, and we were off, my large Mercedes at the head of the convoy, beside me Jojo dressed as an Englishman so as not to be thought a Spanish spy. Jean, who had a mania for costume, was dressed in a medical uniform of his design commissioned from Poiret, his last ensemble before reporting to the army. Paul Iribe, who helped with stage design for the Ballets Russes, outfitted himself as some kind of deep-sea diver. He and Jean had morbid fun dressing for a terrible task. It was their way of facing the dreadfulness of war. War was absurd. And so were their costumes.

The scenes at the front were horrific. A row of men lying on the ground I'd thought were our Senegalese troops at rest turned out to be Germans shot in the face, flies covering their wounds. Trees fluttering with strange kinds of birds on closer look were the remnants of men and animals thrust into the air from explosions. Our ambulances scurried back and forth from the front to Paris with our precious, damaged cargo, some of whom, unable to walk, I carried on my own back up the steps of the city's hospital wards. People didn't believe I could do that, but I did. Jojo, who took a camera with him, captured it in a photograph. I was healthy, strong. After three months—it had never occurred to us the war would last that long—the Red Cross had organized. Our makeshift ambulances were no longer needed, and I donated them to the Empress of Russia.

I crossed the rue de Rivoli into the Tuileries, then walked along the park's gravel paths, the sun rising in secret behind the clouds. I passed a man with no left arm slumped on a chair. Another man nearby stared straight ahead, his eyes blank. Another, crutches resting against a tree, was asleep. Remembering I was wearing Jojo's cloak, I gave each of them money from the stash Jojo always kept in his pockets.

From there, I walked over to the Pont Royal and stood on the bridge and felt the water rushing below me.

That was how I liked to be. Always moving. If not, I would be left behind.

Not anymore. Jojo assured me of that.

But that was what had happened with my first husband, Thadée Natanson. He'd handed me over to the second, Alfred Edwards, to save himself from ruin and pay off debts. Edwards, a very rich and immoral man, was the owner of France's most prominent newspaper. He'd tricked Thadée into a business venture destined to fail. I'd warned Thadée not to get involved, but he refused to listen. Then he begged me to help him by giving myself to Edwards. I felt I had to, as if as a favor for a close friend than anything more. I'd married Thadée in the first place not so much out of love but to escape a domineering stepmother and a father who ignored me. As Madame Edwards, I could afford to lavish my new husband's fortune upon all my artist friends. I convinced Edwards to publish notices about musicians who deserved attention. But once Edwards possessed me, he was on to a new chase. The beautiful Geneviève Lantelme. The actress. He fell in love with her. That was when I would sit at my dressing table, her photo in a frame before me. I hated Alfred Edwards. He was vile, crude, and yet, I still had my pride. I still wanted to be wanted.

And I was. By Lantelme. Curious, I'd gone to see her. I was not one to be easily discarded. At that meeting, she surprised me. She told me she would give up Edwards if I gave her the pearl necklace I was wearing, one million francs, and myself. I was taken aback. She wore her hair long and wild, and she looked at me with a lustful, predatory gaze equal to that of any man. I saw why Edwards wanted her. She was sumptuously alluring. And yet, it simply was not my nature. I gave her the pearl necklace, but that was it.

Now on the bridge, I looked down at the Seine. It was murky like the future, gray like metal, like the machines of this new modern age. Lantelme's last cries had been muffled by the cold swirling water of the Rhine. She drowned after falling from the pleasure boat Edwards originally bought for me. And Edwards had died of influenza less than three years later.

In the end, I was the survivor.

◆ ◆ ◆

A week after the premiere, Jojo and I attended a dinner party hosted by the actress Cécile Sorel.

And to think, I'd considered not going.

Parade, not surprisingly, had closed down early. This, of course, was not a failure but a testament to its brilliance. New ideas, new ways of interpreting the world, had to grow on people. In the meantime, its creators were agitated. Diaghilev had asked for spectacle, and he got it. But he lived like a prince and was always broke. Now, he would have no money. And poor Satie. A simpleminded critic proclaimed he was incompetent, that he had a "complete lack of musical inventiveness." *Parade*, the critic wrote, was a ballet that "outrages French taste." Satie wrote the critic in response, his weapon of choice a series of open-face postcards. "You are nothing but an asshole," Satie boldly scrawled, "and an unmusical one at that." Satie's adjectives only got worse from there. The critic sued for libel. Satie was facing fines and a week in jail.

Only Picasso, who couldn't care less what anyone thought, was on to the next project. If only all could move on so seamlessly. One of his "projects" was the tall, blonde ballerina called Olga. And Jean, who cared about what everyone thought, fluttered about my drawing room every day, talking in circles nonstop until my head spun.

Now, in the bedroom, Jojo adjusted his collar in the mirror, then turned to me.

"Come, Toscha," Jojo said, seeing I was slow to get ready for Cécile's. Satie's predicament particularly worried me. "This isn't like you. You live for storms. Controversy is your element." He put a hand to my forehead as if I might have a fever. "You're not ill?" Jojo had a horror of illness. A man with unending vitality, he couldn't comprehend it.

He took a small box from his pocket that contained a vial and a spoon. He offered me the white powder, the elixir that he said sharpened his brain, gave him reserves of endless energy. He claimed it suppressed fatigue, depression, indigestion, chronic pain, mental weakness, and more. I shook my head, and he took some himself in one quick sniff.

"I'm not ill," I said. "I'm worried. Can you imagine? Prison, at Satie's age?"

"All the more reason to hurry to Cécile's," Jojo said. "The Berthelots will be there. We don't want to miss them."

Philippe Berthelot. Jojo's close friend. He was in the foreign ministry. He knew everyone in government. Months ago, he'd pulled strings to get Jean called back to Paris from the front permanently. Now, he could pull strings for Satie. Jojo prided himself on solving problems. So did I.

And I prided myself on Jojo. I couldn't let him go off to a party without me. We went everywhere together. We were Jojo and Misia. Misia and Jojo. One didn't come without the other. Halves of a whole. A party wasn't complete without the both of us.

Cécile's apartment occupied a coveted spot on the prestigious Quai Voltaire, suitable for a star actress of her long-standing esteem. Jojo and I arrived, trailed by Jojo's man who carried in a crate of Marquis de Goulaine of a rare vintage. Most guests showed up with a bottle. Jojo showed up with a vineyard. Like his enormous murals, he was a man of grand gestures.

I stepped into Cécile's exquisite salon vert with its pistachio-colored antique panels and leopard-skin rugs. Jean rushed to me.

"Darling," I said, hoping he had gossip. "What have I missed?"

"Buffoon," he said, glaring at a man on the other side of the room. I followed Jean's gaze and recognized the person right away: Lalo, yet another critic who'd published a scathing review of *Parade*. "Pretentiously inane," he'd called it.

"How could Cécile invite him?" Jean said.

"Because Cécile casts her dinner parties like one casts a play," I said. "With protagonists and antagonists. It's a matter of opinion which role you fill. But really, Jean, who cares? Critics are critics because they've failed at everything else. You're the talk of Paris. I thought your greatest fear was being ignored."

"You know very well, Misia, I'm fraught with insecurities of every kind."

I made a quick scan of the salon to see who else was there. I counted ten people, most of whom I knew, some I didn't. Jojo had already gone over to greet the Berthelots. Cécile flitted about, a scarf tied oddly around her head. Now that everyone had arrived, she stood in the middle of the room and called for attention. Once all eyes were on her, she pulled the scarf from her head with a flourish. There was a chorus of gasps. Cécile's once-long hair was cut off to just below the ears.

Jean, set on getting back at Cécile for inviting Lalo, was the first to comment. "My dear Cécile, are you preparing for a new role? Let me guess, the elderly Louis XIV without his wig?" He gestured to the bust of the old king on a table behind her, his stone face eying us with mistrust.

"Touché," Cécile said to Jean, good-naturedly accepting his slight as revenge for Lalo's presence.

"But of course," I said to Cécile, realizing now what she'd done, the only explanation that made sense. "You're mimicking a man without his wig by wearing a wig. What a relief. That's not her real hair, Jean. It's a theatrical prop. Oh, Cécile, tell us, what's the name of this latest production? When is the premiere?"

Cécile, smiling, tugged at her hair. "It's not a wig, Misia. It's la mode. It's fashion. It's avant-garde." She turned to Jean. "Your *Parade* inspired me to be modern. You, and my friend Mademoiselle Chanel."

She gestured toward a petite, dark-haired woman I didn't know. But where short hair made Cécile's aging face all that more prominent, the lines and falling jowls, Mlle Chanel, her thick black locks curving in waves, her eyes large and wide, had the more youthful features to somehow complement it.

I waited for this Mlle Chanel to say something. Instead, she was quiet like a sphinx. That she didn't brag and preen like everyone else was off-putting. Not to mention, the simplicity in her gown, the lack of ornamentation, was almost an affront.

As the others fawned over Cécile, I whispered to Jean, hiding my mouth behind my fan. "Mlle Chanel? Have you heard of her?"

He leaned in so we were both behind the fan. "Just that she makes hats," he said. "And something called 'sportswear.'"

"You mean Cécile invited a tradeswoman to a dinner party?" I said. "Now *that's* avant-garde."

From the corner of my eye, I watched Mlle Chanel. Except for Cécile, the other women at the party ignored her. There was something about having someone new in the room to look at that drew me to her. Here we were, three years of war, in all of our drab old clothes, having the same old drab parties. And she was different. Part schoolboy, part duchess. Part gypsy, part aristocrat. Part confident, part shy.

She presented herself in a way I'd never seen before. The lines of her gown, a dark emerald green, were simple, but even from a distance I could tell that the cut and the fit were perfect. She moved with her hips forward, sleekly, like a cat. Not in the short steps of one confined in layers of stiff fabric. One could see the shape of her figure rather than the shape of a corset. Clearly, she wasn't wearing one. And while corsets were meant to flatter, to seduce, seeing the actual lines of her slim waist and hips, seeing them move, was seductive, almost as if one could imagine the body unclothed. Everything about her gave an air of grace and lightness. She wasn't weighed down with the fanciful. She was subtle. It seemed she didn't dress to please anyone else. She dressed to please herself.

It was as if she was the embodiment of the Cubist movement. Stripping everything down to the essential. It was like art itself. It jarred at first, but then one saw the genius behind it.

Such an interesting thought. Could a tradeswoman, a dressmaker, be an artist? An artisan, yes. But one who is reflective of the time?

Yes, that was what it was. Mlle Chanel was living in the current century. The rest of us, except for Cécile, looked like relics from the last one. Now that I'd seen it, I couldn't not see it.

She made all the other women in the room seem stale, including, I feared, me. I caught a glimpse of myself in a trumeau mirror. My blousy bosom. My posture rigid from decades of whalebone. My signature bangs and coiffure. Cut my hair? The hair twisted up in a knot immortalized nine times by Renoir? Never!

At dinner, Jean was seated next to Mlle Chanel, across the table to my right. I could hear him, working hard to charm, his existence one long attempt to dazzle creatures great and small. To my left, Cécile whispered to Winnaretta Singer, otherwise known as the Princess de Polignac. An American heiress to a sewing machine fortune, she'd married into the aristocracy for a title while the titled married for her money. The union was also, everyone knew, a mariage blanc: an arrangement to disguise the couple's true sexual orientations. I listened as she and Cécile discussed Mlle Chanel.

"Where on earth did you find her, Cécile?" Winnaretta asked.

"She makes marvelous hats. And clothing. Not to mention, she's the mistress of Boy Capel," Cécile explained.

"The Englishman?" Winnaretta said. "Polo champion, if I'm thinking of the right one."

"You are. And politician. He's an adviser to Clemenceau."

"Well then, why isn't he here?"

"He was supposed to be," Cécile said. "Called off to England. War work. He's quite high up."

"And he's taken up with a tradeswoman? Odd. Rather daring she's come alone."

"I told her to. We're friends," Cécile said.

Winnaretta snorted. "As much as one can be with the person who makes their clothes. I know you theater people have lower standards when it comes to those with whom you socialize, but really, Cécile."

I laughed. "How funny you are, Winnaretta, for someone whose place in society is derived from the sewing machine."

I didn't know Mlle Chanel, and yet I felt like defending her. Winnaretta was the worst kind of snob, the kind who had not earned the right to be one. She held musical salons of her own, always trying to steal my devotees for herself. Ravel, Debussy, Stravinsky. She'd even had Jojo paint murals for the music room. I wasn't threatened. She tried to lure them away with money, but that was all she had to offer. Certainly not ingenuity or talent.

I turned back to Jean, straining to hear his conversation with Mlle Chanel. Her voice was low. She said something about admiring *Parade*, about being there opening night. Did I detect a trace of the provinces in her speech? I had nothing if not an ear. Whatever Mlle Chanel said about *Parade*, it made Jean preen. He began making faces at Lalo. Once he stuck out his tongue. Mlle Chanel laughed, emboldening him. Knowing Jean, I feared the direction of this conversation. I imagined Jean and Lalo in an escalating confrontation, Cécile egging it on, another of *Parade*'s creators threatened with jail time.

"Lalo," I said loudly more to the table than to him. "Have you heard about the exhibition of French arts Jojo put together in Barcelona last month? Tell me, what are people saying?"

Of course, I already knew. It was a raving success.

"That it was extraordinary," Lalo said. "A true showcase of the best of French art."

"I heard the Spanish government in Madrid wanted nothing to do with it," Winnaretta said. "Afraid the Germans might see a small exhibition to benefit French artists as an act of war."

"My dear princess," said Jean. "There were nearly fifteen hundred works on display. Monsieur Sert has never done anything 'small' in his life. His mind works in grand, complicated schemes."

Jojo's eyes shone. Though Jean often annoyed him, he wasn't immune to Jean's flattery. But the exhibition meant more to Jojo than an opportunity to be praised.

"There were a few ulterior motives," Jojo said, his demeanor turning serious. His voice was low so that everyone had to lean in as he explained the true purpose of the exhibition: to remind Spain of whose side it should be on. The essence of the Latin civilization, of culture, was at stake. It upset Jojo that Spain hadn't taken the side of the French. That was because of the "cowards in Madrid," he said. But he was Catalan, and Catalans were their own nationality. Strong. Rugged. Fearless. The tenor of his voice, his deep concern for France, nearly brought tears to everyone's eyes.

"Dios mío," Jojo said. "Spain is a country full of resources, and France is in its hour of need. They should do something."

"Leave it to you, Jojo," said Jean, "to attempt to single-handedly rouse a nation into war."

"Is it true," Lalo asked, "that the French government tried to dictate which artists would be shown?"

"Leave *that* to Misia," said Hélène Berthelot, who I'd always liked.

"Renoir," I said with a wink, "was well represented. Along with Toulouse-Lautrec, Manet, Rodin, Cézanne, Degas."

"The exhibition would never have taken place," Jojo said, "without the help of Philippe and his government connections. And my lovely Misia, working as she always does so elegantly behind the scenes."

He put his hand over mine and squeezed it.

"From her chaise longue, no doubt," said Jean. "More is accomplished on that one piece of upholstery than at the entire city hall."

Cécile raised her glass. "To French art. French culture."

Dinner went on with more toasts, more boasts. I'd noticed that Mlle Chanel was quiet the entire time, not trying to interject, aware of her place in the social hierarchy. Instead of talking, she seemed to soak everything up.

We gathered after dinner in Cécile's salon rouge. In the rosy glow of the pink-toned paneling and the effects of the overflowing wine, Winnaretta announced that she too wanted her hair cut right there and then.

"Scissors," she said, looking directly at Mlle Chanel. "We need scissors. Surely you have a pair?"

I turned to Mlle Chanel too, not because I expected her to pull a set of pinking shears out from the front of her gown, but because I was curious as to how she would react. Scissors were a worker's tool. The symbol of a tradesperson. But Mlle Chanel didn't blink. Her face didn't flush. She didn't look away. Instead, she lifted her chin slightly and stared back with the amused, superior look of a conqueror.

Of course—the irony!

Winnaretta would never consider inviting Mlle Chanel to one of her musical salons. Yet here she was, asking for a pair of scissors in order to *look like her.*

I stifled a laugh. As I did, the feeling of purpose I'd been searching for rose inside of me. It was the same reaction I'd had before. The first time I heard Stravinsky play a composition for *The Rite of Spring.* The first time I'd seen a drawing by Picasso. The first time I'd heard Cocteau recite a poem. It was hard to explain. I was born with a divining rod in my soul, and right now it was pointing in the direction of Mlle Chanel.

"I have scissors," I said, breaking the awkward silence and surprising all by pulling a small pair of manicure clippers out of my beaded reticule.

Always needing to be the center of attention, Jean inserted himself into the scene. "Perfect," he said. He directed Winnaretta to take a seat in the middle of the room, then began nipping at Winnaretta's tresses with the tiny blades, amusing all of us with his impression of a coiffeur. Except for Jojo, who was scandalized.

"Imagine Venus de Milo without her long locks," he said as Winnaretta's strands fell to the floor. "Cleopatra. Isis! This is blasphemy to the idea of femininity!"

I was happy simply to still have my hair, the twisted knot settled in its usual place on the top of my head. But that wasn't my primary thought. My mind was on Mlle Chanel, on how I could take her under my wing. I could help with the accent. Perhaps she was quiet because she didn't know what to say. Perhaps she didn't know art or music or culture. I could teach her. She had the raw qualities, an eye. And a will. She was a diamond in the rough in need of a bit of polish.

I thought of making my way to her, intent on speaking to her before we dispersed. But what would I say? I'd guided musicians and artists. But never a tradeswoman. Never, for that matter, a woman. Was I sure about this? I'd found myself in the unusual position of being tongue-tied until the evening ended, and the butler brought our wraps. I was drawn to the red cape with a collar trimmed in fur he draped over Mlle Chanel's shoulders. I went up to her, running a finger along the velvet. "Ravishing," I said. "Simply divine."

Before I could blink, she took it off and held it out to me. "Here," she said. "It's yours. I'd be only too happy to give it to you."

"You're so kind," I said, touched by her impulsive generosity. And impressed by her instincts. Cécile Sorel going about town in her creations was good for business. Misia Edwards, I flattered myself, would be even better.

I told her I couldn't accept the coat. What would protect her from the damp on her way back to wherever it was she lived? Ah, I wished I knew where that was. I suddenly wanted to know everything about her. Which was why I decided to call on her at her boutique the next day.

Chapter Three

Paris, 1916

At the rue Cambon, Mlle Chanel was a flash of vitality and charm, greeting me in a tailored day suit that reminded me in part of a man's cardigan. Unexpected yet pleasing.

"Madame Edwards," she said.

"You must call me Misia," I said, handing her vendeuse my wrap. "Madame Edwards was a lifetime ago."

"I'm Coco. That's what my friends call me."

Where she had been intriguing the evening before, she was a delight in the daytime. Her short boyish hair. Her expressive face, square and compact like a nut. Those high duchess cheekbones. That low gypsy forehead. A dancer's long neck. She had a small, snub nose. A Mediterranean complexion. White teeth, marvelous when she smiled.

"Show me everything," I said, clapping my hands together and looking around. "I want to see it all."

"We'll start at the top." She beckoned me toward an array of hats in various colors, each characterized by one extravagant plume or ribbon, not the usual gobs of flower, fruit, and fauna. A well-dressed woman was expected to carry an entire botanical garden or bird mausoleum atop her head with unreasonable poise.

"Simple," I said, liking what I saw. "Yet striking. Not overdone. Not underdone."

"And mine are meant to fit snugly on the head." She put one on to demonstrate, settling it deeply near the brow. "You see? No need for hatpins, those instruments of torture. A woman has to be able to think."

"Torture, indeed," I said, picking up an adorable hat made of suede. "My head has ached since 1905. And this, it's so light."

"Try it," she said, helping me remove the hat I'd worn in, placing this on my head and playing with the fit. As she did, I noticed her hands. Like her slight accent, they hinted at her provincial roots, strong and competent, though her nails were prettily polished. When she was satisfied, she stood back and smiled her endearing smile. "Better, no? Monuments should be in parks. Not on a woman's head. A woman must be balanced."

"Yes," I said, admiring myself in a mirror. "So weightless! My head feels better already." I parroted her words. "A woman must be able to think! Well, I might even forget I'm wearing it."

"Except for the admiring gazes of those you pass on the street. Everyone will see your face," she said. "They'll see Madame Edwards. Not just another passing menagerie."

"Misia," I said again. "Call me Misia."

From there, she showed me suits for daytime like the one she had on. They were soft looking and had pockets in front, unusual for womenswear. Men needed pockets, not women. Or did we? I thought for a moment. Why didn't we have the convenience of pockets? It had never occurred to me before. Yet it had occurred to Mlle Chanel. Coco.

Some of these day suits were beautifully embroidered. Some were cinched at the waist with wide belts, though not too tight. The look was streamlined, nothing stiff or squeezed or pushed up. Open-neck blouses or deep sailor collars peered out from beneath these sweater-jackets. Every buttonhole, every seam, was finished with the utmost precision. Even the inner parts of her garments were magnificently made. She showed me a raincoat with a sable lining. It was as if Coco was giving women a little secret, some bit of luxury all for themselves that only they knew about. And what was more alluring than a woman with a secret?

"This fabric," I said, rubbing a jacket between my fingers. "It's so soft. What is it?"

She leaned forward and spoke in a hushed tone. "Jersey."

I pulled back in surprise. "The fabric of men's underwear?"

"Most people don't ask what it is. They assume it's expensive because it looks expensive. A garment can be made to look luxurious from any textile. It just has to be made correctly."

I couldn't resist reaching out again. This time I ran my hand along the collar of one of the jackets.

"And this fur," I said. "How did you find it? It's so soft. So rich." Expensive fur from Russia or South America was impossible to come by because of the war.

"Rabbit," she said. "Some confuse simplicity with poverty and the overdone with luxury. The exact opposite is true."

I couldn't hide my amusement. She had women of society wearing the pelts of peasants and garments made from the same textile as men's unmentionables. Not just wearing them but buying them for great sums of money. I couldn't think of anything more divine.

"Look at Monsieur Poiret," she said. "He doesn't care about women. He wants to dress us in costumes. In themes."

"I have worn many of those themes over the years," I said, though I hadn't realized they were a "theme."

"A woman must dress for herself. Poiret thinks women should live to dress," Coco said. "I think women should dress to live. A woman must be able to move. Men can. Why shouldn't we? Imagine, a man in one of Poiret's hobble skirts. A man would never stand for such folly for himself."

What an exhilarating idea. A woman must be able to move! Just think of all we could accomplish, I thought, if we didn't have to spend so much time thinking of what to wear and how to get around in it. It wasn't a simple thing to move about as a well-dressed woman. We women weighed ourselves down. We turned our own clothing into obstacles. We needed help to get dressed. Looking around Coco's showroom, it was clear that everything she designed came from a desire for action, for freedom. She was the embodiment of the new modern in a new world that valued moving quickly, mechanical ability, practicality. But in her hands, these cold qualities were elegant. She had an eye for making the functional chic, for being feminine yet rebelling against outdated ideas of what it meant to be feminine.

She was a revolution. A manifesto.

I wanted in.

"I'll take one of everything," I said.

◆ ◆ ◆

I wanted to hear more of what Coco had to say and invited her to lunch at the Ritz, just across the street.

There, I relished the comfortable sensation of my new day suit. Coco had her seamstresses alter one to fit while I waited in the boutique so I could wear it out. The rest would be delivered later. I'd never felt so free, so unconstrained. I'd been uncaged!

Other ladies breezed in for lunch, upper-crust doyennes of the Faubourg, the highest level of Parisian society. They were my friends of a sort. Despite my divorces and bohemian ways, I was granted limited entrée into their world because of our mutual support and fundraising for the Ballets Russes. They respected me because Diaghilev did.

These boring socialites would have no idea who Coco was. As I hadn't until last night. So far, she was known only to the theater crowd. So far. The Faubourg snobs greeted me with a wave or a nod, then whispered when they got to their seats, glancing back at me. I couldn't have enjoyed it more. Neither, I perceived, could Mlle Chanel, who sat primly, fully aware of being noticed as a woman who sold clothes would want to be.

"If it wasn't for my hair"—I put a hand to my topknot—"they might not recognize me at all. Look at them. They're prehistoric. Madame Bouvier in all that black crepe. And her daughter with that wasp waist. I've always thought the sour look on her face was a reflection of her personality. Now I wonder if she simply can't breathe."

Oxygen. Was that the fountain of youth? I felt reborn. Thoroughly modern. A new person.

As the dining room filled and the waiters swirled about, I did most of the talking. I effused about her clothing, the feel, the style. Elegant yet comfortable. Modern yet simple. Her whole being was a revelation: one didn't have to adhere to traditional notions of femininity to be feminine.

"Remarkable. Men have been wearing this fabric every day," I said. I couldn't stop reaching for my sleeve, massaging the cloth between my fingers. I glanced at the waiter as he refilled my tea, wondering if he recognized the material for what it was, a thought that made me want to giggle. Me, Misia Edwards, wrapped in the makings of men's underthings.

"Meanwhile," I went on, "we women have endured against our tender skin starched cotton, metal, bone. It's no wonder we tolerate pain and inconvenience so much more gracefully."

When Coco was showing me her pieces at the boutique, I saw, with the eye of a woman who notices such things, that Coco wasn't as young as she seemed. At Cécile's, in the candlelight, I'd thought she was twenty-five. Today, I was almost certain she could have been a decade older. It was hard to tell, but I would know. Agelessness was a trick I strived for every day with creams and powders.

Across from me at the table, she was quiet. By talking about myself, I hoped to draw her out. French women weren't known for easily opening up to other women. That I did most of the talking at lunch wasn't a surprise. Perhaps because of my Slavic roots, I was different. Yet Coco was a disciplined listener. She gave little away, turning the conversation back to me with a question. By the time our plates were cleared, all I'd discovered was that she grew up in the countryside.

"I was raised in the countryside as well," I told her. "In Brussels, with my grandparents."

"What was it like?" she said.

"It was a place of music, laughter, life, with five concert pianos in the reception hall alone. Seven more throughout the home. A flurry of concerts and guests and feasts."

I talked about my grandfather, the violinist. My grandmother, a Russian aristocrat, beautiful, petite. I studied Coco. Was she bored? No, she was interested.

"Tell me more," she said.

"Grandmother wore jewels from head to toe. I adored her. I learned music before I could speak, musical notes before I could read." I didn't tell Coco that all that was missing was my mother, who'd died in childbirth. My childbirth. And my father. A sculptor. And a womanizer.

"It was at my grandparents' home that poor Zaremski, the composer, died. I saw him, lifeless on the couch where he took his last breath just after playing Chopin's funeral march. He was only thirty-one. Tuberculosis."

"A terrible death," she said, but went no further.

"And it was there I played for Liszt—he was old then, his good looks faded. Well, those golden days were to all come to an end. My father remarried. I was shuffled about between an aunt and an uncle, my father and a stepmother who didn't like me. Nor I her. Paris. Ghent. Paris. Finally, when I was considered unmanageable, boarding school at the Sacre Coeur Convent on the Boulevard des Invalides. It's an apartment house now. Jean lives there! Yes—where I endured endless cold mornings and constant scoldings, Jean lives like a prince and gives poetry readings."

I went on, pausing now and then, still hoping she would interject with details of her own life. Instead, she kept encouraging me to talk, her gaze penetrating. "How wonderful," she would say. Or "Tell me more," or "I love music," or "I wish I could play piano."

All I managed to drag out of her was that she had a younger sister, Antoinette, in charge of her Biarritz boutique. She had an aunt, Adrienne, who was more like a sister and who lived in Paris, the mistress of a baron. She had an orphaned nephew named André enrolled at the boarding school in England Boy Capel attended. Her voice was soft when she said his name.

Her accent told me more than she did. She'd grown up in the countryside, yes, but not in the same circumstances as I. Her skills as a seamstress hinted at a time spent in a convent with a provincial flavor. She had been raised, I suspected, to work or marry. Yet to be here, lunching at the Ritz, lunching with me, the ladies of the Faubourg eyeing us—there was a story to where she'd come from.

She told me how much she loved *Parade*. "And the characters. I was riveted. It was so different. Unexpected."

Like her, I thought.

"I adored how the theme was the everyday," she went on. "The circus performers. So clever and irreverent."

Again, like her. Rabbit fur on a countess. Ragtime in a ballet. "The juxtaposition of the common and the classic," I said.

"Of course, I don't really know about ballet. I have no right to comment. Music. Dance. Art. Culture. Who am I to say? I only know what appeals to me."

"A useful quality when you have good taste," I said. "A quality we share."

"And the reaction of the crowd!" she said. "Why are people so upset by change? They don't like to see things in new ways. Unexpected ways. It made me laugh. They think that just because something has always been done a certain way, that's the only way to do it."

I thought of myself at Cécile's. How at first, Coco's short hair and simple gown had jarred me. Had she gotten me at my own game?

"Most people," she said, glancing around the room, "prefer for everything to stay in its place. Or the place they think it should be in." A mischievous look came into her eyes. She leaned forward and said, "It's more fun to turn things on their head, don't you agree?"

I picked up my cup of tea and raised it. "To women who like to turn things on their head."

My charm offensive must have worked. I was taken completely off guard when, at the end of our luncheon, Coco asked if Jojo and I would dine that very night with her and Boy Capel.

"I know it might sound impulsive," she said, "but he's just arrived back from England this morning. With his war work, he could get called away again anytime. I'd really like you to meet him."

As she spoke, I hid my delight. It could take years to build even an acquaintance with a Frenchwoman, those aloof, guarded creatures. Now, she was inviting me to her home? For a meal? Yet Coco wasn't the typical Frenchwoman. And these weren't typical times. Still, I didn't want to seem too enthused and frighten her off, remind her of her Gallic sensibilities.

"You wouldn't rather have a night alone, just the two of you?" I said. "Especially if you might be deprived of each other again so soon?"

"Oh no. He's taken on a large country house in England recently, in the area of Kent. He's eager to get started on it. I know he admires Monsieur Sert's work. I've heard him speak of it. I wanted to say something at Cécile's but the moment never seemed right. Boy would be very interested to meet him."

"I'm sure Jojo would feel the same," I said. Jojo was never one to turn down an opportunity to accept a commission from a client with more than the means to pay, nor I on his behalf.

"A quiet night so they could talk, at our apartment on the Avenue Gabriel?" The hint of shyness in her voice was charming.

"It would be our pleasure," I said.

I had our driver, Alphonse, take a note to Jojo's studio to let him know of our impromptu dinner plans. Jojo scrawled back that, as predicted, he was keen to meet Boy Capel. Back at our apartment at the Meurice, I passed the time at my secretary writing letters, waiting for him to get home. When he did, he told me more about Boy Capel, that he'd been appointed to various war commissions and councils, posts relating to

Anglo-French relations, diplomacy being a subject dear to Jojo's heart. Boy also had shipping interests and provided desperately needed coal to the French government.

"Yes," Jojo said. "I believe Capel and I have a variety of mutual interests to discuss. For instance"—he suddenly paused, his eyes narrowing—"my dear, something is different about you. What is that you're wearing?"

I stood up and turned to one side and then the other as if I were onstage. "How do you like it? Look at me. I'm modern now."

He smiled. "Toscha, mi amor. You look captivating as always. But you'll never be modern, and I mean that as a compliment. You will always be the archetype of classic femininity." He moved in to kiss me, a hand resting on my waist, then stopped short.

He squeezed, and I jumped. "That tickles."

"What is this?"

"It's me."

"I know that. But where is your corset? There's no moat. No fortress walls. No—"

He stopped short, looking more closely at the fabric.

"This feels . . . familiar," he said.

I was coy. "Does it?"

"Is this . . . ?"

"Jersey? Yes. Mlle Chanel is setting us free with her clothing. It's time women were as comfortable as men. E pericoloso sporgersi, Jojo. I'm leaning out."

As the scion of a wealthy textile family, Jojo was as fastidious about the quality of textiles as he was about wine, food, and everything else. And though he was an artist, he was also, at heart, a traditionalist. A classist. He wasn't necessarily opposed to innovation. But first he had to be convinced.

"Your sudden friendship with Mlle Chanel," he said. "Odd to be so carried away with someone you just met."

"You of all people should know it's not odd in the least," I teased. "I joined you in Italy the day after I met you."

He pulled me closer, running a hand along my hip, no fortress to keep him out.

"There's also Diaghilev. I knew as soon as—"

"—the curtain went down on the first performance of *Boris Godunov*. Surely, Toscha, you're not saying this Mlle Chanel is another Diaghilev? Another *Sert*?" He lifted himself up from the rib cage like a bullfighter bursting with Spanish machismo.

My bullfighter. "There could never be another Sert," I said, my voice low.

"You know," he said, taking me in with a gaze I knew well and pulling me toward the bedroom. "Silk or satin or jersey. It's all the same. The true beauty of a woman is what's underneath."

When Jojo and I arrived for dinner, Boy Capel greeted us. A lovely man. Debonair. Dashing. Handsome but not conventionally so. He was more interesting than that. He had jet-black hair, like Coco's.

"Madame Edwards," he said, bowing slightly as he greeted me, his mustache lightly brushing my proffered hand. "What a pleasure to finally meet you. I've seen the famous portraits of you, though I understand you are as much a mastermind behind them as the beauty in them."

I approved of him immediately.

Jojo and Boy were like old friends, the kind of men who fell easily into new relationships. Both realized they were educated by Jesuits, as if they had some kind of invisible markings or scent that only other students of Jesuits could sense. Both were philosophically minded. Both impassioned by the war. Jojo talked of his textiles, his efforts to help France. Already, they were discussing ways Jojo could help England.

I glanced around, taking in the scene. A person's home revealed so much, like the backdrop at the theater. There were books everywhere, the kind that had been or were being read, not just for pretentious display. Volumes on Hinduism, mathematics, art, by philosophers like Nietzsche and Voltaire and poets like Baudelaire.

The most remarkable feature of the space was how it was dominated by Coromandel screens. Black and gold with inlaid pearl, they encased the room in an Oriental tranquility. They hid the doors, the entrances and exits. The impression was of a cocoon, a love nest. Once you were in, there was no apparent way out.

At dinner, Boy told us about the manor home in England he'd purchased. He asked Jojo if he would consider creating a mural on the dining room walls. We discussed possible themes. "Vivaldi's *Four Seasons*," I suggested. "A season for every wall."

Coco had been quiet most of the evening, solicitous toward Boy, deferential to Jojo and me. So when she spoke next, it surprised me.

"Wouldn't it be interesting to hide the doors in the designs?" Coco said. "To camouflage the exits? I adore rooms like that. It's as if you're really living in the world you made up. You are in control instead of destiny."

"If only," Boy said, putting a hand momentarily over hers. Throughout the evening, I could see they adored each other. The little knowing looks they would give each other. The touches here and there, Coco brushing a loose strand of hair from his forehead. He seemed a steady presence, albeit with an underlying, simmering glamour, like her. It surprised me. Coco wasn't a courtesan by trade, a plaything, the type of mistress men like Boy Capel typically kept. Most kept women didn't work. Their lovers wouldn't allow it. It reflected poorly on them, as if they hadn't the means to provide. They certainly didn't have them read about Hinduism and Buddhism.

Yet here he was. Why?

And he lived with her. Most men of his ilk didn't live with their mistresses. They might set them up, but they had a place of their own as well. A curious relationship. Deliciously intriguing. One could feel the electricity between them. Did she hope Capel would marry her? Did she imagine herself presiding over the dining table at the estate in Kent? For a man of his stature and background, it would be unusual. Did she invite Jojo and me to show Boy she had friends on his level she'd made on her own? I worried. All of his comings and goings. Was there more to it than war work? For her, I hoped not. But nothing was ever as simple as it seemed.

At table, the dinner was exquisite. The wine superb. We continued to discuss the home in Kent. Jojo seemed inspired by the idea. There would be much to draw out and plan.

"Do you draw, madmachelle?" Jojo asked Coco. *Madmachelle.* Jojo's version in his French accented with Catalan of *mademoiselle.*

"Draw?" she said.

"Your designs?"

"Oh no. I take a model and drape fabric around her," Coco said. "The design emerges, I suppose. I must feel with my hands how the clothes fit on the body."

"Ah," Jojo said, nodding. "You're a sculptress."

"I don't think of it that way."

"You should," I said. "Jojo's right. You're an artist. Your fashion is as disruptive as Picasso's new way of painting. You are a constructionist. A deconstructionist. Your medium: textiles. Do you agree, M. Capel?"

"Wholeheartedly," he said. "Coco is a visionary. I've always thought so."

There was a look then on Coco's face I would always remember. Fulfillment. Great happiness. Love. The feeling of being adored and respected and understood, known for who you truly were.

I had that with Jojo. We women knew who we were. But to find a man who wasn't afraid to say it either—out loud—to tell you. That was everything.

Coco had tried, but you couldn't hide doors to keep people from leaving. It might delay the exit, but they would find a way out eventually. You couldn't hold on to a person if they didn't want to stay.

Coco never saw the *Four Seasons* mural. Jojo didn't start on it until after Boy told her he was engaged to marry a Miss Diana Wyndham. Boy loved Coco but was an ambitious man, and marrying Miss Wyndham would catapult his position among the British aristocracy.

When Coco told me, I swooped in. Two years had passed since our initial meeting and our friendship had deepened. And I knew what it was like to be abandoned.

"You have to move out," I said. "You can't go on sharing an apartment with him."

Stoically, she agreed.

I found her a stunning flat near the Trocadéro that a friend no longer needed.

"What is that?" she said, sniffing the air when I took her to see it. She was extremely sensitive to smells.

"I don't know," I lied. It was opium. My friend was an addict. No one was sure if the Germans would take Paris or not. My friend, concerned his access to opium would be cut off by incoming German troops, fled in haste.

"Look at this view!" I said, pulling open the opaque curtains. It was a premier location. The Seine curled and glistened below us as it pushed downstream, a sign that time, for better or worse, flowed on.

I also found her a butler and a maid, a married couple that I knew to be loyal, diligent, and discreet.

"Why do I need them?" she'd said.

"You're rich now. They'll make your life easier."

When Boy was married a few months later, I checked on her every day. She said she wanted to move to the suburbs, and I found her a place. When she didn't answer my calls, I checked with the butler. I sent meals to the rue Cambon. All she wanted to do was work. She threw herself into it more than usual. When she was invited to the Alps with friends, I persuaded her to go.

"But I have a thousand worries," she said.

She came back refreshed, as I told her she would.

Boy Capel was not the only man in the world.

I introduced her to others. Even Boy noticed the change in her. Yes, Boy. He was married. He still came back.

But there was a part of her, a lightness, that died. The hope that he would marry her, that she was different, that the world was different. Then the realization that it wasn't. What does that do to a person? We are born soft into this world. Then the hardness accumulates.

She was no longer the woman I'd met at Cécile's. But who was she?

On a cold night in December, I received a call from Coco's butler. Boy Capel was dead, killed in a car accident. Just thirty-eight years old, taken in the prime of his years.

"I'll be right there," I said, but the butler told me she was gone. She'd left to go to the scene.

I waited for her to come back. She wouldn't see anyone. Not even me. I went to her house again, and she'd had the shutters painted black. Neighbors stood outside pointing and scowling. Black shutters? It was uncommon. But she'd had a need to pronounce her loss to the world. Perhaps she wanted everyone else to feel it too. Did that make her feel less alone? I went inside. Her room too was painted black.

I sat with her as she wept.

"I've lost everything," she said. "Everything."

When she managed to get out of bed, she went straight to work. That was all she did.

"Work is the only thing I've ever been able to count on."

She was a ghost, quieter than normal, rarely going out. Jojo and I finally married the next August, eight months after Boy's death, and I insisted she come with us on our "honeymoon" to Italy. She had never been.

Jojo was astonished. "Never? Ah, madmachelle," he said to her. "You shall see. There is no better place to heal the soul."

As I had done in Rome, Coco followed Jojo through museums and churches like a disciple. Eventually, I would retreat to the hotel or to a restaurant with friends, but Coco and Jojo were tireless. "He's fascinating," she said to me later, real color in her cheeks, hands gesticulating. "He knows everything. All of the interesting things no one else tells you. Why Carpaccio painted this. Why Titian painted that. Their troubles. Their triumphs. Who they hated. Who hated them. The secrets. There are whole worlds in those pictures. He makes paint on a canvas or a wall come alive. He makes the world come alive."

Yes, that was my Jojo. He made her come alive.

We took Coco to our favorite antique stores and junk shops. I was not one for talismans, but they were, and while I looked at Italian porcelains, he taught her about rock crystal, Jojo pointing out those he believed had powers to protect or heal. We went to fine restaurants. We went to small villages where we joined locals roasting pigs on the side of the road. He taught Coco about wine. "No, no, no," he said when she ordered a glass of Orvieto. "You can't drink that. It has no soul. Besides, it only costs three lira." He put a glass of Château-d'Yquem beneath her nose. "Now this, madmachelle. This! Smell the sap! The bouquet! Yes!"

We went to Padua and the Basilica of Saint Anthony, the patron saint of lost things. Jojo thought she should experience Donatello's altar. But inside, she experienced something else.

"Did you see him, Misia?" she said to me later that evening. "That elderly man bent over at the altar? His forehead touched the floor. His face, I can't forget it. He was in so much mental anguish that it made me feel ashamed. I was standing in front of the statue of the saint and felt an energy grow inside of me. I felt Boy. He was there, from the other side. I heard his voice. He told me to stop feeling sorry for myself. He told me it was time I decided to live."

Chapter Four

Paris, 1925

I have always had a keen sense of smell. Better than Coco's, though she would never admit it. Chanel No. 5? It was I who discovered the secret formula of the Medicis and gave it to her. I'd had to *convince* her to create a perfume.

Now, another unexpected scent entered my life. I was waiting at our apartment at the Meurice for Jojo to come home from his studio. It was the end of his workday, a time I anticipated each evening as the sun ceded to the iron collage of rooftops over Paris. Jojo and I had the same routine. He would change, we would go to Maxim's, we would dine, meet friends, enjoy wine, champagne, perhaps everyone would come back to our apartment, or we would go to someone else's, a typical night of laughter, conversation, music. Coco might join us with her latest lover, Grand Duke Dmitri, or Picasso, or a South American horse breeder, or even Stravinsky. She had been "living" and then some.

"Toscha—hola! Toscha!" Jojo called to me as he walked in the door. Mezzo scampered to greet him.

"Here," I called from the salon. At the piano, my fingers danced playfully over a few notes of Beethoven's cheerful *Turkish March*.

He came in and greeted me with a kiss, his beard lightly scratching my face. He smelled as he always did of his studio, a soup of linseed oil and turpentine, paint and ink and acetone. But as I breathed him in,

I was surprised to find that on this night his typical fragrance carried a new note. A scent I couldn't place, yet familiar. Unpleasantly familiar.

I followed him like a bloodhound into the bedroom, Mezzo spinning like a top along with us. I sat on the edge of the bed as Jojo changed and talked about a mural he was painting for the ballroom of the Hotel Wendel. The theme was the Queen of Sheba visiting King Solomon. He always consulted me over his projects. This time, he went on about the complexities of layering sepia glaze over silver sheets flecked with gold, a process that would normally interest me. Instead of listening and sharing my thoughts, my mind worked to pinpoint the invisible intruder winding its way around my nose.

What was that smell?

I was accustomed to the floral or Oriental signatures of women's perfumes. With one whiff, I could take the measure of any woman. Worth's *Dans la Nuit*? A woman with more money than taste. Coty's *Muguet des Bois*? An unimaginative woman who couldn't think for herself and had her perfume chosen for her at the department store counter. Guerlain's *Pour Troubler*? A woman desperate to be interesting.

I was interesting. I didn't need a scent for that.

I also wasn't naive. Jojo was a lusty Spaniard. This was Paris. Trivial liaisons were so common they even had a name: the *cinq à sept*. From five to seven every evening, a hush came over the city as mistresses with faces strategically veiled slipped between dark entrances and creaking doors to the places of their appointed rendezvous. But in all the years we'd been together, less than a handful of times had I ever been suspicious that Jojo indulged in the cinq à sept. Those few occasions, I'd never mentioned any lingering traces of perfume. Why would I? I had never felt threatened.

Then why on this night did I feel a tinge of apprehension? This new scent made me uncomfortable. It wasn't floral. Not Oriental. Rather, it was earthy, almost damp. It was . . .

"Sculpting clay?" I said, blurting it out as Jojo fastened his cuff links.

"What?" he said, dropping one to the floor.

No wonder I was disturbed. It was the scent of my father, dead now many years. We were never close, yet he was still present in my mind more than he'd ever been in person. Cyprien Godebski was a sculptor. Town squares throughout Europe were garnished with his renderings of village heroes. In Halle, Belgium, one was of my grandfather, the well-known cellist. My entire life, my father tried to turn me into one of his statues, shape me into what he thought I should be, then put me on a stand somewhere out of sight.

Why would Jojo smell of clay? He wasn't a sculptor. He was a muralist. Working with sepia glaze.

"Darling, are you making something with clay?" I asked. "A model, perhaps, for a mural?"

All I could see was the top of his head. He was bent over, looking for the lost cuff link. When he stood again, his face was red as if all the blood had rushed to it.

"No, no. Not me. A sculptress came to the studio today out of the blue. A young refugee from the revolution in Russia. From Georgia to be precise. The Republic."

"What do you mean she came to the studio?"

Only the consecrated—Jojo's male assistants and models—were allowed into his hallowed space of scaffolding, ladders, projectors, cameras, templates, and drafting boards. Creating enormous murals was a complicated proposition and for him, a jealously guarded secret. "Your assistants always shoo unknowns away. How did she get through?"

"Well, you see, Toscha," he said as I helped him fasten his cuff link, "I was there alone. I'd sent everyone out on errands. There was a knock on the door, and I answered it. I never do. I happened to be near it. I assumed it was the delivery of those new brushes I ordered from Italy. Then this girl, she was rather disarming, said she'd seen my name on the door, she knew who I was, and was looking for advice. She held a sculpture in her arms, a work in progress, an aviation trophy she'd been commissioned with, that's all. She looked helpless. Her family lost everything, like so many others. The madmachelle is a princess of some kind."

Paris was seething with various sorts of penniless Russian nobility who'd fled the Bolshevik takeover, now scraping to get by, many of them desperate. I felt for them. Coco employed them. Grand Duke Dmitri, her latest lover, as press secretary. His sister as an embroiderer.

"And did you help her, Jojo?"

He shrugged. "What could I do? I'd already let her in. I did what I could. I had to get back to my work. You know that. I'm swimming in commissions. What a wonderful problem to have. And it's all thanks to you, my love." He kissed me on my cheek. "Now, why don't we go, yes? Our table awaits. Did you hear that? My stomach. I've been thinking all day of what I'll have tonight, debating between lobster thermidor and beef bourguignon. What should I choose?"

I smiled and took his arm. "I know you, darling. You'll end up having both."

A few weeks later, I scanned the newspapers for the latest reviews and came across one of a sculpture exhibition. I remembered the Russian sculptress. Jojo was lying on the divan nearby, reading his own stack, when I asked after her, thinking he'd tell me he'd never seen her again.

"She's doing quite well," he said. "The aviation trophy is coming along."

I looked up from the newspaper. "But how do you know?"

"Didn't I tell you? I've lent her a space to work in the studio."

"Darling, what?" Surely, I'd misheard.

"The Russian princess. I let her take a little corner in the back to finish her trophy."

I tried to keep my voice light. "But . . . you're letting her work there? You never do that. As you always say, you require concentration and deep, uninterrupted thought."

"Yes, yes, but this is merely temporary," he said. "She has no place else to go. Her family has taken up at the Hotel Versailles on the

Boulevard du Montparnasse—very shabby—while they try to get back on their feet."

"Shabby? It may not be the Meurice," I said, reclining as I was in my chaise longue in the midst of our suite of rooms with its extravagant view over the Tuileries, "but it's hardly a shack."

"Ah, you should see it now. It's gone dreadfully downhill."

I stared at him. His eyes darted back to the newspaper. "You've been there?" I said.

"I stopped in only to deliver a drawing I did for her. A model for the trophy."

He went on, talking about the benefit to her of using his studio with its high ceilings and open spaces. He said she'd been chosen to show her work—three busts—a couple of years ago in the Paris Salon of 1923 when she was only seventeen.

Only seventeen? That meant now she was . . . nineteen?

I drew in my breath. Jojo was twice her age.

"You know, Toscha, she's working on a bust of that Japanese actor, Sessue Hayakawa, the one in all the Hollywood pictures. He sits for her back at the hotel."

At the hotel. Where Jojo had been. "Did you meet him?" A Hollywood star. To think Jojo hadn't told me *that* when we told each other everything.

"Very briefly."

I shook my head. It was all so perplexing. Jojo's studio was his hallowed sanctum. Not long after we'd returned from our first trip to Rome, I'd casually dropped by, wanting to see how he worked on those enormous murals of his.

The studio was an open, airy space, three stories high, necessary in order for him to manage his large panels. I'd walked in to find Jojo with a camera circling three men who were on a scaffold completely nude, posed in a frozen pantomime. Two of the men flanked an elderly gentleman with a protruding belly who leaned back awkwardly, his face looking up toward some invisible yet seemingly terrible force. Their muscles were flexed, faces pulled with expressions of anguish, man-parts dangling. It was barely afternoon. I was so surprised, coming in from the street with no context, I'd burst out laughing.

It was an unfortunate reaction. "Senora!" Jojo said sharply, realizing I was there. Later, I learned this was one of his techniques to work out in advance the complexity of muscle and movement. In this case, it was a study for a biblical scene, the Condemnation of Christ by Pilate, to be installed in the Vic Cathedral.

And I'd laughed. I still felt guilty for distracting him.

Not anymore.

"You know, Toscha," he said, "she mentioned how much she would like to make your bust."

"Mine?"

I didn't want to be sculpted. I'd turned down Rodin innumerable times. I knew my limitations and had no interest in subjecting myself to the chisel. My cheekbones were high, but I was certain my round face was not the sort to be effectively reproduced in that medium. I feared I would look like a ball of dough.

And then there would be that damp, pernicious smell of sculpting clay.

What was this girl after?

I laughed at myself for being so sensitive. What was I thinking? It was not the girl who bothered me. It was the reminder of my father.

"Maravilloso!" Jojo said when I told him I would come by the studio the next day at three to meet the girl. "You'll adore her. And Roussi will be thrilled to finally meet you."

"Roussi?"

"The Princess Mdivani. Her name is Roussadana. People call her Roussi."

Rrrrrroussi, he said with his Catalan accent, those long rolling *r*'s.

At the appointed time, Alphonse pulled up to the door of Jojo's studio. From the back seat, I watched a young woman dash out. She was tall, blessed with the grace of youth and long limbs loping across the street like a startled deer. She glanced quickly at the car, then blocked her face with her pocketbook. How strange. It was raining, and I watched as she faded off into the gray as if a wisp of a cloud.

I didn't know what to think. Was that her? Why would she run off?

Inside, Jojo was flustered. "I'm not sure what happened," he said. "She said she had some kind of appointment, one she'd forgotten and couldn't miss."

"How unfortunate," I said.

"Yes," said Jojo. "She did want to meet you."

I looked around, finally spotting a table that appeared to hold the dreaded sculpting clay and the tools of a sculptor. "Well, at least I can see her work."

I headed toward it.

"Oh," Jojo said, following behind. "I think she wanted to show it to you herself. Perhaps you should hold off until—"

I didn't break stride. "Why would I do that?"

"It's rather a raw talent," Jojo said. "In need of some formation and guidance and . . . she is young, you know."

Yes, I knew. Nineteen.

"Yet she's shown in the Paris salon," I said.

"Yes, her busts."

I stopped in front of the table. On it was a rough model of the figure of a man standing on a rock. In one hand, he held the beginnings of what was to become a biplane, aiming it toward the sky like a javelin. Next to the sculpture, a drawing in Jojo's hand of the same was tacked up on the wall. The concept was clear, its epic theme quintessential Jojo: man bearing a heavy burden resulting in the triumph of humanity.

But the execution—

He looked at me expectantly. "What do you think?"

"What do I think?" I said, spinning around, a smile pasted on my face. "I think it's tremendous." Tremendously bad.

It was completely uninspired. Amateur. There was no poetry. No grace. Nothing clever or new or different. I knew art, and this wasn't it. Surely Jojo saw that. Or did he see anything at all besides a young, beautiful damsel in distress?

◆ ◆ ◆

"Have you heard of a Russian family called the Mdivanis?" I asked everyone I knew.

A young Russian composer named Dukelsky who had come the next afternoon to play for me. His answer: *Nyet.*

Diaghilev, who came right over when I told him he needed to hear Dukelsky play and who immediately heard the choreographic possibilities. But as for the Mdivanis, his answer was the same. *Nyet.*

And Lifar, the Ukrainian dancer who came with Diaghilev. *Nyet.*

I went to the rue Cambon to ask Coco. She had never heard of them. She asked her salesgirls who had come from Russia, former aristocrats themselves now in need of work. They had never heard of them. Nor had Dmitri or his sister.

Back at the Meurice, I phoned the Hotel Versailles and had the operator connect me to the Mdivani rooms. I introduced myself to a woman with a Russian accent who said her name was Princess Nina Mdivani.

"Oh, then Princess Roussadana Mdivani must be your sister," I said. "I was so sorry to have missed her yesterday afternoon. We had an appointment. I'm told she left in a hurry. I do hope everything is all right. I understand she wants to make my acquaintance. The desire, naturally, is mutual. Is she available tomorrow? What time shall I come by?"

Princess Nina hesitated. "Did I mention I have a gift to deliver?" I said. "A token of friendship." The prospect of a gift was all it took.

I secured the invitation. I was to be received by the sculptress and her sister, Nina Mdivani, at the Hotel Versailles the next afternoon.

The day we were to meet, I spent extra time at the dressing table. I didn't know what to expect from the Mdivanis, but in an abundance of caution, I thought of Coco's mantra: "dress like you are going to meet your worst enemy." I pulled out an ensemble from her most recent collection, a slim skirt, a collarless jacket with a silk camellia at the collarbone adding a feminine touch, and a thin belt. The sculptress/refugee would not be dressed in Chanel, the very pinnacle of fashion.

Alphonse had the car ready. It felt good to be au courant, all thanks to Coco.

I swooped into the Hotel Versailles like I was Napoleon invading Russia.

Yet this Roussi had her bulwarks. I was forced to run the gauntlet before even setting eyes on her. Opening the door to the suite was the sister, Nina. Where Roussi was blonde, Nina was dark-haired. Where Roussi was tall, Nina was petite. She wore, to my surprise, what I recognized as an expensive Lanvin dress, polka dotted with a wide lace collar and drop waist. Jojo had made it sound as if they had just crawled out of the gutter. Clearly they had means of some kind. Nina's manners were formal. Her face was fine-boned and pale. She did not smile. Her posture was erect, her chin lifted, her movements self-conscious. I had the sense that she did not come from nothing, but as of yet, not that she was of an aristocratic class.

"Charming to meet you," I said, ignoring the coldness in her eye as she took my measure. It didn't bother me. She and her sister may have been princesses. I was the Queen of Paris.

I casually handed her what was purposely and obviously a very expensive, exquisite bowl of blue Venetian glass. "My husband and I go to Venice every season and bring back so many pieces. It's ridiculous to hoard them all for ourselves."

"But you are too generous," Nina said, still not smiling, yet clutching the bowl close as if I might change my mind, which told me a bit more of their economic situation.

"I'm not generous at all," I said, holding her gaze. "My husband becomes enamored of every pretty piece he sees. He insists on bringing them home, then quickly forgets about them. I end up doing the sorting out, that's all."

Nina scowled. I smiled. A man stepped up, and she introduced him as her fiancé. Mr. Huberich. American. An international lawyer, Nina said with pride. He was tall and stern and at a minimum, twenty-five years her senior. Now I understood the Lanvin dress. The nice hotel suite—it was not, contrary to Jojo's description, shabby. Mr. Huberich also did not smile, but in my experience, lawyers rarely did.

"Madame Sert," he said by way of greeting, and I liked the way those two words resounded throughout the room.

Now where was this Roussi?

Nina and Mr. Huberich led me from the entry to a sitting room. To my disappointment, Roussadana wasn't there either. Had she flown the coop again?

But her handiwork was on display. The bust of Sessue Hayakawa was in progress on a table. And to my great surprise, the man himself, stretching. He appeared to be just getting up from a sitting. I almost couldn't believe my eyes. I'd convinced myself the girl had been lying to Jojo about making a bust of him, especially after seeing the aviation trophy in progress. Why would the famous Japanese actor, the esteemed Hollywood matinee idol, sit for an unknown like Roussadana?

Yet here he was. Cheekbones like cliffs. Angled jaw. Perfect lips. Eyes that smoldered. Now *this* was a visage made for the sculptor's knife. His whole being emoted sexual appeal. But if the trophy was any evidence, Roussi was unlikely to capture his true essence. I looked again at the bust in progress. With one glance, my suspicions were confirmed.

Anyone with some training could claim to be a sculptor and make a passable bust. But not anyone, and not Roussadana, could make it so you could sense the bones beneath the skin, so that you could feel the complexities of the spirit. The bust was flat.

"Enchanté," M. Hayakawa said, coming toward me as we were introduced, bowing slightly. He wore an expensive, perfectly tailored suit. I told him I admired his pictures. He tilted his head and smiled a dazzling Hollywood smile. Near him was a decidedly intimidating and enormous sumo wrestler who thankfully wore a kimono over his loincloth. His features were pinched as if he too couldn't stand the smell of sculpting clay. His arms were folded over a barrel chest. I supposed his purpose was to fend off swooning flocks of women. I'd heard he himself was in love with the actor, that his guardianship was more than perfunctory.

In any event, I made sure not to swoon.

Where was Roussi?

Finally, she emerged, the princess-sculptress entering the room with, of all things, a tiny monkey riding on her shoulder. She was tall, with a coltish quality to her, as if she wasn't fully in control of her limbs. Her hair was of a flaxen tone. When she smiled, her lips curved up as if she had secrets, amusing ones. Whereas Nina's dark, suspicious eyes seemed to absorb light, Roussi's emanated it.

"Pleased to meet you, Madame Sert. And this," she said, smiling at the chimp, "is Poki."

If she expected me to shake the creature's hand, a fidgety thing costumed in a red-and-gold vest of Oriental brocade, I did not.

For a moment, I forgot my equilibrium. A monkey. A sumo wrestler. Two princesses. Had I stepped into a José María Sert mural? The scene before me would have blended in with the dwarfs and giants, the trapeze artists, the elephants and the palm trees, the characters of folklore or myth that populated Jojo's fantastical allegories. Art was supposed to imitate life and not vice versa.

Suddenly, I remembered what happened when Napoleon marched into Russia. He lost.

"Poor little refugee girl," Jojo had said. "She had nowhere else to go," Jojo had said.

Far from it.

She had resources. She was not alone in the world. And this suite of rooms was suitable enough for her to sculpt M. Hayakawa's bust. The aviation trophy could be completed here as well.

Was Jojo not being honest with me?

"Enchanted," I said back to Roussi.

M. Hayakawa and his bodyguard said goodbye. Mr. Huberich walked out with them. I took a seat, not going anywhere. The two sisters exchanged a glance, then sat down as well. This was my chance to probe, to find out who these Mdivanis really were.

"My husband has told me a bit about you," I went on as Nina poured tea from a samovar, "but I'd like to learn more. I'm always interested in my fellow countrymen. I've spent most of my life in France, but was born in Saint Petersburg. My father was a sculptor. He was there overseeing the reconstruction of the palace at the time, as a favor to the tsar."

"Our father was an aide-de-camp to the tsar," Nina said. "And our mother a lady-in-waiting to the tsarina. And we're Georgian. Not Russian. Not since the revolution."

Really? To deny Russia's artistic, literary, and musical heritage for a minor national affiliation? What did anyone know about Georgia or Georgian nobility? Maybe that was the point.

"And now you are in Paris," I said. "Is the chimp Georgian too?"

"Poki is from Senegal," Roussi said. "By way of Constantinople."

I knew, without need for explanation, the family had fled, as many Russians had before them, to Constantinople after the Red Army invaded Georgia.

"While Mother and Nina appealed to the embassies for aid," Roussi went on cheerfully, "Alexis and I took advantage of being unsupervised and roamed the ports like street urchins. A Senegalese sailor gave us dear Poki as a gift."

"Alexis?"

Roussi's face brightened. "Our brother. I'm a year older, but we're twins, I know we are. Is that possible? Why not? We share a soul. We always know what the other is thinking. We don't even have to speak. We are practically the same person."

Roussi's tone was playful. In deep contrast to her sister's. Nina glared at Roussi, a warning look. Perhaps Nina had instructed Roussi not to speak, that she, Nina, the older sister, would take charge.

Yet Roussi kept talking as if describing a grand adventure, ignoring Nina's glowering.

"Alexis and I stayed at the port from morning to dark. The sailors let us explore their ships. They gave us trinkets from China and Africa. Alexis became a shoeblack to earn money, imitating the servants who shined our shoes back in Georgia. We spent everything he made at the confectionaries! Isn't that hilarious? They wouldn't accept cotillion favors."

I raised an eyebrow. Cotillion favors?

Nina stepped in, clearly hoping to quiet Roussi. "In our rush to leave Georgia, there was a misunderstanding with respect to our trunks."

Roussi laughed. "The trunk with the family silver and Caucasian petroleum shares got left behind. Instead, all we had was a trunk of perfumed sachets. Worthless."

Nina squirmed. Roussi's enigmatic smile didn't crack. Such an odd story. And how odd to share it with a stranger. There were subjects not to be spoken of in polite company, financial matters one of them.

But it was somehow endearing. Roussi seemed willing to discuss anything—unlike her sister. Roussi was a one-woman, three-ring circus. I waited for her to go on. Her delight in her story was contagious. Lured in, I wanted to hear more despite myself. But Nina, all business and vitriol, was finally able to shush her.

"We weren't without resources for long," Nina said. "Mother and I were received at all the embassies. We made arrangements to come to Paris in a matter of months."

I remembered that their mother, Jojo had told me, had passed unexpectedly just after they'd arrived in Paris. Perhaps that explained Nina's motherly smothering. Yet her tone and the lift of her chin grated me. "Mr. Huberich has taken up our cause," she said. "He's helping us negotiate the return of the petroleum shares. All will be restored soon."

I smiled. "Mr. Huberich must be a great comfort, in so many ways."

Nina didn't respond.

"And Princess Roussadana," I said, turning to her, "has found comfort in sculpting."

"Roussadana is very talented," Nina said. "She's just finished a bust of the Prince Consort of the Netherlands. And now, M. Hayakawa. Once she finishes, she'll be leaving for California. She's been commissioned to do a bust of Charlie Chaplin."

Chaplin? California? Could it be true? The beloved actor could have his bust made by anyone in the world. Why this untalented unknown? Surely, she was telling tales.

"She'll join our older brothers there," Nina said. "The Princes Mdivani. They're in Hollywood. Organizing investments in the Venice oil fields. They have degrees from the Georgia Engineering School. They're in the petroleum business."

"And David's going to be in a picture show," said Roussadana. "Just for fun. Isn't that hilarious? Serge might too. Too bad Alexis isn't there. He was made for the screen. But he's in England. At Oxford."

I sat up in surprise. "Shining shoes?"

Nina's eyes narrowed. "At university."

"Well." Roussadana laughed. "He mostly plays polo. Everyone wants him on their team. We played all the time as children. On the grounds of our home, the governor's palace!"

"It was an idyllic childhood," Nina said.

Hollywood. Oil investments. A polo-playing, Oxford-attending shoeblack. This was becoming more and more absurd. It couldn't possibly be true.

And yet, I'd seen M. Hayakawa with my own eyes. Perhaps these older brothers were influential. They were, after all, the Princes Mdivani. Americans were gluttons for aristocratic titles. Perhaps they had sent M. Hayakawa Roussi's way. Perhaps they actually knew Charlie Chaplin. Perhaps there were other Hollywood stars to come.

Americans could be clamoring to have a bust made by her, no questions asked. Certainly, Hollywood didn't care about taste or art. Hollywood cared only about spectacle for spectacle's sake.

It was apparent, I thought, looking at the monkey posed regally on Roussi's shoulder, the Mdivanis had a knack for that.

I stood to go. It occurred to me that her talent may have been more as a sculptress of stories than of clay, embellishing her family's background. I couldn't altogether blame her. There was a theater to her as there had been to Jojo when I first met him. It amused me. And it would certainly amuse him. I hoped there was no more to it than that.

"Darling," I said to Jojo that evening at Maxim's after we'd settled in at our usual table, and I waited for him to absorb just the right amount of Château d'Yquem. "I visited Princess Mdivani today. She's charming, in an unusual way."

I watched his reaction carefully. He looked surprised, pleasantly so. "I thought she might interest you," he said. "She's young but has potential."

"To think," I said, "she's going to America to do a bust of that funny little Charlie Chaplin, no less."

"And do you know, Toscha? The Chaplin fellow might be in need of a mural to go with his bust. An opening into Hollywood's drawing rooms could be profitable. Roussi herself had this idea."

"Did she?" I lifted my glass and took a sip to tamp down a sudden flash of aggravation. Surely Jojo was not listening to her for advice. That was my job. My place. I was Jojo's tireless promoter. Since we'd met, his career rose steadily thanks to the wealthy connections I'd made as Madame Edwards. Being devoted to him meant devoting myself to his success. Commissions had come in worldwide. The United States. South America. All over Europe. As the former Madame Edwards, the wife of a rich and powerful newspaper magnate, I knew people in high places. I talked up his murals. I was always running into someone building or redoing a palazzo here, a villa there. Jojo was appreciative of the advice I gently gave him, suggestions, for instance, on color and themes, on which commissions to take, which to turn down.

"You're already popular in America," I said. "The Palm Beach commission was a great success." The moment the words came out of my mouth I regretted them. A dark look passed over Jojo's face.

Somehow I'd forgotten the Palm Beach commission was a sore subject. My intention in bringing up Palm Beach was to point out I myself had secured his first American project. It had been installed in Florida the previous year. All thanks to my ear for opportunity, one that came through the friendship I'd cultivated with that tiresome Princess de Polignac, otherwise known as Winnaretta Singer. Winnaretta lived in Paris yet had deep connections to the Palm Beach crowd.

But a few months ago, after Jojo's murals were installed, the servants of the Palm Beach estate had gone on strike, claiming that living with the panels—eight of them twenty feet high depicting the travails of Sinbad the Sailor—left them unable to sleep and plagued with nightmares. It was in the newspapers in Palm Beach and the society pages in New York. All forty servants walked out while a ballroom full of dinner guests sat at the table waiting to be served.

"Weaklings," Jojo said, glowering.

I'd forgotten how this still irked him. "Now don't grumble, darling. The Sinbad panels were a great success with those who matter."

To soothe him, I recited some of the praise from memory. "'Sert knows the elephant as a naturalist, birds as an ornithologist, the sky as a poet. He is a master of composition. He has a dazzling sense of color.'" Still, from across the table, he was scowling. "Jojo, darling, the New York art world would agree that the servants' reaction is a tribute to your genius. A testament to the realistic quality of your work."

"A testament to their utter lack of cultivation," Jojo said, a hard edge in his voice that was tinged with hurt. "When I think of the time I'd dedicated to those panels, the quest for perfection. Take my glorious pyramid of writhing elephants, their trunks outstretched, trying to pull poor Sinbad from a tree and stomp him to death."

"Your vision for that scene was brilliant," I said.

"I worked for months to get the perspective just right. The strength and power of the elephants' limbs. The fierceness of expressions."

"You put everything you have into your work," I said, still trying to redirect him. "You always do."

"And the panel depicting the giant ogre, gripping a butcher knife in one hand, about to feast on a sailor in the other. Do they think it was easy to capture his murderous nonchalance? I must have done a thousand studies of a clawing hand at varying angles to ensure it was realistic. Not to mention the terror on the sailor's face."

"All the work you do in your studio with live models," I said. "No one comes close to your understanding of the musculature of the human and animal physique."

He sat taller, his chest puffed out.

The hurt in his voice was gone, replaced with indignation. "Apparently the American servant class has no knowledge of medieval Persian and Arabic lore. They have no idea Sinbad's adventures are roughly based on the experiences of merchants from Basra traveling to the East Indies and China to trade. Exaggerated, yes, but only to show the triumph of man against death. Sinbad was resourceful, a man of action and endurance."

"The murals are inspiring," I said. "Emboldening. You're an artist, Jojo. Your creations move people. It evokes deep emotion. Your life's work isn't to entertain. It's to illustrate the grand themes of the human condition. That's why you've been entrusted with the decoration of the Vic Cathedral. With the palaces of royalty. This controversy in Palm Beach—you, my love, are too great to be distracted by small trivialities."

Like this Roussadana.

He took a deep breath, smiled, and reached for my hand across the table. "What would I do without you, Toscha? You always see the forest when I'm lost painting the trees."

"And what sublime trees they are," I said, taking his hand and squeezing it.

He was in a better mood now, and I was relieved. It pained me when any artist I believed in thought lesser of themselves. I knew how demoralizing it was. Thanks to my father, I understood rejection. I understood unfair criticism. I knew how it felt to have your talent rebuked. But with Jojo, it pained me the most. We felt what the other was feeling. We were connected.

The waiter came, setting steaming plates before us. Jojo dug into them with his usual voraciousness. He was a man of many appetites, who wanted to try everything. It was up to me to channel him in the right directions. I was proud that I could do that. When we were in New York, I'd overheard some of the New York critics commenting that the Sinbad murals were truly marvelous but more suitable for a public space such as a grand building, a gallery or museum, than a private home, intimating Jojo's work might be too sensational for everyday consumption. I'd been keeping that criticism to myself all this time, thinking it might offend him. Now, I saw the possibilities it offered.

"You know, Jojo, you were such a success in New York. I think there could be opportunities for serious commissions there. Why not? Public buildings or the like."

"Imagine," he said, taking in my suggestion. "The juxtaposition of a classical theme against the lobby of a brand-new skyscraper. So much new, open space. Ah, Toscha. Yes, yes. I like this idea. A completely blank canvas. A blending of the New World with the Old World."

"It would be perfect," I said, vowing to set out feelers again.

When the orchestra struck up the first notes of after-dinner music, Jojo finished off the last of his wine. He stood, a mischievous expression on his face as he fox-trotted with an invisible partner to my side of the table, making me laugh.

"To the dance floor, senora," he said, ushering me up, his hand steady on the small of my back in a way that made me feel claimed. I reveled in it. What he lacked in stature he made up for with a low center of gravity, with rhythm, Catalan swagger, swaying hips. We danced, and I felt that frisson between us that had been there from the day we first met.

Chapter Five

The next morning, the glow from the evening at Maxim's coalesced into a bolt of lightning as I realized Jojo had already left for the studio. I vaguely remembered him rustling me, his beard scratching my cheek as he kissed me goodbye.

I rose in a flurry. I had tasks as well. I was still working with Dukelsky on his compositions that Diaghilev was turning into a production called *Zephyr and Flora* to premiere in Monte Carlo. And there were arrangements to make for an upcoming fete I was hosting with my friend Princess Radziwill—Dolly, as I called her. Beneath the Pont Alexandre III bridge, with its extravagant sculptures of nymphs, cherubs, and winged horses, we had converted at great expense a barge on the Seine into a dance hall. There would be velvet banquettes. Crystal chandeliers. Champagne fountains. A jazz band. I even had the barge electrified.

But it wasn't simply a party. It had a purpose. I'd recently been captivated by the work of a group of struggling Polish painters. They'd come to Paris to partake in the avant-garde art communities of Montmartre and Montparnasse. Because my father was Polish, I considered Poland one of my countries of origin, though I'd never lived there.

I'd hosted a lunch at the Meurice for the Poles and my wealthy friends who bought their paintings on the spot. Now, the barge was to be both dance hall and gallery, an exhibition of more of the artists' works. All of Paris would come—at least all of Paris I cared about. If everything went according to plan, they would buy the Polish artists' extraordinary paintings. Talent would have the recognition it deserved. Art and artists would progress.

"I invited Roussadana and her sister to the party."

"You did what?" Coco said, her voice distant over the telephone line when I told her. She was out of town with her latest love, the Duke of Westminster, known by his nickname Bendor. "Why would you invite them?"

"So they can see what real art is."

Coco laughed. "I know you, Misia. You want to keep an eye on her. You want to see how she and Jojo are around each other. And you can show her that you are Misia, and in your world, she's completely overmatched. And you know what? I don't blame you. I would do the same thing. I just wish I could be there to see it."

The boat party began with a storm. Bursts of torrential rain. High, ominous winds. Distant thunder and flashes of light.

"Like Otello's arrival at port in Verdi's opera," Jojo said, safe and dry in the expansive luxury cabin where he enjoyed an aperitif with Prince Radziwill.

"If only the source were an organ and a thunder machine," I said, looking out at the quay with Dolly and hoping the weather wouldn't put anyone off from coming. But I knew my friends. It was 1925. This was the glittering season.

They would come.

Thankfully, we had no plans to actually sail. And when the first of the gray, heavy clouds began to close in, I'd pilfered staff from the Meurice for the night. They were out on the quay now, lined up and waiting, an entourage of royal umbrella carriers. Dolly and I watched until we saw movement on the steps from the bridge leading down to the river, umbrellas heading this way. Yes, guests were coming, arriving just as the wind and rain momentarily died down to a breeze and a drizzle, though the sky still flashed with white and distant thunder growled.

Quickly, I checked my reflection in a window, running a light hand over my fresh Marcel waves. My dress was Chanel, of course, a bright, audacious red, the kind a man might want to sink his teeth into, like Eve and her apple. Sleeveless with a square neck, the design was horizontal tiers of delicate, sparkling fabric that lightly swished and swayed when I moved, brilliantly drawing attention to my figure instead of distracting from it. Coco was a master at that trick of subtlety. Jojo had noticed, giving me a lusty look before we left for the party, running a finger along the darling red velvet belt that hung below the waist, growling under his breath. "I want some of that," he'd said. On my head, I wore a jaunty feather. Around my neck, pearls. I was flirtatious. Confident. Modern.

On the boat, Jojo came beside me to greet the first arrivals. Strains of jazz rode the gusts from the incoming storm across the quay as guests descended toward the barge aglow in electric light. Jean, dressed in a captain's uniform. Next, the fairylike artist Marie Laurencin and Fernand Léger. Cécile Sorel, the actress. Paul Morand, the diplomat. Aristocratic friends like the Count de Beaumont and the Princess Bibesco. I'd even invited the Murphys, that American couple, but not their writer friends—they were too unpredictable, always drunk and fighting. The fashionable women were bare-armed in clinging dresses with metallic fringe, the men in black patent shoes and tuxedos, their hair glossy and parted down the middle.

Then Pierre Reverdy, the poet, always brooding. He asked after Coco because they used to sleep together and sometimes still did, when Bendor wasn't behaving. There was Satie, the umbrella he always carried in a pocket so it wouldn't get wet. With his grizzled goatee and damp gray velvet suit, he looked like a swamp rat.

Then Picasso with his now wife, Olga—I had been a witness at the wedding, Coco had made the gown—who looked tired and limped from an injury. Had they been fighting? Picasso often came over to visit me and complain about his marriage. Ballet took much out of her, but so did being married to Pablo, subject to his moods. I loved him dearly but knew he could be cruel.

And Stravinsky, so dapper, who also asked after Coco, giving my heart a pang. He was still not over her. One of our first arguments, between Coco and me, had been because of him. I was so furious with her for breaking his heart. We didn't speak for weeks.

Then Diaghilev appeared just as a bolt of lightning crossed the sky, his jowly face pale. He had a terrible fear of water. A fortune teller told him he would die near the water, and he was certain she was right. His entourage of strapping male dancers surrounded him like a life raft.

"Ah, Misia," he said, his voice shaky, "only you could invoke a typhoon to liven up a party. It's diabolical. Demonic. Unholy."

Diaghilev made his way toward the hors d'oeuvres. Jean came up behind him. "I don't think he need be so jittery," Jean said. "He's grown rather buoyant these last few years. If he falls in, he'll float all the way to Le Havre. Young, handsome sailors in uniform will fish him out, much to his delight."

Just then, another bright flash of lightning filled the sky, followed by an ear-shattering crack. Inside, electric lights flickered, the wires buzzed. With a loud pop, the barge was thrust into darkness. There were a few screams, then murmurs, then laughter. The Poles, unfazed, kept playing. The waiters kept pouring.

"There," I said, directing one of them to a cabinet where I'd seen old lanterns stockpiled. I had another waiter put candles—I'd found a stash of those too—in empty wine bottles, the supply gathering by the minute. The setting was more enchanting than before, the gaiety reaching new heights helped along by Jean. He amused everyone, carrying a lantern and sticking his head through the portholes with a frightful expression, claiming we were sinking.

The dance floor was crowded, the barge rocking in the waves that bashed against the quay, occasionally foisting people into one another's arms. It was too dark to see who danced with who, intrigue all around. The appearance of Sessue Hayakawa caused an additional thrill. I'd sent a note to his hotel to invite him. Why not? Everyone swooned over the handsome actor except Jean, who swooned over his samurai bodyguard. I looked to see if Roussi was with the actor. She wasn't.

She wasn't anywhere. I searched the dark corners, keeping an eye on Jojo, his booming voice in conversation with the diplomat set between sniffs of the white powder he carried in his breast pocket, as popular now as the cocktails imported from America our waitstaff served. Everyone thought they were so new, but Thadée's brother had them at a party back in 1895—how could I be so old? Toulouse-Lautrec was the bartender and nearly killed us all with lethal concoctions of liqueurs based solely on their colors—oranges, yellows, and greens—rather than common sense.

"Misia!" a familiar voice called out.

I turned to find Colette. She'd probably been at that party in 1895. We were both girls. Now, we greeted each other with the affection of people who'd known each other when. She was accompanied by a woman with a cropped hairstyle and wearing a tuxedo. Colette must have met her at Le Monocle, the nightclub for women who loved women.

"But where is Bertrand?" I said. For Colette, love was interchangeable. Men. Women. Boys. Over the past four years, she'd been living with her second husband's son. She'd very famously made him a man when he was sixteen and she decades older.

"We've broken up," she said. "And how are you and Jojo? I was just visiting with him. He seems different, especially vigorous, like a younger version of himself."

I suddenly felt off balance and not from the rocking of the boat. Were people noticing a change in Jojo? Was I the last to know?

Colette immediately sensed my discomfort. I was angry with myself for giving it away.

"The old bastard," she said, her broad, pleasant face wrapped in a scowl. She and Jojo also knew each other when. Had they gone to bed together then? Probably. She put a hand on my arm. "Don't tell me he's just like the rest of them. Don't let him take you for granted, Misia. He wouldn't be half the man without you."

Her concern touched and mortified me at the same time. Well, I thought, centering myself. Jojo wasn't like "the rest of them." He certainly wasn't like Willy, Colette's selfish, overbearing first husband who'd taken credit for the wildly popular Claudine novels she'd written, published under his name and not hers.

Jojo was different. He would never take me for granted.

At that moment, the Poles burst into a rowdy Russian folk song. As the music's pace picked up, the male dancers from the Ballets Russes—Diaghilev's entourage—threw off their jackets and swarmed the floor. They wrapped arms around each other in a Cossack dance, squatting and kicking in dizzying circles. Everyone clapped along and cheered and wished they had such gymnastic ability, the youth, the knees—to be able to move like that. Jean attempted to join them but toppled over. He was immediately scooped up and carried about in a pas de deux shoulder sit by one of the dancers—Serge Lifar, the best of them all—much to Jean's delight.

I looked on, Jojo joining me, an arm around my waist.

A private, spontaneous performance from the dancers of the Ballets Russes was just the sort of entertainment that people had come to expect at one of my parties. He leaned in. "You did it again, Toscha. Amazing. You have conjured the fabulous."

Eventually, the evening shifted toward its natural decline. Jubilation faded to a satisfied, wrung-out kind of exhaustion. I looked out one of the portholes to the east. Could it already be dawn? The rain had stopped. A pale streak of yellow light peeked up over the horizon.

Guests drifted off with the sunrise, the sky a Monet watercolor of oranges and pinks. Picasso left, Jean's captain hat atop his head. Olga had departed hours ago. I said goodbye to Reverdy, Marie Laurencin, Diaghilev, and Lifar. Satie and Stravinsky walked out holding each other up, eyes bloodshot. Colette danced up the quay to the bridge, music still playing in her head, her companion at her side. Then the Polish painters with their instrument cases. One after another guest said adieu. *The party of the season,* they said. And *one that will be remembered* and *impossible to top.* Only Jean remained. He was curled up on one of the banquettes asleep or in an opium fog, I wasn't sure which, oblivious to the fanciful mustache Picasso had drawn on his face with my eyebrow pencil.

The event was a success, every painting sold. But Princess Mdivani hadn't showed up. She hadn't sent a note with an excuse. Nothing. I attributed it to her youth, her upbringing. She didn't know any better.

An avalanche of fatigue filled me. Suddenly, I could think only of my bed, my soft pillow, the cool sheets, Jojo undressing me, the red dress tossed over the back of a chair, the two of us entwined, then sleeping until dinner. Instead, in our bedroom back at the Meurice, Jojo took out his vial and spoon and sniffed the white powder. He splashed water on his face. I watched as he changed clothes, not into his silk pajamas but a fresh suit.

"Where are you going?" I said, surprised.

"The studio. The panels for the Vic Cathedral . . . so much to do. I believe I've figured out the problem of the perspective on *The Homage to the Orient and Occident.*"

"Wonderful," I said. "And will the princess be there as well, or has she completed her special trophy?"

"The princess? I suppose she may be. She seems in no hurry to finish."

Jojo kissed me—could he feel my gritted teeth?—and then he was gone.

◆ ◆ ◆

After he left, I fell into a spiral of sleeplessness.

Something felt off, something more than the association between sculpting clay and my father. I needed to be sharp. I needed my beauty sleep. I could not have Jojo come home from his studio to faded glory, not if youth was still in the picture.

Yet the more I thought of the dreaded consequences of the lack of sleep, the more agitated I became. Sunlight pushed at the closed draperies, shamelessly intruding along the edges. Street noise reminded me that it was daytime, and Jojo was at his studio, possibly with her. I tossed and turned, disturbing even Mezzo, who jumped off the bed for the tranquility of a cushioned chair.

I pushed my sleep mask to my forehead and went into the bathroom for the bottle. I hoped it was still there. I hadn't taken morphine since the Count and Countess de Beaumont's last fancy dress ball a year earlier. After all-night masquerades and other festivities, Jojo and I sometimes availed ourselves of the magic elixir floating in that bottle to ensure a sound, refreshing sleep. Acquired from the pharmacy, our potion was purely for medicinal purposes. Only in more recent years was a doctor's prescription required. But those too were not hard to come by. The healing qualities of morphine were well known.

The bottle was there.

In a drawer, I found the mother-of-pearl case that held my hypodermic syringe. I pulled my nightgown up, baring my thigh, and winced at the pinch of the needle as it punctured the outer layer of my flesh, a slight discomfort accompanied by a great sense of relief. I lay back against the pillows with a sigh and descended into a dreamy, bottomless bliss.

While Jojo was at his studio, I'd been spending hours each morning at my piano advising Francis Poulenc. Dear Poulenc. He heard music in poetry. I heard poetry in his music. Mutual friends had told me of this shy, unknown young man who longed to play his ballet for me but was too embarrassed to do so. I invited him to the Meurice to play at my piano. He waited, so nervous, for the right moment when no one else was there. When he played, I was charmed by what I heard. I suggested a few tweaks, then presented it to Diaghilev, knowing he would be charmed too. Now, we planned to use it for the score for a new ballet to be performed by the Ballets Russes. Soon everyone would know the name Francois Poulenc.

It was exactly one week after the barge party. Late one afternoon, after a morning with Poulenc and an afternoon with Diaghilev and rehearsals for *Zephyr and Flora*, I arrived home. As I rested before dinner, Aimée told me Jojo was on the telephone, calling from his studio.

His gravelly voice had a deeper tone I recognized.

"Darling, did you just wake?" I said. Jojo sometimes took his siesta at his studio. The making of great art could be exhausting.

"Yes, yes. Just a little catnap. But the work is going very well. Very well. I've got some studies for Vic I'm close to finishing today. The Adam and Eve panels. I'm afraid if I stop now, I'll lose all momentum. I called at Maxim's—told them we'd be a bit later than usual but to save our table. You understand, don't you, Toscha?"

"I understand. I'm thrilled you're making progress."

"I am too. Don't worry. I won't be terribly late. I'm famished."

Famished. The word took the wind out of me. I wanted to pretend I hadn't heard it. I *needed* to pretend I hadn't heard it. But I had.

I kept my voice even but said goodbye quickly. I sent Aimée out on an errand with Alphonse. I needed to be alone. My knees wobbled. I had to sit. Unsettled, I went to my dressing table, then to my writing desk, then finally to the piano. My fingers trembled over the keys as I tried to play a happy, light aria, as if that could make impending doom go away.

Had he just said he was famished?

I'd barely begun to play before my hands collapsed on the keyboard in a cacophony of clashing notes.

He had.

I knew Jojo better than he knew himself. As a lover, I was familiar with his habits and quirks in bed. First, we would make love. Then, in the exquisite sweetness of the "afterward," we would hold each other close, our minds and bodies slowly returning to the conscious world. But there would come a point when he could lie still no more, when, like a conqueror who'd earned his feast, he would heartily announce, "I'm famished!"

In the kitchen, he'd slice off pieces of his treasured Iberico ham or take out a plate of fresh tomatoes and mozzarella he'd bought from a street vendor and drizzled with a balsamic glaze. He'd feed me little bites as if I were a bird, alternating between himself and me, putting the fork to my mouth, his hand beneath as he had in Rome.

Now, images I didn't want to see scrolled through my mind. Roussi and her long, smooth limbs, her youthful, acrobatic energy. Jojo, post-lovemaking, spent, as she curled up around him, her flaxen hair fanned out, mingling with the dark brush of his barrel chest.

I'm famished.

That was what he said to *me*. That was our special language. To hear him use the same expression as when we finished making love?

Intolerable.

I slammed the cover over the keys and got up from the piano. I had a driving urge to go to the studio and demand the Georgian interloper leave. What a release it would be to tell Jojo how I felt. To not have to play this game any longer. To demand Roussi's expulsion.

Yes. I would do it. I'd waited long enough.

I needed to change clothes, to look exquisite yet formidable. Regal. Poised. *Modern.* In my room, I began pulling out clothing, tossing outfits about the room. This navy Chanel ensemble? Beautiful, but too subtle for my mission. This suit from Poiret? Too dated. A pale pink day dress from Worth? Too insipid. I went through all my Chanels. Patou, Lelong, Molyneux, Jenny, Renee, Callot. No matter the dressmaker, everything was wrong, wrong, wrong. Where was Coco when I needed her? In Scotland, with Bendor.

After I'd flung half of my wardrobe across the bed, the floor, and the lampshades, I caught a glimpse of myself in the mirror. Red-faced. Eyes crazed. Mania had seized me.

I dropped to the edge of the bed, realizing how close I was to losing the control I'd been practicing these past few weeks. An old feeling of desperation shook me. I was desperate when I'd begged Thadée not to leave me. I was desperate when I did the same with Edwards. I was so very desperate I'd even gone to Lantelme, pleading with her to stay away. None of it worked. Instead, I'd driven them away.

I could not be desperate with Jojo.

No one would want that pitiful, raging woman in the mirror.

A crueler thought pierced me. Was this what my mother had looked like all those years ago, after she'd opened a letter not meant for her?

Mezzo, who'd been watching from behind a pile of discarded couture dresses, jumped in my lap, sensing I needed consolation. I gathered him to me. The drama of my birth was a part of my heritage I could not escape. My father had gone to Saint Petersburg after accepting the commission to redecorate the tsar's palace. My mother, carrying me then in her womb for eight months, had stayed behind in Belgium in the comfort of my grandparents' luxurious villa because everyone said that would be best.

Then, in the frozen stillness of winter, my debut into this world imminent, a letter bearing the Imperial Russian stamp arrived. My mother wasn't supposed to see it. It was from Saint Petersburg. She thought it was for her, from my father. Anxious to hear from him, she'd opened it without looking at the addressee.

But it was for my grandmother, from her younger sister Olga. In the letter, Olga confessed to having an affair with my father, the man who had married her niece. Cyprien had seduced her, she'd said, and now she was with child.

My mother, racked with grief and turmoil, came undone.

She left the house before sunrise one morning, leaving Belgium for Saint Petersburg despite her delicate state. It was December, Russia buried alive beneath layers of deep snow and ice. Traveling alone, she spent hours in the polar cold, waiting in drafty train stations, riding in cars that jolted and shuddered. After a long journey, she arrived at my father's doorstep at the end of her tether. There, she collapsed. Inside, she gave birth to me, then drew her last breath.

I knew none of this until I was eighteen and soon to be married to Thadée. My precious grandmother, whom I adored, was on her deathbed at the villa, and I'd come from Paris to Belgium to be with her. I'd never seen her so still except when she would listen with deep rapture to the music of the great composers who came to her salon. She gave the same attention to me when I played the piano as a child. I could never forget that proud, beatific expression on her fine-boned face. She was petite, pretty, always dressed in exquisite clothes and laden with jewels, a woman always moving about, planning feasts and musicales that included Liszt, Rubinstein, Richter, von Bülow.

It was from her I learned by example to do for artists what she did for musicians. Give them a place to play, to create, to conspire. A place to forget their troubles. This, she said, was the calling of angels.

What a shock it was to see her so fragile, as if she might float away. In her jewel box, I found her ruby necklace. She let me clasp it around her dainty neck. I hoped it would weigh her down, keep her there on earth with me.

Then Olga arrived from Saint Petersburg. Olga demanded I leave the room. I did, stopping outside the door to listen. Grandmother, grasping some last strength, was furious Olga was there. They spoke of my father, what had happened, my grandmother reliving the details of my mother's grueling journey.

I was in disbelief. Why had no one told me? Olga pled for Grandmother's forgiveness. Grandmother accused Olga of treachery.

There was no forgiveness in her voice. But Grandmother blamed herself as well for not stopping my mother. She thought my mother would come to her senses before she got far and turn back. But she didn't.

I hadn't known any of this. My mother had died in childbirth. That was all I'd ever been told.

"If she had been patient and stayed here, in Belgium," Olga said, "if she hadn't chased after him, she would be alive. To travel at that time of year, alone, with child! What was she thinking? Her death was self-induced."

"How dare you," Grandmother said, her usually melodic voice a ferocious rasp. "I blame you, and I blame Cyprien. Who does such a thing with his wife's aunt?"

"Cyprien would have come back to her in time, Sophie. He left me eventually. I lost the baby. All she had to do was wait. She had the upper hand."

"She didn't even get to hold Misia in her arms," my grandmother cried. "Her own daughter. To never know a mother's embrace."

I couldn't bear to hear any more. I burst into the room.

"Get out," I said to Olga. "Get out."

She did.

If only I could use those same words now with Roussadana.

The fates were surely laughing at me. I was born into a love triangle. Now, my life appeared to be an excruciating series of them. How to break the curse?

I had to do the opposite of my mother. The opposite of what I'd done with Thadée and Edwards. I could not confront Jojo and make demands. If my mother had stayed and waited for my father to come back to her, perhaps everything would have been different. Instead, she'd let anguish overtake her.

I could not let anguish overtake me.

I set Mezzo down and went to the piano once again.

The first movement of Beethoven's Sonata No. 17, *Tempest*, exploded into the air as my fingers rolled like a tidal wave over the keys. There was a tempest within me, a tumult building inside.

Conflict. Yearning. Broken chords ascending.

Beethoven's agony over the realization he was going deaf, the worst fate he could suffer, was the expression of my overwrought soul. What was the worst fate I could suffer? Losing Jojo.

"Break the piano," the composer passionately instructed a pupil who'd once asked how to play the beginning of the piece. I wanted to break Roussi. My instinct to play Beethoven was no coincidence. I could imagine his growing feeling of isolation as sound became muffled around him, lips moving but he couldn't comprehend the words. He'd watched helplessly as the world went on without him, deafness edging him out.

The flurry of my hands slowed into the second movement of the piece. Here, I held each key a fraction longer as Beethoven's rage and my own receded to bleak, resounding melancholy. Why had Jojo opened the studio door that very first day when she knocked? He never answered the door. But that day, that one day, he did. To a vision of youth and loveliness. A "princess" in need of aid. Who wouldn't let her in?

In the third movement, the frenetic rage of the first was replaced by a building sense of control, of calm resolve. Rage turned to defiance. Loss to triumph.

I played, and the notes worked their magic, funneling the chaos of my mind. To create music was to grapple with emotion, composers working as translators of our souls, somehow reining in their amorphous depths between stanzas. I needed to rein myself in.

Defiance. Triumph. Beethoven would not surrender to the whims of providence. Nor would I.

I would be in control. I would *allow* their affair. I would be kind. Magnanimous.

An unconventional approach, but my life had never been conventional. For me, convention didn't work. I knew Jojo would give her up if I demanded it. And I knew from experience that people wanted what they couldn't have. As Coco said, men especially. And so I would give her to him. Because soon enough, he would not want her.

Meanwhile, I would be above it all. Beneficent, generous, patient Misia. Letting Jojo have his momentary fun, a mirage of youthfulness, a burst of virility as he grappled with getting older. How exciting for Jojo. This little interlude with Roussi was a gift I was giving him. He would understand that. He would appreciate it. He would love me even more.

No, I didn't do things the way normal people did. But for better or for worse, I wasn't normal. My intuition had served me well all these years. There was a reason I was who I was and had accomplished what others hadn't. Roussi, that shiny object, would eventually dull. All I had to do was quietly bide my time.

I rose from the piano to bathe and dress, to have Aimée fix my hair, to meet Jojo at Maxim's, to watch him eat ravenously, to act as if all were perfectly well.

After dinner that evening, we were home alone. Usually we might be relaxing beneath the stars on our balcony overlooking the Tuileries, my feet on his lap, his strong painter's hands massaging them. Instead, there was a distance between us. He knew me well enough to sense I was not completely myself at dinner. Yet as he sometimes would, he didn't ask me what I was thinking.

Now, I was at my writing table returning some correspondence. He was in the library, shuffling papers around his desk, when he came out holding something in his hand.

"Look, Toscha," he said. "Look at what I found. One of the photographs I took during the war when we were driving the ambulances. Do you remember?"

He held it out. It was me, carrying a wounded man on my back up the steps of the hospital.

The war was when he'd first started working with cameras.

"What a picture this is," he said. "The genius of the camera. How it captures you. My Misia."

The image was blurry, smudges of black and white. The injured soldier was draped across my back. "He couldn't manage on his own," I said. "All the orderlies had disappeared. He was in pain. There were others there on the pavement, standing about. But no one offered to help him. So I did. Why not? I was strong, invigorated by the work we were doing."

"I'd been in the hospital," Jojo said. "I walked back out to find you. And there you were, midway up the steps. I was astounded. Amazed. I took the picture right away. You were incredible. Never afraid to do what others will not. You don't hesitate. A person is in need and you help. You do what needs to be done no matter what."

"I remember I had no idea you were there with your camera. My attention was on ensuring I didn't trip over my long skirts and harm the man further."

"I was there, and I'm glad I was. It struck me so much, seeing you like that. I should have gone to help you. I realize now, so much later, why I didn't. That moment. Of all the portraits famous men have made of you, of you sitting at your dressing table. Or sitting at the piano. Or sitting in a garden. This, Toscha. This, on the hospital steps, is the truest portrait. The one that captures your essence. It's the image that defines you."

He paused for a moment as if to draw back emotion. I was quiet now myself, caught up in the sentimental and his feelings for me.

When he continued, his voice was low. "You've carried many men on your back, mi amor. You've helped so many by lifting them up. Renoir. Diaghilev. Stravinsky. Cocteau. But no one more than me." He put a hand to my cheek and cupped it, his eyes holding mine. "Where would I be without you?"

"And I you," I said, putting my hand over his. "You are the only man who has given me the freedom to be me. Who's proud of me for what I do, not resentful or jealous. Oh, darling, where would we be without each other?"

Jojo was back. Reeling himself in. He didn't want to lose me. I just had to endure.

Chapter Six

Monte Carlo, 1925

On my way to Monte Carlo for the premiere of the Ballets Russes's *Zephyr and Flora*, I should have been exhilarated. Instead, I was forlorn. At the last minute, Jojo hesitated about going. It was just before Alphonse was to take us to the Gare du Nord station, where we would board the exclusive overnight train, affectionately nicknamed the "blue train" because of its sumptuous blue sleeping car trimmed in gold.

I had noticed as we were getting ready that Jojo was distracted. He'd come home from the studio seeming vexed. My jaw tightened— imperceptibly, I hoped—as I thought of time wasted helping "the princess" with her sculpture. I wondered if this change of heart had more to do with her than deadlines. Had he been lying to me of his progress these past weeks?

"There is still so much to do," he said. "I'm anxious, Toscha, very anxious. There's the Wendel panels. And the Jeu de Paume exhibition will be here before I know it."

"Yes, but . . ."

I'd done this to myself. I'd spoken to friends in the art world and arranged for an exhibition of his panels at the Jeu de Paume the next May. Large and soaring, this was the kind of venue that could properly display his work. I wanted to inspire him to finish, a deadline to light a fire, force him to make choices. And take his mind off Roussi.

"Oh, darling. I know. But wouldn't a break help? Renew your stores of creativity? And you love Monte Carlo so." I forced a sympathetic smile on my face and into my voice. I must not—not!—sound clinging.

"I do. And especially with you. But . . . I fear I'd be preoccupied the entire time. A black cloud over the festivities. I don't want to ruin this especial moment for you, for Diaghilev. You must go and enjoy yourself. Coco will be there. And Jean. You won't even notice I'm not."

A claw with long talons lived in my stomach, digging my insides out. "Of course I'll notice. Everyone will. You bring life wherever you go. All our friends will be so disappointed if you're not there. Especially me."

He pulled at his beard, looking down at the floor. Finally, he sighed and with a weak smile said, "Yes. Yes. What am I thinking? If you really want me to, I'll go. I want to be by your side always. Alphonse, are my bags ready?"

"Yes, Monsieur Sert. Shall I take them down to the car?"

"No," I interjected, trying not to sound exasperated for it was too late now. I would feel overwhelming guilt keeping him from his work. "Just my bags, please, Alphonse. Monsieur Sert will stay here."

Alphonse left, and the entire trip crumbled before me. I would be unhappy if Jojo did come, unhappy if he didn't. I had to remain composed and hide all disappointment, reminding myself that I was acting out of generosity. I could still insist he come. And he would. I had the power. Our tender moment the night before, remembering the war, told me so.

"You're right," I said to him. "You must stay in Paris. Actually, I insist."

His shoulders, which had been around his ears, relaxed with relief. Too much relief. "Are you sure, my love?"

"Absolutely sure."

"Will you forgive me?" He said this in such a sweet way, putting his arms around me, kissing my hair. I savored the feeling of him holding me, my own arms around his solid frame. It steadied me, absorbing the warmth of the man I loved despite his faults.

"There's nothing to forgive," I said. "I would despise myself if I were to keep you from creating when you feel the need. Especially over a small premiere that means more to me than you. You're so busy with the Hotel Wendel commission. And the Vic Cathedral panels. You have to concentrate on those."

"You know me as no one else does," he said. "Only to you can I admit the difficulties and fears. You're the only one who knows my struggles."

◆ ◆ ◆

Taking the train by myself, I was somber. Usually upon boarding, Jojo and I would go to the dining car for a five-course meal, but I decided to skip dinner. I didn't care to be seen alone at the moment. I had no appetite anyway.

With Aimée's help, I settled into my berth. Until now, I had so many fond memories of traveling from Paris to the coast. This very train had inspired one of Jean's genius ideas for a ballet, *Le Train Bleu*, performed by the Ballets Russes last year. Jojo was with me for that premiere. Lighthearted, the ballet poked fun at the wealthy Parisians who took this exclusive car to the Côte d'Azur. Coco conceived the costumes, which were bathing suits and tennis wear from her collection. Bronislava Nijinska conceived the choreography, which was more acrobatic than balletic. Picasso painted the curtain with two of his nearly naked Amazonian women running hand in hand along the beach, black hair flying behind them.

Thinking about it now brought on raw feelings of melancholy and a desire to go back to a time when I was so splendidly unaware of Roussadana's existence. As the train coursed along, farther and farther away from Paris and Jojo, I wished I'd insisted Jojo come with me.

It was a relief when I remembered Aimée had packed my brown medicinal bottle. I would take an early dose and sleep the whole way.

◆ ◆ ◆

Stepping out the next morning, I breathed in the sun-gilded air to fortify myself. A premiere was what I lived for. The anticipation. The stakes. How would the ballet be received? I didn't need the gambling tables of the casino. This was my roulette.

Immediately upon checking in to the Hôtel de Paris, I was presented with an enormous flower arrangement from Jojo that brought on more questions than delight. Was it a token of guilt or appreciation? Or both? There was also a stack of messages from Diaghilev.

Have you arrived? Where are you? Haste!! Haste!! Come right away!

Why aren't you here yet? Disaster has struck! Hurry!

Madame! Whatever you are doing, could it be more important than this?

Surely you are in Monte Carlo by now?

"My god, woman," Diaghilev said when I arrived at the theater. "Are you purposely torturing me?" He wore his summer uniform. A straw hat, white trousers that stopped at his ankles, a black jacket. He twitched with nerves as if trying to escape the severity of his always-starched collar, his head turning this way and that. A camellia peeped obliviously from his buttonhole.

I couldn't tell him I'd been delayed at the hotel dressing table, wondering how to take ten years from my face. There, disaster had struck as well.

I stood at alert, ready for action.

"Massine is trying to change the choreography. Lifar twisted his ankles. Yes, both of them. The third viola hasn't shown up. Jean and Coco are bickering nonstop over what's more important, the libretto or the costumes." Diaghilev raised his straw hat and dabbed at his forehead with a crumpled handkerchief.

I touched his arm. "I'll talk to Massine. Lifar will pull through. I'll send Jean out to look for the third viola. He probably won't find him, but that will solve the bickering. No one will notice the missing viola except us. What else?"

"The set," he said. "I'm sure there's some catastrophe there too."

He strode off in that direction, and I surged into action. I scolded Massine. *No new choreography!* I checked in with Lifar, who insisted with a grimace his ankles were fine. I found Jean with Coco, who was adjusting the hem on one of the ballerinas' sequined skirts.

"Where's Monsieur Jojo?" he asked immediately, as if he had the supernatural ability to pinpoint the most fragile areas of my mind. Jean was exceedingly perceptive, one of the qualities I normally admired in him. But nothing was normal now. Surely he didn't know the truth?

"Jojo wasn't able to come," I said in a too-abrupt tone. "So much work to do. Important commissions. You know."

Jean's eyebrows lifted in surprise. "Monsieur Jojo didn't come to Monte Carlo? But he always comes. Brash, decadent, extravagant Monte Carlo. This is his element."

I wished Jean would keep his voice down. "Making great art is his element," I said. "And it was I who insisted he stay."

Before Jean could say more, I sent him on his quest for the missing viola, then walked quickly toward Coco. When she saw me, she looked up with a sympathetic smile, the one person who knew exactly why Jojo stayed behind.

On Bendor's yacht before the show, Coco and I toasted the evening to come with coupes of champagne. She was radiant these days, and I was glad to see it. She wore loose-fitting, wide-legged pants and a short-sleeved shirt. With her cropped hair and bronzed skin, she could have been a member of the yacht's crew. She loved the way the tan made her pearls look whiter. I was certain everyone in Monte Carlo would soon be wearing the same, including me. I'd already cut my hair, lopping off the old-fashioned topknot Coco referred to as my "mandarin orange" and succumbing to the trend. The effect on Coco was enchanting. After years of heartbreak, Bendor was good for her. She loved the British sporting life, and with Bendor there was plenty of it. I didn't care to fish, as Coco did. Or ride horses. Or play tennis. Or any of that. Perhaps that was why Bendor and I had yet to warm to each other. He was somewhere belowdecks. He'd come out to say a polite but stiff hello and that was it.

I was relieved that Coco and I were alone. We lounged on the deck in the sun's embrace. Around us, limestone cliffs spilled down from the sky like the palm of Mother Nature's generous hand opening into the sea. Fragrances floated in from the brush—wild lavender, thyme, rosemary, juniper. The shore ribboned around the coast like the curves of those oddly proportioned women in Picasso's imagination and canvases.

"Drink," Coco said. "Champagne always smooths out the nerves."

I took a gulp. "My nerves are more than about the show. You must tell me, are people talking? Jean is suspicious. Do people know about Jojo and that girl? I can't stand the thought!"

"No one has said anything to me. I haven't heard a word."

"Colette noticed. She knew before I did! You should see Jojo. He went to the tailor the other day and came home wearing a new style of trousers. They're extra wide. High waisted. A look I've seen of late on younger men. Much younger."

Coco laughed. "I hope he doesn't make a fool of himself. He's enamored not of the girl but of thinking of himself as young again. He'll realize the delusion before long."

"Will he?" I took another taste of my champagne, then told her about the telephone call with Jojo, how he'd used the word "famished" and what it meant. I lowered my voice. "It was as if I were right there in the room with them. Ghastly."

"And he, naturally, has no idea he gave himself away. That's because the affair is nothing to him."

"It certainly feels like something to me. A dagger to my heart."

"But you can't think like that. It's not personal. You know how this works. You should take a lover of your own," Coco said.

I scoffed. "I don't want one. I'm simply not capable. I want Jojo." I didn't understand the point of lovers. Perhaps that was why I took Jojo's wanderings more to heart. Though in the case of Edwards, except for Lantelme, I hadn't minded at all. He had proclivities I'd found exceedingly distasteful. For these, it was I who insisted he engage a mistress. Alas, in that case, we were both happy.

In this case, I was utterly miserable.

"The key in these kinds of things is discretion," Coco went on. "Fidelity in affairs of the bedroom isn't expected as long as fidelity to discretion is. This is what worries me, Misia. Jojo is being discreet, with the exception of the pants. Ha! It's you who isn't playing by the rules. Inviting her to the barge party. What were you thinking?"

"You know very well that I am not good at being discreet. I'm trying, but it's not in my repertoire."

"I understand it's difficult for you not to be pulling all the strings," Coco said. "But for once in your life, you must be patient. You must stay behind the scenes. Don't go to visit her. Don't invite her to parties. Don't speak of her to Jojo. When he speaks of her, change the subject. If you continue to acknowledge her existence, she will continue to exist. You must bury her in silence and complete indifference. Bury her before she buries you!"

To remain silent was so hard to do. But that was the tactic Coco had taken when she was new to Paris, living with Boy Capel as his mistress. As did so many men, Boy had small affairs on the side. They bothered Coco, but she ignored them. "He always comes back to me," she'd said. She had his heart.

Just as I had Jojo's.

When Boy told Coco he had gotten engaged to the Englishwoman, Coco hid her devastation. Instinct told her not to complain. Not to cry. Not to make demands. Instead, she relied on dignity.

Looking at her now on Bendor's yacht, I could see how the years had chiseled her. Back then, before Boy's engagement, she was softer. Easier. Spirited, but optimistic. Back then she glowed. Now, she glittered.

I never once saw her crack. A woman worth having, she said, couldn't appear to question her worth. Coco was a wonder to watch, especially as I had had no such dignity with Thadée, with Edwards, with Lantelme. When Boy married, she remained stoic, focusing on her work, taking on lovers of her own more to show Boy she could than for pleasure. Boy still came to stay with her, little by little, then more and more. She welcomed him as if nothing had changed. She never asked about his wife or delivered ultimatums. She loved him, that was all. He'd hurt her but not enough that she could stop loving him.

"The best thing to do is nothing," Coco told me then. "I have the higher ground. All I have to do is hold it and wait."

That was what Coco did, and Boy came back. He decided his marriage had been a mistake. He wanted to marry Coco.

She did everything right. Then destiny stepped in.

Boy left her home in Paris a few days before Christmas, very early one morning to drive to Cannes. His wife was to meet him there from England for the holiday. He told Coco he would ask for a divorce. Through self-control and dignity, she'd won him back, though what happened next was pure Greek tragedy.

Halfway to Cannes, his automobile spun off the road. He was killed instantly.

Now, so much had changed for her. With Bendor, she was happy again.

And I was the one in need of counsel.

She poured more champagne into her glass and mine. She slumped back in her chair holding the stem—with me, she let her guard down as well and was not always so poised. "You know," she said, "it actually occurred to me that you might have had it in your head to invite the young princess here for the premiere. As your guest. That way, you would have known she wasn't with Jojo."

◆ ◆ ◆

At every premiere of the Ballets Russes in the past, I'd held court in the foyer, Jojo at my side. But I couldn't preside in the foyer alone. I made my way to my box with Coco and Bendor, holding my head high. I wore my tiara, as I often did for a premiere, though Coco begged me to take it off, calling it vulgar because she considered it excess and to her, all excess was vulgar.

But on this night, I needed my crown. This was not the time to relinquish it. People were used to my tiara. They expected it. I smiled as I waved and nodded to friends and acquaintances. For some, it seemed their gaze lingered longer than normal.

I took a seat in my box. The best box, as always, in the house. Was that Winnaretta brazenly looking up at me through her opera glasses? When I looked back, she turned away quickly. Perhaps she was admiring my ensemble? A Chanel gown of gold lace with scalloped edges, a low belt, and a scoop neckline. Coco always dressed me to my best effect. I may not have been a lithe nineteen-year-old, but I was still a force on my own. So was Coco, who sparkled like the night sky in a gown of delicate black sequins.

I was relieved when the lights dimmed and the curtain lifted. All eyes turned toward the stage. Dancers practiced at rehearsals. They performed at opening night. They leaped higher. Stretched farther.

Lifar was magnificent, bounding seamlessly through the pain of the twisted ankles. But in his role, he was no longer mortal. He was Boreas, the cold north wind, an interloper conniving to separate the oblivious

Zephyr and Flora, husband and wife, with a devious, seductive charm. Boreas schemes to draw them apart. Then, with the single shot of an arrow, he kills Zephyr. Triumphant, he sweeps the distraught Flora into his arms. She is his.

Or so he thinks.

In come the Muses, ballet-stepping across the floor in Coco's sequined shifts. Zephyr's love for Flora could not be so easily extinguished. With the Muses' help, Zephyr was revived. They tied Flora to Zephyr's wrist so she could never be lost again. Boreas was punished. Zephyr and Flora were forever afterward together.

After the last act, the crowd rose with cheers and applause. I did too, clapping for more than just the performance. Oh you gods of the theater, I thought, always whispering in my ear. *Don't worry, Misia. Roussadana is no more than a fleeting north wind, a momentary gust. She will pass into the hinterlands soon enough, never to be heard of again.*

After the show and the curtain calls, the standing ovations, backstage there were embraces, tears, laughter. Diaghilev and Massine reconciled. Coco and Jean walked together, Coco fussing over him, worried as we both were he'd disappear into Monte Carlo's opium dens later. We went to celebrate the premiere's success with a late supper at the casino as we always did. But where was my generous Jojo hosting and calling for bottle after bottle, plate after plate? I missed him.

At the head of the table, Diaghilev feasted, spilling sauce on his tie. Everyone went over the performance. Lifar was a wonder. Dukelsky's music glorious, the missing third viola forgotten. Coco's costumes groundbreaking. Braque's stage set magnificent. Even the lightmen and the soundmen, who Diaghilev had shouted at so many times during rehearsals, were heroes.

Beside me, Coco moved closer. She had an expression that gave me pause, coal burning in her black eyes.

"This!" she said, gesturing around the table and speaking in a low hiss. "This would not exist if not for you. You know, Misia, sometimes I think you boast too much. It chafes me. Until I remember you have to boast."

"I have no idea what you mean."

"Otherwise, no one will recognize what you do. The end of the show. The curtain call. All the applause for the performers, the musicians. Then the crowd turns, as they always do, looking for your box. But not for you. They're looking for Diaghilev. They clap until he stands, waves his hat, that silver streak in his hair reflecting the stage lights."

"Coco, what is your point?"

"Performance after performance. You bring the composers to Diaghilev. You bring the ideas. And he gets all the credit."

"He deserves it."

"So do you. Your name should be in the program. Your name should be in the reviews. People should clap for you too."

"That's not important to me. That's not why I do it."

Coco put her name on everything. I put my name on nothing. I admired her for insisting on recognition. Fearlessly demanding credit. But we were different that way.

"You do the same for Jojo," she said, shaking her head. "You do everything for him. And he does whatever he wants."

I had an epiphany on the train back to Paris. I remembered Coco saying she thought I might have invited Princess Mdivani to Monte Carlo. I would never do that, but it did give me a different idea. I should invite Princess Mdivani to luncheon.

I didn't know when Jojo's infatuation with Roussadana would blow over. In the meantime, I couldn't have everyone in Paris speculating. Who had seen her go in and out of Jojo's studio? Did he talk about her to others, praising her sculpting skills, so that they may think she had other skills he found praiseworthy?

I had to nip speculation in the bud. If people saw me out with Princess Mdivani, no one would suspect a thing. Everyone knew Misia Sert would never socialize with her husband's paramour.

Would she accept my invitation? She did.

When she arrived at the restaurant, she immediately addressed me as "Misia," an informality that at first rankled me. Who did she think she was? Had she no manners? Perhaps this rendezvous was a mistake. Soon enough, though, I realized I was the anachronism, stuck in old-fashioned mores. Me—who had lived my entire life on the premise that rules were meant to be ignored.

"Oh—I apologize," she'd said almost immediately in that unselfconscious way of the truly young. "How rude of me. I should have asked—do you mind if I call you Misia? To be known by just one name, well, that is the very definition of success, isn't it? The very summit. One says 'Misia' and everyone knows immediately it's you. To address you formally seems an insult."

Unable to deny the truth of her explanation, I could only laugh, my guard lowered slightly, and insist she call me Misia.

She had a way of seeming harmless. She'd been in Paris two years and still had a country milkmaid aspect to her despite an effort to appear artistic. She wore a jacket that looked like Lanvin, probably her sister's courtesy of Mr. Huberich. An embroidered blouse perhaps from the markets of Constantinople. A skirt that didn't match the jacket though it complemented it in tone and fabric. Her hat, a felt cloche, was pulled lower over her right eye than her left so it gave the lighthearted effect that she was winking at you.

I was anything but lighthearted, though I pretended to be.

I hated to admit it, but I admired the way she'd outfitted herself, haphazard as it was. She looked interesting. Many of the refugees hadn't the means for extravagance. They paid no attention to their appearance, hoping to draw sympathy. Instead, they were avoided.

Roussadana seemed to inherently understand the usefulness of looking appealing. Her attire flattered her and vaguely reminded me of my initial impression of Coco when I'd first met her during the war, how her unique style stood out as fresh and new.

I was the cultivator of the fresh and new. Everyone knew that. I could see she piqued the interest of those around us. When I introduced her to curious friends who came by our table, she offered an irresistible dimpled smile. "You know all the best people," she said after they left. "Look at how they come to you."

She told absurd anecdotes as she had at the Hotel Versailles. When our sole meunière came, she held up her left hand and claimed that the Eastern-looking gold-and-emerald ring she wore had come from the belly of a trout she'd once caught fishing with her brothers in the river that ran outside their estate in Tiflis, the capital of Georgia. She leaned toward me and said in a whispery singsong voice that she was certain the fish had once been a Hindu Indian queen cursed by the gods for committing some wild indiscretion. She spoke of Alexis, the favorite brother, repeating what she'd told me before. "We are two people, but we share the same soul."

Sitting in the reflection of her succulent youth, the effect was not what I expected. Instead of feeling older in her presence, I felt younger, as if I were soaking in her liveliness. Around her, the air changed. The light changed. *I* changed. I felt like a more interesting version of myself.

No wonder Jojo was taken with her. She must have made him feel this way as well. He'd even bought those silly pants. She was "especial" as he said, one of those Spanish words still peppering his speech.

She ordered what I had because "I know you only have the very best—of everything." She complimented my ensemble, saying she'd always looked in the windows of Chanel but hadn't the courage to go in. She had a childlike quality as if she hoped for direction, as if she thought I might take her to Chanel and dress her up, introduce her to society, give her a Parisienne sheen.

The idea intrigued me. I had always been a Svengali of sorts, shaping people, exerting control. I could control her right out of Jojo's life. Unlike Svengali, my motives were never sinister but derived from love. And there was no one I loved more than Jojo.

◆ ◆ ◆

When it was time for Jojo and I to leave for our annual season in Venice, I was ready for the monthslong break from the Princess Mdivani. She hadn't left yet for California. She had another commission from that American flyer. I didn't understand how one kept Charlie Chaplin waiting, if he were in fact waiting, but the trip was apparently put off until she could finish the second aviation trophy.

On the day of our departure, Alphonse packed the limousine with our multitude of trunks.

Our Rolls-Royce had been specially altered for travel according to plans Jojo had drawn up years ago. Not the latest model, but perfectly equipped for us. We had extra storage as well as reclined seating for two in the back. This for our annual long journey—"our madness," I called it. Three months of receptions, balls, concerts, revelry. For almost twenty years we'd been making the pilgrimage to Italy, and especially Venice, every summer since our first trip to Rome.

"Darling, are you ready?" I said to Jojo from inside the car.

"Yes, yes," he said with a slight scowl. Usually, he was the impatient one, haranguing me for taking too long. I was always worried I'd leave something important behind. This time, he was the one acting that way.

I had the odd feeling that someone was watching Jojo and me from the shadows of the Meurice's front entrance. Roussi's eyes. Why did I feel them boring into the back of my head? The situation with her was making me lose my senses. Coco had actually thought I might invite the girl to come along.

"Don't do it, Misia," Coco had said.

"Do you even know me? I would never. Venice with Jojo and all of our friends is far too sacred for that."

"Do I know you?" Coco said. "These days I'm not sure."

Well, dinner at Maxim's was one matter. Evenings there—I had invited her several times—had been uneventful and, thanks to Roussi's youthful vivacity, pleasant enough. But my strategy for keeping gossip at bay didn't involve Venice. A very small part of me feared Jojo would decide at the last minute not to go, just as he had for the premiere in Monte Carlo.

But Venice didn't compare to that. Our annual trip was sacrosanct. It was the treasured respite during which Jojo replenished his creativity, travel a necessity for Jojo not just for pleasure but for new ideas. Venice was where he communed with his Tiepolo, Tintoretto, and Veronese. He roamed about their most cherished city studying the layers upon layers of architecture, design, and decoration.

Finally, he slid in the back beside me. Mezzo settled happily between us and that was that. Alphonse shut the door, then took the driver's seat. The great engine roared, and the car moved out into the traffic. I could breathe. We were going back to the way it had always been. Just the two of us. I'd longed for that. We would reconnect and when we returned, Roussi would be wiped from his consciousness altogether.

Italy was our place. Where our love always blossomed. Our lucky charm.

I turned to Jojo, surprised to find he still had a worry line between his brows. An artistic dilemma? Problems with a commission? These he always shared with me. I knew all of his troubles. What was this about?

"Darling," I said, taking his hand. "We're on our way to our Elysian fields, our Oceanus banks. Our place of perfect happiness."

He lifted my hand and kissed it. The muddy pools of his eyes held mine for a brief moment, just long enough for me to perceive a ripple of sadness in them and fear he was thinking of Roussi.

Oh, Venice—preening in the moonlight, drowsy in the morning mist, shimmering in the afternoon sun.

Floodwaters came and went. We, like Venice, still stood. Roussi—
any sadness in Jojo's eyes surely had nothing to do with her. And if it
did, he would soon forget her. We were in Venice!

As was all of our inner circle.

Diaghilev and his young lovers, vying for his attention: Lifar, the
dancer; Kochno, the librettist.

Our musicians: Stravinsky, Poulenc, Auric, and Milhaud.

Our Coco, on and off Bendor's yacht.

So many others, friends we'd collected over a lifetime.

Jojo and I stayed in our usual suite of rooms at the Hotel Danieli.
Every morning, we slept late. After, we lingered at a table at Florian
or sat on the Lido with friends beneath the glorious sun, Mezzo in
Jojo's lap. We drank exquisite wine, ate exquisite meals. We saw the
opera. We went to all of the parties, in lavish costume or fancy dress,
joining the caravans of gondolas making grand entrances at palaces and
palazzos alight with torches, fountains, servants. The Princess di San
Faustino. Countess Morosini. The Princess de Polignac. The Count
de Beaumont. Count Volpi. The Viscount of Noailles. Each had their
night, all trying to outdo.

Everything in Venice was as it had always been.

Almost.

Jojo usually held court wherever he went. In the passages and sacred
spaces of Renaissance churches. At cafés with friends. I'd overheard him so
many times passionately describing the sensuality of Tintoretto's use of color,
the violent brushwork, the plunging perspectives. Or the revolutionary
talent of Annibale Carracci, who "might never have been discovered had
he not, as a young boy, quickly and precisely drawn portraits at the police
station of the throng of peasants who'd just robbed his father."

And Veronese. Jojo recited from memory from the court transcript
of 1573, when the great painter was brought before the Holy Inquisition
for heresy over his raucous version of *The Last Supper*.

"The priests were outraged that such a sacred occasion would
be depicted with jesters, drunks, buffoons, and the like," Jojo said.

"He actually had one of the apostles picking his teeth with a fork! Yes! Thankfully, Veronese was a clever man with a flexible mind. He changed the name of the painting to *Feast in the House of Levi*. The problem was solved for all."

But this summer, from the beginning, Jojo was uncharacteristically distracted, his mind far off. There were few long dialogues, little exposition. I tried to nudge him out of it.

"Jojo, tell us more about Veronese and the Inquisition. So fascinating. Did they really ask him to replace an image of a dog with Mary Magdalene?" Or "Jojo, tell us, won't you, about the feud between Titian and Tintoretto?"

"Yes, yes," he would say with momentary enthusiasm, starting in until his voice trailed off. I worried others noticed his unusual preoccupation, but they seemed too caught up in their own. Lifar and Kochno would start arguing in Russian, Diaghilev breaking it up. Or Diaghilev would complain about Cole Porter who brought "that idiotic jazz noise" to Venice.

Or Coco would talk about Jean, who now professed he wanted to be a priest.

"He told me he takes communion every day," I said. "It's always extremes with him."

"Yes," said Coco. "He's exchanged the opium pipe for the wafer. I hope it lasts. I've spent a fortune paying for his cures."

I feared I might need a cure. A cure for Roussi. I would willingly pay a fortune for that.

There was something more insidious plaguing me, something secret, something in the deepest of my darkest places. Much worse than Jojo's somber mood.

The first time we made love on this trip, he gave his usual attentions to me, attuned as always to my pleasure. I reached mine. But soon thereafter, I realized Jojo, my ardent lover for so many years, hadn't reached his.

With him, it was easy to tell. In the peak of lovemaking, my Jojo roared like a lion in the jungle. But not now. Instead, our unsatisfactory grappling fizzled out. We settled into an embrace, giving in to it like a sigh of relief. Whatever *that* was, it was over. Any lingering glow drained out of me. I had a disconcerting feeling of being exposed, naked before a stranger. I'd been so stupidly unselfconscious, assuming he was enjoying our togetherness as much as I. But he wasn't. He was somewhere else. Thinking of someone else.

Roussi was here in our bedroom.

Venice, my treasured Venice. Crumbling facades. Masquerades. Games of pretend. The past and present colliding. An allegory for my life.

But during the day, as I walked about, I saw Venice for what it was. A miracle. Improbable. Unlikely. Buildings standing up in the water like reeds. What held them up? How had this city survived? Venice was eternal. My husband sought eternity with a younger woman, a silly little nothing without an ounce of talent. A child playing with clay. Sexual attraction alone waned. Quality did not.

I was quality. It was I who suggested to Coco that she make a perfume. It was I who suggested to Diaghilev that he make ballet. I was confidante to Renoir, Bonnard, Vuillard, Toulouse-Lautrec, Proust, Picasso, Satie, Stravinsky, Cocteau, and so many·more.

I was Misia. I was the Queen of Paris.

I was eternal.

Chapter Seven

Back in Paris in late September, I told Coco my plan. "I mean to see to it Jojo and Roussi are together as much as possible."

"That's a terrible idea," she said with a sigh that carried through the telephone line all the way from Bendor's hunting lodge in Bordeaux. "The cauldron of your mind never ceases to amaze me."

"It's a superb idea," I said. "You know what anguish Venice was. Away from Roussi, Jojo pined after her. You saw him. So glum. Without her there in front of him, I'm afraid his imagination put her on a towering pedestal, complete with halo and gilded wings. Jojo must be with the girl to grow tired of her, to discover who she really is. She doesn't understand art. She doesn't understand culture. Her idea of theater is the puppet shows in the Champ de Mars. She goes to them all the time. She thinks they're hilarious."

"But what you're doing is perverse," Coco said.

"It's not perverse," I said. "It's strategic. The more she's with Jojo and me, the more ridiculous she'll look to Jojo. He'll see she doesn't belong in our world. Finally, the spell will be broken. The bubble will burst."

"Yes, but whose bubble?"

◆ ◆ ◆

I invited Roussi to everything, not just luncheon or dinner at Maxim's, and she accepted, accompanying Jojo and me to the opera, the theater, a concert. Jojo seemed pleased to see the two of us getting along so well. I invited her to stop by the apartment from time to time.

"Whenever you're nearby," I said. "Whenever you like."

"Oh, I would adore that," she said, her smile so wide I thought I saw fangs.

Roussi visited, between this and that, when Jojo wasn't home, her ways informal as if our drawing room was her drawing room, chatting on about the latest marionette shows or about riding the carousel in the Tuileries or about her brother Alexis at Cambridge, a conqueror on the polo pitch and with the ladies. Sometimes she'd come in bursting with vitality and exertion, her hair damp from swimming at one of the indoor pools. I was appalled by how easily she broke the rules of decorum, then appalled at myself for being appalled, having to remind myself again that I'd made a life of not following rules. Sometimes I felt sure she knew she had this power, that she did it on purpose, though her movements appeared loose and spontaneous. She lounged about on the furniture, even my chaise longue, shoes off, feet up, always exhilarated from some recent adventure.

Have you seen Josephine Baker perform, Misia? You absolutely must go. I can't wait to take Alexis when he visits. She wears nothing but a skirt made out of banana peels! It's hilarious!

Or another time: *Oh, Misia, my feet are killing me. Alexis and I, we danced all last night! Do you know how to do the Charleston? I'll teach you!*

Once, she glided in on a pair of roller skates, laughing hysterically, saying she'd skated all the way from the Trocadéro, her cheeks flush with the outdoors. I watched in horror as she twirled around on our parquet floors, narrowly avoiding crashing into all of Jojo's collections, the priceless Louis XV commodes, the fragile antique porcelains, the ancient architectural fragments, the enormous crystal rocks scattered all about, the antiquities he bought in Italy that turned our apartment into a deluxe version of Aladdin's cave. Mezzo skittered behind her, barking with unusual ferociousness mixed with glee, jumping a full two feet in the air.

"You must show Jojo when he gets home," I shouted above the commotion. Certainly, he would be horrified.

"But I already did," Roussi said with delight. "I went by the studio. He told me to come here and show you. He said you would be so amused."

I forced my smile not to crumble. I tried to picture her as Jojo might. A young woman, a princess, with natural vivacity, a reckless air. How glittering she looked even in the ridiculous.

◆ ◆ ◆

Eventually, Roussi visited almost daily, bursting in, then settling down, curling up on a chair, her large eyes focusing on me.

"Tell me every detail of your afternoon, Misia. Who did you dine with? Where did you go? What did you do? I want to know it all."

I didn't tell her every detail. Just the broad outlines. "I went to Picasso's studio. He wanted to show me some canvases." Or "I had Poulenc and Diaghilev over for luncheon." Or "Jean came by. He's written a new play and wanted to read it to me." Or "I met Coco for tea at the Ritz."

She asked so many questions.

What did you wear?

Chanel.

What did you eat?

Oysters.

Who did you see?

Lady Abdy. Princess Radziwill. The Baroness d'Erlanger.

Who were they wearing?

Mainly Chanel.

She listened attentively to my answers, absorbing every word. Why? She reminded me of Proust. He used to sit so quietly and watch me, filing details of my conversations, mannerisms, and dress away in his head to memorialize in his notebooks later. And then in his great work,

Remembrance of Things Past. The dazzling Princess Yourbeletieff. The cunning Madame Verdurin. He'd modeled two characters after me. One wasn't enough.

But what was Roussi filing this information away for?

"She wants to be you," Jean said one afternoon, entering the apartment just as Roussi was leaving, a sneer animating his pointy face. "She wants to take your place."

"Darling," I said to Jojo as we were dressing for dinner at Maxim's, where Roussi would join us. I'd been waiting for the right time to broach a sensitive topic. "Roussi tells me you're using her chimp as a live model for some of the scenes in the Wendel ballroom."

He glanced at me, then looked away quickly. "Yes, yes. Roussi asked me to. I thought it would add some authenticity. And why not immortalize the little fellow?"

Why not? *Why not?* Because Jojo had more important matters to attend to than such trivialities. He knew that as well as I. Hence, not meeting my eye.

"Jojo. You can paint a monkey blindfolded. She mentioned you'd been working on it for a few days."

A creature common to his murals, he'd done so many. Thick brushstrokes of black, brown, and white. Stronger swirls here and there to make the shoulder, the chin, the head.

"And I thought you'd finished the ballroom," I said. "The Vic Cathedral panels must be coming along then if you have time for that?"

I was concerned. For months now, he'd told me he'd been making progress on the panels. As he did with all his murals, he worked on the panels here, in his Paris studio, to ship them and have them installed later once completed. He started with charcoal sketches and models that would later be scaled in size through the use of a grid on large panels.

He worked with a team, sometimes with up to eight assistants. The work was complex, expensive.

It was to work on the Vic Cathedral panels that he hadn't joined me in Monte Carlo for the premiere of *Zephyr and Flora*. That was what he said. But I knew him. He didn't come home in the evenings bursting with details of what he'd accomplished that day as he usually did. He didn't spend hours detailing what he would accomplish the next day.

Instead, I found out from Roussi he was painting monkeys.

Roussi. She was the culprit. She was standing in the way of Jojo completing his life's work.

He did not have time to paint monkeys.

"The Vic Cathedral panels," he said, his voice turning to a growl. "The damn Vic Cathedral panels. Toscha, you know me too well. They are not coming along. Not at all. And so . . . I paint monkeys." He collapsed into a chair.

I went to him. "Tell me."

"Es frustrante," Jojo said. "Frustrating. I begin with one idea, work furiously, then rethink, begin again, go back to the first idea. I've been trying to finish this commission for two decades now."

"That's not your fault." There were extenuating circumstances. One being the patron who commissioned him passed away. Thanks to church bureaucracy, it took a great deal of time for the contract to be renewed. When it was, Jojo had changed his perspective. His techniques had evolved. He felt compelled to start over. Then war broke out.

"I'm not young anymore," he said. "What if my ideas aren't good? What if I can't execute?" There was an anguish I recognized in his eyes, the kind I'd seen before in others, the insecurities of a creator.

"You must remember," I said, my role to build him up. "It's a struggle. A battle. Art that isn't agony—that's not great art. And you are a great artist, Jojo. One of the greatest. Every painter, every composer, every writer, fears that once they've completed a work it will be their last, that they won't be able to create something worthwhile again. But they do, darling. They do. As will you. It's grueling but rewarding. You know that. Once you finish, it will be glorious."

"I finish, and that's when the reviewers come in. Their voices live in my head, tearing down all I worked to build."

I knew those voices. They called Jojo a mere decorative painter. They said his work was anachronistic. Unimportant. Self-indulgent. Even in our avant-garde crowd, Jojo was considered an outsider for his adherence to classical motifs, his unwillingness to sacrifice traditional concepts of beauty for experimentation as Picasso did. Though Jojo was at a peak in his career, offered exorbitant sums to "decorate" palaces near and far, he took these criticisms to heart.

"Not only that," he said, "Vic is a *cathedral*. A house of God. Not a dining room or a salon."

"Yes, a cathedral," I said. "That's why it's been entrusted to you. One that is just outside of Barcelona, your beloved city. And you, a Spaniard, a Catalan, a Jesuit. You were meant for this, Jojo. You and only you are able to conceive of the magnificence this space requires."

Jojo sighed. After a moment, he took my hands in his. "Do you truly think so?"

"I do. I know you, my love. I know what you're capable of. I know what you've achieved. I know how brilliant you are. Don't you remember what I said when we first met? Only you are daring enough to paint a cathedral now, in modern times. Only you are bold enough to take on a work of such monumental proportions and meaning."

He embraced me. "What would I do without you, my Toscha?"

I was alone in the apartment late one afternoon when Roussi arrived.

"Nina's going to have my head," she said brightly. She had been at Angelina, the popular teahouse down the street. Her eyes were bright with merriment as she described how she had set the chimp down in order to pick up her cup of hot chocolate. She had turned her back for just a moment. The next she knew, Poki was atop the counter, helping himself to the elaborate pastries. He threw those he didn't like about the sophisticated teahouse to the shrieks of customers and shouts of staff. Roussi related that she was laughing so hard, she was helpless to stop him.

"I told them to send the bill to Mr. Huberich. It was the only way they would let me leave."

She'd already told this story to Jojo, she said.

"What did Jojo think?"

"He thought it was hysterical."

"Did he?" Surely not.

She had another tale to tell a few days later. Again, I was alone. Was it a coincidence she always visited when Jojo was at the studio? I prayed he was turning her away to work on the Vic Cathedral panels. Perhaps he sent her away, regretting that he'd allowed Roussi free passage into his private studio in the first place. Did he see what a mistake that was?

This new story was of she and her brother Alexis, each a passenger in a separate open automobile—three-seater Citroëns—circling around the Place de la Concorde. The siblings were attempting to hold hands across the gap, standing and leaning out from the back seats, the two autos careening dangerously close. The roundabout was in complete pandemonium, she said. Everyone honking, yelling, angry, having to pull over to avoid collision and stay out of the way. A few up over the curb, drivers shaking fists, cursing.

"But we did it!" she said. "Alexis and I grasped hands. It was thrilling. Round and round we went. Who else can say they did that?"

When I was her age, I was reviewing submissions for a literary magazine. Toulouse-Lautrec had drawn me for the cover. I was sitting for Renoir.

I hadn't had to resort to spectacle for attention.

Did Jojo know? Yes. He came home that evening in a state, telling me I must talk sense to her, how terrible it would have been if she or anyone else had been hurt. He certainly didn't find this story "hysterical."

"You see," I told Coco later when she called. "The more Roussi talks, the more she gives herself away."

"Yes," Coco said. "As someone who likes to disrupt. Someone intent on turning everything upside down."

◆ ◆ ◆

Nina, Roussi's horrid sister, was finally to marry Mr. Huberich on October 19, a week away. I couldn't imagine tying myself to such a man. All he did was clean up other people's messes, most recently the one made by Roussi's chimp at Angelina.

As the wedding date neared, Roussi cavorted more than ever around the city, usually with Alexis, sometimes with two young women her age, attendants in Nina's wedding. One of them was another Georgian princess, according to Roussi. The other was a young American opera singer with some success there who was sure to fizzle out here. Along with them was the singer's fiancé. A much older man, a Mr. Harmon. This was the man who happened to have commissioned the aviation trophies from Roussi. The American flyer.

"You know," she told me one afternoon, whispering though we were alone, "he proposed to me first. But I told him I was married to my art. That's my priority."

Her "art." I held my tongue.

She was jittery. Her lips moved when she wasn't speaking. Jojo must have offered his spoon to her back in the studio. She smoked cigarettes more and more. She ate nothing, or everything, emptying our pantry. She was full of momentum, bounding in and out of the Meurice. There were gown fittings, celebratory teas and luncheons with her and Nina's American friends. And there was some ulterior motive to this hive I couldn't decipher. Some underlying narrative. I sensed a web of intrigue. Older, wealthy American men lurking about looking for young mercenary brides. They'd found each other!

Then one day, a few weeks after the wedding, a complete surprise. I was alone at the Meurice. It was just after luncheon. I wasn't feeling well and ate in bed. Stravinsky was to come later to play a new piece for me. Jojo and I were to dine with Picasso and Olga that night. Before the appointed time, Roussi burst in, waving a paper in her hand.

"I'm going to America," she announced with excitement. She thrust the ticket at me. "It's all booked."

I held the paper in my hand. There it was. Passage aboard the *RMS Mauretania*, November 29, 1925. Three weeks away.

She hadn't spoken of it in so long. I presumed the Charlie Chaplin bust was a hoax. It still could have been, but at least she was leaving. The great weight I was carrying suddenly dissolved.

"I'm thrilled," I said. "For you, of course. They will adore you in America, I'm certain. You're just their type. It's the land of opportunity."

"And opportunities are cascading in. Mr. Harmon made a fortune in real estate in New York. Well, he's put together an itinerary for me. Friends all along the East Coast who want their monuments done."

Monuments. This was what she called her busts. It was clever. Didn't every man believe he deserved his own monument?

"Then off to California," she went on. "Charlie Chaplin, you know. Isn't he hilarious? And my brothers will be there in Los Angeles, Serge and David. They've made all sorts of friends in Hollywood who will want their monuments done too. Wealthy men. Important men. You know, Misia, I may never come back!"

There was something intentional behind her statements so excitedly presented. Some silent agenda.

That night, when Jojo came home, I couldn't help myself. "Isn't it wonderful?" I said. "Roussi's going to America. Remarkable—so many commissions already lined up. Coast to coast. Her career is certain to take off. And Charlie Chaplin!"

He scowled. "It's ridiculous. She's doing perfectly well here. I don't see why anything has to change."

My chest tightened. I'd hoped I'd find something in his reaction, a sign he was tired of her and glad she was going.

"Well," I said, "her Mr. Harmon has set up so many opportunities for her there."

"It's a terrible lapse in judgment for her to take him up," he went on. "All I've done for her here. Artistically. What does America know about art? Her decision seems impetuous."

The tightness released. Ah. Yes. This was Roussi. Slowly it was dawning on him.

◆ ◆ ◆

"People think I'm going to America to find a husband," Roussi said, sinking into the divan one morning, two weeks before she was to leave. I was still in my dressing gown on my chaise longue, reading the theater reviews, and it was just she and I. Her statement stopped me. I wondered if she meant Jojo.

"Naturally," I said. "You're at that age. Why wouldn't you be?"

"I'm wedded to my art. But any suitor may have his monument made. The man who pays me the most for that will have the best chance. But nothing guaranteed—except the monument!"

Of course. To Roussi, sculpture was about manipulation, not art. It was never about art.

She told me that as part of the trip, there would be the delivery of the aviation trophies. A dinner. A reception. She would be honored. Her brother David would attend as her escort. If only Alexis could be there, she said. David was the connection to Charlie Chaplin in Hollywood, so she said. She talked about her other brother there too.

"Serge is still putting together oil interests in California. Everyone is asking him to. He and David have degrees from the Georgia Engineering School in Tiflis."

"Ah," I said, remembering Nina had mentioned this during our first meeting and doubting anyone in that family had a degree from anywhere.

"David was in a movie! Isn't that funny? I told you he might be. An actress friend recommended him to a studio . . . I think she might hope to be more than a friend. Really, though, Mother must be spinning in her grave. Her son on the stage . . . she would think it so inappropriate for a prince. It's really only for fun."

"Mmmm, of course," I said.

"I'll be going to Palm Beach. Mr. Harmon has friends there. Then Palm Springs . . . it's in the desert. Did you know that?"

"I did," I said.

"America has everything," Roussi said.

I smiled. "I hope for you that it does."

There was a moment of quiet. Then, out of the blue, with a flat tone in her voice, she said, "He loves you, you know."

I was startled. Mr. Harmon?

Jojo. She was speaking of Jojo.

"I know," I said. I had to refrain from snapping. I didn't need Roussi to tell me Jojo loved me.

She didn't say anything else. Instead, I noticed this girl with boundless energy suddenly seemed tired. Her tone had been irritated, not warm. That was because in that moment, her mask had slipped. I saw something new. I saw that perhaps the reason she came to visit me so often was to keep an eye on me, to assess my mood and standing.

To measure the situation with Jojo. Just as I was with her.

To see if she was winning or losing.

I was winning.

November 29. Finally! We saw Roussi off, Jojo and I, saying goodbye as she stood on the platform waiting for the train that would take her to the port where the *RMS Mauretania* awaited, a frigid wind blustering through. Her round face was whitish-blue, bloodless from the cold. She looked miserable and uncharacteristically uncertain. The animation, the high spirits, were gone.

She and Jojo avoided eye contact. They barely spoke to one another. I did all the talking.

"Be sure to send a telegram from the ship. And do write. We want to hear all the thrilling details of the evening your aviation trophy is presented. All the rave reviews."

"I will," she said through chattering teeth. Jojo was quiet. Was he angry that she was leaving? Relieved? Both? Either way, she was leaving. Feeling generous, I threw my sable coat over her narrow shoulders. She didn't protest as I had those years ago when Coco had thrown hers around mine. I knew what Coco would say. *She's Russian. She always thought of it as hers in the first place.*

What else did she think of as hers? Jojo. I shivered as I watched her board the train, but it wasn't from the cold. To see my coat walking off was surreal. As if it were me, as if I were watching myself leaving Jojo behind. As if it were the two of them watching me go.

But it wasn't. I slipped my arm through Jojo's as the train disappeared. Roussi was gone.

At first, I was relieved. But when Jojo and I arrived back at the Meurice, it was too quiet. That night, our table at Maxim's felt empty.

I looked continuously toward the door out of habit, half expecting Roussi to come floating into the room at any time with some "hilarious" story of why she'd been unable to board the ship. *You wouldn't believe what happened—it was hysterical!*

I was so used to her constant intrusion, I was unsettled without it.

"Do you think she'll be all right?" Jojo asked over foie gras and a bottle of Sauternes.

"Quite all right. She'll be with her brothers and family friends."

"Yes, yes. Of course," he said.

Why on earth did he worry about her? It revealed his delusion about who and what she was. How could he not see it? She'd survived a revolution. She was certainly capable of surviving America.

I drank more wine than usual. So did Jojo.

Across the table, Jojo was gazing off. He was thinking of her too, both of us adrift from each other. I feared once again he might put her on that marble pedestal with halo and gilded wings.

Sometimes, the more absent a person was, the more space they took up.

◆ ◆ ◆

The next night, I made sure friends joined us at Maxim's.

Diaghilev with his troupe of Lifar and Kochno.

Jean, with the aroma of the opium den, his infatuation with the church fading, his addiction renewed.

Poulenc, with more musical ideas, thrumming the beat with his knife and fork.

Marie Laurencin, her hands flecked with paint.

Stravinsky, dapper in an enormous beret and rimless glasses.

Picasso too, with all his he-man energy, without Olga, who he said was unwell.

And Coco, now back in Paris.

"Is she gone?" Coco whispered as soon as she sat down.

"I think so," I said.

"You think? Hasn't she sent a telegram telling you she's on board?"

"No."

"That's rude," Coco said.

"That's Roussi. But she's never been on a transatlantic ocean liner. I suppose she doesn't know it's the thing to do."

I kept one eye on Jojo as he conversed with Diaghilev. I also watched, amused, as Coco avoided the gaze of Marie Laurencin. The year before, Coco had engaged Marie to paint her portrait and hated the final result so much—it portrayed her as soft and feminine—she refused to pay.

But Coco wasn't avoiding Picasso. She alternated between concern for me and flirting with him. She pulled a cigarette from her case and gazed at him. How provocative was that cigarette in her mouth as he lit it, her hand over his on the lighter as he leaned in, eyes on eyes. Surely, they wouldn't start things up again as they had a few years back. Picasso always said Coco was the only woman in Paris who had any sense. But this was nonsensical. She was happy with Bendor, wasn't she?

"What are you doing," I said to Coco in a low voice. "Not that again."

"Why not? Bendor has his infidelities. I'll have mine."

"Picasso's dangerous. I've told you before. You should stay away."

"He is dangerous," she said, taking a sultry puff of the cigarette. "That's what I like about him. There are so few men who actually frighten me."

I shook my head, then asked about the collection. She talked on and on, filling me in on her work as she chain-smoked, her plate pushed away, her dinner barely eaten.

"The new perfume," Coco said. "It's doing very well."

She told me next about the Wertheimer brothers, her partners. "It's a collaboration. The Galeries Lafayette say they won't carry my perfume unless I can give them a larger quantity. They say they can barely keep bottles on the shelves. So the Wertheimers take over production and we share the profits. It's easier on me."

Then back to Bendor. "Did you see what they printed in the British papers about us?" she said. "'A French couturiere may be the next Duchess of Westminster.' Reporters. So vulgar. They ask me about it all the time. As if that's all that matters."

"And what do you say?"

"Nothing. It's insulting. They should ask about my collection."

Insulting or tantalizing? I knew Coco better than anyone. Deep inside, she longed to be married but acted the opposite. And to be a duchess? What a delicious slap in the face that would be to all who had snubbed her years ago and called her a tradeswoman. Yet she had risen so far above that now by sheer will. Yes, the question was insulting.

"Here's what you say," I told her. "Anyone can be the next Duchess of Westminster. There can be only one Coco Chanel."

"Ha!" she said. She raised her glass of champagne to me. "Exactly."

◆ ◆ ◆

"To the Boeuf!" I announced on the fourth night after dinner. Still no onboard telegram had arrived from Roussi. At least, not that I knew of.

And so to distract, to Le Boeuf sur Le Toit, Jean's cabaret, though he didn't own it, he just made it popular. Nights at the Boeuf were always a scene, a haze of smoke and music and bon vivants where we drank champagne and cocktails. Jean played with the band he'd put together with Milhaud, Auric, and Poulenc. He sat in the middle, banging on a drum lent to him by Stravinsky. Jean could draw, he could write, he could keep a beat on the drums. But he couldn't get over the loss of Radiguet, his young lover who'd fallen ill and died so suddenly two years before. Jean didn't smoke opium for fun.

Coco had arranged the funeral all in white: white flowers, white coffin, white parade horses.

Coco had a special relationship with death, as if she were its appointed usher. I wondered if that was why Coco took funerals so personally, the transition, the passage, as if to make sure the deceased made it safely to the next world. Her sister, Antoinette, who she had been very close to, who had helped her from the beginning with her business, had died in Buenos Aires several years earlier. Coco wasn't there to give her a funeral, to bury her. It was just after Boy was killed in the auto accident. She hadn't attended that funeral either. She couldn't bring herself to do it.

A sense of closure she didn't have for herself—perhaps it was her gift to others.

At the Boeuf, the world came alive. One dressed up: dinner jackets for the men, evening gowns for the women. Here one found the avant-garde, café society, European artists, American writers rough around the edges, poets in large cloaks and black hats drinking absinthe, businessmen buying drinks for well-disguised prostitutes. There were beautiful people, rich people, those who were both and those who were neither. There was Isadora Duncan, drunk, dancing freestyle to the beat of Jean's drum.

And there was Coco, sitting on Picasso's lap, a wicked smile on both their faces.

Ah, Jojo. How I loved him. He had his faults, but he wasn't wicked. His arm was draped over my shoulders as we talked with Jean Hugo, Victor Hugo's great-grandson, Jojo's voice raised above the din to be heard. His shoe tapped to the music. The cocaine energized him. It elevated his mood. It should have elevated mine, but there was something off, something discombobulating.

That Picabia painting over the bar. That was it. Jean had hung it there years ago alongside his own drawings and those lent by Picasso, which Picasso had since taken back, leaving empty, forlorn-looking spaces on the walls. As a result, the Picabia stood out even more. Picabia had asked visitors to his studio to contribute something to a canvas. The result, a collage of scribbles, newspaper cutouts, signatures, and adages.

And at the bottom right, the image of an eye, stark and unblinking.

I should have stayed away from Jojo's spoon. My mind was working too quickly, fast but also slow, all at the same time, convinced anything was possible. The eye was alive. There was a person behind that eye. Roussi. Keeping tabs. Measuring. Assessing. I almost believed it.

Was she on the ship? Or was she here, lying in wait?

That eye—watching. Plotting.

To sleep that night, just a bit of morphine. It was the only way to rest.

Finally, a telegram arrived at the Meurice, addressed to M. and Mme Sert.

When Jojo came home from the studio, I shared the news. "Roussi's arrived in New York, darling. Isn't it wonderful? She'll be the toast of the town."

"Yes, yes," he said irritably, not looking at me.

My heart thudded to a stop. "You already knew," I said.

His eyes met mine, then darted away as if he realized he'd revealed something he shouldn't have: confirmation, as I'd suspected, they were communicating, going around me as they always had.

"She sent a telegram to the studio," he said. "Just to say, the aviation trophies. They've arrived in one piece."

"What a relief," I said, and it was. But the relief was only partial, as I wondered what she really said in that telegram. And if Jojo was sending messages back to her. Roussi held a stronger grip on Jojo than I'd let myself imagine. But she was gone now. Where she should be. Someplace else.

December in Paris was another time of parties, of high spirits, night after night a social whirl. I ensured Jojo and I went to every dinner, every ball. By January, Roussi would be a memory, dissolved in the season's effervescence, lost behind the transatlantic mists.

For Christmas week, Jojo and I traveled to Biarritz with close friends, the Berthelots and others of the intellectual crowd Jojo favored. Anticipating the trip, I'd imagined him having long, stimulating conversations about politics and religion with Philippe Berthelot. I imagined us breathing in the revitalizing sea air. I imagined the vastness of the ocean adjusting narrow perspectives. We would renew our bond emotionally, sensually, coming together in bed as one, completely in sync. I imagined deep, satisfying sleep, our bodies merged, the rhythm of the tides soothing.

But Biarritz was quiet, damp, cold. Jojo was distant, as he'd been in Venice. We'd made love the first night we were there, but it left me with a feeling of sadness and dissatisfaction. His roar was more a purr. He hadn't said he was famished. In fact, over the past weeks, he had lost a bit of weight. It felt as if there was less of him for me.

The morning after Christmas Day, while Jojo was out roaming the streets and boardwalk with Mezzo, I searched the pockets of his clothing.

His overcoats. His jackets. His trousers. Nothing. Until I came to the black wool dinner jacket flung on the back of a chair. In an inner pocket, I felt a piece of paper. I pulled out a folded-up square of stationery.

It was a letter. Addressed to Roussi. Written in Jojo's scrawling hand.

Roussi, Come back. I can't live without you. I will say it now: I love you and only you.

The words drew blood. I felt as if I'd been struck, my entire being hit by some overwhelming force. Instead of crumpling, I was paralyzed. From living and breathing to rigor mortis in one fell swoop. I read the letter again. And again.

I love you . . . and only you.

I would never have believed words could hurt so much.

But they did. The realization that Jojo, my Jojo, could write those words to someone else, turned the world into a place I no longer understood.

Yet I simply could not believe that he loved her. Here was the evidence in my hand, but I knew in my heart it was false. I, who saw the essence of everything before anyone else, could not comprehend that Jojo might actually love someone other than me, that Jojo would let this one young woman annihilate twenty years of love.

I slowed down my thoughts, trying to understand how this man I trusted so implicitly could have written something so inexplicable. When might he have written this? How long had he been carrying it around? There was no date. It must have been penned in an emotional moment likely stirred by the fact that Roussi had left. A few sentences of impassioned verbiage, that was all it was. That did not necessarily prove anything at all.

And why did Roussi leave? An epiphany came to me. *I will say it now . . .* Jojo had written. *Now.* This implied he would not say "it" before she left: that he "loved her and only her." That explained the tension between them in the weeks before her departure. I saw it so clearly now. She had given him an ultimatum, telling him if he didn't make that declaration, she would leave. And he'd refused. Because he didn't love her and only her.

He loved me.

This letter. This proclamation. It was just a ploy to convince her to come back. A lie. He did not mean it. And of yet, Jojo hadn't posted it. But he still could. He was just a weak moment away. And if he did, would that entice her to come back?

I could not let those words live uncontested. I had to *do something*. I would never leave Jojo. I loved him. And I couldn't approach Jojo face-to-face. That would make too much of it. If I acted as if he were truly in love, he might believe he was. If I confronted him, some aspect in his face might change. His eyes might dart away from mine out of guilt. There might be pity or regret in his gaze. I would see what I couldn't bear to see: that he actually did believe he loved her.

I wasn't brave enough for that.

I went to the writing table. There, I picked up a pencil and dashed a warning across Jojo's false declaration. Not a demand. Not a threat. Just an observation from the person who knew him best.

Impossible. It is me you love. To confuse what you feel for her as love is a mistake.

With what I hoped was an air of calm I went out to join the Berthelots sitting by the fire in the drawing room. When Jojo came back from his walk, I greeted him as if nothing were amiss. I knew he didn't love Roussi.

That evening, he wore his dinner jacket at the table. He had to have seen what I'd written on the letter. Yet he said nothing. Nor did I. It was better that way, better to smother Roussi, hold her down until she could no longer move, no longer breathe.

Chapter Eight

Paris, 1926

Back in Paris, I was in demand. I was a woman of importance.

Diaghilev needed me as always. He sought my opinion on his new choreographer, a promising young man named Balanchine, who he brought to dance in my drawing room.

Kochno, along with Lifar, needed me too. To help manage Diaghilev. Cole Porter had been making generous donations to the Ballets Russes motivated by his continuing yet unrequited crush on Kochno.

"Infuriating. Insulting. Diabolical," Diaghilev raged. "Who does that idiotic crooner think he is?"

Jean needed my help as well. His new play, *Orpheus*, was scheduled for the stage in June. Coco was making the costumes. She'd done them for his production of *Antigone* a few years before because Jean "could not image the daughters of Oedipus badly dressed." Likewise, Jean insisted, Orpheus must be chicly attired.

But Coco and Jean's friendship had been stormy during rehearsals for *Antigone*. Coco was certain her costumes, which reflected her latest collection, were what people really came to the theater to see, not the actual play. With no play, Jean asserted angrily, there would be no costumes. They hurled hurtful words at one another—especially Coco—all of it culminating in an unfortunate incident with Antigone's cloak.

It was exquisite, the result of months of painstaking work by an elderly knitter, a Russian woman Coco had hired. Part of Jean's script called for Antigone to fall through a trap in the floor. But at dress rehearsal it was discovered that with the cloak on, the heroine wouldn't fit in the opening. Coco argued Jean should remove that scene.

"Who cares about your script," Coco said to Jean. "It's ridiculous anyway."

"All you care about are your bits of wool," Jean said.

Coco sneered. "If Sophocles could hear you, he'd be laughing at you."

She'd turned back to the cloak, noticing then a small imperfection. Frustrated, she pulled at it and the cloak unraveled, all of it, strand by strand into a wasted pile of yarn. The old knitter began to weep.

This was how I felt. One tiny frustration away from unraveling.

After his experience with Coco during *Antigone*, Jean asked if I could help keep the peace with Coco for *Orpheus*.

With that in mind, I set out for the rue Cambon with Mezzo one afternoon, curious to see what Coco was planning. Inside, the boutique thrummed with clients and salesgirls. I waved to all and quickly passed through, going directly to Coco's private quarters upstairs. There, I found her sitting on the floor, her tortoiseshell glasses low on her nose as she studied a pile of sporty British tweeds and tartans, woolen golf sweaters, and houndstooth coats.

"Is Bendor hiding under there?" I said, poking at the mound with the tip of my shoe.

"Bendor is still in Scotland," she said. "Do you know, he will only wear old clothes? Like these. He refuses to wear new ones. He thinks of old clothes as old friends. The man won't put on new socks until his valet has soaked them for days in water to soften them."

"I never have understood the British," I said. "Nor have they understood me."

"It's not the British. It's Bendor," she said as Mezzo crawled into her lap. Dogs universally loved her. "It is, I've realized, another of the luxuries of being as rich as he is: the ability to own only clothes so well made they last forever."

She held up a sweater knitted with patterns in alternating colors, something one might wear on a trek through a boggy heath on a wet, frigid day, a venture I'd never undertake. It frankly didn't look like much to me, but Coco always knew what should come next in fashion, just as I did in the arts.

"Feel this," she said. "Isn't it exquisite? It's made in a place called Fair Isle, one of the Shetland Islands. Bendor has scores of them he's been wearing for decades. I've borrowed a few for myself. They're soft and warm like a cocoon. This is quality, Misia. A textile that gets better with age. Imagine."

"Yes. Imagine," I said.

She held up a woolen jacket in muted browns and greens. I could picture Bendor in it, striding across the grounds of one of his many sporting lodges with a fishing pole, if he actually carried such things himself. "And this. Touch it. Quality, again. Practical and beautiful all at the same time. Luxury without ostentation."

"There," I said, running a hand along the lapel. "You put your finger on it. What I don't understand about the British, that is. What's wrong with luxury *and* ostentation?"

"The British despise ostentation. But what is lacking in their brand of luxury is elegance. It doesn't come to them naturally. Luckily, I'm stepping in. Bendor's putting up a textile mill in the Highlands for me. I'm going to have it make a softer wool for women, more feminine, but just as sensible as the men's. A French twist on British practicality."

"And a modern twist on *Orpheus*?" I said. For *Antigone*, the costumes mimicked Coco's Russian-influenced fall/winter collection of the time, which was in turn influenced by her then lover, the very soigné Grand Duke Dmitri Pavlovich, who'd fled the revolution and with his elegant good looks ended up in Coco's bed. This time, it was Bendor's turn.

She nodded. "Exactly."

"After *Orpheus*," I said, taking a seat on the divan, my usual spot, "society women everywhere will be going about looking like the Duke of Westminster."

She stood. "Misia, you know me so well."

"I do," I said.

"And I know you." She put a hand on her bony hip and scrutinized me as if I were a bolt of jersey cloth. "What's wrong? You've lost weight."

Her expression turned to a mix of concern and approval. She was always nudging me to diet as she did with all her clients. She herself constantly worried about her figure, going off from time to time on slimming cures. To her, loss of appetite was a silver lining to any romantic crisis.

I had to confess what I'd discovered in Biarritz, the letter I'd found in Jojo's pocket. I wanted to tell her. It was a burden to keep it to myself.

"I was putting away his dinner jacket," I told her as she settled into a chair, feet curled beneath her, Mezzo in her lap. "A piece of paper fell out." I didn't want to admit, even to her, I'd gone looking for it.

"Misia," she said, tilting her head knowingly. "You don't 'put away' dinner jackets."

I acknowledged the truth. I'd gone through every pocket. Then, defiantly, I recited for her the letter, burned as it was in my soul. *Come back. I can't live without you. I will say it now: I love you and only you.*

"He didn't mean a word of it," I said. "What he wrote—it's a lie. Meant only to convince her to come back so he can feel young again. He's a man who believes in abundance. In having it all. Roussi isn't a threat."

"Oh, Misia. Don't be so sure. Russians like Roussi exist solely to plot coups."

"She's America's problem now," I said. "One can't continue to plot a coup from the other end of the earth."

"But what about when she comes back?"

"She's not coming back," I said.

◆ ◆ ◆

Mid-January, a letter with an American stamp arrived at the Meurice informally addressed to "Misia." I knew before opening the envelope it was from Roussi. Only she would address a letter so irreverently. Could she not bear to write Madame José Sert? Inside, I found a clipping from an American newspaper I'd never heard of, the headline in bold:

Princess Here! Princess Roussadana Mdivani, noted sculptress, to present a cup, her own work, to round-the-world flyers.

I burst out laughing. How many lies could a single sentence contain? *Princess. Noted sculptress. Her own work.*

A greeting in Roussi's hand was scrawled across the top: *Kisses to you and Jojo!*

The nerve of this girl, still determined to maneuver from afar. But what was her purpose? To keep me off balance? To taunt me? To taunt Jojo? Did she think the idea of these "round-the-world flyers" would make him jealous?

She'd addressed this just to me, thinking I'd show it to Jojo. Sending it to him herself would make her look silly. But it begged the question: What was she sending to him?

A pang of panic ran through me, riding on a thought I'd been trying to avoid. I didn't know if he'd written her or not, if he'd ever sent a letter.

I love you and only you.

Surely, I thought, one of these round-the-world flyers would want to marry her, make her an offer she couldn't refuse. By sending this clipping, she was just trying to hedge her bets. To keep a toe in Jojo's pond. To play games with me, push me into becoming the shrew who would then push Jojo away.

I tore the newspaper clipping to pieces. I threw it in the fire. Hands shaking, I watched the pieces curl up and turn into smoke. Jojo would never see it.

As the weeks passed, Jojo did seem to be recovering from his Roussi addiction. His appetite was back in the bedroom and at the table. Oh, those glorious words: I'm famished! We made love. He roared. He was hungry. Hungry for me. Hungry for work. Hungry for conversation with friends at dinners and parties. I watched with amusement one evening at dinner where, preceded by an old-fashioned chilled Pernod, he devoured partridge, washed it down with his favorite burgundy, and for dessert ordered another partridge. The exhibition at the Jeu de Paume was just a few months away. My instinct in arranging it was right.

Now with Roussi gone, Jojo was making the progress that had eluded him. I knew from the charcoal stains on his fingers when he came home in the evenings. The smell of sculpting clay had dissipated. We were back to linseed oil and turpentine. To discussions at dinner about technique and themes. Of all those who needed me, he needed me most.

Everything was going to be fine. Roussi would find a suitable man in America. She would be happy at last. And so would I. I could hardly wait until June. The exhibition of the Vic Cathedral panels wouldn't be just Jojo's triumph. It would be our triumph.

More weeks passed. More pathetic clippings arrived.

Princess Mdivani in Palm Beach . . .

Princess Mdivani in Miami Beach . . .

Princess Mdivani back in New York . . .

Princess Mdivani to be guest of so-and-so.

I wouldn't have bothered to open them but for the hope that one would contain at last the news I was waiting for. An engagement announcement.

Meanwhile, as Roussi traversed the eastern coast of America in search of the highest bidder, Jojo and I were exactly where we should be. Together at Coco's, there in the center of one of the biggest parties of the season.

Her home on the prestigious Faubourg Saint-Honoré almost felt like ours as well. She had moved in not long after Jojo and I took her to Italy. The apartment had enormous rooms with paneled walls and high ceilings. Jojo had helped her decorate. Coco understood proportion on the female figure; Jojo understood proportion in large spaces. The two of them chose Louis XIV furniture from antique stores, then moved on to the Paris flea markets where they found crystal balls they turned into lamps. A glass-topped table held up by golden shafts of wheat. A collection of old tarot cards she set out on a desk. A small bronze frog on the mantelpiece, its mouth open as if about to catch a fly, symbolized good fortune, love, and health.

While I'd chosen the piano—a Pleyel, the preference of Mozart and Stravinsky and Saint Saëns—Jojo had chosen the Regency divan that dominated the drawing room, upholstered in orange velvet.

"Yes, yes, madmachelle," he said when Coco was unsure of the bold color. "Orange has many uses. It absorbs natural light. It draws the eye. Bellini used it to evoke distant hills at the horizon. Did you know that in Northern Renaissance paintings, orange is a symbol of prosperity?"

"Jojo decorates like a Renaissance painter," Coco said, agreeing more to the symbol of prosperity than the color. Everything had to have meaning.

Jojo installed mirrors that extended all the way to the ceiling, making the drawing room seem more expansive and luxurious at the same time. They reflected, too, the view to the courtyard and beyond to the extensive gardens of topiary and fountains that reached all the way to the Avenue Gabriel, the street where Coco had lived with Boy in his bachelor apartment when I'd first met her.

It was no coincidence. Coco was always hoping to conjure ghosts, going with Jean to séances at people's homes, Coco trying to reach Boy, Jean trying to reach Radiguet.

This home connected her to the time she'd been the happiest. And then the saddest.

Boy was gone, yet his spirit lived on. Coco made sure of it. The same Coromandel screens from the Avenue Gabriel apartment lined the walls here. At the flea markets, she bought whole collections of rare books to build on those Boy had given her. Overhead, soft waves of light diffused from the chandelier she'd had custom made by Baccarat and hung with crystal charms, more tokens of her past and superstitions. Her lucky number five. Her interlocking Cs. Those Cs didn't stand for just *Coco* and *Chanel.* That's what most people thought. But I knew better. They were *Chanel* and *Capel.* Through that symbol, she and her lover were forever secretly linked.

Now, for the party, champagne cascaded from fountains. Russian caviar chilled in enormous soup tureens. There were trays of foie gras canapés, cornucopias of exotic fruits, lobster, oysters. Centerpieces of enormous rock crystal. A jazz band played in the entrance hall. Positioned about the house were staff periodically diffusing Coco's latest perfume into the air.

Out in the courtyard, Jojo was buoyant, directing Picasso, his fellow Spaniard, as he played at being a bullfighter. Lifar and the other young male dancers were the bulls. Jojo stood atop a garden chair, arms moving like a conductor. On the ground, Picasso's shirt was unbuttoned, revealing his bare chest of which he was so proud. Coco had dressed him in one of her short bolero jackets embroidered with gold and silver threads—she kept a room here for him whenever he didn't feel like going back to the country, where Olga was staying.

As matador, Picasso waved a red silk scarf Coco gave him in one hand. In another, he brandished a small wooden chair, legs out like sabers, shouting all the while "Ole!" The dancers, with mock seriousness, charged at him, performing acrobatic twists and turns while Picasso attempted to knock them down with the chair. But Lifar and company were too slippery, avoiding his thrusts every time. It was Picasso who should have been the bull, aggressive as he was, always looking for someone to gore.

I was glad Diaghilev couldn't see. He'd be apoplectic if Lifar or any of his other dancers were hurt. Instead, Diaghilev was perched on the orange velvet divan in the very center of the party next to me. The Count and Countess of Beaumont flitted by, chins in the air. I had to laugh. A few years before they'd refused to invite Coco to their spring ball because she was a mere "storekeeper." In solidarity, Jojo, Picasso, and I refused to go. We stood outside the party among the chauffeurs, Coco in tow. The four of us taunted the guests, urging them to come to the Boeuf instead. At least half of them did, including Diaghilev. The Beaumonts were furious.

"Now look at them," I said to Diaghilev. "They have no problem drinking a storekeeper's champagne, do they?"

He put a hand on my arm. "Forget the Beaumonts and their predictable tired balls. Remember the gala we threw at Versailles, Misia, the Hall of Mirrors? We outdid ourselves. They could never top that."

"Never," I agreed. "We should do it again. Why not? A reprise."

"Yes, we will! We must! We'll stage another ballet there . . . who will write it? You'll find someone for me, won't you, Misia? But that's the best part. Someone new. Someone fresh. To astound." He took a sip of his champagne. "To turn the world on its head."

I took another glass of champagne from a passing waiter. My eye caught the motion of Jojo, coming inside from the courtyard, his cheeks ruddy, his eyes bright. There was no lost, faraway look in his eye as if he were thinking of Roussi. Man Ray approached him, seeking him out as people always did. I watched as the two men conversed with enthusiasm, about photography certainly. Then Princess Violette Murat joined them. She was a royal Bonaparte, a hash smoker, and according to rumor a lover of Marie Laurencin, so oddly proportioned with her head that seemed to rest directly on her shoulders, no neck in sight. Proust used to say she looked more like a truffle than a violet. She was a quality princess. Man Ray a quality artist.

Yes, I thought, surely Jojo understood he was where he was supposed to be.

◆ ◆ ◆

April. May. Roussi's clippings continued to arrive.

> Princess Mdivani to do important sculptures.

> ... of Charlie Chaplin ...

> ... of Calvin Coolidge ...

> . . . has been commissioned to do the Queen of England ...

Was any of this true? Certainly not. It was ludicrous.

And then one day in May, finally, an engagement announcement but not the one I was hoping for. Prince David Mdivani was to marry the actress/vamp Mae Murray, commonly known as "the girl with the bee-stung lips." The maid of honor would be Pola Negri, the actress. The best man would be Ms. Negri's fiancé, Rudolph Valentino.

"I'm sure Mae Murray is more than thrilled to add 'princess' to her calling card," said Coco when I told her.

"And I'm sure the Mdivanis are thrilled to add a bankable Hollywood starlet to the cabal," I said.

Coco looked up. "Perhaps it's true love?"

We both burst out laughing.

◆ ◆ ◆

Jean's *Orpheus* opened at the Théâtre des Arts. My mediation between Jean and Coco had been successful. In addition to the Bendor-style costumes, she'd dressed the character of Death in a pink muslin ball gown and a chinchilla coat. This coat did not come unraveled. Neither did anything else. The show was a hit. Jean was floating, certain he was the earthly channel through which the gods spoke.

Coco's Bendor costumes were a hit as well. All the international society ladies would flock to the rue Cambon to ensure they would be dressed as English dukes for the winter season. "Bendor's textile factory will be working at full capacity," said Coco with a pleased look.

"You'll make the richest man in England even richer," I said.

After the premiere, we celebrated at the Café de la Paix, our usual long table beneath the mirrored wall. Jean gave a speech, thanking everyone, glancing at his reflection as he did.

"His next play should be titled *Narcissus*," Coco said to me under her breath.

I laughed, then glanced in the mirror myself. How chic I felt dressed in one of her new black evening dresses. Black was her latest obsession. She was turning out black wool dresses for day. And for night, black silk or chiffon. My gown had a drop waist and glass-beaded rectangular strands of different lengths hanging from the shoulders and the bottom of the skirt. Hers was sleeveless, made of metallic lace and alternating sequins of black and gold in a horizontal zigzag pattern that worked its way to the skirt. Together, we dazzled.

"All this black," I said. "I suppose your inspiration is Bendor's maids and butlers. What's next? Gardeners? Stable boys? Shoeblacks?"

Suddenly, a jolt. Picasso pounded the table with his fist. Silverware chimed, glasses wobbled, wine teased the rims of glasses threatening revolt, some spilling over, staining the tablecloth pink.

"And you call yourself a Catalan," Picasso said to Jojo in a low growl, eyes bulging with challenge. I assumed they were having one of their usual quarrels over some principle of aesthetics.

"Dios mío. Why must everything for you be as simple as possible?" Jojo said.

"Why must everything for you be as complicated as possible?" said Picasso.

For two men from the same part of the world, two artists, they were vastly different, brilliant but in completely opposite ways. I appreciated them both. Unfortunately, they didn't always appreciate each other. I thought it must have been painting techniques they were debating this time. Or color palettes. Or style and form. I thought wrong.

"Not just simple. Pure. True," Picasso said. "Botifarra. There's a reason it's the most popular sausage in Catalonia. It's pure. It's true. A workingman's meal. Hardy."

Jojo scoffed. "Hardy? You speak of hardy? That's Iberico ham. Yes! The product of wild boars bred in the most rugged of conditions. A lifetime roaming over the mountains, feeding on acorns. Do you dispute Pliny the Elder, who praised their superior quality in the year 77? Or Columbus, who took Iberian pigs with him the second time he crossed the Atlantic? Surely not. I must inform you, senor, that Iberico ham has been considered a delicacy for centuries. Meanwhile, your sausage does nothing but fill stomachs."

"Iberico ham is a delicacy for the delicate," Picasso said. "Botifarra—a plain and simple sausage, sold on every street corner, not fussy, not complicated—is for the strong!" Picasso lifted his short arm like a boxer showing off biceps.

Jojo raised his chin. "Iberico ham is for the strong. The entire ham is buried in salt for two weeks. Then a year curing in the mountain air. More years curing in a cellar, all to reach peak flavor. Oh yes, you can taste it, my friend. The land, the sky, the air of Spain. The flavor of life!"

Picasso laughed. "Overcomplicated. Overwrought. Like your murals."

Jojo's eyes flashed. Picasso's words summarized the chorus of critiques that played constantly in Jojo's head. I knew how he would respond. The two had gone down this path many times before. "Says the canvas painter. Your imagination is confined to a rectangle. You could never conceive an entire room. Walls and ceilings. The logistics. The arithmetic."

These were my words, spoken to Jojo when his spirits were low.

Picasso sat back, crossing his arms in front of him. "My work isn't decorative. My work is important."

Jojo laughed. "You throw paint on canvas. My work is the very walls of palaces, the naves of cathedrals." He looked to me.

"Yes. Cathedrals," I said. "In two days, one of the most important museums in Paris will exhibit a testament to that."

Jojo gave me a wink. Picasso complained, though with a knowing smile flickering across his lips. "And you, Misia, to betray me. The witness at my wedding. The godmother to my child. The only woman I trust."

At that, Coco, jealous of my friendship with Picasso, pursed her lips.

A waiter approached Jojo carrying a package in butcher paper. Jojo, who must have sent him on this errand when the argument began, undid the string as if opening the Holy Grail. Inside, delicate slices of Iberico ham, red and glistening, shone in the light of the empire chandeliers. Jojo distributed the thin, sheared pieces around the table, dictating how they were to be consumed.

"No, Jean," he said. "Don't chew. It's very especial. You must let the morsel dissolve in the mouth."

Then to Coco: "You see, madmachelle," Jojo said with complete seriousness as she took a bite of her portion and held it on her tongue. "This isn't ham. This is an orgasm!"

The table erupted, everyone wanting a piece now, including Picasso.

"Monsieur Jojo," Jean said with mock alarm. "You sound like a Surrealist."

"Never," Jojo said. "Iberico ham, my friend, the sensation, the taste, is one hundred percent real."

I loved hearing this version of Jojo. This was the old Jojo, the man who came alive sparring, arguing, debating. The Jojo before Roussi.

◆ ◆ ◆

The afternoon before Jojo's exhibition, I had a strong craving for a Mont Blanc, the melty meringue and sweet whipped cream.

I could have sent Aimée to Angelina to fetch it for me. Instead, I chose to go myself. The tearoom was just next door, and the June weather was so pleasant. The sky was a clear, beneficent blue. The flower beds in the Tuileries Garden burst with shape and color and lusciousness. The trees were full with leaves carrying on a continuous whispery conversation among themselves, gushing with gossip. I imagined all they knew, observing from high above.

It was the sort of day Manet or Renoir or Pissarro would paint, setting up an easel on a nearby balcony or bridge, each with their own perspective. I brought Mezzo along, and he pranced beside me with extra enthusiasm. The Jeu de Paume was not far away, at the edge of the Tuileries where the garden met the Place de la Concorde. I'd gone by the day before to see Jojo's murals in final form, and they were breathtaking. I thought with great satisfaction of Jojo busy inside with finishing touches.

At Angelina, I'd ordered my Mont Blanc and was walking with it toward the door when I nearly ran into a familiar silhouette. Lanvin dress. Large straw hat. Insolent chin. Princess Nina Mdivani. Or rather, Mrs. Nina Huberich. I'd last seen her that afternoon at the Hotel Versailles when I first met Roussi. It surprised me she would show her face here at Angelina after her sister's rogue chimp nearly ruined the place. But the Mdivanis had no shame.

"Madame Huberich," I said, enjoying the fact that now that she was married to a "commoner," she was no longer to be addressed as Princess.

"Madame Sert," she said, spitting it out as if acknowledging my position as Jojo's wife was distasteful to her. She had teeth like a wolf, pointy incisors. I was about to say "good day" when she pounced.

"I'm sure you've heard. Roussadana is quite the success in America," Nina said.

"Is she?" I said in as dismissive a tone as possible.

Nina persisted. "She says she's written you."

I smiled. "Madame Huberich. I receive so much correspondence on a daily basis. I have time to read only a fraction of it."

"Well," Nina said, "if you did read it, you would know that many, many prominent American men are begging to have her make their busts. She's so talented. But her time is limited. She has to narrow it down."

"I didn't realize they had such a dearth of capable sculptors in America. How wonderful that she's found a place where she can be properly utilized."

I took a step to continue on my way when Nina said, "I'm sure she'd be happy to tell you all about it herself. She'll soon be in Paris. Her ship arrives next week."

I hoped I didn't give away my shock. Roussi was supposed to stay in America until she found someone to marry. That was my plan. I'd thought it was hers. And now here was Nina, an overconfident, victorious expression on her annoying little face. Not so soon, I thought to myself, blood simmering. I would be the victor. Not her.

Not Roussi.

I feigned sorrow. "Such a pity," I said.

"A pity?" Nina pursed her haughty lips, tilting her tiny head.

"All those prominent men and not a clear highest bidder among them." I waited a beat. "For her monuments, of course."

Nina smiled slowly, revealing once again her wolf teeth. "But Madame Sert," she said. "I'm afraid you misunderstand. There have been numerous high bidders. Especially when they heard Roussadana studied under your husband." Now she waited a beat before continuing. "My sister is coming home to consider her many options. Surely you remember from days long ago that youth has many options? A beauty like Roussadana, gifted, high spirited, has a long list of offers to consider. In America, and in Paris."

Nina brushed past me toward the counter with an air of superiority. "Good day, madame," she said over her shoulder, this time leaving out the "Sert."

◆ ◆ ◆

Back at the Meurice, I imagined a newspaper clipping, the heading: *Princess Mdivani, the noted—no premier—sculptress, the beauty raised in the palace of Tiflis, returning to Paris to consider her options!*

And Jojo. What did he know?

Did he know she was returning and didn't tell me? I would ask when he got home. Part of me said not to. Don't act as if it means something. That was the old me. The new me was tired of playing dumb.

In the half hour before Jojo's arrival, I rose from my chair. For dinner, I put on my red Chanel gown, the one I'd worn to the barge party that he'd been so complimentary of. I fixed my hair and face in the mirror. I thought of a line from Jean's script for *Orpheus*, one that had been spinning trails through my mind.

Mirrors are the doors by which Death comes and goes . . . And if you look at yourself in a mirror all your life, you'll see her at work, like bees in a glass hive.

The bees buzzed all around me.

I rose and went to the balcony. Soon, the sun would set. The days had grown longer. The sky hinted at a pink sunset. Surely that was a sign of something good. I imagined my grandmother as the light behind the clouds. The fiery gilding to their edges. How I wished she were here in her red ruby necklace orchestrating where everyone should be, who should sit next to whom as she did back in Belgium hosting her musical salons. I knew where she would put Roussi—on the next train to Siberia.

Light still lingered outside when Jojo arrived from the studio. I was quiet, unusually so.

"What are you thinking, Misia?" he said in a low voice, his head tipped to the side, his brown eyes slightly hooded.

"Did you know Roussi is coming back to Paris?" I said.

Oh, the way he looked at me. I could read that face of his. Usually full of expression. Now, it was expressionless, placid as the pond in the Tuileries on a windless day, children's toy sailboats unmoving. Which meant he had thought about this moment beforehand. He had calculated how to handle it, how to handle *me*. It was as if he'd drawn it all out by hand first as he did his murals, before painting the final version.

"I received a letter from her a few days ago," he said calmly. "At the studio. She mentioned she might return. Didn't I tell you? I could swear I did."

"You didn't tell me."

We looked at each other, so much unsaid between us. Now, I thought. Now was the moment to tell me the truth of their relationship, whatever it was.

"Well, with all the preparation for the exhibition. I've been so busy, Toscha, it simply slipped my mind."

This was a lie. I could hear Coco: *Yes, it's a lie! Misia, wake up!*

But I was awake. More than I wanted to be. In my heart, I knew what he was doing. He didn't want to hurt me. And I was torn between not wanting to be hurt and wanting to beg him to tell me the truth. Did he love her? Was he anticipating her return? Maybe they had been corresponding this entire time. Maybe he had sent a version of that letter I'd found in his pocket in Biarritz. *Roussi, Come back. I'll say it now. I love you and only you.*

But I still couldn't believe that, now more than ever. Biarritz was six months ago. I stared at him. What I saw was that he was afraid to lose me. Words were trapped in my throat. Because I, likewise, wasn't prepared to be lost.

I needed him.

He spoke carefully. Intentionally. "I assumed, perhaps, she might have told you herself. She said she'd written you."

"Did she?" Anger flared. So they *had* corresponded. "She didn't write me," I said, my voice snippy. "She sent silly newspaper clippings. And you know, Jojo, I am not one to aimlessly put pen to paper. Unless it has a purpose. I don't have time to sit and write for the sake of writing. Or read pointless newspaper clippings. I mediate. I arrange. I convince. I correspond solely to get things done. Things of importance."

"Yes, yes. I do know that. That is one of the qualities about you I admire. Everything you do has a purpose." He took me in his arms and held me close, his chin resting on my head. "Well, it's my fault," he went on. "I should have told you about the telegram. I'm sorry. Are you upset? Please don't be upset. She's coming back. But it means nothing. Nothing at all to us. I simply forgot to mention it."

Nothing at all to us. That was an admission. A confession of sorts. It hurt and soothed at the same time. Surely, he wouldn't say this if he didn't mean it. Safe in his embrace, I felt that old trust I'd always had with him, that he wouldn't hurt me. He knew how I'd been hurt by Thadée, by Edwards, by my father. I could never believe he'd let me be hurt again. That *he* could do the hurting.

That night at Maxim's, friends joined us at our table. My red dress blazed like Grandmother's ruby necklace. Jojo was boisterous, debating with Picasso the best place to buy turpentine, glancing at me from time to time, looking me up and down with a lusty gaze or a quick wink or even a little growl. What would happen when Roussi returned? I couldn't get out of my head one truth I knew for certain. Russians. They never gave up. They never went away. Especially if what they wanted belonged to someone else.

But Russian blood flowed through my veins too. I would never give up. I would never go away.

The Jeu de Paume whirled with political leaders, wealthy patrons, high society, and journalists from the majority of the press publications with serious art criticism sections. *L'Illustration. Le Figaro. L'Intransigeant. La Veu de Catalunya.* The crème de la crème of the Paris art and literary world mingled at the feet of Jojo's breathtaking panels. In sepia and gold, the scenes with Saint Peter and Saint Paul, with the Four Evangelists, soared upward so that one felt on par with the clouds, arrived at the gates of heaven. Everyone marveled.

Such luminosity!

The use of color—exquisite!

Such a potent imagination!

As if we were in Venice, admiring the work of Tiepolo!

Magnificent. Monumental. How does he do it?

I loved to see Jojo the center of attention. I was at his side as he presided in the middle of the salon. I listened as he accepted congratulations and answered questions, his voice deep and authoritative with its melodious Spanish tones. His hands gesticulated, so supple, so talented. The hands of a magician.

"Between mural painting and easel painting," Jojo expounded to a group of writers, "there is the same difference as between poetry and prose. Yes! That is how I think of it. Painting the walls of a building, you see, is like a poet writing a sonnet. There are limitations. Rules! But for the muralist, the architecture imposes the discipline. You see? I am a poet with a paintbrush."

To journalists, he simplified: "You must understand. Catedral de Vic is a classical building. Sadly, it's been altered too much over the years. It's lost its character. Its identity. Yes, yes. My task, you see, is to bring it back to life, to raise it from the dead, like Lazarus."

To architects, he pontificated: "The Catedral forces me to respect the principles of its construction. The pilasters in the walls, the arches, the domes, the flat and curved surfaces. Think of that, gentlemen. Just think of it! All must be painted."

To artists, he instructed: "Each surface, you see, has its own independence conferred by its structural framing. Each requires a subject of its own. But, of course, all must agree with the others. Coherence. Coordination. All just as our limbs articulate to form the human body. Yes!"

He was magnetic. Expressive. A vivid presence. People leaned closer to hear him speak. They nodded their heads. They absorbed his words and ideas. All wanted to be around the force that was Jojo, charisma flaring out of him. He was on the stage. A stage I'd built for him.

He was the man who drew the King and Queen of Spain to Paris. They were coming the next week for a private viewing.

Tonight, I was the queen. I wore my tiara and a silvery Chanel gown with fringe. Beforehand, he'd presented me with a diamond necklace. "My angel," Jojo said, as he clasped it at the back of my neck, his fingers grazing my skin. I was his angel, there beside him at the Jeu de Paume, reinforcing his points and his brilliance, greeting, chatting, charming. "You see," I said to the critic for *L'Illustration*, "the windows of the cathedral are small, cramped. Jojo specifically uses metal as a base to draw in more light."

Though they dominated, the Vic Cathedral panels weren't the only feature of the exhibition. We also included a mural he'd painted on several wood panels to be installed later in an American home. The image was of a Mediterranean village atop a hill as viewed from a distance. Sublime. Atmospheric. A reminder to attendees they could commission Jojo to create scenes for their luxury homes.

"So unique," I heard the critic for *Le Figaro* say. "The way Sert uses silver and sepia on lacquered wood. His virtuosity is impressive. A man who is a follower of the Renaissance tradition and at the same time, a passionate seeker of novelty."

Tradition. Novelty. How quickly those words took me out of my dream state.

Old. New. Yes, that was Jojo.

Somehow, in the exhilaration of the opening, I had almost forgotten Roussi was coming back.

◆ ◆ ◆

That evening, we celebrated at Maxim's. Jojo, me, Diaghilev, Lifar, Jean, Picasso, Coco. So many toasts to Jojo. To me. To all of us there. To life and love and art, always art.

"Come to the Meurice!" Jojo called out as we shut down Maxim's, inviting our group and anyone else in earshot to our apartment. We weren't ready for the party to stop. I wasn't ready.

There, more drinks. More toasts. Loud bursts of laughter. A glass breaking. More laughter. A haze of cigarette smoke, of wine and champagne, of no one wanting the evening to end.

"Play something, Misia," Diaghilev said.

After that, a chorus of voices: Yes. Do. Play, Misia.

I took a seat before the keys. "What shall it be?"

Lifar spoke up, definitive. *"Afternoon of a Faun."*

"Debussy," Jojo said. "Do you know he first aired the piece that would turn into the ballet at this very piano? It was Misia who discovered it. She was the first to hear it. He'd been inspired by a poem of Mallarmé, an old friend of hers." There was pride in his voice. How I loved this man.

Lifar had a mischievous look on his face as he climbed atop my piano and reclined provocatively on his side. With his thick, slicked-back dark hair, his bronze skin, his white teeth, he looked like a panther. I began to play, and he slid gracefully to the ground. He removed his jacket slowly, seductively, that superb physique transforming into the dance of the Faun, half man, half goat, a forest creature who spends his time in the pursuit of nymphs.

I knew the piece by heart. I played and watched as Lifar twisted and turned. He was wistful. He was whimsical.

He was erotic.

I glanced at Jojo. He was watching me. I knew that look. Lifar might be a panther. But Jojo was a lion.

Meanwhile, everyone was entranced. Usually, Lifar was onstage. Far away. Here, one could reach out and touch him. And Lifar knew how to play to the crowd. He slipped the long silk scarf from the neck of Isadora Duncan. She had been at Maxim's with a friend and had joined our table. Diaghilev was annoyed. She'd once proposed marriage to his former lover Nijinsky, saying, "Think what wonderful dancers our children would be . . . prodigies!" To Diaghilev's delight, Nijinsky had retorted that he didn't want his children to dance like Isadora.

That was years ago, but Diaghilev didn't forget. I wondered if it riled him now that his current lover, Lifar, was playing with her scarf.

Not just playing. As called for by the choreography, he let the scarf flutter to the floor. Then, he crouched down. He acted as if he were mounting it, his imaginary nymph, his body pulsing over it to the rhythm of the music. My hands played the final notes. I teased a bit. Pausing, Lifar freezing. Then I sped up. Lifar sped up. Everyone laughed.

But to close out, I had to let the beauty of the music take over. My hands languished over the final notes, sensual, suggestive. I could play to a crowd too.

But now, I was playing for Jojo. This was the moment. The culmination of pleasure. Lifar's beautiful face looked up to the heavens in a silent moan of ecstasy. I glanced again at Jojo, the piano keys still sending vibrations to the tips of my fingers. The look he gave me made a warm pooling sensation in the emptiness just below my rib cage. We would have our own ecstasy once everyone left.

Lifar stood. He bowed dramatically as our friends cheered and whistled. Diaghilev moved closer to him, as if to remind everyone Lifar was his.

Jean sidled up to me, his voice low. "Who else could offer in their drawing room the spontaneous performance of Serge Lifar performing as a faun making love to Isadora Duncan's scarf? You are genius, Misia. Simply genius."

It wasn't me. It was a collaboration. The physical beauty of Lifar. Of the dance, choreographed by Nijinsky. Of Mallarmé's poem that inspired it, my old friend who closed his eyes and listened to me play piano for hours when I was young and married to Thadée. Of Debussy's score. Some had called *Afternoon of a Faun* indecent when it was first performed in public. And yet, it was just a faun, whimsical, natural, feeling, not thinking. It simply showed the animalistic desires of men. Not love, but pleasure.

Chapter Nine

Paris, 1926

She was back. Jojo told me himself. Roussi had visited him at his studio. How in character for her first act to be to impose herself in his sanctuary and offer herself to him. Did he take her up on it?

Jojo met my eye when he told me. That was good. "She's been commissioned to make another aviation trophy," Jojo said. "That Harmon fellow again."

That Harmon fellow. Jojo said his name with distaste, but I liked the sound of it. Harmon must have still been pursuing her. Perhaps Roussi was the real trophy he hoped to acquire. He might be engaged to Roussi's friend, the American opera singer, but that engagement was likely just a way to have an excuse to be around Roussi.

When she didn't call on me that week or the next, I was surprised. Maybe she was interested in Harmon now. Maybe she went to Jojo for help, to ensure this next trophy spurred a new proposal. Maybe they weren't sleeping together again, going right back to where they'd left off. I remembered the tension between them. Roussi leaving was an ultimatum, and she'd lost.

Roussi had been in Paris two weeks when at last she turned up at the Meurice. Aimée let her in.

"Misia!" Roussi said, rushing into the drawing room and wrapping her arms around me as if I were a treasured friend. Or so she wanted me to think. Thankfully there was no monkey in sight. Mezzo, terrified of the creature, was relieved, though still cautious, eyeing Roussi from the comfort of his plush bed beside an antique Italian commode. He knew as well as I she was not to be trusted.

"Roussi," I said with false warmth. I felt that rush from her charm, her aura, that invisible intoxicating something she atomized into the air as Coco did her perfumes. She stood back, taking me in. I expected she was looking to see if I was any closer to my deathbed. I was not.

But was she?

"You're ill," I said as she coughed several times into a handkerchief. She waved a hand. "Just a cold," she said, her voice raspy. "But look at you. Exactly the same. You're even wearing Chanel. Always so loyal." There was a hard edge to her voice.

I smiled. "You say that as if loyalty were a fault."

I assessed her clothing. I couldn't name the designer she was wearing, and I knew them all. She didn't have the resources for that. As always, she tried to make up for it by being original, and it worked. She wore a little beanie-size cloche on her head with a brooch pinned front and center. Her hair was shorter, though the style now was longer. It suited her. She knew how to appeal. She knew how to stand out.

She went on. "I've been away so long—seven months—I feel as if centuries have passed. But here, at the Meurice, time always stands still, doesn't it?"

"Here at the Meurice, we are timeless," I corrected.

She pulled out several photographs of David Mdivani's wedding party, variations of the one she'd sent me from the newspaper with Valentino and Pola Negri, now ashes in my firebox. She pointed out David, the groom. He was tall like Roussi, with light hair that went back from his face in gentle waves. They had the same eyes, heavy-lidded. The same pose. The same faraway gaze, as if they were always looking around you for something better.

She pointed out Serge. He resembled Nina with black hair and a piercing "what's in it for me" gaze. He was tall, like David, both the sort who took up a lot of room, though Serge was broader. An overcoat was draped across one forearm, a cigarette fixed between his lips, an appraising, slightly predatory expression on his dark face. He looked quick to laugh, quick to take offense, quick to judge.

"Aren't they dashing?" Roussi said.

"But where are you in the photographs?" I said. "Surely you were part of the wedding party."

"Oh no. I was too busy in New York."

"For your brother's wedding?"

"The courtship was only three weeks. They're so in love, they couldn't wait. I had so many engagements I couldn't possibly get away on such short notice. Mr. Harmon had arranged for me to meet so many prominent people. Lunches and dinners and balls. It was a whirlwind."

Harmon. Again.

"David and Mae will be in Paris soon. We'll have a grand dinner here. A feast! Champagne. Caviar. Everything. You must meet them. You and Jojo. Can you imagine, Misia? David and Mae might even want to commission a mural from Jojo. For their California estate. Wouldn't that be wonderful? Just think, his work is so beautiful, so stunning, everyone in California will want him. Valentino. Pola Negri. Maybe they'll even want him at the studios, for stage sets. He's done them here, after all."

"Jojo painted backdrops for the Ballets Russes," I said. "One wouldn't call them stage sets."

"Oh no? It seems the same to me." She coughed, then kept on. "Well, Alexis will be in Paris soon too. I can't wait! I miss him terribly. And if David's marriage ruins Alexis's prospects, I'll strangle him. East Coast society looks down on Hollywood."

I stifled a laugh. East Coast society? And the Mdivanis? But I shouldn't make fun. If it would take Roussi away from here, I was all for it, as preposterous as it sounded.

"Alexis has so many dear friends from Oxford. One of his American friends there is simply begging Alexis to marry his sister, Louise. She's one of the Van Alens. I'm sure you've heard of them. They're part of the

Astor family. The Dutch side, in New York. All of that means nothing to me, but that's what Mr. Harmon said. Alexis adores Louise but isn't sure he's ready to settle down. All he wants to do is play polo."

Her enthusiasm was overdone. The distracted look in her eyes didn't match her animated tone. Perhaps it was because she didn't feel well. Perhaps it was because she came back to find Jojo and I so perfectly aligned.

Yes. It reminded me of her behavior just before she left for America, when she couldn't get Jojo to declare his devotion to her and only her. That too-excited edge in her voice. That intonation of false high spirits as she bantered on. She was once again trying too hard to appear carefree.

"Your necklace," she said, homing in on the diamonds strung around my neck. "Is it new?" Behind her smile—gritted teeth.

I put a hand to it. "Yes," I said. "A gift from Jojo. He gave it to me just before the Jeu de Paume opening. To show his appreciation. The opening was such a marvelous evening for us. The critics can't stop raving about it. But I'm sure you've seen it for yourself."

She sat back on the divan and yawned. "No. I haven't had time."

She'd had time. She simply didn't want to see it. It was a collaboration between Jojo and me. Our triumph. Like an insolent child, she couldn't stand it.

"What a pity," I said. "It's been the event of the summer. Even the King and Queen of Spain have come to view Jojo's panels."

"How marvelous. Jojo is revered in Spain. He told me that himself. Did you know he doesn't have to take off his hat in the presence of the king? Well, I saw the panels in progress," she said. "As he was working on them. In his studio." She paused to emphasize that. *His studio.* Her words stung. So much that I couldn't respond.

"Oh, Misia, did he tell you? I have a new aviation trophy to work on now. Mr. Harmon has commissioned another one. He's in Paris to form an International Aviators Aid Society. So generous with his fortune. Well, I wish I could stay longer. I have so many stories to tell you from America. But I have an appointment with a physician. This dreadful cough." Thankfully, she rose to go.

"I hope he can help you," I said. "All these commissions you have—as you said, you don't have time to be indisposed. Pity you didn't make it to Hollywood. I imagine Mr. Chaplin is impatient for you to complete his monument."

She looked at me. Was she glaring?

"Impatient," she repeated with a hard tone in her voice. "Yes. That's the right word. That sums everything up."

She came by again a few days later, still with a cough. She seemed meek, softer than her last visit, maybe from the illness. I had Aimée boil water for tea.

"What did the physician say," I said to Roussi.

She looked up at me with her sad, childish eyes. There were bags beneath them. "The physician insists I go to Switzerland. To consult a specialist."

"Are you going to?"

"I don't know. Nina's living in London. I don't want to bother her. And I'm afraid to go by myself. I don't have anyone else. Would it be possible for you . . . Do you think you could . . . I'm afraid, Misia, and you always know what to do."

After Roussi left, I went straight to the rue Cambon to tell Coco I needed a new wardrobe and quickly, the best she had for the Alps.

"What are you thinking, Misia?" she said when I told her the purpose. "Why would you agree to go? You cannot trust her."

"No, but she'll be with me, away from Jojo. Oh, I know she has an agenda. I agreed to take her to find out. Maybe Jojo has rejected her since she's been back. He despises illness. Maybe she's interested in Mr. Harmon. Or I can convince her to be. She mentions him often.

Perhaps she wants my advice. My counsel. Why else in the world would she invite me to accompany her to Switzerland?"

"I know why," Coco said. "To push you off a cliff!"

◆ ◆ ◆

As I was the one who took care of so much for so many, Jojo must have thought it natural I'd take Roussi to Switzerland. "Yes, yes, Toscha," he said. "It does seem the right thing to do."

With the Jeu de Paume exhibition still going through July, he was busy. I was busy too, helping Diaghilev with ballets. Consoling Coco over Bendor's infidelities. Watching over Jean as he sank deeper into the opium. But taking Roussi to Switzerland was important. The world must see that if I considered her any kind of a threat to my marriage, I certainly wouldn't travel with her.

In Berne, we shared a suite of rooms. Roussi spent most of the first two days in and out of sleep. The specialist had put her on strong medication. How odd it was to see her unmoving, this youth who was always in perpetual motion. I stayed at her bedside, hoping for semicoherent ramblings in which she might mumble something revealing about her relationship with Jojo or about herself. Some delirious truth that would expose the real Roussadana.

The third day, we took walks outdoors so she could pry open her lungs with the crisp mountain air. There was so much talk of her brothers.

"Alexis is invited to play polo all over England . . . all the best players want him on their team."

"Serge has become close to Pola Negri, the actress who was engaged to Valentino. He died during surgery for tonsillitis. Such a tragedy."

"Serge is appearing in a film. It's called *The Volga Boatman*, just a small part, for fun. Isn't it hilarious? A newspaper article reported 'he's distantly related to the late tsar and formerly possessed of fabulous wealth.' Well, he still has wealth. Oil interests, you know."

At least now, Roussi was much improved. Her cough subsided. She recovered so rapidly it made me wonder if she had actually been as sick as she'd let on. Was it an act? But youth recovered quickly, I told myself. There was no reason to be suspicious.

I heard Coco in my mind: *There is every reason to be suspicious.*

The afternoon before we were to return to Paris, Roussi wanted to stop for tea at a confectioners. I thought she might thank me for coming to Switzerland with her, for standing by her when anyone else in my place would have done the opposite. I noticed a strange air of triumph about her. I presumed it was for conquering, at last, her cough.

I was wrong.

At a café table, we sat across from each other. I sipped my tea. I bought a tin of marzipan candies. I always had the little roses from Fauchon at home. Roussi devoured them. This time, she pushed the box away and sat tall in her chair as if she had an announcement.

"Misia, darling, darling Misia. You have been so good to me. I simply can't deceive you any longer. It's time you knew the truth. For your own sake."

This was a surprise. "Oh? What is it you think I should know?"

"What has been before your face for so long. Jojo loves me. In fact, he wants to marry me."

"Excuse me?"

"Jojo and I are in love. We want to get married."

I stared at her for a moment, these improbable words bouncing off the walls of my mind, then was surprised to hear myself laugh. How ridiculous she sounded. She hadn't been here for six months. And she comes back and announces they are in love and want to marry?

She faced me unblinking. "There's nothing funny, Misia. This isn't a joke."

"I imagine it isn't—to you." I thought of the letter in Biarritz, my stomach cramping. Surely, Jojo hadn't sent some variation of it, declaring his love. And if he had? That wasn't real love. That was delusion. Lust.

"Roussi," I said in my calmest voice, though beneath the table, my legs were shaking with anger. "You are naive. I'm afraid you mistake his intentions."

She sat up taller. She smiled, a pitying smile. "It's you who is naive, Misia. You who have put your head in the sand all this time. We love each other. And you stand in the way."

The audacity of her. Did she truly believe she could convince me Jojo didn't love me? I nearly laughed again. A wild laugh. I understood then why she begged me to come to Switzerland. My instinct was right: she wasn't as ill as she'd let on. She purposely wanted to isolate me. To keep me away from Jojo so I couldn't immediately ask him if what she was saying was true. This was one of her ploys. Tell the world some extravagant lie, like she was making a bust of Charlie Chaplin or the Queen of England. That way, maybe it would come true.

"You need to accept it," she said, reaching out a hand. "You're making this all much more difficult. Forgive me, Misia. We both love you so much. Neither of us intended for this to happen."

I smiled, shaking my head. "Roussi, my dear. You have a crush. How can I blame you? You're drawn to Jojo's masculine appeal. Jojo is desirable in so many ways. But you—he desires you in just one way."

She looked down. She played with the buttons on her glove. "When I first met you, Misia, I was intoxicated. Your power. Your fame. Your aura. I didn't see how I could be worthy to take your place." She looked up. "I believed the man who suggested it was just flattering me."

I could have lunged across the table and broken her neck. It was Roussi who was full of "suggestions." She didn't fool me. If Jojo had truly condoned such a thing, he would have told me first. He would never have agreed to let Roussi do this on her own.

Somehow, I managed to feign patience. "There is a difference," I said, "between fantasy and reality. Jojo indulges his fantasies. He makes things up. He creates whole worlds in his mind. He plays in them, but he doesn't live in them. He lives with me, in the real world. His wife. Any suggestions, if made, are pure fantasy."

She leaned forward. Her smile disappeared. "Poor, blind Misia. So loyal. To a fault. It *was* Jojo who suggested it. You must face it. He loves me, and I love him. You are the only obstacle to our union."

Her voice was lilting, smooth like the sugar in the marzipan candy. Behind the sweet tones, Roussi meant to hurt me. She wanted me to react. She hoped to gain some kind of leverage over me with this declaration by making it here, in Switzerland, away from Jojo.

Perhaps she thought I'd believe her and throw myself off a cliff.

"You had no luck finding a fiancé in America," I said. "That's why you came back."

"I came back because Jojo begged me to. I could have made a very good marriage in America. Many of them. But he told me he would die if I didn't return. The simple truth is he doesn't love you anymore."

Coco said Roussi wanted to destroy me, then climb atop the rubble. I would give her nothing to destroy. I would take the joy out of it for her. I called her bluff.

"He would not for a moment consider leaving me," I said. "But if he really wants to marry you, I won't stand in the way."

She sat back, a gleam of victory in her eye. "He does. You will soon see. He does."

The little idiot. She was not as clever as she thought. I had the higher ground. As Coco said, all I had to do was hold it. My other marriages had been civil as was required in France. But Jojo was a devout Catholic. We had married in the church. As such, our marriage was indissoluble. He knew that.

Not that he would have any interest in dissolving it.

Roussi had no idea that even if he wanted to marry her, he couldn't.

We retreated in silence back to our suite, anger boiling inside me. In my room, I took an extra large dose of morphine. How dare she. I slipped into bed, exhausted. Outside, it began to drizzle. In the rhythm of the rain and rustling of the trees, I heard traces of Debussy's piano solo *Gardens in the Rain*. I didn't want to think of Debussy now. It was too grim. When I was married to Edwards, I'd supported him and his wife for so long, until our falling-out, unreconciled to his death. Perhaps he was haunting me, seeking revenge. He'd divorced his wife. Left her penniless. In the Place de la Concorde, she'd tried to kill herself with a revolver by firing at her chest. She didn't succeed, though a bullet remained lodged in her vertebrae. Behind Debussy's back, I'd continued to give her money. When he found out, he never spoke to me again. So much talent. So little heart. I never understood how he could leave his wife alone, forgotten and destitute.

I knew Jojo would never do that to me. Thadée and I had been friends more than lovers. And Edwards had never loved me. He simply wanted to acquire me.

I of all people knew how it felt to be married to someone who didn't love you. Jojo loved me. The question was whether he thought he loved her as well.

In the morning, I was calmer. Traveling back to Paris, we were polite. Roussi, cheerful and apparently certain of her position, didn't bring up the subject again. I, certain of mine, didn't either.

At the Meurice, I waited for Jojo to return from the studio. The time had come to be frank. I knew he would reassure me.

"She told you what?" he said, rising abruptly from the divan. He was indignant. "Marry her? I never said anything of the kind. If she said I did, she misunderstands. I would never leave you. The thought is absurd."

He took my hands. He looked into my eyes, pleading. How I loved those eyes. They knew how to touch me inside, bore right into all the tender places.

"I am sorry, Toscha. She's young. Impulsive. Please, please don't be upset. I beg you. Please tell me you know I would never leave you. It's impossible. You are the only woman who could ever understand me. How I hate to see you upset."

"That letter. The one I found in your pocket in Biarritz."

"I never sent it. You saw it."

"Did you send one like it?"

He dropped my hands and lifted his chin in the air, jaw thrust forward, the Catalan posture of honor. "Absolutamente, no," he said, a hand to his heart. "I swear to you. Never. Please. Tell me, Misia, tell me you believe me."

There was anguish in his eyes and his voice. He took my face in his hands. Why was this girl coming between us?

"I believe you," I said, tears streaming. "I do."

Jojo pulled me to him, his arms tight around me, one hand pressing my head against his chest as if he could somehow fuse us together. He held me like that for a long time, his grip tight, so that I had the sense of the two of us clinging for dear life in a strong wind, the kind that blew everyone and everything away.

I didn't know what he'd said to Roussi, but it was as if the confrontation in Switzerland had never taken place. Weeks passed, and Roussi said nothing about her and Jojo being in love. Not one word about marriage. He had shut her down. But he hadn't given her up. He wanted us both. He was content with the way things were. As Coco liked to say, what man wouldn't be?

Roussi continued to come by the apartment whenever she pleased. I welcomed her. I still would rather have her in my sights than out of them. She played up to me as usual, hugging me, kissing me on the cheek, determined to make me believe she loved me, that she would do nothing to purposely harm me. She was deferential, devoted, especially in Jojo's presence. She chatted on and on about dinners and parties she went to celebrating her brother David and Mae Murray, the new Prince and Princess Mdivani, who were now in Paris for their honeymoon. She spoke incessantly of Alexis, his polo-playing accomplishments, his future marriage, how so many young socialites were in love with him. "He knows I have to approve," she said. "He does whatever I tell him to do."

Roussi's energy, as always, was infectious. Sometimes, she came to dinners with us. Sometimes, we went to social gatherings together. I despised myself for enjoying the attention she brought to Jojo and me, the Georgian princess who now garnered so much interest, who everyone wanted to meet, whose brother had married a Hollywood star. And weren't all of those Mdivani brothers—the princes—so handsome and debonair?

Parisian society knew who she was now. She and her brothers were in all the papers. Reporters, especially American ones, were everywhere, snapping pictures of them. Roussi was attracting attention as the younger sister with her joie de vivre, her lovable eccentricities. She had two monkeys now, the new one from an old organ grinder. She took them out around town, perched on her shoulders or her lap. She'd taught Poki to dance while the new monkey, Tika, went around with a little tin cup collecting coins.

"Isn't it hilarious?" she said, using her favorite term, and people thought it was. She dressed them in matching outfits I helped her pick out, I paid for. I paid for anything she wanted. I took her to the rue Cambon.

I knew my generosity seemed insane. No one would understand why I would spend exorbitant sums on my husband's paramour. But then, wouldn't it make them doubt she was his lover? And I needed Roussi to need me. As much as she needed Jojo. It gave me a sense of control. If she was dependent on me, if I was so generous to her, how could she steal my husband?

Roussi was the Georgian princess who shimmered and shined, who saw every moment as an opportunity for fun, who radiated gaiety, who went about as if something wonderfully exciting was about to happen to her and everyone around her at any moment. People were drawn to her. Even Coco couldn't help but fall under her spell. I didn't mind. It meant Coco could help keep an eye on her.

Roussi was trying to prove to Jojo that she could take my place.

Jojo knew she could never do that.

I acted as if all was normal. The current situation was a compromise I could manage. It was peculiar, yes, but I had never been conventional. I'd never lived how everyone else had lived. I told myself the war with Roussi was over. We had settled into an entente.

"Peace?" Coco said over tea at Fauchon, her eyebrows raised. All we talked about was problems. She had many of her own. Business disputes with the Wertheimers over her perfumes. Bendor and his wandering eye. "Jojo is perfectly happy having both of you just as it is. He likes the status quo. It's Roussi who doesn't. She'll do everything she can to force him to make a choice."

Venice, at last, our annual trip at the end of August. I was thrilled to have Jojo to myself again. Was it too good to be true? Such an odd thought—he was my husband. Yet it was a thought that reflected reality. There was a third person in this marriage.

But I was safe in Venice, our collection of little islands. If only there were a way to draw up all the bridges, I could keep her out. And Jojo and I, we would stay there together, forever in paradise.

Roussi was in Paris with Alexis, continuing the celebration with David and Mae Murray who were the toast of the town, still darlings of the press.

I searched for regret in Jojo's eye that we left Roussi behind. He could have been disguising it. Since the debacle in Berne, he seemed to be careful about my feelings. He didn't want to upset me. He didn't want to upset either of us.

On hot afternoons, we drew the curtains for our daily siesta, our Venetian tradition. The city was a feast of sights, so that when you closed your eyes, you still saw a kaleidoscope of colors and shapes. Then in bed, we were for each other a feast for touch, for sensation.

On our strolls we always stopped to gaze upon the Lion of Venice, the ancient, winged sculpture high on a granite column in Saint Mark's Square. Jojo would teasingly pinch my side or wink or say something suggestive. Jojo had a huskiness to his voice that was as effective as a finger tracing my collarbone, that brought on that warm feeling below my rib cage like an inlet, a hidden cove where I floated in turquoise waters, sensation rippling through me.

The lion was the symbol of Venice. We laughed about that. It was everywhere. *Especially in our bedroom,* I would tell him in a low voice. On this trip, he was back with his roar. A roar just for me. A roar that came from the pleasure I gave him.

"What did you like the best?" he would ask after, wanting to know how he'd pleased me.

When I told him he would smile, happy. His eyes were soft like the smoothest brown velvet, the underside of a truffle, a rabbit's coat, the acorns that made up the Iberico ham. "Ah yessss," he would purr, nodding in agreement. "That was my favorite too."

His pleasure was mine. Mine was his. We were inseparable.

We made our usual excursions outside of Venice during our stay, bringing along friends like Coco, Diaghilev, and others who'd also come to Italy for the season. First, we went to Ravenna to see the Byzantine mosaics, where Coco took notes for her jewelry designs. We took another trip by train to Naples, a city filled with hidden treasures, including one of Jojo's favorites, a panel in the Church of Santa Maria del Parto called *The Devil of Mergellina.* I was glad to see him animated.

"Do you see, madmachelle?" Jojo said to Coco, who hadn't been to Naples before. He pointed to the figure of the Archangel Michael, sandaled feet holding a creature half serpent, half woman to the ground.

"This is a very especial painting. Can you see why? Satan is portrayed as female. Yes! A woman. A she-devil. And not just any 'she.' Look closely. This is the face of Vittoria d'Avalos. But who was she? Ah, a very beautiful and seductive Neapolitan noblewoman. A woman who had the nerve to fall in love with the bishop of Ariano Irpino, a Catholic priest, a man who had taken a vow of chastity before God. Yes, yes. A priest! Well, this woman was determined to have her way with him. She concocted a powerful love spell to enchant the churchman. Can you imagine? Who would do such a thing to a priest?

"Well, it worked," Jojo continued. "The bishop fell in love with her, yes, and, devoured by passion, broke his vow of chastity. Terrible! Even worse, he found it quite enjoyable, naturally. He wanted more and more. Yet his soul was in peril—if not already lost. He knew he must break the spell! But what to do? Well, our bishop managed to find a monk, an expert in exorcism. This clever monk advised the bishop to commission a special painting of Saint Michael driving away the devil. The colors must be mixed with a mysterious balm, a recipe, sadly, lost to history. To complete the exorcism, the bishop was to have the artist portray Satan with the features of guess who? Vittoria d'Avalos. Yes! And it worked! Signora d'Avalos's demented spell was broken! The bishop was set free!"

My eyes went to Coco. Hers met mine. We were thinking the same thought. The devil was a woman. The devil was Roussi. It was a matter of time before the exorcism.

◆　◆　◆

Our Venetian delight ended. Back in Paris, Roussi talked incessantly of Mr. Harmon. The man crept into nearly every conversation, particularly when Jojo was with us. My hopes rose. Mr. Harmon was the answer. This American man, older than Jojo, was throwing dollar bills around Paris to impress her.

Mr. Harmon hosted a luncheon today at the Plaza Athénée, and I chose all the guests. He hosts the most entertaining musicales too . . .

Mr. Harmon took me to tea and showed me the plans for the most magnificent clubhouse he's building in the Bois de Boulogne for the International Aviators Aid Society . . .

Mr. Harmon says that in every country, it is the elite of the nation's manhood that takes to the air . . .

Mr. Harmon bought me this diamond bracelet as a token of friendship. Isn't it stunning? I had him buy one for Poki and Tika too, so we would match!

"You know, Misia," Roussi said one afternoon, stopping by the Meurice just after luncheon when Jojo wasn't there. "Mr. Harmon is still engaged to Miss Keltie. You remember her, the opera singer? But he keeps hinting that he still wants to marry me instead, saying that I've always been his first choice. Isn't that funny?"

"I doubt it's funny to Miss Keltie," I said. "But all the same, you should consider it. To have the elite of manhood want to make you his bride. That would make you the elite of womanhood."

Truly, I couldn't help myself.

She looked at me, her singsong voice gone. "I'm twenty-one now, Misia. I won't wait much longer. I need someone to take care of me. It's time. Time for my real life to begin. Jojo and I love each other. But . . . he can't leave you. It makes him feel too guilty."

So this had never been about Mr. Harmon. She was using him to make Jojo jealous. Taunting Jojo to try to force him to choose.

"He can't leave me," I said, "because he loves me. Guilt has nothing to do with it. Jojo is a man who does as he pleases. Surely that's obvious to you now. He's greedy. Selfish. He wants everything and thinks he should have it."

"Then why do you allow it?"

"When you love someone, you love them for their faults too. You wouldn't understand. You don't know how to love anyone. Except yourself. And Alexis. Jojo loves me. He merely wants you."

She stared at me for a moment as if not sure how to react. Then she laughed. She came to me and kissed me on the cheek.

"Oh, Misia," she said, the singsong voice back as she moved to the door. "You're so droll. I never know what you'll say next."

Chapter Ten

Paris, 1927

Spring came and with it there was to be another Mdivani wedding. Almost a year after David and Mae Murray wed, Serge Mdivani was to marry the exotic actress Pola Negri, a much bigger star than Mae. Hollywood would have two Princess Mdivanis.

"Serge has never loved anybody as he loves Pola," Roussi said when she told us the news. "And you only need to look at Pola to see that she loves him too."

The entire Mdivani clan descended on Paris for a celebratory dinner at the Plaza Athénée. When Jojo and I arrived, we were ushered upstairs to the largest suite and a view of the Eiffel Tower. Affable General Mdivani, Roussi's father, immediately came over and greeted us. David and Alexis Mdivani as well. They backslapped Jojo. They shook his hand. They clustered about him as if they were all old friends and I a potted plant. How comfortable they were together. I felt my heart harden into a knot. I wondered how Jojo was so familiar with them. Something had transpired behind my back. Jojo had been seeing them more than I knew.

Soon, a throng of American photographers and reporters were let into the suite. Roussi and Nina surrounded Pola. Serge cleared his throat and professed his love for Miss Negri for the newspapermen. Roussi, on one side of Pola, was smiling, her gray eyes unusually bright.

I saw her kiss Pola several times on the cheek, then press her own cheek against Pola's, just as she so often did with me.

Ah. I'd never understood why Roussi doted on me as she did, but I'd grown used to it. Now, I saw the behavior for what it was: a tactic to endear herself, to trick, to get what she wanted. From me: my husband. From Pola: her earnings, her name, her fame.

Nina, on the other side of Pola, had an arm firmly around the actress's shoulders. As usual, Nina was not smiling. I had the feeling that if Pola tried to run, Nina's hand would quickly seize her neck in a death grip.

As for Pola, the imperious, black-haired beauty appeared older than Serge by a decade. Her skin was snow white, her nails painted red. She wore a blue velvet suit from French couturiere Callot Soeurs. Pola was no ingenue, but as the Mdivanis swarmed around her like ants on a cream puff, she had a look in her large, green eyes as if she wasn't sure what she had gotten herself into.

It was a look I recognized of late from my own mirror-gazing.

After Serge's brief speech came the sudden flurry of the photographers' magnesium flashes, blinding bursts and pops. Then Alexis picked up the phone and called for champagne—Dom Pérignon—and caviar. "Fresh," he instructed loudly. "Not pressed."

I glanced at Mr. Harmon, who naturally was there as well. I remembered how he hosted his musicales here, according to Roussi. All this, I presumed, was going on his tab.

The newspaper people lingered, hoping to get more from Pola Negri and this exuberant family of princes and princesses. The Mdivanis were exciting. Magnetic. They had the bearing of movie stars themselves. Boisterous and interesting, they bragged about polo, horses, gambling, oil, playfully arguing and gaining an advantage over each other. Very Russian. They made people want to be around them.

And Jojo—I observed that he was caught up in it too. Jojo was always attracted to larger-than-life characters. They populated his mind and his murals. Aladdin. The King of Siam. Don Juan. He had a passion for life, and they were so lively, as if they hadn't a care in the world except whether the caviar was pressed or not. Colors were brighter around them. Contrasts crisper. Including the contrast between Roussi and me.

Thankfully, I was modern in one of Coco's little black dresses. American *Vogue* called them the "Chanel Ford" because like the Ford automobiles they were black and made it easy for women to move about from place to place. Coco believed in always being "presentable," and in these, you were instantaneously. Everyone wanted one. I already owned four. I was also wearing her recent perfume, *Bois des Iles*. I wasn't a movie star or a princess, but I was *Misia*, for God's sake. My face might be older, but it was still the face immortalized by the Impressionists. But much of that was in the last century. *The last century!* This new one was already more than a quarter of the way over.

There was not a soul here who interested me. No one here cared about art or music or theater. These were not my type of Russians. There was nothing refined about them. Nothing subtle or poetic or intellectual.

Roussi appeared before me, peeling me from Jojo's side. "Darling Misia, you absolutely must meet Pola's mother," she said. "She's from Poland, you know. Just like you! She says in Poland everyone knows who you are. She can't wait to meet you. She says you're the Polish Queen of Paris."

Silver-haired Madame Kielczewska was seated on a chair near the reporters. Meanwhile, across the room, Jojo remained in the inner circle, now in conversation with Roussi's precious Alexis. Who wouldn't want to talk to Alexis? I heard Jojo speak of him several times as Alejo, a Spanish endearment. How did he know him well enough for that? Alexis wasn't technically the most handsome of the brothers, as Roussi liked to claim, but he had a convincing swagger, a rogue appeal that gave him the strongest magnetism. Golden hair with tousled curls. A boyish, friendly expression that made you want to please him, spend money on him. He looked like fun, with the same air of pending adventure as Roussi. Of the siblings, they were the most alike. Twins, as Roussi said.

I would have politely left Madame Kielczewska to her own devices. I would not allow Roussi to attempt to relegate me to the antiquities section. We spoke in Polish. Growing up with a Polish father and grandfather, I had an ear for language just as I did for music. I quickly realized a perch next to Miss Negri's mother, who had just been interviewed by a newspaperman, could be advantageous. She looked as dazed as Pola. She went on, still in Polish, about how they didn't expect the press to be there, that the newspapers had reported the engagement a few days ago before the couple was actually engaged, catching her little Pola unaware. Mme Kielczewska didn't trust Serge Mdivani.

"He is pushing her into this," she said. "Her Valentino still warm in the grave. The American public, they are furious with her. This engagement will ruin her. They adored Valentino. And she does not even love this Prince Serge Mdivani. She told me herself. She said, 'Mama, I don't love him. He just will not go away.'"

My whole body clenched. How familiar that sounded.

I listened to Madame Kielczewska with one ear, David Mdivani another. Behind me, he was taking questions from a newspaperman who'd asked when Mae would arrive in France.

"She's not coming," David said. "She's not going to the wedding."

"Not going?" the reporter said with surprise.

"Neither am I," David said. "What? Me wait for the wedding? It can't be done. I'm flying to London tomorrow to rejoin Mae. Then on Saturday, Mae and I sail for Africa from Southampton. We're going big-game shooting. We made an appointment to kill a lot of animals in Africa—lions, tigers, elephants, crocodiles, polar bears, camels—everything."

Polar bears in Africa? Camels as big game? The Mdivanis said whatever they wanted and expected people to accept it. That was part of their game.

I heard Alexis tell one of the newspapermen he wouldn't be at the wedding either, that he had to get back to London to resume his studies. "I'm at Oxford, you know."

Then Roussi. "Of course I'll be at the wedding," she said. "I wouldn't miss it for the world. I love Pola like a sister. I may have to leave early, though. I have a possible engagement in Spain. I've been commissioned to make a statue of Commander Franco, you know, the aviator."

What? This was the first I'd heard of such a thing. Surely, it was Mr. Harmon's doing. How annoyed Jojo would be to find out the man was intruding on his territory: Spain. As Roussi passed by, I gently took her arm.

"How marvelous," I said with as much sincerity as I could muster. "You didn't tell me Mr. Harmon had arranged a commission in Spain for you."

She tilted her head, a smile flickering on her lips. "But it wasn't Mr. Harmon," she said. "It was Jojo. I thought he would have told you. You see, Misia. There are things you just don't know."

I dropped her arm. She walked off, back to Pola, embracing her, holding her hand. I went to Jojo and pulled him aside. I'd had enough. I repeated what Roussi told me about the statue of Commander Franco. "Did you arrange that?" I said in a low voice.

"No, no," he said. "Not at all."

"Not at all?"

"I mentioned it to her as a possibility. Nothing more. Since she's making a name for herself in aviation sculpture. I'm acquainted with Commander Franco. I told her I could suggest it to him but as of yet, I haven't had a chance."

"That's a relief," I said.

"Why do you say that?" I was surprised by the stern way he looked at me.

He should know why I said that.

"Is that wise to entrust her with it?" I said. "Are you sure she's capable? You have your reputation as an artist to think of."

"I know what I'm doing," he snapped. "I'm perfectly capable of judging her abilities for myself."

I stood back. I raised my chin. "Of course," I said stiffly. "Yes, you are, darling. I didn't mean to imply that you weren't." I waited for his expression to soften. For him to say something conciliatory. But he didn't.

I told him I was tired and was going to leave. I would not stay for the dinner. He didn't argue. He didn't offer to come with me. At home, I was nauseous. I was suffocated. If only I could be sick. How physical my reaction was. In the bathroom, I filled my needle, then stabbed it into my thigh, wanting quick and complete relief. I was so overcome with anguish I lay down on the hard floor. I curled up into a ball, my eyes staring at nothing. It was the only way I could stop the spinning in my head.

I would never forget the look on Jojo's face when I told him I was leaving. It was a look of relief. In my mind, Roussi's voice: *There are things you just don't know.*

◆ ◆ ◆

The marriage ceremony was in a small village just outside Paris called Seraincourt. Pola Negri had acquired a château there the year before with her starlet earnings. Soon, I was sure, Pola's château would be recast as the château of the Prince and Princess Mdivani, going down in Mdivani folklore as having originated with them.

A wedding was still a wedding. I was sentimental. In the car on the way to Seraincourt, I took Jojo's hand. I hoped he would say something meaningful about our own wedding, remembering fondly our ceremony at the Church of Saint Roch in the rue du Faubourg Saint-Honoré after so many years of waiting for the right moment.

There was no waiting for Mdivanis. For them, there was no time to lose.

We went first to the town hall, where in accordance with French law, the mayor would perform the civil marriage. A large mob of journalists and photographers was already there. Inside, filling the mayor's office, there were just twelve of us, including Pola's mother and godfather. Nina Huberich, unsmiling, to whom I didn't say a word. Clifford Harmon, looking at his watch nervously. Jojo and me. We were crammed in a small space, a situation made even more uncomfortable as we waited for the general and Roussi, who had yet to arrive.

Outside the town hall, we could feel the press of the waiting spectators. "It looks like nearly two hundred newspapermen," Serge said, peering out the one window. There was a hint of pride in his voice. "I would say at least three hundred cameramen."

"So many," Pola said, complaining. "How did they find us? You didn't tell them, did you? I wanted a quiet wedding."

"Darling," Serge said, "you're a movie star who is now about to be a princess. They were certain to track you down. This is international news."

Pola had certainly not dressed in the manner of one who wanted a quiet wedding. She wore a sleeveless Lanvin gown in white chiffon and velvet embroidered with pearls. A cape trimmed in sable graced her shoulders. She held an enormous bouquet of white lilies of the valley. Her neck and wrists were swathed in diamonds and emeralds. Her bobbed hair was so black it looked midnight blue. She knew the photographers would be there. This was what Hollywood expected.

Where were the general and Roussi? This was just like her to hold everyone up. Roussi was to be Pola's attendant.

"Roussi is already like a sister to me," Pola insisted, mirroring Roussi's words about her. "We must wait."

The room was stuffy. Filled with subplots. I just didn't know what they were. Serge patted at his forehead with a handkerchief. Like me, he seemed to want to get it over with. Like Harmon, he continually glanced at his pocket watch. The swarthy bridegroom wore a perfectly tailored cutaway and white spats, a silk hat atop his dark hair. He kept leaning in and speaking in low tones to Harmon, the best man, who glanced about, watching for the late arrivals, shifting his weight from foot to foot. Beside me, Jojo was perspiring too, using a finger to wipe and flick sweat from his brow.

Earlier, I'd approached Pola's mother, hoping she might give something away, but she didn't. Her attitude had changed. "They're in love," she said of her daughter and Serge. She spoke of the general, how charming he was, and I wondered if she wasn't a little bit in love as well. The Mdivanis had gotten to her.

Finally, after an hour, the general arrived. Alone.

"Roussi's not coming," he announced. "I tried to persuade her . . . she couldn't be convinced. She's . . . not feeling well."

What little air was in the room disappeared. Roussi was the linchpin, the mastermind of the event. She was the one who had drawn Pola in, who had convinced her of Serge's love. She was the reason Jojo and I were here. She was the reason Harmon was here. Now, as always, she was playing a game.

"How odd," I said to Jojo. "She was perfectly fine when we saw her this morning."

"Yes, yes," he said, looking away, annoyance in his voice.

My eyes went to Mr. Harmon. His face had flushed red. Serge and Nina exchanged a glance. I was sure Jojo knew something about the reason for Roussi's absence.

At least now the ceremony could take place. The mayor, bald with a walrus mustache, presided. It didn't take long. When it was over, the doors of the town hall were flung open to the cheering crowd. The newlyweds stepped forward. Serge swept his bride into his arms with a flourish.

"Kiss me, princess," he said loudly as if he had practiced it, and, to the accompaniment of three hundred flashbulbs, the newest Princess Mdivani did.

◆ ◆ ◆

At the château for the reception, we gathered in the garden. Once again, the press and photographers arrived.

Champagne was offered about. An orchestra played half-heartedly. Where were all of the esteemed guests? The film stars. The celebrities. As expected, no Alexis, David, or Mae. Or Roussi.

A few more photographs were taken, and then the newlyweds left almost immediately for Deauville, Mr. Harmon their driver. I heard Pola say she was disappointed Roussi wouldn't be able to make the trip with them as planned. She supposed Roussi would announce her engagement later.

Engagement?

I understood now Roussi's ploy, why Harmon was upset. Roussi had ditched him. It had all been another plot. She was trying to make Jojo jealous, to get him to make a choice. *If you don't leave Misia, I'll marry Harmon.*

Jojo stood his ground. I was the victor, yet I didn't feel like one. Jojo's mood was somber. Roussi wasn't there, and it was as if I wasn't either.

What a strange reception this was. It had just started, and everyone was leaving.

There was a reason the siblings didn't care about attending. To the Mdivanis, weddings weren't sacred. They were transactions to get what they wanted.

In August, Jojo had our Rolls-Royce remodeled to fit three passengers instead of two. Roussi was accompanying us to Venice.

"It's always interesting to see the world through fresh eyes," Jojo had said when he first proposed the idea of Roussi joining us. "It's useful for my work, no doubt. New perspectives. New ideas."

I knew what Roussi was thinking. A new wife.

I had become part of a harem. I tolerated it for Jojo's sake, for the love I had for him and I knew he had for me. I tolerated it because it was temporary. With Roussi nearby, Jojo's mood was lighter. He engaged with the world again, with me. He ate and drank with his usual gusto. And he made love to me once again as he always had. No longer yearning for her, he was happy once more with me. He was a man loyal to the classic, though able to dabble in the modern, a man who appreciated the silver and the gold. Our closeness, his tenderness that I could tell in my heart was real, assured me. I knew him. He could never grow tired of me. But he would of her.

We took a side trip to Florence to show Roussi the Duomo. Roussi brought along new friends she'd met in Venice, a group that included several attractive young men of means. I let myself hope that she might fall in love with one of them and settle with someone her own age. I clung to every thread of possible salvation I could.

One hot afternoon, she was off with these friends. Jojo and I had a bottle of wine at lunch, then retired to our suite for siesta. Shutters closed to block the harsh afternoon light, we fell into bed, like old habit, something we'd avoided on this trip with Roussi always near, always underfoot.

I'd let him undress me, reveling in the feeling that he wanted me, that all his attention was on me and only me. He always moved smoothly, a master of undoing buttons and clasps. Two steps ahead, he had an erotic mind, and I knew he was already choosing from his many scenarios, mentally then physically arranging us in lovemaking as he did the characters in his murals, positioning me, himself, for maximum enjoyment.

"Do you like that?" he would whisper.

"I do. Do you?"

"Yessss."

Soon I was lost in the pleasure he was bringing me, his bulk now poised on top of me, his skin warm and alive as I caressed him, as his muscles rhythmically tensed then released, tensed then released. Yes, I was his wife. I was his wife! He was not leaving me. Beneath him, I was tense too, deliciously so with pleasure building and building and . . .

The floor creaked.

I glanced down. There was Roussi, on hands and knees.

I gasped. She was crawling toward us as if trying to go unnoticed, tears running down her face.

"Roussi!" I shrieked. "What are you doing?"

Jojo spun off me. "Roussi?"

I sat up. "Get out," I said to her. "Get out!"

Roussi rose from the floor, her whole body shaking. She ignored me and glared at Jojo. "How could you do this to me?" she said, her voice low and trembling. "How could you?"

I was confused, mortified. To be so exposed, so vulnerable, in front of her. She turned and fled from the room. Jojo slid out of bed, calling after her. He dressed quickly and moved toward the door.

"Where are you going?" I said.

"To find her."

"What? Are you serious? Jojo, don't leave," I said. "She's unhinged to do such a thing. What was she thinking?"

"She's upset," he said. "I must talk to her. To calm her. I'll be right back."

"I'm upset too," I said, but he didn't seem to hear me. He was gone, and I was alone, too stunned, too hurt to move. What had just happened?

He returned thirty minutes later in a posture of defeat.

"I couldn't find her," he said. "She's disappeared from the hotel."

"Why are you so concerned?" I said, furious. "She brought it upon herself."

"She had no way of knowing what we were doing."

"She certainly did. We are husband and wife," I said. "She should have turned around. She should have never come in. She should have knocked."

"Misia, why are you being so unkind?"

"Me? Unkind?" I was baffled. How could Jojo not be on my side? She crept into our room, and I was the one in the wrong?

Fury consumed me. She had disrespected me from the moment she stepped into our lives. But this. This crossed a line I couldn't ignore. And Jojo. The concern in his eyes, his gestures, told me everything. He was worried, but not about me. Not about the infringement on my—on our—privacy. He was worried about her. She made him feel as if we were the adulterers. As if by making love to his wife, he had betrayed *her*.

"She's gone too far, Jojo. I've accepted a lot. I've been discreet. But this . . . Jojo, what is happening? Why are you defending her?"

He put his head in his hands. "I don't know. Misia, I don't know."

Chapter Eleven

Venice, 1927

Roussi came back eventually. I knew she wasn't about to take the first train back to Paris and disappear from our lives forever. She'd invested too much in Jojo. I didn't know what conversations she and Jojo had outside my presence, but I presumed he made promises and declarations to appease her as she manipulated him. I presumed he'd been doing that all along. A man tells a woman what she wants to hear when he wants something from her.

We returned to Venice, and the three of us went about the rest of our time in Italy as if nothing had changed, attending dinners and parties and balls, my smile forced, pretending on the surface the debacle in Florence hadn't happened, that everything hadn't, in fact, changed. But I knew it had.

She was chipping away. Jojo was slipping away.

The sanctity of our bed was the one hill she had yet to take.

"Russians," Coco had said. "What's yours is theirs."

Roussi considered the marriage bed hers. I was the trespasser.

But I was not so easily dislodged. No wonder Roussi was frustrated.

The drive back to Paris in September was long. Jojo seemed preoccupied and uncomfortable. Roussi slept most of the way. All that plotting someone else's demise must have been exhausting.

◆ ◆ ◆

We were back in Paris not a week when I returned home after lunch with friends to find Roussi and her lawyer brother-in-law, the expressionless Mr. Huberich, in my drawing room. Aimée, flustered, whispered that Roussi had insisted on waiting for me.

Roussi rushed up to me smiling brightly, kissing me, hugging me. "Misia! Where have you been? Doing something important, I'm sure. I have news to tell you . . ."

She led me to the divan and had me sit down. She sat next to me, very close, and took my hand, her gray eyes peering into mine. "It's all settled. You don't have to worry. Not about anything. Jojo and I will never leave you. We'll still all be together. Nothing will change."

"What do you mean?" I said.

"Mr. Huberich, as I'm sure you know, is a recognized international lawyer. He knows a way to go around the church so that Jojo and I can be married, as we both have wanted for so long. You said if that was what we wanted, you wouldn't stand in the way. Do you remember that, Misia? In Switzerland. That's what you said. Now, it's all been arranged."

"What exactly has been arranged?" I said.

"Your divorce. And following that, our marriage. Tell her," Roussi said to Mr. Huberich, and he proceeded to explain. A divorce for Jojo and me to be followed eventually by a civil marriage for Jojo and Roussi. It was a way, he said, to circumvent the Catholic canons prohibiting divorce.

"A decree in The Hague is perfectly legitimate under French laws," he said.

The Hague? What did The Hague have to do with Jojo and me? I listened as if I were watching from my box at the theater, my opera glasses on. Who was it onstage? What was this scene? I heard my voice as if it were an actress speaking, someone else playing the part of me.

A thought occurred to me. I was the monkey at Angelina. I was the mess Huberich was cleaning up this time.

"If this is what Jojo truly wants," I said, "then as I promised in Switzerland, I won't stand in the way."

I knew what Jojo wanted: to go along as we were. Which was impossible. Roussi had made that clear when she crawled into our bedroom in Italy.

"Oh, Misia, it is what he wants. It just can't be helped. You are such a dear. We'll travel together to The Hague. I couldn't bear to think of you doing that alone. You and me and Mr. Huberich will go to file the petition. I won't leave your side. You won't have to go through anything alone. Because we'll still always be together, me, Jojo, and you."

She was soothing, like a daughter, a caring friend, stroking my arm and speaking in cooing tones as if she weren't at all the source of the affliction. Her manner was hypnotizing. Her ministrations eventually calmed me despite that I was fully aware the divorce would be for her sake and her benefit, to get what she wanted: to be the new Madame Sert.

But she could never take my place. She could never be me. All of this—for a piece of paper that meant nothing.

After the two plotters took their leave, I phoned Jojo at his studio. Hands trembling, I asked him to come home immediately. He did.

I hid my distress. I had to appear calm and unworried as I told him Roussi's plan. "Did you know about this?" I said.

He drew himself up. "Absolutamente no! I had no idea."

"Not at all?"

"Roussi mentioned something about Huberich looking into various laws regarding marriage and divorce. Ways to go around the church. She'd said something about The Hague. I certainly never agreed to anything. Did she say I did?"

"It was just like in Berne, Jojo. She said it was what you wanted." He may not have said yes to Roussi's plan, but he didn't say no.

"But how could I possibly want that?" he said, his tone distressed just as it was when I'd told him about what Roussi had said to me in Berne. "Please don't be upset. Please tell me you know I would never leave you. You are the only woman who understands me. And I understand you. We are meant to be together. No, Toscha, no. We cannot get divorced. You are my wife. My dearest friend. My confidante. We have so much history together. Our life, all of this—" He motioned around the room to all of our furnishings, the antiques, the paintings, the objets d'art we'd collected over the years. "No, no. It would be absurd of me to marry a woman of twenty-one at my age. It would be uncouth of me to leave you at your age. Absolutely unthinkable."

All these reasons pouring out of him. They revealed to me a devastating truth. He had been thinking about leaving me. He had been debating with himself.

I felt the blade of a knife, slitting me open from the inside.

He sat me down on the divan just as Roussi had. He took my hand in his, looking at me imploringly, like a rabbit caught in a trap.

"Tell me to stay, Toscha," he said, as if it were so simple. "If you tell me to stay, I will stay."

"Why?" Coco said. I'd gone to her home on the Faubourg needing consolation. She'd been lying on the orange divan rereading *Wuthering Heights*. When I told her all that had happened, she sat straight up. "You always tell people what to do. You've spent your entire life ordering people around. And now of all times, when it matters the most, you won't?"

I was depleted, weaving in and out of panic and resignation. "I've spent my entire life helping people get what they want," I said. "If Jojo wants the divorce, I won't stop it. He has never said he doesn't want the divorce. Not once. And of all his reasons we should not divorce, he hasn't said the most important one." I looked down. It was hard to say. "He hasn't said he loves me."

Just as he hadn't that last time I'd confronted him after the trip to Berne.

"Misia. Don't be ridiculous. Jojo doesn't want a divorce. He wants everything the way it's been. And if you don't tell him to stay, all he'll hear is her telling him to leave. She'll tell him you don't love him enough to fight for him but that she does."

I was adamant. "He has to decide to stay for himself."

"He can't. He doesn't know what he wants. He can't think clearly. Women like Roussi put ideas in a man's head. They manipulate. She's causing all this disruption. All this distress. And when she's with him, she's telling him she's doing it for them. Because she loves him so much and they are meant to be together. She doesn't mean it. She doesn't love him. She wants to beat you. She wants to win. Women of her type use everything in their arsenal, and men are helpless against it. Youth, sex, adoration, the promise of eternity. If only I could bottle it."

"Chanel No. 6," I said. "With a hint of sculpting clay."

A few weeks later, catastrophe picked up speed. I was in a car with Roussi and Huberich going to The Hague. Jojo had tried to stop me many times, always with the same reasons. My age. His age. Our past.

Everything but the reason I waited to hear.

I didn't need Jojo to tell me he loved me for myself. I knew that he did. But if he couldn't say it to me, that was the barometer. It meant he was already gone.

It meant he was already imagining a life with her. In his mind, he was sketching the scenes in black charcoal, envisioning how they would come together on the big panels, the final rendition. This new, exciting commission. He was wrapped up in it.

He looked distressed when I said goodbye. "Don't leave me, Misia," he said. But the car was waiting. Still, he let me go, as if I were going to the Netherlands to look at the tulips.

That was because he knew as well as I did a divorce in The Hague was no more than theater.

The production even came with a costume.

"I brought you these," Roussi said, once we got there. She handed me black, shabby clothes that looked like they'd come from a flea market, certainly not, as Coco would say, "presentable."

"I hope, darling Misia, you don't mind wearing them. It will make everything easier. For you, of course. Huberich says it's better if you look poor. He says that way they don't ask too many questions. You don't mind, do you, dear Misia?"

I started to laugh. "Do you really believe, dear Roussi, that a change of wardrobe can take away my power? You think by dressing me in rags I will shrivel into nothing? I will no longer be Misia? Jojo will no longer love me and I him?"

She shrugged. "It's the lawyer's advice."

"Ha! You mean the producer's advice. This is theater. It's the only reason I agreed to come. I'll wear them. I'll wear them to prove even more this excursion is parody. You're simply too greedy to see."

In a private room, I slipped out of my expensive Chanel dress and coat ensemble for Roussi's washerwoman outfit. When I came out, she was gloating, there in her gray Vionnet suit that I'd paid for. I didn't care. This wasn't me. I saw as if from a distance, peering over the railing of my theater box at the stage. I was playing a part, the wardrobe change confirming it. In "character," I registered my application for "divorce" with Huberich's help. How he loved pushing paper, telling me where to sign. Once I scrawled my name, Roussi's demeanor was doting. Adoring. As if she thought she'd actually won.

"We will always love you, Misia," she said. "You will always be a part of our lives."

"Yes, you keep saying that," I said, annoyed.

She knew how to play into one's insecurities. For Jojo, age and virility. For me, being abandoned. Until Jojo. He was different. He loved me. He appreciated me. He needed me.

He would stop this before it went too far.

Divorce in The Hague meant nothing.

Back in Paris, I went as if in a dream state. The court prescribed a waiting period of three months during which the married subjects were to make an "attempt at reconciliation," which was ludicrous since Jojo and I still lived together at the Meurice as if nothing had changed. We still went to dinner every night. We still enjoyed each other's company. I waited for Jojo to say the three words that would make me tell him to stay. I waited for Roussi to realize that now that she would get what she wanted all this time, she didn't want it.

"This Hague idea," Jojo said. "It's a sham, Toscha. An absurdity. We married in the church. Some Dutchmen with gavels can't change that. If you would just tell me to stay . . ."

"If a life with Roussi is what you want," I said, "I love you too much not to give it to you."

And I love you too much to let this go on any longer. That was what he could have said, but he didn't.

The allure of Roussi, of the Mdivanis, was overpowering. Roussi was always around to remind him of that. Looming. Pushing. Charming. Manipulating fate itself.

One afternoon when Jojo was at the studio, I went into his study seeking a letter opener as mine had dulled. I was surprised to see the photograph he'd taken of me carrying the soldier up the hospital stairs during the war resting on top of his stationery. Had he been looking at it again? Why? What was he thinking?

Where would I be without you, Toscha?

I studied the photograph, the wounded man propped on my back, his arms clinging to my neck and shoulders as I leaned forward, balancing his weight.

It hadn't occurred to me then that there were many men who would be humiliated by that. Men who didn't want a woman's help. But that had never been Jojo. Not with me.

"You are a magician," Satie had said to me when we were working on *Parade*. But to others he often called me names meant to be unflattering, to hurt. Aunt Trufaldin. Aunt Brutus. Bitch.

"Misia is a lovely cat," he told everyone who would listen, "so hide your fish."

A man I did much for and would again. It was said I could make or break a man just by a nod or shake of my head when looking over a new piece of music. He like so many others blamed me at times for their failings when my critiques were simply to make them better. Jean had. Proust had. Picasso too. They accused me of interfering with their creative vision. One of the two characters Proust modeled after me in *Remembrance of Things Past*, Madame Verdurin, was not complimentary. Toulouse-Lautrec, when angered with me because I critiqued his technique, painted me as a madame in a brothel as revenge.

I laughed when he showed it to me, though inside it stung.

The photograph from the war was blurry. You could sense the movement, the feeling of being caught between one space and another. You could see the outline of my body, my form, my long skirt of the time, my waist held in by a corset, the man like a sack over my shoulder. He was not a large man. I was not particularly strong. But as Jojo said, I got things done when they needed doing.

The feeling of movement, of time passing. We were living ghosts, each moment fading into the next, moments we could not hold on to. A person who is there, and then who isn't.

That afternoon, I returned to my desk, but I couldn't concentrate. Old wounds from my father had reopened.

I liked to think that when I was young and sat as muse for my artists at the home Thadée and I shared with them, it was a purely generous act on my part. In truth, it was selfish. I needed to be seen. That was how I could sit for hours under their gazes. To my father, I was invisible. But there, in their endless paintings and drawings, was proof I existed.

It was Renoir who worked the hardest. After the divorce from Thadée, when the others shied away, he came to the home I shared with Edwards to attempt portrait after portrait, determined to capture what he called the alchemy of my outward appearance and inner vibration. "Your essence, Misia," he said. Even when he was overcome with arthritis, when his assistant had to place his brush in his fingers, he tried, yet was never satisfied.

All I needed was the attempt. That was what touched me. He tried.

"Come with me to Scotland," Coco said. "You need to get away from Paris. You're not thinking straight. You need perspective. You're always there for Jojo. This way, maybe he'll realize what it would be like without you."

I didn't want to be apart from Jojo. But we were at an impasse. Coco was right. My absence could show him the reality of casting me aside.

In Scotland, Bendor had purchased an old, run-down estate called Rosehall, as if he needed another one. But this was for Coco. She took me to see it. The home was dark and cold, like everything in Scotland, but she was going to brighten it up. She had carte blanche to redo it however she liked, and she wanted my opinion.

"You should hire Jojo," I said. "You know he can do wonders."

If I brought Jojo another commission, that could bring him to his senses and remind him of who I was, who we were.

Coco clucked her tongue with disapproval like an old peasant woman. "Always looking out for him. Is he looking out for you? No. I won't hire him this time. I'm furious at him for what he's doing with Roussi. And I want this house to be different. Everything Bendor owns is ridiculously masculine. Coats of arms, coats of armor, shields on the walls, portraits of scowling ancestors literally everywhere. I want Rosehall to be like its name. Soft and floral. I want pretty wallpaper on the walls. Not circus murals with Roussi's monkeys. I'm putting in a bidet. I've had to have one shipped from Paris. They don't know what they are over here."

Soft. Floral. This was not the usual Coco. "You're talking about this as if it's more than just a house," I said.

There was a hard look on her face, and I knew I was onto something. "Maybe it is," she said. She took her cigarette case from a pocket, pulled out a cigarette, then lit it. Behind the gray veil of smoke, Coco's dark eyes flickered. "We've been trying for nearly a year."

"Trying?"

She sighed. "For an heir. For Bendor. I've told you he wants one."

"But do you?" I was surprised. I didn't think Coco wanted children. And surely it was too late.

"I do."

My heart felt like glass shattering. I could hear the longing in her voice. A husband. A child. To her, that would be the acknowledgment she pined for. To be respectable. To be like everyone else. To belong to people who had to claim you when her father would not. Few saw Coco's domestic, maternal side. She had a nephew she doted on. She'd supported him from a young age, after her sister had died, as if he were her own. He had married, had children. She was an aunt but not a mother. There was a difference.

My friend who wore pearls draped over her chest like armor. Her round earrings and buttons like shields. The cigarette she wielded like a flaming sword. The curtain of smoke a shield too, as if to say don't get too close. All of it was to hide who she really was. A person who wanted to be soft but life had never let her.

"I know what you're thinking," Coco said. "I'm forty-four. He thinks I'm thirty-four. But even at my age, women have been known to have children."

Coco always appeared younger than she was. I was the only one who knew her true age. It was one of her many secrets. A secret that now worked against her. The chances of her being able to give Bendor a child were slim.

"I've seen doctors," she said. "Specialists. In the bedroom, I do the most humiliating gymnastics. Practically standing on my head. You would laugh uncontrollably if you could see it. I'm trying everything, Misia."

Everything. She would lose him if she didn't succeed.

"If I don't give him an heir, he'll find someone else to do it."

"Someone younger," I said. "A replacement. Like Roussi. This is maddening. Would Bendor really do that? Surely not."

Doctors told me years ago I was unable to have children due to a quirk of my anatomy. With Thadée, Edwards, I hadn't wanted them. With Jojo, he hadn't wanted them. That's what he'd told me.

"Bendor's devoted to you," I said. Just as I'd believed Jojo was devoted to me.

"He's a duke, Misia. He has a line to pass on. It's the one job he has."

Now I understood this "Rosehall." It was her attempt to bring out her feminine side, dainty and girlish. Coco Chanel didn't wait for the gods to determine her fate. If she had, she couldn't be Coco Chanel. She had to do something whether it made sense or not. If she could create that mood around her, perhaps the most womanly of creations would follow: an heir growing inside her, the next Duke of Westminster. Her relationship with Bendor depended on it. If she could give him an heir, he would marry her.

The next Duchess of Westminster. I knew Coco. I knew she hoped for the title despite all she'd accomplished on her own. "There can be only one Coco Chanel," she told the reporters.

But that Coco Chanel was a woman who longed to be loved just like every other woman, who wanted to have someone to call her own, the promise of respectability and a man who, unlike her father, made a vow to never leave her. I wanted her to have that. I understood her despair.

Coco was a woman who only had lovers. I was a woman who only had husbands.

Yet there really was no difference. Husbands left just as easily as lovers. There were no guarantees either way.

I could stay only a few days. I was bored in the countryside. I didn't fish or ride, activities Coco relished, freezing rain or not. I missed Jojo, my piano, my view over the Tuileries, Mezzo, Mont Blancs at Angelina, marzipan roses from Fauchon. Diaghilev sent endless wires. Where was I? When was I coming back? There were pieces he wanted me to play for him. He preferred my interpretation of the music over the composers.

Back home, I asked Jojo if he needed advice on what kind of wedding ring to purchase for Roussi. He hesitated. Yes, it was an odd question given the situation. But who else would he ask? My need to be needed was maniacal. He had always consulted me for everything. And I wanted her to know I'd chosen it. Every time she looked at it, I wanted her to think of me. Every time Jojo looked at it, I wanted him to think of me. I would haunt them, though on the surface my behavior was such that I seemed to welcome their future marriage.

He said yes. He would value my opinion.

Coco was appalled when I told her.

"But this proves more than anything the divorce is a farce," I said. "He'll go along with it all for now. He wants to. But he'll tire of it, and then he'll come back to me."

We were merely pretending to divorce.

Certainly, it would be too cruel to agree to let me help choose a wedding ring if he thought the divorce were real.

◆ ◆ ◆

The clock was ticking. Time marching ahead. The appointment to finalize the divorce at The Hague was nearing.

"Toscha," Jojo said, a few days before we were to leave. "There's still time. If you swear that I am the man of your life, I feel I cannot leave you. It would be impossible to go."

I immediately tensed. His plea struck me the wrong way. Twenty years of all we'd been through together, and he needed me to tell him he was the man of my life to stay?

He was the one with the power. He was the one who could stop this. He didn't have to go to The Hague. He didn't have to go through with the divorce. He could tell Huberich to call it off. He was trying to shift responsibility for this whole debacle onto me. As if it would be my fault he left because I didn't say the right words. Not because he left.

◆ ◆ ◆

"I want to shake you, Misia," Coco said over the phone. "He *is* the man of your life. Why can't you tell him so and end this once and for all?"

I tried to explain the unexplainable. "Any love he has left for me will be gone if I am the one who keeps them apart. He'll weary of Roussi and when that happens, the love Jojo still has for me will resurrect. But he'll only have that love for me because I didn't keep him from what he wanted. You didn't keep Boy from marrying Diana Wyndham because you knew it was inevitable. And then he came back to you."

"Yes," she said. "And then death stole him for good."

◆　◆　◆

At The Hague, I would not costume myself as a washerwoman this time. Not in front of Jojo. Coco chose a silk dress in a black-and-white check pattern. She put a black crepe coat with matching lining over my shoulders. The look was elegant and restrained.

Roussi watched over Jojo and me as if we might run into each other's arms at the very last moment to turn her plan awry. But I couldn't look Jojo in the eye. Eventually we were called into a room, just Jojo and me. The court required us to sit on opposite sides. The atmosphere was dismal. Sinister. Waiting outside the room were Roussi, Huberich, and Nina—dreaded Nina—there to ensure my demise.

Finally, the moment came. The judge asked Jojo if he wanted a separation from me.

"Yes."

It was his voice, but I couldn't watch as he said it, the word uttered with no hesitation. The word echoed in my mind.

It was all I could do not to crumble. I realized then I believed he would say no. I believed he would be unable to go through with it.

As if by magic, we were divorced, at least in the eyes of The Hague, a place we were not citizens of. A place in which we had never resided. So far from Paris, I knew no one. It wasn't real.

Divorced. How could that be?

We stayed in the same hotel, but now I had a room alone. We all had dinner together, me, Jojo, Huberich, Roussi, Nina.

It was humiliating, but I didn't know what else to do. I had to hold my head up. I was Misia. I was Madame Sert. One moment in a foreign court couldn't make me no longer Jojo's wife. The Mdivanis were in a celebratory mood, all at my expense. For me, this was unthinkable. A situation you would vow to never find yourself in. Your husband of a few hours ago was going to dinner, and you'd dined together every evening for twenty years, and so to not be at the table together actually felt much stranger.

I tried not to feel lost. To be generous was my plan all along. But I was losing my way. Who was I now if I had to pretend not to be married to Jojo?

What had I done? Why hadn't he said no? Why hadn't he said he loved me? Should I have said all he wanted to hear? *Stay, my darling. You are the man of my life.*

Was it too late?

I couldn't manage another minute. I left the dinner early. At the hotel, Roussi came to my room to comfort me. Roussi, not Jojo. How I longed for him to come and take me in his arms, to tell me he'd come to his senses and the nightmare was over. But the nightmare was right there in my room fawning over me, and despite everything, I welcomed her. I needed to read her as much as she was trying to read me. She'd separated Jojo and me, but she hadn't won yet.

Nevertheless, she played the beneficent victor. A much easier role than the one I was playing. "It couldn't be helped, Misia," she said. "I love him so much. So, so much. And he loves me. Please don't cry. We love you too, we won't leave you. We're only happy because of you and your generosity. We'll always be together, the three of us."

I was certain it was Jojo who made her come, who made her pledge these strange oaths. Jojo made her say what she did. She went along with it because she saw his distress. If she was rude to me, if she pushed me out, that would be the one thing she could do that would make him leave her. She knew that, and so she came to me to keep the peace. These assurances that they wouldn't leave me were his. To assuage his guilt. For him, he would still have us both. We just traded places.

She came to keep an eye on me as well, still watching over me because she wasn't married to Jojo yet. She wasn't yet the new Madame Sert.

Back in Paris, Jojo came with me to the Meurice. He packed a suitcase. How uncomfortable it was. How wrong. He embraced me. He patted Mezzo on the head. "The Lutetia's not far, Toscha," he said, but to me it was. The hotel was across the river, on the Left Bank. He was going there to live with Roussi. Then he walked out the door as if he was just off to the studio for the day and would be back in time for dinner. We'd lived together twenty years, and he was gone.

Just one suitcase. He left everything else behind, the furniture and art and priceless collections he assembled, all of his carefully curated possessions. I told myself he could only have done that because he knew he was coming back. He was going on a short trip, that was all. Everything would all be here just as before, waiting for him, like me, when he was ready to come home.

Chapter Twelve

Paris, 1928

Coco stomped around the apartment at the Meurice, that Aladdin's cave now without its Aladdin. "You can't stay here," she said. "It's a mausoleum to you and Jojo. How can you stand it?"

I was paralyzed. Afraid if I left, I might miss Jojo. He might call. He might come by. In the evenings, I was always waiting for him to "come home" from the studio. In the mornings, I expected to see him next to me in bed. I expected to hear his voice. Instead, silence tormented me. The forlorn expression on Mezzo's face didn't help. He wondered where Jojo was too, waiting by the front door or going from room to room.

"But if I leave, how will Jojo find me?" I said.

"Jojo knows where I live. You're moving in with me. He'll have no trouble finding you at all. Now where's Aimée? Tell her to pack your bags. There's room for her too. Don't you remember, you were the one who made me move out of Boy's apartment when he told me of his engagement? And you were right to do it. You have to turn the page."

But this was different. Jojo might be "engaged," but it wasn't a real engagement. Not like Boy's.

◆ ◆ ◆

At her Faubourg apartment, Coco was the Mother Superior running an orphanage. She had a weakness for lost souls. I had become one of them, just as Picasso had stayed with her when he needed time away from Olga and as Stravinsky had when he had no money. She had been lovers with each of them.

Now, along with Coco's German shepherds and terriers, Mezzo and me, Jean was there with his young lover, Jean Desbordes, the two of them incapable of taking care of themselves, light as air, unearthly, living on opium.

Coco had a room made up for me, decorated in soothing beige, comfortable and luxurious with the softest sheets and a fur blanket at the foot of the bed. I immediately let Jojo and Roussi know where I was. It gave me an excuse to phone them. Not wanting them to know the truth, I told them Coco needed help managing Jean and his condition.

At Coco's, everything reminded me of Jojo. The divan upholstered in orange velvet. The enormous mirrors he'd had installed floor to ceiling. The furniture he'd chosen. He'd even painted a gilded, eleven-leaf screen *Vision of Naples* for her dining room. How could I live without him? I proceeded through my days feeling as if my body was stuck with large needles so that if I moved at all, the sharp points would dig in deeper. I was imprisoned within myself. I felt a dull, constant ache all over as my mind thought of them living their lives, enjoying themselves, laughing, intimate, not thinking of me.

Roussi phoned daily, chirping away, grating. "Did you know, Misia, that Roussadana means 'lighthearted'?"

How marvelous not to have to bear the burden of whatever name means "deep thinker," I thought.

All of her talk of "we will never leave you, Misia"—so far she was true to her word, though I knew her intention was to check on me as always, ensure my whereabouts and that I wasn't plotting behind her back to foil her plans with Jojo. He still phoned me every day to talk about his commissions just as we had at home together. He needed me.

I met Roussi for tea or luncheon often, or she came by Coco's apartment at teatime. She spoke mainly of marriage, how with Serge and David now settled, it was important Alexis make a good marriage "as the rest of us have."

"As *you* have?" I said.

"Oh, of course we're not married yet, not officially. Sometimes I forget. It does feel like we are. You have made us so happy, Misia. We love each other so, so much. Mr. Huberich has submitted the paperwork to The Hague. Then we'll go once everything is through."

My every nerve was on edge. "And when do you expect that to be?"

"Mr. Huberich isn't sure. It could be several months. No later than the end of summer."

Summer. Venice. *Our annual trip for the past twenty years.* What would become of that? Would we all go together again, our roles reversed? No. Never. Jojo would break from Roussi before then, surely. He could not let this ruin our Venice.

If Roussi didn't phone, I would phone her. Determined to continue to be involved in their lives, I asked questions with feigned detachment, as if I were merely an interested friend. Where did they plan to live? What was the status of the paperwork? Did they intend to take a honeymoon? Where would they go? I wanted to keep up with what she and Jojo were doing, how they were doing, something I could not do if I didn't talk to or see her.

I offered to take her shopping for her bridal trousseau. The best way to be close to Jojo was to be close to her. It gave me a sense of control. When I told Coco, she was apoplectic.

"You are telling me that you are taking the woman who is planning to marry the man you still consider your husband to shop for a new wardrobe?"

I feared Coco might barricade me in my room.

"The divorce isn't real," I said. "The marriage, if it happens, won't be either. It will be a pretend trousseau for a pretend marriage."

"It *is* real. Look at you. You're miserable."

"I'm miserable because I miss Jojo. Not because I think he will never come back. I know he will."

She gave me a skeptical look. I didn't blame her. She wanted me to move forward. Sometimes hopeful self-delusion was the only way to do so.

"Listen, Coco," I said. "They can't get rid of me easily. You know me. I'm a meddler. I always meddle in people's lives."

"You've certainly meddled in mine," she said with a pointed look.

"If it wasn't for my meddling, you never would have gotten out of bed after Boy died. If it wasn't for my meddling, there would be no Chanel No. 5."

"Listen to you boast," Coco said.

"I'm not boasting. I'm taking credit as you once told me to do. If it wasn't for my meddling, there would be no Ballets Russes, no Nijinsky, no Balanchine, no Lifar, no Satie. Arguably, no one would know Renoir, certainly not as they do now. Or Bonnard. Or Vuillard. Or Van Gogh. Or even Proust. What would *Remembrance of Things Past* be without Princess Yourbeletieff and Madame Verdurin?"

"All of that is different," Coco said. "All that has to do with art."

"And this has to do with my life. If there has ever been a time for me to meddle, it's now."

◆ ◆ ◆

Jojo and I dined alone together at Maxim's when Roussi was busy with family affairs, her mission to marry Alexis off taking much of her time. Dinner with just the two of us was more relaxed, easy to slip into old ways, but still strange. On the one hand, it felt natural. Comfortable. We enjoyed each other's company. Our conversation flowed easily. His projects, commissions, gossip about our friends. I felt our connection so strongly.

But when the meal was over, when we used to go home together, it was time to part. That was when reality struck. He kissed me on the cheek but didn't embrace me as closely or as long as he once did. That embrace—or lack thereof—told me everything. He went his way, and I went mine. I'd had some hope he would take my hand. We would go back to the Meurice. Bar the door. Change the locks.

But that didn't happen.

The wound reopened, that great open scab. I was the fool. He was leaving me for the arms of someone else. Bounding toward her, actually. The feeling of intimacy I'd had with him at dinner must have been one-sided. It took all I had not to completely despair. But beneath that despair, there was certainty. I was certain he loved me.

"You're giving too much of yourself away," Coco said when she found me upset. "You're always helping him. Let him see what it's like living without you. He must miss you to appreciate you."

I told her I'd asked him if he still wanted me to help him find a wedding band.

"Yes, yes," he'd said. "But I don't know when. I've been so busy at the studio lately. I have models for a scene of Italian fishermen from the seventeenth century."

An idea wound its way through my thoughts ever since. "Could it be," I said to Coco, "perhaps he isn't so sure about the engagement?"

"Oh, Misia," Coco said, shaking her head, pity in her voice.

In Coco's drawing room, I sat at a table where Coco had spread out her costume jewelry–making tools and supplies. Mindlessly, I played with wires, twisting them along with my thoughts. Jojo would come to his senses. This "divorce" was just temporary. A divorce in The Hague meant nothing. Marriage in The Hague, if it came to that, meant nothing as well.

Our marriage wasn't over. *Twist.*

It would never be over. *Twist. Twist.*

Never. *Twist.*

I added more wire as my thoughts churned until what I held in my hands resembled the shape of a palm tree, a long, slender trunk, a glorious crown. I'd always loved palm trees. Tall. Exotic. Above it all.

Yes, that was how I must be. Regal as the palm tree. Above it all. I covered the wire with tarnished silver foil. I glued on tiny crystal beads over that, one next to the other, precise, focused work. Hours had passed and I'd forgotten temporarily about Jojo and Roussi.

I thought Coco would call what I'd made silly. To my surprise, she was enamored.

"This is magnificent, Misia," she said, examining my beaded tree. "So unique. How did you think of it?"

"I didn't. Pain and misery thought of it."

"Through which all great art is made, as you always say."

"This isn't great art," I said. "But it's something to do."

My tree needed a stand. The next day, Coco's jewelry maker drilled a narrow hole in the middle of a fist-size chunk of one of the many pieces of rock crystal that Coco had, most of them given to her by Jojo and me. Voilà, a fanciful bibelot for the tabletop. Coco brought home more wire, more beads, more crystals, heaping all on the table.

"You'll have me making trees until kingdom come," I said.

"Idle hands are the devil's workshop," she said. She wanted to keep me busy. She hoped activity would keep me away from Jojo, from wedding band and trousseau shopping, from further humiliation.

It did. Concentrating on twisting wire and gluing beads was a relief for my brain, relief from the constant whorl of Jojo and Roussi, Roussi and Jojo. From chaos to palm fronds. This was the outpouring of my suffering mind, wild with flailing tentacles. As if to tame them, I bejeweled them, adding semiprecious stones here and there, imitation diamonds or opals or turquoise. Soon I had a small jungle. My beautiful trees, confined in their beautiful rock crystal prison. Stuck, like me.

Coco liked them so much, she sold them for a ridiculous amount at her boutique. "Americans are especially taken with them," she said. I knew she was trying to encourage me to "work," I who had done so much in life but never actually had a profession.

After Boy had died, she'd done little else but work. She did the same when she realized Grand Duke Dmitri would never marry her, a dressmaker, and they parted. Now, I noticed she was spending more time in Paris than usual.

"Work is the only thing that has never let me down," she said as she had before, and I feared the sentiment now applied to Bendor.

Jean and his young lover, Desbordes, slept late. Desbordes's name was Jean too, so we called him Jean-Jean, to distinguish between the two. When awake, they wandered around in stained dressing gowns with holes burned by cigarettes. "The uniform of an addict," Jean said. In the room Coco gave them, Jean's pencil drawings covered the walls, mainly profiles of Jean-Jean as he slept. Opium paraphernalia littered the floor, and the room smelled of the telltale burnt chocolate. The room had a view of the Champs Élysées, but I doubted they ever saw it. Curtains always drawn, they avoided daylight.

"Sun is the opium of happy people," Jean declared upon emerging midafternoon from his slumber, cringing and shielding his eyes with his hand.

Jean drew not just on walls but on scraps of paper, on napkins and newspapers. He was a master of space and angles. Simple line drawings of me scowling as I made my trees. Of Coco, standing, hips thrust forward, on attack, scolding Jean for taking opium, for wasting his talent, for not eating, for talking too much. He always drew her with a cigarette in an overly wide mouth, smoke pluming upward.

Jean-Jean was soft spoken. Jean talked all the time. They wore their hair the same, long and feathery, with no part. Lucid, they read poetry or excerpts from their manuscripts to each other. Or to me as I made my trees, or to Coco and me as we dined or had tea, which sometimes we nearly spit out as Jean-Jean emotionally recited lines from his manuscript called *J'Adore* such as "I touch the tree and a branch stands up" and "When I think of nothing, I think of love rising."

The Faubourg town house was never empty. It was a gathering place, and friends were always coming in and out. Colette. Christian Bérard, the illustrator. Daisy Fellowes, society vixen. Max Jacob, the poet. Jean Hugo. Our Lifar. Picasso, who Coco compared to a hawk.

Coco adored entertaining. She hosted lavish parties, inviting Paris society, British aristocracy, our artist friends, Bendor's friends, her wealthy clients from North and South America, the Vanderbilts, the de Hozes. Because of her home's location near a number of fashionable clubs, it was a hub for all. Coco was glamour, her townhome the peak of Parisian elegance, lanterns illuminating her gardens, jazz bands in the drawing room. She had a cook, footmen in livery, maids, a butler. Sometimes Stravinsky played the piano. Sometimes I did. Even Jean and Jean-Jean changed out of their stained dressing gowns and put on cravats and cutaway coats.

Sometimes Jojo and Roussi came, people whispering behind their backs and mine. I knew what people said. Coco told me the outlandish rumors. That Jojo, Roussi, and I were a ménage à trois. That Jojo and I had imprisoned Roussi in the Meurice and kept her as a slave. That Roussi and I had been lovers, and now I was spurned. There were those at these parties who felt sorry for me and avoided me. Those who never liked me anyway and looked at me with judgment and mockery. Those who came up to me and stayed at my side no matter what, like Colette and Cocteau and Coco. The entire situation was awkward and excruciating. But I simply wanted to be around Jojo and Roussi. I was the one who invited them. I was an addict, just as much as Jean and Jean-Jean.

◆ ◆ ◆

Jean became obsessed with Barbette, an American trapeze artist from Texas. He took me to see Barbette at the Moulin Rouge, where the performer soared through the air in daredevil feats as a woman, then revealed himself at the end as a man. Jean had commissioned Man Ray to take photographs of Barbette getting ready for his show, wearing his blond wig with Marcelle waves. Barbette's face made up with rouge and lipstick. Barbette's bare chest and arms masculine and athletic.

Fluidity, the state in-between, fascinated Jean. Nothing was black or white. Nothing was right or wrong. We—humanity—were trapped in a cage. Jean believed mirrors were doors out of the cage, but we had to figure out how to open them. That was the purpose of art. To open minds. To open doors. To find our way out of the human condition.

"Everything is an illusion," Jean said. "Identity is simply a role one chooses to play."

He was always posing in front of the floor-to-ceiling mirrors that lined the walls of Coco's apartment. *Mirrors are the doors by which Death comes and goes . . .* What did he see? Did he see death at work, the bees buzzing around him? Coco was having a doctor come to the house regularly, a specialist in treating opium addicts. She'd given Jean an agreed amount of time to take himself off opium. If he didn't comply, she would send him to treatment. Jean's face was gaunt, his frame thinner. The doctor gave him morphine to help cure him from the opium.

But he didn't want to be cured. Instead of taking the morphine, he gave it to me.

◆ ◆ ◆

"It's enchanting, Misia. Magical. I can't wait to show it to you."

I looked up from the beaded tree I was fashioning, this one a sort of weeping willow, to find Coco exhilarated. She and Bendor had just purchased a property on the Riviera, she explained, near Roquebrune-Cap-Martin. It was down the road from Lord Rothermere's, where the Prince of Wales stayed. And Winston Churchill, who people said was tiresome, complaining about the Germans night and day as if there might be another war.

"Perfect," I said. "By all of Bendor's friends."

"And the view," Coco said. "It's high on a hill with the most spectacular panorama of the coast. I know exactly where I want the house to go. All the architects tell me I can't build on that spot, that it's on too much of a slope. But that's where the prettiest vista is. I don't care what they say. I'll find a way."

I listened, thinking that building a villa together didn't sound like a couple on the verge of parting. Or did it? A last effort, a last push. She had consulted more specialists and midwives on how to conceive. She'd gone to fortune tellers and tarot card readers for advice. Yet her bedroom endeavors still hadn't brought forth a child.

But Coco did always find a way. If she built a house, maybe she could build an heir?

The idea seemed similar to Rosehall in Scotland except closer to home for her. An easier commute to Paris. A gentler climate. A place where Coco could be domestic with Bendor. And away from London, a source of another more recent problem.

"I'm calling it La Pausa," she said. "It will be a place to pause, to rest."

"But, Coco, you don't rest. Even when you're resting, you don't rest."

"One can be occupied and rest at the same time. There will be a tennis court," she said. "And an art studio for Bendor. He's always wanted one. A place where he can pick up painting."

"And drop something else?" There had been talk of a love interest in London.

"There are always rumors, you know that," Coco said.

Bendor was known for having lovers on the side. He was twice divorced and had been married when he began pursuing Coco. He was the richest man in England. He was a duke. Accordingly, he was a target of women everywhere. His affairs were not a new concern. Coco usually ignored them with her typical nonchalance.

"Why would I want the kind of man who wasn't wanted by other women?" she would say.

I'd always felt the same about Jojo and his affairs, those meaningless cinq à septs, as long as they didn't come too close. Until Roussi, they never had.

This "she" was in London. Was she young? Fertile? Once I'd asked Roussi if she and Jojo planned to have children, something I could never give him. How it pained me to ask. She laughed. "Children! But I already have my little monkeys!"

"Have you said anything to Bendor about this woman?" I said.

Coco scowled. "Not directly. But he knows I'm not pleased. All I've ever asked for is discretion. My golden rule. He tries to make up for it by giving me gifts. Gifts I don't want."

"What kinds of gifts?"

She sat down across from me, playing with one of my trees. "A few days ago, we were in Monte Carlo. On the yacht. We were sitting on the deck, and he handed me a small velvet box. Inside, a string of pearls. How proud he was of himself. They must have cost a fortune. I held them up, studying them, dangling the necklace in the air as I admired it against the blue of the ocean. Then I let it slip through my fingers, pearl by pearl, and drop into the sea."

I gasped. "You didn't."

Her voice was hard. "I won't be bribed."

"What did he do?"

"He stood and walked away. He didn't say a word."

"I'm surprised he didn't jump over the side to try to fetch it."

"Bendor? You mean order his crew to do it? His wealth is limitless. That necklace was nothing to him. It's not much to me either. He must have forgotten I'm not like other women. I can buy my own strings of pearls. Well, the next day, he made a concession."

She paused for a moment and when she spoke again, her voice was lighter.

"He took me to look at property on the Riviera. He knew I've been wanting a place there, a real home. I'm tired of staying on the yacht or in a hotel. That's when we found that enchanting piece of land in Roquebrune, and we bought it. Together. It will be the first home that is our home. A place that isn't a part of his past, where he can forget about all of his obligations."

Obligations. Like an heir.

The night after she'd shown me her plans for the new villa, I stayed awake in bed, my head spinning as usual with thoughts of Jojo and Roussi. What were they doing? Was Jojo happy? Or were they arguing, realizing their incompatibility?

Normally I would reach for morphine. Instead, I felt the need for a different kind of medicine. I left my room and sat at Coco's piano. I began to play softly, my favorite pieces, my fingers brushing the keys, my eyes closed. After a bit, I heard footsteps. It was Coco, coming downstairs. She wore white silk pajamas, the latest rage. I wore a matching pair. All of the fashionable women did.

She motioned for me to keep on. "Please. Don't stop," she said. She looked tired. Wan. "It's so lovely."

She curled up on the divan and closed her eyes. One of her terriers settled in next to her. Gigot, her Great Dane, a beautiful, enormous creature, plopped with a thud on the floor nearby. I played snippets of this and that, whatever came to mind, each a fond memory, a person, Liszt, Satie, Beethoven, Stravinsky. Old and new. I tied the compositions together like pearls on a string, an ode to Bendor's gift at the bottom of the sea, pearls returning to their natural home just as the piano was mine.

When I could play no more and the last note receded, Coco broke the silence. "I've longed to have any kind of musical ability my entire life. It's all I've ever truly wanted. To perform. To have everyone adore me and applaud for me. I only ended up making hats and clothing because I wasn't good at anything else."

"Well, turns out you're very good at that." I could feel her heart was as heavy as mine. I rose from the piano and joined her on the divan, waiting to see if she would say more. I treasured the moments Coco revealed her true self to me.

"I did perform for a little while," she said. "Believe it or not. In Moulins. I was twenty-one. I sang at a cabaret. Isn't that sad? Don't laugh. I was terrible. But the soldiers loved it. I sang a silly song about a dog named Coco and did a silly dance. That's how I got my name. The soldiers clapped and shouted. They pounded the tables, saying 'Coco, Coco, Coco.' They made me think I was good."

This surprised me. She told everyone that "Coco" was a nickname her father gave her, a term of endearment. The father who left for America and never came back.

Sometimes lies were more for ourselves than other people, certain truths we couldn't stand to face.

She toyed with a ring on her little finger, gold and topaz. As long as I'd known her, she wore it. It looked like a child's ring. She said a gypsy gave it to her sister Antoinette, and Antoinette had bequeathed it to her before she died. Her sisters, her family life, were another mystery she rarely spoke of, that she held close and protected.

"I thought I'd be the next Mistinguett," she continued, speaking of the adored cabaret star. "I moved to Vichy, the resort town, to audition for the big shows. I was a fool. I paid a man all the money I'd earned in Moulins for voice lessons and costumes. He tricked me into believing I had a chance. I fell for it."

She'd never told me any of this. She spoke so little of her life before Paris. She focused only on the future. The next collection. The next season. I had a sense the past hadn't been good to her.

"And you, Misia. So much talent. Do you know what I would do if I could play as you do? I would leave everything behind. The rue Cambon. Biarritz. Deauville. Cannes. London. I would let it all rot, and I would play in the grandest venues in Europe to packed crowds. I wouldn't think twice. I would take the stage and mesmerize them all. I would revel in the applause. I would wrap myself up in it like a fur coat. I would let myself feel adored."

"But you are adored," I said. "You're Coco Chanel. Everyone wants to be you. To look like you. To live like you. And it has nothing to do with any man."

"Men listen to you, Misia. Serious men. Important men. Brilliant men. They seek you out for advice. And Jojo. You've made his career. He knows that. That's why he tells you not to leave him even as he goes off with Roussi. All men want from me is my money to support their cause. There's not a single one who would take my advice unless it was to tell them which perfume to buy for their wife or mistress."

She reached for her silver case on the table. The lighter in her hand clicked. Flame burst as she lit a new cigarette. She inhaled deeply, then blew the smoke toward the ceiling.

"I have a secret to tell you," she said, smiling. "Before we ever met, I observed you in your box at the theater. At the premiere of the Ballets Russes's *The Rite of Spring*. Before the war. I was a different person then."

"That was 1913. You've never told me you were there."

"I was with Boy, before I knew anyone other than him."

"What a night that was," I said, remembering the riots.

"I was mesmerized that people could be so passionate about art. And I was mesmerized by you, Misia. That a person like you could exist, sitting up in your box like you were perched on a cloud, surrounded by other divinities. Diaghilev, Stravinsky, Jojo, Jean. I knew then *The Rite of*

Spring existed all because of you. The men respected you. They listened to you. I'd never realized a woman could have that power."

She rested her cigarette on the edge of a crystal ashtray.

"Yes," she went on, "there was Misia. The Queen of Paris. I knew who you were. I read about you in the newspapers and magazines. Misia, a presence in her box in the very center, leaning over the rail, her eyes affixed on the stage. You didn't care about being seen. You were interested only in the performance. It was the first time I'd encountered a woman who cared so deeply about an idea."

She picked up her cigarette again and held it toward me, offering. I took it.

"Then we became friends," I said. "And you learned that I was human. What a disappointment. Life is fraught with them."

"You were an inspiration. You still are. I see someone who claims her place in the world. She tells people who she is and not vice versa. She is a woman who does what she wants, her way. She is free. Understood or not, she is a force. And she is a creator."

I was astonished. "But, Coco, do you hear what you're saying? You're describing yourself."

"Do you think so? I'm a tradeswoman," Coco said. "I know nothing about art. Fashion starts out beautiful then becomes ugly. Art starts out ugly then becomes beautiful."

"But they both revolutionize. They change the way people live, hopefully for the better," I said.

"I just make clothes. But you. The way you play the piano. You open people's hearts. Look at me. I just opened mine, and I rarely do that. You have such a talent. You need to perform. People need to hear you. You need to be onstage."

"It's too late," I said, remembering my old piano teacher, the respected Fauré. I'd started with him when I was fifteen. My weekly lessons had been the sole bright spot during my isolation in the convent school in Paris where my father and stepmother had shipped me off.

"It's never too late for men," Coco said. "Look at Jojo. Prancing about with Roussi. You need to show the world who you are and what you can do on your own. I'm my own muse. I always have been. It drives me. You see the genius in so many. Why can't you see it in yourself?"

◆　◆　◆

Coco dozed off, but I couldn't. There was a reason I didn't perform. There was a reason the scent of sculpting clay made me nauseous.

I was seven years old, sitting on Franz Liszt's knee at one of the Pleyel pianos at my grandparents' villa in Belgium. My small but deft fingers played a Beethoven bagatelle to the predinner crowd gathered about the salon. They were the usual friends, relatives, musicians, composers—the circle of artists that swirled around my grandparents and the musical kingdom they'd created. My father was there too with his wife. I remembered the servants in their starched white aprons listening in the doorway, the smell of roasting meats and crusty bread ribboning in from the kitchen.

I didn't need to read the music. I knew it by heart. There were twenty-four pianos spread across my grandparents' villa, at least one going at practically all times with Beethoven or Bach or Wagner. I didn't study music. I absorbed it.

At the end, I'd barely lifted my hands from the keys when Liszt raised his arms, looked up at the ceiling painted with clouds and allegories, and lamented for all to hear:

"Ah! If only I could still play like that!"

Everyone burst into applause as he set me on the floor, people smiling at me, clapping, nodding with approval. My grandmother, petite, pretty, with a beguilingly authoritative Slavic charm, beamed. I felt like a star. I made a little curtsy, in the midst of which, I heard my father say in a voice for all to hear, "A shame she's not a boy."

His words reverberated through my mind as all other sound faded. I didn't understand. I had always been precocious and spoiled, certain of my own power. What did it matter whether or not I was a boy? I never thought it meant that there were certain things I couldn't do.

My father's declaration went straight to my soul, piercing it. I barely knew him. He was always traveling for commissions. Conversations with me were few and far between so that what little he did say had import. Well known for his works shown in the Paris salon, for public monuments like the statue of my grandfather holding his cello, he was less known for how he sculpted me. Not with his hands but with his words.

Five Roussadanas. Ten Roussadanas. Twenty Roussadanas. In the mirrors of Coco's fitting room, Roussi multiplied like images on a kaleidoscope. This was the content of my nightmares, but it was real and I had brought it upon myself.

She was charming to all of the vendeuses as they pulled out day suits and dresses and evening gowns for her trousseau. Coco sat on her stool, elbows on her knees, cigarette lodged between her fingers as if it were one of them, her tortoiseshell glasses sliding down her nose. She studied Roussi from head to toe, her form, her dimensions, bust, waist, hips, shoulders, neck, back width, front length. She held up various colors before Roussi, white, champagne, black, gold. Roussi gushed, flattering Coco, who wasn't immune.

This fabric is absolutely divine . . . this dress is so charming. All of these ensembles are perfect. Beyond perfect. Exquisite. Better than Lanvin. Than Vionnet.

This was the way to Coco's heart—disparage her competitors. Coco liked what she heard. I could tell by her expression. She also liked what she saw. Roussi was lean. Tall. Flat chested. And she was sleeker since she'd been with Jojo. Monied. Her flaxen hair was dyed blonder. The young Princess Mdivani wearing Chanel was good for sales.

Her girlish effervescence had attracted Coco just as it attracted Jojo and me. Coco needed to appeal to the young. We were the older generation now. Chanel couldn't be considered stale. Roussi was modern, just what we always sought out.

Wouldn't it be hilarious to have matching sets for Poki and Tika? I simply must dress them in Chanel.

Roussi modeled each ensemble before me as if I were her mother. How annoying. Each dip of the knees and vivacious twirl was a reminder that she was what my husband desired instead of me.

"What do you think, Misia?" Roussi asked. "How does this look?"

"It's perfect on you, naturally. You have no hips."

I didn't mean that as a compliment, but in this age of "flappers" it was. Roussi was one client Coco would not have to scold to lose weight.

The parody continued. Jojo's mural with the seventeenth-century Venetian fishermen was complete. He hadn't been having second thoughts about going through with the masquerade in The Hague. We met at Cartier, and I helped him pick out Roussi's wedding ring and her first ruby necklace, de rigueur for any Russian bride. The hard faces of the gems, the bold cuts, the cold, glistening metals in their cases, reminded me of who I was. *I* was in control. Roussi would wear what *I* chose. *I* was letting him have her. He even needed me to shop for her. Pathetic. She was at my mercy, not otherwise.

I picked the most expensive rubies I could find. She'd need them after he left her.

August approached. Had the marriage paperwork come in? Would Jojo go through with it? I waited like a figure in a wax museum, an eerie facsimile of myself.

What about Venice? Our Venice? We should be preparing to go. Planning excursions and stops along the way.

Nearly every day, I visited the hotel where Jojo and Roussi played house, the suite slowly filling with Jojo's new finds from the antique stores. Our apartment at the Meurice remained unoccupied, the treasures he'd collected with me unclaimed. A mausoleum, as Coco said. Jojo was usually at the studio. Roussi was often on the telephone, talking with Alexis. Jojo, I overheard, was paying for his education at Oxford. What? Who had paid before? Huberich?

Roussi convinced Jojo to buy a new car. The "last word" in automobiles, Roussi called it. What torture it must have been for her to ride in our ancient Rolls. Marrying a princess had its obligations, conspicuous luxury apparently one of them.

Aviation trophies out of the picture along with Mr. Harmon, she told me she wanted to sculpt Lifar. "Put in a word for me, Misia, won't you? I know he'll sit for me if you suggest it."

She told me she and Jojo were planning to take an apartment after they were married. "Which do you think is the best location, Misia, the Place du Palais Bourbon or the rue de Rivoli?"

About Alexis and his marriage prospects: "As long as it's not another Hollywood actress . . . he's too good for that. Louise Van Alen, did I tell you she's one of the Astors from New York? She still has her eye on him."

About David and Serge selling oil interests in Venice Beach, California. What had happened to the petroleum shares Huberich was supposed to secure? Those "lost" in the trunks? They were never mentioned.

When I would see Jojo separately, I would try to read him. Was he happy? Did he have any doubts?

"You know, Toscha," he would say when I saw him. "If you would just . . ."

If I would just what? He didn't finish.

Say the word.

You see, Roussi, I thought to myself, *I have the power. I simply choose not to use it.* I could end my own agony. But just as with the divorce, he had the power too. I needed him to end it on his own.

◆ ◆ ◆

Venice.

It was as I feared. There was no talk of our annual excursion to Italy. Jojo never mentioned it. Nor did Roussi.

"You wouldn't really go with them, would you?" Coco said over dinner at the Faubourg.

"You came with Jojo and me on our honeymoon to Italy," I said.

"It wasn't really a honeymoon. You'd lived together for ten years. And Boy had just died. You and Jojo brought me there to save me, to bring me back to life. This is different. I could never imagine going on a trip with the man I love and his new wife."

I shook my head. "Sometimes life becomes what you could never imagine."

◆ ◆ ◆

Over the telephone, Roussi was breathless.

"Oh, Misia, it's finally happened. The paperwork came through. Jojo and I are going to The Hague for the civil ceremony. Finally! August 18. Jojo and I will be married. It's all because of you and your generosity. How unselfish you are to allow us so much happiness."

Was it odd that my first thought was of what I would wear? My brain stuck in old patterns, I assumed we would all go together.

But I wasn't invited.

Jojo phoned not long after. "Do you know?" he said.

"Yes, Roussi told me."

"It's what she wants."

"And you?"

He gave the usual reasons not to leave me, all but the one that would have changed everything.

"I wish, Misia," Coco said, "that you weren't so stubborn."

◆ ◆ ◆

It was tormenting when they were gone. I couldn't think of anything but what they might be doing, what Jojo might be thinking. *Come back to me,* I thought in whispers in my head. Surely, this wasn't real.

Then, the afternoon of August 18, a wire arrived for me at Coco's. The sender was Mme Sert. How could that be? *I was Mme Sert.* I saw the addressee. Mme *Misia* Sert.

They were married. I dropped to the floor.

The Princess Mdivani thought she could become Jojo's wife all because of a piece of paper signed by a judge in The Hague.

But it was artificial, like Roussi. Like her sculptures, her "art." A degradation of the sacred.

How could Jojo do this to me?

When at last I could stand, I took a full dose of Jean's morphine, and I went straight to bed, where I stayed an entire week.

Chapter Thirteen

La Pausa, 1929

Coco threw open the curtains and forced me out of bed. "We're going to La Pausa," she announced, and then she made me eat. She told Aimée to pack for me, draw me a bath, dress me, fix my hair.

"This is what we do for each other," she said, reminding me of those terrible days after Boy Capel died, when she'd refused to leave her bedroom and had the walls and shutters painted black. I'd used morphine for the same effect. The unconscious state was the only state I could manage.

"The sun will do you good," she said.

On the way there, all I thought of was Jojo, our trips to Monte Carlo, flickering memories of jubilance now turned to dust.

We arrived in Roquebrune, to my first sight of the villa. Coco had taken the train to Monaco at least one time per month for the last year, sometimes round trip on the same day, to oversee the construction. Now, in record time that only Coco could achieve, it was nearly done. The home was her vision. Bendor had given her carte blanche.

And it was stunning. La Pausa looked as if it had been there forever, the roof covered with aged tiles, the architecture simple but sublime like her clothing. I was surprised to find that the interior was uncluttered with just a few unadorned pieces of large, heavy seventeenth-century oak furniture scavenged from Bendor's estates. The palette was beige, including the piano "for you to get ready for your recital, Misia," Coco said, still pushing me to perform, to have a raison d'être that wasn't Jojo. Beige to her was relaxing, and this was a place to relax.

At the center of the home was an austere yet elegant curving stone stairway. A replica, she said, from a convent near where she was raised by aunts. Aunts or nuns? I suspected the latter. She'd had the architect go to this convent to copy it.

There were three living rooms, a dining room, two kitchens, and staff quarters. Everything was splendid. Coco and Bendor had their own bedrooms with an adjoining white marble bathroom. Coco's headboard was tall, wrought iron, affixed with large metal stars as if she slept among the heavens, perhaps the heavens would bestow upon her a son.

In total there were seven bedroom suites. There was a suite for me, generously appointed. There were two cottages, one for guests, the other for Bendor's watercolors.

As yet, the watercolors were untouched. Bendor was absent, fishing in Scotland, Coco said.

For the garden, she'd brought in ancient olive trees, a cheery orange grove, a sea of lavender that waved in the Mediterranean breeze, climbing roses along the walls beginning their ascent.

We stood on a promontory at the back of the property, looking at the extraordinary view. The home was high up, lodged upon a cliff, an allegory. All that she'd built, all that she'd dreamed of, her relationship with Bendor, would it stand or would it crumble? Coco fought for a foothold in unsteady ground like my jeweled trees, their short roots cemented into quartz. If not balanced, they would topple over. Life, it seemed, was always on the verge.

The coastline below stunned. An endless swath of tranquility in sapphire blue forcing the eye out, a statement, a message to look forward, not backward, to possibility, the future. That was always

Coco's way. I supposed that was what had appealed to her about this perch.

By creating so much beauty, she hoped to drive away misery.

◆　◆　◆

At La Pausa and then back in Paris, I was untethered. Jojo and Roussi were in Italy, without me. How dare they! I waited constantly for them to send a wire. Surely, they would. I thought of them every second of the day, what they might be doing. Was it everything Jojo and I used to do? Lunching on the Lido. Strolling about the alleyways. Siesta in our room, curtains drawn. I was furious. It was unbearable. She didn't just steal Jojo from me. She stole Venice!

Finally, a wire came. They asked me to meet them in Genoa for a cruise around Greece and Turkey. It felt like a miracle. I was risen from the dead. Jojo had to be behind this. He missed me.

"You're not going?" Coco said.

"I am," I said, enlivened.

"Why?"

"Why not?"

"No one understands you, Misia. Not me. Not Jean. Not anyone. I don't even think Jojo understands. The way you behave. The choices you make. It's incomprehensible."

"They don't understand me because I willingly bare my soul to the world. Others fight their longings because of pride. But I have no pride. I have only love. It surprises me too, to realize how indestructible my love for Jojo is. I can't tame it. I can only try to live with it."

◆　◆　◆

The cruise was a fiasco.

They'd forgotten to book two first-class cabins. I had become an afterthought. Or not a thought at all.

Roussi and I shared the luxury cabin. Chivalry forced Jojo to take one in third class. His quarters were cramped, the bed uncomfortable. He complained about his back. But I wondered, had he forgotten on purpose? Could he not sleep with her in a supposed marriage bed knowing it was me he was truly married to?

I was uneasy rooming with her as if she might try to suffocate me in the night. While I changed in the bathroom, she dressed and undressed in front of me, showing off her young, exquisite body, her taut stomach, the tender swelling of her breasts, her pliant skin, semitranslucent, entirely flawless, as if made like the Venus de Milo of Parian marble, the favored material of ancient Greek and Roman sculptors. Her exhibitionism was like shots fired, as if to say *look at me, this is what I give to Jojo that you cannot.*

On the ship, people noticed her. She still cast her spell. They gazed at her with interest as if she were someone to watch. Her liveliness made strangers smile just by being in her presence. Now, she seemed to have an added sparkle. It wasn't just the diamonds glittering around her neck and wrists, gifts from Jojo. She was a flower emanating a mind-altering scent. An insect secreting an invisible cloud of some potent chemical, a mind-altering spritz, transfixing all who breathe it in and rendering them helpless.

Despite all, I intuited she was jealous of me. I had power that was more than physical. Flowers could be picked. Insects could be squashed. The young grow old. She was afraid of me, and that was what made her dangerous. She wanted to keep an eye on me still, to see how Jojo and I interacted, assess her evolving position in this game.

I started undressing in the room. I wanted her to see my figure, the shapely legs I was known for, my full breasts that Renoir pleaded with me to reveal, that Jojo loved for almost more years than she'd been alive.

As the cruise neared Constantinople, we sat at a table on the deck. Roussi retold ludicrous stories in her singsong voice of her time there after the Bolshevik revolution, the Mdivani family escape from Georgia, the discovery of the trunk with cotillon favors instead of petroleum shares, when she and her "twin" Alexis roamed the docks like urchins. She told a new tale, of a grandfather who had a wooden leg from fighting the Turks. In Georgia, he lived in a palace.

"Ah, the Turks," Jojo said, and I could tell by his voice he was about to embark on one of his history lectures, Roussi and I his pupils. "Do you know of the famous Catalan soldiers who sailed to Constantinople in the fourteenth century? A magnificent tale. It was just after the War of the Sicilian Vespers. Yes, our men sailed all the way from Catalonia to here. Why would they journey so far? A very especial mission: the emperor of the Byzantines requested their aid to save his people from the Turks. He knew the mighty strength of the Catalans. And as expected, the brave Catalans defeated the Turks. Absolutamente they did. There could be no doubt. They saved the Byzantines with their cunning, sacrificing themselves. And how were they rewarded? With gold, silver, jewels? No. With treachery! The Byzantines betrayed them. The emperor's very son had our Catalan leader murdered, along with a thousand of his men in cold blood."

Betrayal. How familiar this sounded. Roussi listened with fake rapt attention. She loved stories, mostly telling them. I had heard this one before.

"But the remaining Catalans did not run home defeated," Jojo went on, his voice booming with pride and passion. These were his ancestors. "No. Those Byzantine buffoons. Our Catalan heroes took revenge, righteously killing their enemies, plundering, pillaging, taking cities everywhere in what we now call Turkey and Greece until they took the greatest prize of all. The birthplace of the gods and goddesses. Of art, literature, philosophy. Have you guessed it? The duchy of Athens! Yes! Men of Catalonia controlled Athens for decades! Ah, how I wish I could have been there to see it, to live and breathe it."

"But you can be," I said. An idea had been brewing in my mind as he told his odyssey. "You can re-create it. Wouldn't this be the perfect motif for the Barcelona town hall commission?" This commission was recently bestowed upon him as a result of the success of the Vic

Cathedral paintings at the Jeu de Paume. It would be a part of his legacy, and he had been anxious, searching for a noble motif. "You can depict the Catalan revenge in all its glory on those four walls; that can be your theme."

"Toscha. Yes! I'd been contemplating a biblical theme, but this is much preferable. A more fitting scenario for the city hall of Catalonia. Bold, dramatic. Toscha, it's ingenious. Why hadn't I thought of it myself?"

I was enjoying Jojo's praise when Roussi suddenly clapped her hands. "But you did think of it, Jojo. Thanks to me mentioning my grandfather who fought the Turks. Wouldn't it be hilarious if you painted an old man with a wooden leg in your mural? Like you included Poki in the ballroom for the Hotel Wendel?"

I frowned, just as Roussi did every time Jojo called me "Toscha," his old endearment. She should keep her mouth closed, I thought. This was not her territory. There was nothing "hilarious" about Jojo's art. Poor girl.

But then he turned to her. I could see the way she looked at him drew him to her, her eyes wide and seemingly innocent, an adoring nymph gazing up at "the man in her life" on his throne.

"Yes, Roussi," he said. "Why not? An old peg leg would fit right in, wouldn't it? A nod to your ancestors just as it is a nod to mine."

If I thought marriage would weaken their bond, I was wrong. I sensed a great invisible expanse between them and me now, a distance that hadn't been there before based on experiences they'd shared without me. Intimacies I wasn't privy to. Roussi was the so-called wife, sharing the marriage bed, while I was now the one on my knees, crawling in, desperate not to be left out.

◆ ◆ ◆

My heart was becoming a ball of iron. Dark and heavy. I didn't know it anymore.

Months passed and back in France, still Jojo and Roussi continued to carve a life together.

Months during which I accompanied Roussi to look at apartments for her and Jojo. She begged me to, telling me I always knew the best places. "What would you choose," she'd ask me, "if it were you?"

Jojo consulted me constantly about the Barcelona city hall commission over the phone, or came to see me at Coco's, or when I finally moved out to my old apartment at the Invalides, where I'd lived briefly after my divorce from Edwards. There were conversations we had again and again, Jojo, uncertain, pulling on his beard, telling me he was thinking of paintings in sepias and reds over a background of gold, but was that too predictable? He could hear Picasso in his mind, laughing.

"Picasso is from Barcelona," I said. "They didn't ask him to paint the room at city hall, did they? They want you. They want Sert. They saw your work at the Jeu de Paume."

"Thanks to you," he said.

"If you want to do something different, play with the perspective. That's Picasso's game, but you do it your way. The Sert way. Optical illusions, perhaps?"

"Ah, Toscha, yes. Brilliant. Optical illusions. A wonderful idea."

It should be simple for him. We were living one. The illusion we were not married, that he and Roussi were.

I was not an idle person. My days were filled with substantive tasks and engagements. Dinners, luncheons, and soirees with distinguished friends. I was still consulted by others for my taste in music and art. No one consulted Roussi for that. No one consulted Roussi for anything.

Diaghilev summoned me as he always did to play scores he'd received for those hoping he'd find them "astonishing." I played, and Coco's voice whispered to me. *You should perform.*

But what would be the point of that?

Diaghilev was feuding with Stravinsky, who'd contributed compositions to a rival ballet company. "Provincial boredom, Misia," Diaghilev said after he'd seen the reviled production. He looked weary. His eyes were glassy. His face and stomach bloated. "Tiresome. Tragic. Moribund. Pure horror."

How perfectly he had summed up the life I was living.

And Coco too. At La Pausa, I would overhear Coco and Bendor argue over rumors of his dalliances. Coco still never demanded total faithfulness, just discretion. I would hear doors slam. I would hear the car engine start then fade away as Bendor drove off alone to the casinos in Monte Carlo, where he would stay all night.

For all of these months, Jean lived comfortably in a detoxification clinic in Saint Cloud, just outside Paris. Too comfortably, Coco was beginning to think. The clinic was fashionable and expensive, just like Jean. Coco, his benefactor, was paying the exorbitant bill, yet the patient seemed cured.

There, when I visited him, he presided in bed like a sultan, surrounded by papers and books and scribblings, gruesome ones from the first few weeks when he'd been physically purged of his addiction. Contorted bodies and faces with open mouths and bulging eyes. Jean called them cries of pain in slow motion.

Now, he'd gained weight, color, was alert, awake, writing away like a fiend.

"You look well, Jean. Too well. If Coco sees you, she'll make you leave," I said. To drawings from Picasso and a plant from the American Gertrude Stein, I added a box of marzipan roses from Fauchon. He'd asked for sweets because he thought they helped bring on dreams. "Are you taking up permanent residence?"

"You have to help me, Misia," Jean said. "I'm getting so much done. I can't leave now. This is almost like a jail, forcing me to put pen to paper. I've never been so prolific. You must tell Coco I look ghastly, I beg you. Tell her I've taken a turn for the worse. Where has she been? Thank god not here. She hasn't visited in weeks."

"She's with Bendor all the time," I said. "Following his schedule of fishing, hunting, going to the races. I'm going with them on a cruise soon, to the Dalmatian Coast. She's afraid to leave him alone. His eye can't wander far if she's near. He's been sloppy lately with his . . . associations."

"And Coco," Jean said. "A woman who considers sloppiness one of the seven deadly sins." He took a bite from one of the marzipan candies, then went on.

"Tell me, Misia. Is it true? I've heard Stravinsky is a troublemaker these days, telling Coco I only pretended to need the cure in order to have time to write. Stravinsky, who siphons money from Coco and has for years! I thought he was my friend. You can't trust anyone. Please, Misia. You must defend me. I'm almost finished with a new novel. I'm calling it *Les Enfants Terribles*. You're not in this one so you don't have to worry. And I've finished a journal of my cure. Very profound. I'm calling that *Opium*. The doctors tell me I'm their favorite patient because I'm the only one who can verbalize how addiction feels. And if I were to leave, how will you get your morphine? I have some for you now. The doctors don't notice. We're in this together, Misia, aren't we?"

We were. I wanted him to write and to be productive. In exchange, Jean slipped his morphine to me.

"Don't take too much," he warned, the addict advising me how not to get addicted. I told him I only took a small dose at night, to sleep. "Good," he said. "Regimented portions, at regimented times. I've had doctors tell me that is how to reduce your chance of dependence. Some have told me if you inject it in food, you have less chance of getting hooked. Like these innocent little flowers. What if you injected a bit of morphine into one? Would you feel better or worse? Sweet dreams, perhaps? That's a thought. Well, the problem is the drug. Be careful, Misia. One may take it, but eventually it wants to take you."

I was careful. I could stop whenever I wanted. I had before. I saw my current morphine usage as short lived, terminating simultaneously with the partnership of Jojo and Roussi.

And it was just to sleep. Life was backward, everything reversed. Each evening, thanks to the medication sluicing through my veins, I fell into a deep slumber. And each morning, I woke to a bad dream.

◆ ◆ ◆

"It's extraordinary, I suppose," I said, my voice flat as I looked out from the deck of Bendor's yacht at the Dalmatian Coast, that long stretch of steep limestone cliffs, untouched islands, and turquoise waters just across the Adriatic Sea from Italy.

Coco sighed from her lounge chair beside me. "Yes, I suppose it is."

We were two women who had achieved so much in art, in business. We were well known. We were wealthy. We were fashionable in Coco's wide-legged sailor pants and striped fisherman shirts, our skin magnificently bronzed—even I had succumbed to the "suntan."

But we were miserable.

On this cruise, I served as buffer between Coco and Bendor, a distraction so they could put off acknowledging their growing rift. They both knew but couldn't acknowledge that the relationship would end soon. While Coco and Bendor were in Monte Carlo a few weeks before, he'd invited a certain young interior decorator to a party on the yacht. "Did he actually think I wouldn't notice?" Coco had said. "Did he think I didn't know?"

Furious, she'd insisted the woman be escorted off. The next day, hoping to make amends, Bendor offered Coco an enormous emerald. Had he not learned his lesson? He presented it to her on the deck.

"I threw it overboard," she said.

Despite the tension, they had difficulty letting each other go. I certainly understood. They had been lovers and companions, close friends and confidantes for many years, not husband and wife but living as if they were such. And yet time was so cruel, welding two people together as if they were one, conjoined limbs, lungs, hearts, then tossing in a plot twist.

There was no easy way to un-weld.

This was another summer without going to Venice. Without Jojo. My ability to bear pain astonished even me. If only these see-through Adriatic waters, crystal kaleidoscopes in every cerulean shade, were enough to take my mind from where I ought to be—with him.

"Those pristine islands," Coco said as we floated by. "They should be beautiful. But all I see is how barren they are."

"And all those old forts and castles and citadels," I said, "left to crumble, ignored. They should be romantic. Instead, they look destitute. Why does everything glorious turn to ruins?"

We were moored just outside Hvar when a radiogram arrived from Venice. At first, when Coco told me, I thought it was from Jojo, asking me to join him and Roussi, though I knew they were in Spain. Could they have had a change in plans? My heart beat faster. Lethargy disappeared. But Coco's expression was anxious. The message was from Diaghilev. *Am ill. Come at once.*

Bendor's yacht turned west for Italy. In Venice, Coco and I rushed into the Grand Hotel, past the familiar marble, the frescoes, the chandeliers. In his room, Diaghilev was prostrate, feverish, shivering with cold, wearing his dinner jacket beneath the blankets to stay warm.

Coco, who reacted to distress with action, went immediately to fetch a doctor, scolding Lifar and Kochno for not calling one sooner. But they couldn't be blamed. Diaghilev, a despot who hated doctors, told them not to.

I sat on the edge of the bed, taking his damp hand in mine. He was so pale, at first I had the nonsensical idea that someone had put stage makeup on him. But it wasn't makeup. It was his incomparable life force in retreat inside of him. I had to bring it back. I had always been his gatekeeper. Could I keep death at bay?

"My dear, dear Misia," he said, his usually commanding voice faint. "You look so lovely in white. You must always wear white when I'm gone."

"But darling, you won't be gone. Don't talk like that."

"Stravinsky," he said. "Why did we ever argue? I love him. We are brothers. Will you tell him for me?"

"No, darling, no. You'll tell him yourself. When you recover."

"I have always aspired to live life a certain way," he said. "With savoir faire. Nothing banal. But look at me. Death is banal. What a disappointment. Death should astonish, shouldn't it? It's *death*, after all. It should be moving, majestic. It should be . . ."

A moment of hope came over me. This was my Diaghilev, speaking of his next production, his vision of how it ought to be. The new season. Better than the last. He would tell me we needed to line up the librettist, the composer, the dancers.

But words failed him. He looked lost. Tired. Suffering physically, this man who had so much stamina. At last, it had given way.

This wasn't theater. This was reality, cold and implacable. How sad that in the end, we were all just human.

The doctor diagnosed blood poisoning, the result of abscesses that had plagued Diaghilev, a consequence of diabetes he'd had for years and did nothing to mitigate. It was imperative I reach Jojo. I felt an intense need to share this news with him. It was Jojo who had introduced Diaghilev and me. For so many years our lives had revolved around the Ballets Russes. Only Jojo could understand what a tragedy this was to me, to the world. He would want to know Diaghilev was on his deathbed. But he was somewhere in Spain with Roussi. I sent wires to every hotel I could think of. I wrote that it was urgent. Jojo would wish he could be here, in Venice, at Diaghilev's side. But he didn't respond.

In his final hours, before he went into a coma, Diaghilev sang quietly to himself, as if he were already gone. His voice was faint, but I recognized the melodies. Tchaikovsky's *Pathétique*. His last symphony.

As long as I'd known him, Diaghilev spoke of how he admired it. We'd agreed it was the most sorrowful piece of music ever composed. A sense of indefinite falling. A feeling of complete despair. And the last movement: it was the sound of a soul giving up, fading.

I did nothing but cry.

Finally, a telegram arrived from Jojo. He'd received one of my earlier wires and sent best wishes. Best wishes? That was it? I threw the paper to the ground. Was he so distracted by Roussi he didn't care Diaghilev was dying? Or had he read it at all? The response seemed classic Roussi. Surely Jojo could not be so cruel.

It was too late anyway. Diaghilev had always thought he would die near water, and at dawn, he did. In its own way, it was perfect, a ray of Venetian sun reaching through the window, gathering up his soul, and flying it away.

With Lifar and Kochno, I watched through a haze of tears as Coco adjusted the collar of Diaghilev's shirt and fixed the sleeves of his dinner jacket, gentler with him than she was with her living models. She draped his white silk scarf around his neck. She brushed his hair, arranging his gray streak away from his forehead in a swoop as he liked. She applied subtle touches of rouge to his cheeks and temples. She filed and buffed his nails. With a straight pin she secured a white rose to his buttonhole. Then with more straight pins, she gave him back a bit of his youth, attaching the loose, lifeless skin of his jowls behind his ears as if taking in a collar.

◆ ◆ ◆

A week had passed since Diaghilev's funeral. I was at La Pausa with Coco, dabbling at the beige piano. I'd started injecting small doses of morphine after lunch just to numb the pain of his loss. I was still overcome with it, wallowing in melancholy and nostalgia, afflicted with constant sadness and sudden bursts of tears, when Jojo finally phoned.

"I'm so sorry, Toscha. To lose Diaghilev—devastating." His voice crackled over the long-distance line. Nonetheless, I could hear the grief in it. "If only I could have been there. I can't forgive myself."

Anger toward him dissolved. It was Roussi who'd responded so callously to my wire. It was terrible to think she could be so selfish as to keep the news from Jojo until Diaghilev was dead. But of course, she was. She knew of the bond Jojo and I shared because of Diaghilev. Like me, she might have thought our connection with each other could be renewed. A side trip to Venice was not on Roussi's itinerary.

"The greatest magician the art world has ever known," Jojo said. "How strange it will be without him. Especially for you, Toscha. How are you coping?"

I wanted to cry with relief. He understood. More than anyone else, he understood what Diaghilev meant to me.

"Twenty years," I said, thinking not just of Diaghilev but Jojo too. Our love was sealed over *Boris Godunov* after we returned from that first daring trip to Rome. "It's impossible to believe he's gone. I pick up the telephone with something I must tell him, then remember I can't."

Jojo was quiet. I wondered what he was thinking. I had hope, so much hope. The two of us mourning Diaghilev. Maybe at last, we would go back to the way we were, the way we should be.

◆ ◆ ◆

A few days later, Jojo phoned again. This time, his tone was different, hesitant, almost shy. "Misia. There's something . . . well . . . it's really just a formality at this point so I shouldn't think you'd mind . . . but she . . . Roussi . . . we are married now, as you know, everywhere except in the church, so it seems only appropriate . . . a small favor . . ."

He was stammering.

"It's actually a simple process," he said. "It should be no trouble at all. Just a brief meeting. But . . . but Toscha, if it's too much, then never mind. If you don't feel that you can go through with this, just say so. Especially now . . ."

Did I hear tears in his voice? Was he crying?

"Tell me, Jojo," I said with dread. "What is it?"

"I've put in an application," he said with a deep sigh.

"For what?"

"An annulment."

◆ ◆ ◆

Sometimes, you can be so hurt you cease to feel.

In Paris, a letter came, a summons from the archbishop.

Coco came with me to Notre Dame. I had no idea what to expect. She was made to wait outside. I was brought into what looked like a courtroom where four priests in red robes waited to pronounce their judgment on me. It was The Hague part deux, except with a Bible. I was told to put my hand on it and vow to tell the truth.

One of the priests read a statement that supposedly had been written by Jojo. It said that he had married me for the purpose of producing an heir, realizing after the fact I was physically incapable. I couldn't believe what I was hearing. It was a lie. And Roussi, I knew, took care not to become pregnant. *I'm only twenty-three. I've got my art. My monuments. And I have to get Alexis settled. I really just love animals . . .* She was a child herself.

Or that was her act.

How long could hope live in the human heart? I still believed Jojo might come out from behind one of the wooden doors and in his stentorian voice stop all this nonsense and swoop me into his arms.

With great solemnity, the priest read aloud from Jojo's statement about my "inadequacies," the scientific details of my anatomy, my intimate parts, the womb that couldn't carry a child. These were confidences only Jojo and a close circle of friends knew. He must have told Roussi. And Huberich. How could he? I forced myself to stare at the Bible, frozen with horror as the priest's voice echoed through the chamber, in my mind resounding throughout the great cathedral. The gargoyles, the martyrs, the angels. I imagined them shaking their stony heads, listening to yet another sad tale from the centuries. The flames in the candles silently flared with the scandal.

How could Jojo put me through this? I was hollow and forsaken, my insides a vast empty space of "inadequacy."

I had to escape. The priests put papers before me. I signed them as fast as I could, too mortified to argue or object, and rushed out.

"Jojo couldn't have written that statement," I told Coco back at her Faubourg apartment. "Roussi did. Or Huberich. Jojo could never do that to me."

I'd collapsed onto the orange divan. Coco sat at the desk where I made my jeweled trees, angrily twisting and untwisting an extra piece of wire, her bracelets and necklaces clanging. The grounds for the annulment— the inability to carry a child—was for her too a wound still open.

"You give Jojo too much credit," she said. "Whoever wrote it, he knew what it was going to say. I will always be grateful to Jojo for how he helped me after Boy's death, but this is despicable. Why did you agree with the statement? You should have said no. Any normal person would have said no."

"Jojo and I are still validly married no matter what a firing squad of men in The Hague or the Catholic Church determine."

"Oh, Misia," Coco said. "I don't know if you are mad to believe as you do or if you are actually the strongest person I know."

Was I mad? Was I truly the only one who didn't believe my marriage was annulled? I thought of the tragic Empress Elisabeth of Austria, walking along the Rhône in 1898 when an anarchist bumped into her and and pierced her heart with a needle file so small she didn't realize at first she'd been stabbed. Yet she kept going, walking, walking, slowly growing weaker, unaware of what was happening.

Coco suggested I should go to New York to live.

"What a preposterous suggestion," I said. "Me, leave Paris?" I would never go to New York. Leave Jojo and Roussi? Impossible.

"Fira needs help starting out. Who better for that task than you?"

Fira Benenson. She was a mutual friend who had recently opened a dress shop in the heart of New York's fashion district. She was Russian, from wealth, another escapee of the Bolshevik revolution, but in her case a beautiful, gracious woman with a true sense of style. She imported European clothing and wanted to provide a Parisian experience for New Yorkers, the same quality worn by the private clientele of the Paris couturiers. That naturally included Chanel.

"Fashion is your forte, not mine," I said.

"You've helped me. You can help her. You help people get their start."

"In the arts."

"You're always telling me fashion is art. More importantly, people will adore you in New York, and you deserve to be adored. A real Parisienne. Misia Sert. The Queen of Paris. Wouldn't that be a fine thing? They won't know what to do with themselves. They will all want to know you or at least be seen with you. You can tell them all about Proust and Renoir and Toulouse-Lautrec and Coco Chanel—ha! You'll be invited everywhere. An envoy of taste. Of European sophistication. Too busy to think about Jojo and Roussi. That's the most important part."

◆ ◆ ◆

Jojo would never agree to the move, I was certain. He needed me, my advice and consultation. New York was too far. Fira was offering an immense sum for my services. That would horrify Jojo. His wife—or former wife, in the eyes of The Hague and the archbishop—working for a living! I went to the apartment he and Roussi shared, the one I helped them find. I went to tell him I was moving as if it were a foregone conclusion, though I knew he would not allow it. I thought of telling him this as more of a test that I was confident he would pass.

He failed.

Inside their apartment, I felt immediately heartsick. Looking around, I saw that I had receded further from his life than I'd let myself realize. Where at the Meurice, every piece of furniture, every painting, every token, represented some part of our life together, here all was alien to me. Everything represented some part of their life together, shared journeys and events I wasn't privy too. Or modern furnishings Roussi had chosen that had no soul. I expected Jojo to protest when I said I was going to New York, to tell me he needed me. Put his foot down and insist that I stay.

But why would I expect that? He'd just asked for an annulment. That was Roussi's doing. And Roussi was there. I should have told him in private. Now, it was too late. Roussi filled the void of silence, gushing loudly. "What a thrilling idea, Misia! You'll be perfect for such a thing. Misia, the Queen of Paris, in New York. Like a traveling exhibition but better. Not just a Renoir portrait from the turn of the century, but the real person!" She fluttered about as if she weren't intentionally disparaging me. She embraced me. She sat by me. She caressed my arm.

"What will we do without you?" she went on. "We'll visit, won't we, Jojo? We're going to miss you so, so much. So very much."

She couldn't wait for me to go.

And Jojo? Jojo couldn't look at me. I had the disorienting sense he felt abandoned, as if he were the one who was wronged, as if I had somehow let *him* down.

"It's over with Bendor," Coco said. I joined her for a late dinner in her private quarters at the rue Cambon a few days before I was to sail for New York. There was no emotion in her voice. Her eyes were bloodshot, not from crying, but from staring at fabrics and seams for hours on end. She did what she did in times of crisis. She worked. "We're going to remain friends," she said. "But romantically, it's over."

I shook my head. "I'm sorry," I said.

We sat together late into the night, smoking, talking. Men came and went. In the end, it was the two of us.

Roussi and Jojo saw me off at the boat train. Roussi insisted. She wanted to make sure of my departure. She gloated. "Do you remember, Misia, when I went to New York for my monuments, and you and Jojo saw me off? Isn't that funny?"

Funny? What was truly hysterical was me. The fact that I still believed there was some chance Jojo would stop me and tell me not to go, throw himself between me and the train.

Later, in my cabin on the ship, delusion finally left me. How small I felt on that ocean liner, alone and completely out to sea, going farther and farther from Jojo. I'd never intended for this to happen. But he hadn't stopped me. All along, he'd never stopped any of it.

Chapter Fourteen

New York, 1929

I "consulted" at Fira's boutique, Verben, around the corner from the Plaza Hotel, where Fira put me up. My job was to hold court in a plush chair and talk about the latest in French fashion as outside, American cars screeched and honked their way down Fifty-Seventh Street. Fira hoped my presence would draw in more clients, even some of the society women who every year went directly to Paris for their new wardrobes and could supplement during the in-between times at Verben.

In the evenings, she paraded me around to parties, dinners, and the like. We went to places called speakeasies, unmarked doors at the end of dark corridors, where they served wine and other spirits because in this very strange country, one of life's greatest joys, as Jojo would say, was outlawed.

Roussi was right. I was a museum piece. A living memento of the past. For Fira's sake, I smiled as if I was interested in these Americans when I wasn't at all. My heart was in Paris. My mind reliving the trip Jojo and I took to New York together for the Sinbad exhibition. Now, the men talked incessantly about something called the stock market. The women did too, anxiously going on about the men worrying about the stock market. I found it all horrifically dull.

There was one spark of excitement. At the Central Park Casino, a piano player, a handsome young man named Eddy Duchin, was with the orchestra. He played jazz intuitively, composing as he went along with remarkable talent. Was he another Poulenc? Stravinsky? I had a piano brought up to my suite at the Plaza. I had him teach me his jazz. Then, one day I said without thinking, "You must come to Paris. I'll introduce you to Diaghilev. He'll adore the way you play. He'll ask you to compose something for him, and you'll become the toast of Europe and . . ."

I stopped myself, horrified. For one shining, exquisite moment, I'd lived once again in a world that still had Diaghilev. Remembering he was gone was like losing him again. Tears streamed down my face. The poor boy helped me to a chair. Aimée quickly ushered him out.

I didn't ask him back again. There was no Diaghilev. There was no point.

◆ ◆ ◆

Impending disaster. That was the mood of the Americans.

At the Plaza, a disaster of my own.

A letter arrived. It was a formal announcement, the kind sent to masses of people. Cold. Impersonal. It said that Jojo and Roussi had married in a religious ceremony in a Spanish church in Paris. Perhaps that was why Roussi was so thrilled to see me go. Jojo didn't even phone to tell me. I knew it was coming. Roussi would settle for nothing less. Was this why Jojo was so quiet? I remembered again his expression of abandonment.

Did these Americans wonder why I started wearing dark glasses indoors and out, day and night? Perhaps they thought it was the latest in Parisian chic.

I went about in a stupor until one evening at a dinner party, I overheard men at my table discuss a prestigious new hotel that was to be built. It would be the revamped Waldorf-Astoria, the old one bulldozed, the new one taking up an entire city block, forty stories high, a gathering place for American and international elite with over two thousand rooms. Despite the circumstances with Jojo, my mind did what it had been doing for two decades and thought of the great expanses of walls that would need decoration. Ballrooms and dining rooms and suites in need of art, themes, atmosphere, touches of European sophistication.

The architects were the same who had designed the Breakers Hotel in Palm Beach. How fortuitous. I'd met them there when Jojo had installed the Sinbad panels, his work that was controversial with the waitstaff in Palm Beach but applauded in more sophisticated circles in New York. We'd visited with the architects when they'd come to his exhibition at the Wildenstein Gallery. Back then, I'd overheard them speak highly of his work. They were the ones who'd said that Sinbad murals were truly marvelous but more suitable for a public space such as a grand building.

This Waldorf-Astoria would be a grand building.

I thought back to that conversation Jojo and I had during one of our magical nights at Maxim's, before I'd ever heard the long rolling *r* of *Rrrrrroussi* on his lips. It was the night I had inadvertently mentioned the Sinbad commission, how to soothe him I'd brought up the possibility of serious commissions in New York. Modern New York, where they were erecting tall buildings of steel. I remembered exactly what Jojo said, the light in his brown eyes, how the idea of a classical theme against the lobby of a skyscraper thrilled him. A blending of the New World with the Old World. The juxtaposition.

This would be his opportunity. *This* was why I was in New York.

It was destiny.

What did it matter that he and Roussi were married in the church? It was invalid just as the annulment was. Jojo and I were still connected. I was still meant to be in his life.

I sent him a wire telling him of this hotel. He responded soon after, more than enthused. He was in Barcelona, staying at the Ritz, installing the panels for the *Catalonian Revenge*. Was he thinking of me as he oversaw the installation? How it was my idea though Roussi tried to lay claim? Surely, he must have been.

This commission was preordained. In New York, the architects and I were once again in the same circles. At dinners. At parties. The Central Park Casino. They maneuvered their way to me. Did I remember them?

I did. I spoke of Jojo and his latest work, how in demand he was, all of the praise he was receiving in Europe, as I always did. It was like breathing. "Did you know," I told them, "the King of Spain came specifically to see Jojo's exhibition at the Jeu de Paume? Panels for an important cathedral near Barcelona."

Did I think he would consider the Waldorf-Astoria, they asked. It was just a hotel but important to the city.

"Well," I said, "he's quite busy now installing panels in the famous city hall in Barcelona, a very important building." Taking their cue, I bantered the phrase "important building" around as others had "stock market" all these weeks. The architects wanted their hotel to be considered an "important building." What better way than with a José Sert mural?

"He may have another commission soon, for the King of Spain," I said. "For his palace in Madrid."

It went without saying *that* was an important building.

I had the architects on a string. And Jojo too. He was always checking in.

Imagine, Misia, the juxtaposition of the old and the new.

I didn't have to imagine that, I thought, wondering if he only called when Roussi wasn't there.

I'd been in New York just a few months when the stock market all had been speaking of "crashed." It was October 1929. The night before, the restaurants and speakeasies were shoulder to shoulder with nervous crowds, the feeling that no one would sleep. Then the next day, chaos descended, American men on the streets everywhere, shouting in their brassy voices. The avenues were jammed with cars, horns honking, everyone trying to get to Wall Street, to trade shares.

Shares? Paper, I was told, that represented money but wasn't actually money. And if you couldn't change the paper for money at the stock exchange, what did you have?

Worthless paper.

I saw well-dressed men crying in the streets. There were rumors of ruined investors jumping off buildings to their deaths. I prayed they were just rumors.

◆ ◆ ◆

New York was muted in the aftermath of the crash. The men, their clanging American voices, were now low and tense. All were cautious, unsure of how to proceed. Banks were failing, but not all of them. Fortunes were wiped out, but not all of those either. Surprisingly, the financiers of the Waldorf-Astoria were untouched.

They told me they were going to make Jojo an offer for a prime spot in the new hotel: the gala dining room. They wired him at the Ritz in Barcelona. The amount they proposed paying Jojo was more than he'd ever made before for a single commission.

I longed to celebrate with Jojo as we had in the old days. But that would go to Roussi, who had done nothing. Surely, Jojo wished I were with him. That he had me to discuss ideas for the new project, something Roussi could never do. How invigorated he must be. He would be thinking of a motif. He would want only to discuss it, to throw out possibilities. Something epic as always but perhaps light, I would suggest, to distract from the darkness of America's new precarious financial situation. Ideas swirled through my mind. I even took notes, not wanting to forget them. Don Quixote? He loved the story of Don Quixote. He loved the absurd and fanciful, a thought that made me falter. That described Roussi.

Coco's question: *Why did I help him?*

Because it was the one way I hoped I could still hold on to him.

◆ ◆ ◆

Ironically, the crash was a boon to Fira. If they could no longer afford to take expensive trips to Paris for their seasonal wardrobes, the ladies of New York society would go to Verben, where Fira imported the best of Paris, the best of Chanel. She'd proven she could. She'd imported me.

Now, it was time for me to go home.

Coco and her driver retrieved me in her Rolls from the Gare de Nord when I returned to Europe in December, the city covered in a soft layer of snow. Paris was so much gentler than New York, though Coco's news wasn't.

"Bendor's engaged," she said flatly.

"No!" I was indignant. "How dare he. So soon. Oh, Coco. Do you think he could be doing it just to make you jealous? To get you to go back to him?"

"Not at all. Her name is Loelia Ponsonby," Coco said. "Twenty-seven years old. English. From a noble family. Presumably fertile. I hope for her sake. I can't see why else Bendor would be interested in her. He proposed, then left her immediately to come see me." Coco paused imperiously, then took a long inhale, then exhale, on her ubiquitous cigarette. "They met two months ago."

"Just two months?"

"He's not getting any younger, though the women he chooses are. Last week, Bendor brought her by the rue Cambon as if he wanted me to inspect her and approve. I looked her over. She was terrified."

"Naturally," I said. Coco was intimidating. I wondered if Miss Ponsonby reminded Coco of the young English noblewoman Boy had married instead of her, history on repeat. Did it pain her? Of course it did. But Coco wasn't as vulnerable as she was back then. She was older, wiser, jaded, still layering clanging necklaces and bracelets like shields to protect her. She wore talismans and all kinds of crosses. Byzantine. Maltese.

"I made her sit on a stool at my feet," Coco said with a laugh. This was her exterior, the part she showed to the world. I knew on the inside, it hurt. "The girl was all nerves, telling me she'd been given a Chanel necklace as a Christmas present. I asked her to describe it, then told her it definitely had not come from me. She had been duped. Tricked. I would never have such a thing as *that* for sale."

"She must have wanted to die on the spot. What did Bendor do?"

"Smirk. He found it all very amusing."

In February, Bendor and Miss Ponsonby were wed. The British politician we were reading so much about lately, Winston Churchill, was Bendor's best man.

There was a new Duchess of Westminster, but it wasn't Coco.

Just as there was a new Madame Sert.

Chapter Fifteen

La Pausa, 1930

The next summer at La Pausa, guests came and went. Coco invited people from the fashion world. The American editor of *Vogue*. The British editor of *Marie Claire*. Musical friends, like the young pianist Marcelle Meyer, who played with Poulenc and Stravinsky and Les Six. And Jean out of the clinic now but for how long? Jean-Jean had already wrapped one of Coco's cars around a tree, the two of them lucky to walk away. He and Jean argued so much Coco found a separate villa for them nearby. It was too much to have them in the same house without the opium elixir.

In the mornings, everyone slept in. Nothing happened at La Pausa until noon. That was when the day began, with a feast of pastas and cold roast beef set out on a long table with hearty breads, bowls of nuts and sweet figs, fresh lemons and limes from trees that spread their limbs across the property. No waiters in livery here. You served yourself. At Coco's, you lived according to Coco's philosophy of life. You took what you wanted when you wanted it. If you wanted more food, you got up and got it. If you wanted more wine, you poured it. You didn't wait for anyone to do anything for you.

The atmosphere was informal. Rough linens for place mats. Thick hand-blown glasses for drinks. Flowers picked from the gardens. The beige of the decor emphasized the vistas out the windows, the long stretches of lavender, light blue sky, deep blue sea.

Midday, cars with drivers waited at the ready to take those down the mountain who wanted to swim to the beach and those who wanted to shop to town. Others stayed and enjoyed the grounds, the olive groves, the lavender fields, the goat paths, the tennis court.

In the evenings, I played Mozart and Beethoven and Stravinsky. Sometimes a little of Eddy Duchin I'd learned in New York. And, if Lifar was there, *Afternoon of a Faun*. Ever since his erotic dance with Isadora Duncan's scarf years before in our apartment at the Meurice, it had become a command performance at parties. He would start on the piano, then slip down to the floor, that superb physique transforming into the dance of the Faun, half man, half goat, the whimsical forest creature in pursuit of nymphs. Then, after the applause, we would all talk of poor Isadora Duncan who'd died a few years before, strangled to death in Nice when one of the long scarves she always wore got tangled in the hubcap of her car as it drove off. A cruel death. I wondered if it was the same scarf Lifar had pretended to make love to back at the Meurice.

We rarely went out after dinner. Instead, we gathered late into the night around the fireplace. Coco and I told stories from the past like a comedic act, finishing each other's sentences. We talked about the making of art with Diaghilev. The arguments. The triumphs. Coco and I were the entertainment, playing parts so we didn't have to play ourselves. Our very miserable selves.

Remembering Jean's warnings, I tried to limit my morphine use to just a few evenings a week. But some nights and even afternoons, alone and in despair, I was unable to stop thinking of Roussi and Jojo together and what they must be doing. I imagined them making love. But I also imagined them growing closer as companions, enjoying each other's company in general, their emotional bond growing.

That was what hurt the most. The pain of it was so excruciating I wished I could claw my brain out of my head just to stop thinking of it. But all I could do was reach for the needle.

As I fretted over Roussi and Jojo, Coco fretted over her accounting books. I feared that the financial gloom that began on Wall Street had spread to Europe. Chanel was luxury, and people didn't have the money they once did for that. She started cutting prices, firing staff.

"I have a thousand worries!" she said. There were few options, until one night, while Coco and I were at the casino in Monte Carlo, we were approached by Dmitri, Coco's onetime Grand Duke, who'd inspired her collections with Russian themes. That night, he introduced us to Samuel Goldwyn, a successful Hollywood movie producer. With the swagger of the self-made and an accent of the Polish ghettos that to me gave away his origins, M. Goldwyn told Coco he wanted to make her famous in America.

She scoffed. "I'm already famous in America."

"I want you to come to Hollywood," Goldwyn said.

"My business is here," Coco said. "I don't need Hollywood."

"Americans need a reason to go to the picture shows again. I want my stars to wear Chanel on and off the stage. Gloria Swanson. Greta Garbo. Marlene Dietrich. Ina Claire."

Coco waved a hand. "Ina Claire already wears my clothes."

Goldwyn smiled, revealing a gap between his front teeth. "I'm not asking you to move. Just come to Hollywood, say twice a year. That's it."

Coco balked. "Twice a year? I certainly don't have time for that. Do you have any idea what it takes to run a fashion house, M. Goldwyn?"

"It takes money," he said. "And there's not as much of that going around right now. It's got to be hurting you. Listen, I'll pay you five hundred thousand dollars a year."

I hid my surprise. This was five times the amount Jojo would receive for the Waldorf-Astoria. An immense sum, particularly in times like these. I looked at Dmitri. He gave a slight nod. Dmitri wouldn't have introduced M. Goldwyn if he didn't know the producer could back his offer up.

Coco shook her head, dark curls swaying. "No," she said.

Goldwyn stood back, crossing his arms in front of him. "One million dollars then. Plus traveling expenses."

One million dollars. It was unheard of. An astounding amount. Ten times the Waldorf commission. Certainly, that would be a great boost to Coco's accounting books. But she was quiet, her hand on her cigarette case, unmoving.

What was she thinking? How much she hated being dependent on a man, I was certain.

Finally, she sighed. She looked up at him, her eyes like black ice. "I'll think about it."

◆ ◆ ◆

Coco took her time considering Goldwyn's offer, negotiating back and forth, finally agreeing when she felt that the arrangement would be on her terms, not his.

"Misia, you must come too," she said. "I need you. Four weeks in America by myself? With Americans! Alone! I couldn't bear it. All that smiling and laughing and enthusiasm. All that forthrightness. And the constant optimism and compliments."

"What if it was to wear off on you?" I said with a pretend gasp. "Coco Chanel. Giving out compliments? You're right. I must go. Your French soul depends on it. The Chanel brand depends on it. I'll be your constant reminder to frown and smirk and criticize. Though you'll not need any reminders."

"You're not mistaken," Coco said. "But I will need you to help me through it. I must get out of there in one piece. The Chanel brand does depend on that. It's settled. We'll have a grand time making fun of everyone. And I mean everyone. Now, I don't dread the trip so much. That Goldwyn. If he thinks I'll be his hired seamstress, his costume designer, he needs to think again. I'm not even going to bring my scissors. I'm not making one dress. Not in Hollywood. This is a collaboration on which I am still determining whether or not to collaborate."

I understood her hesitancy. She had learned to be wary of men in the business world. Since she'd gone into partnership with the Wertheimers, her perfumes had been making a fortune. Especially for the Wertheimers, who refused to renegotiate her original 10 percent share of the profits. Coco had been arguing with them for years to no avail. It was her name. Her genius. Her nose. Her image and reputation in the ads. She hired lawyers to sue them. In return, they kicked her off the board of directors.

She would take her time before rushing into another business alliance. Meanwhile, in Hollywood, I intended to look for opportunities for new José María Sert commissions with Hollywood luminaries. To do something constructive was just what I needed. Perhaps the homes of Mr. Goldwyn and his moving-picture friends might be in need of decoration with a European flair. Or even stage sets. Yes, I had once looked down on that when Roussi mentioned it. But the industry was changing. Movies had sound now. People were beginning to flock to the "talkies" as an escape from their dreary lives. What were Jojo's murals if not an escape? The world could enjoy the bountiful fruits of his imagination and talents in movies just as it would Coco's dresses. All leading to more commissions. More opportunities for him to make art. To show his genius and his vision.

The thought made leaving Paris for four weeks, leaving Jojo and Roussi behind, worthwhile.

When Roussi learned of the planned trip, she was suddenly interested in me again. Where I would be going, what I would be doing.

I knew why. Pola Negri had moved back to Hollywood, though not with Serge. After the crash, he'd left her. She'd had to sell her château in France to pay bills, move back to California, swallow her vixen pride, and shimmy up to the movie moguls because she needed to go back to work. Serge wasn't going to support her. All his "petroleum interests" he would keep to himself.

"You know, Misia," Roussi said, one afternoon at my apartment, "Pola Negri roped Serge into marriage just so that she could be called princess. Pola promised Serge she would stop working. She knew very well a prince cannot be married to a working actress. Can you imagine!

Engaging in love scenes with other men! So humiliating to Serge. He had no choice but to ask for divorce."

Roussi's short hair was in charming disorder. Her large eyes were sleepy, her voice languorous, her elongated body like a character in an El Greco painting.

"Of course, he had no choice," I said, wanting to seem on her side so she would keep talking. "It makes perfect sense."

"This had been building up for a long time," Roussi continued. "Pola was spending all of Serge's money! Poor, poor Serge! Always too generous. He's been so successful with his oil business, he and David. They have oil leases over six lots in the Venice oil fields. Everyone in Hollywood is begging to be in on the investment. Everyone!"

"Naturally," I said, noticing that she didn't inquire after me and my well-being. Did she ever? She didn't talk about Jojo. All Roussi could talk about was Serge, as if justifying his actions to me would justify them to the world. I supposed I was practice for her, a way to get her lines just right.

"Have you heard of Mary McCormic, Misia? Why, Pola drove Serge straight into her arms. Pola was drinking all the time. Vodka day and night. She was so cruel. Blaming him for the stock market crash, as if he could control it. Miss McCormic, you know, is a highly esteemed opera singer. Opera is so much more respectable than motion pictures."

"I wonder if I might run into Pola when I'm there," I said. That was what Roussi was worried about.

"If you do, just remember, Misia, Pola's an actress. She's prone to drama. She craves attention. You simply can't believe a word she says. Serge has learned that the hard way."

Chapter Sixteen

Hollywood, 1931

Coco and I boarded the *SS Europa* on a freezing day in late February to make the crossing. In New York, we stayed for a week at the Pierre hotel lounging in Chanel silk pajamas while Coco recovered from the flu. From there, we were whisked away by a custom luxury express train car decorated all in ivory and stocked with champagne and reporters, courtesy of Mr. Goldwyn. We made stops along the way, in places called Indiana and Iowa, Coco using her atomizer to spray the crowds that gathered at the stations with her latest scent. It took four days to get to California. Four days! What a country, so many long stretches of nothing. It was far too big.

"If I'd discovered America," I said to Coco, "I wouldn't have told anyone."

In Hollywood finally, at Union Station, Goldwyn had Greta Garbo waiting to greet us when we arrived along with more reporters. Coco pulled out her atomizer and squeezed. Everyone cheered. Coco told them she had agreed to go to Hollywood to see what "the pictures have to offer me and what I have to offer to the pictures." She wore a salmon-pink suit in jersey, a white blouse, a salmon-pink beret with a brooch fastened to it, layers of pearls, low heels. I wore jersey too, but in pale blue, and diamonds instead of pearls: the necklace Jojo had given me after the Jeu de Paume exhibit.

There were parties and dinners and a lavish affair at Goldwyn's Hollywood mansion, which Goldwyn proudly described to me as "Italianate."

"It's certainly not Italian," I said.

Everything in Hollywood was a stage set. For picture shows. For life. There were pretty girls everywhere. Coco whispered in my ear, "This place is like an evening at the Folies Bergère. The girls are beautiful in their feathers, but there's nothing to add."

Marlene Dietrich. Gloria Swanson. Claudette Colbert. And a young actress with a simple style and a throaty voice named Katharine Hepburn. No airs or artifice, Coco was taken with her. "She has a future," Coco said to me.

There were directors like George Cukor with whom I talked up Jojo's murals.

And there was Pola Negri. She'd heard I was in town. She sent me a note, inviting me to tea.

At three in the afternoon the next day, I arrived at the door of Pola's home on the beach in Santa Monica. Pola greeted me with a glass of vodka in her hand.

"Your home is lovely," I said as she ushered me in.

"This place?" She waved her free bejeweled hand in a dismissive way. "It's not mine. I'm leasing it. I had to sell the mansion in Beverly Hills because of Serge. Despite what the Mdivanis say, it was Serge who spent all *my* money."

Each time she said "Serge," it sounded as if she were simultaneously thrusting a knife in his heart.

She took me to her sitting room. There, an enormous portrait of Pola in a green gown dominated a wall. I recognized the artist. Tade Styka, another Pole, made a living churning vanity portraits.

"Here, darling," she said, handing me my own small glass of chilled vodka. There was no tea in sight.

"Na zdrowie," I said, the Polish version of "cheers" as we settled into chairs upholstered in velveteen yellow-and-black tiger print.

"Na zdrowie," she said back, and from there, she spoke only of Serge. She wanted to talk, one Polonaise to another, she said. There were rumors. The Mdivanis were telling lies. She wanted me to know the truth of who they were.

I was certainly interested in that. "But why me?" I asked.

"Because you will understand." Pola wore fashionable hostess pajamas in beige. Her green eyes flashed like mirrored knives, slick green steel. Silky black hair peeked out from under a scarlet scarf knotted around her head gypsy style. She was barefoot, her toenails painted a brilliant orange, the same for her fingernails. Exoticism was her appeal, and she played it up. She was no fool. So how did she get fooled by Serge Mdivani?

"I will start from the beginning," she said. "Serge and I had been friends. That was all I wanted. I made that clear. Then he turned up wherever I was. Chicago. New York. Always pretending to have business. Always with gifts. A corsage of orchids. A diamond brooch. Expensive dinners. I laughed it off. I said to myself, 'Pola, he is suave, handsome, younger than you by several years. This is a compliment, no? Why not enjoy? You'll be gone soon anyway.' I was going to Europe for two months. To my château to spend time with my mother. Then, I was on the sundeck on the *Mauretania* to make the crossing, and I hear a familiar voice. Serge! He took the chair next to mine. He said he'd had an urgent message from his father that he was needed in Paris immediately. 'Such a coincidence,' I'd said, suspicious. 'Uncanny,' he said with a mischievous grin. I suppose I thought it was a romantic gesture, the lengths he was willing to go."

I took a sip of my vodka. The Mdivanis had a knack for turning up in convenient places, I thought, thinking of Roussi knocking on Jojo's studio door that fateful day six years ago.

"It turned out, I was happy he was on board," Pola said. "He was a good companion. He protected me from throngs of strangers. I called him my cavalier. He was debonair. Always thinking of me and making my life easier. As a famous movie star, people continually approached me with varying motives. He acted as my guard in a way, putting off opportunists, and I appreciated it, not realizing he was the greatest opportunist of all. His concern seemed to be my happiness. Oh, I knew he wanted to marry me. He told me so several times. But I was not interested. I wasn't over Valentino. You know he'd died, so tragically, on the surgeon's table, his tonsils inflamed, just months before.

"Then next I knew, the ship had docked. Serge used my fame to get us through customs and into a waiting car. He'd arranged everything, saying the car would be much nicer than taking the boat train. We went straight to the Plaza Athénée, straight into the clutches of the entire Mdivani family.

"It was there I discovered to my horror that while I was at sea, the newspapers in Hollywood had printed that Serge and I were engaged. When I found out, I was appalled. I said to myself, 'Pola, you know very well the newspapers print what people feed them. Who fed them this? Would Serge do such a thing? Could he be that conniving? No. He was harmless, wasn't he?' But at the Plaza Athénée, I was overwhelmed by Roussi and Nina. Then the press arrived. Serge announced I was to be his future bride. You were there, Misia. What did you think?"

"I thought you looked overwhelmed," I said. "And it was quite a celebration, for the Mdivanis."

I remembered how I'd left early after the shock of watching Jojo so familiar with Roussi's brothers, the way he seemed relieved I was leaving. I took another sip of my vodka, though I could have downed the entire glass.

Pola stood and went to the window with its expansive view of the beach. "I thought I would be able to get out of it," she said. "When everything calmed down. But you know the Mdivanis. Nothing is ever calm. Everything is constantly moving in the direction they want it to go as they charm and charm and charm. They push you along with no time to catch your breath. Particularly Roussi. How dazzling she is, no? With all her eccentricities and her little monkeys dressed in Oriental brocade. She treated me as a sister from the beginning. She was always speaking of Serge, telling me of his wonderful attributes. She convinced me it was love."

"And so you married," I said. "You seemed blissful at the wedding. What happened?"

"What happened? The real Serge came out. It started on the honeymoon. We went to Deauville. From there, we were to go on a yacht. Instead, Serge went straight to the casino. He spent all his time there. Everyone was always willing to lend credit to a prince. Especially one married to a movie star. He left me, Pola Negri, alone in his bed. That had never happened to me before. Then, every morning, I awoke to a sky-high bill for his losses. Apparently, I'd married the unluckiest man in the world."

She paused. The rim of her glass was red from her lipstick. She refilled it, then mine, and returned to her seat.

"The honeymoon was a catastrophe," she said. "All we did was argue. But I told myself, 'Pola, everything will improve once you are back in California.' There he would be back to the way he was. Affectionate. Loving. He had his oil interests. He talked about them all the time. He invested my money. Mae's money. He and David had just set the business up. Soon, royalties would come rolling in, he said. He was going to make millions. Relying on me for money was only temporary, he said. But we came home, to Hollywood, and he didn't go back to work at all. No. Instead, he came with me to the studio every day, hovering, breathing down my neck. Watching to make sure my love scenes weren't too intimate. That there were no real feelings involved."

"But you had to act as if there were. Surely, he could understand that," I said.

"Misia, you know how the men are. Especially the Russian men such as the Mdivanis. They must be in charge. They must be respected. Particularly, as he would say, a man of his station. A prince!" She shook her head. "Then some people at the studio accidentally called him Mr. Negri. Mr. Negri!"

"And did such people remain unharmed?" I could picture large, swarthy Serge raging at such an insult.

"They did, but I did not. He was so rude and condescending to everyone, the studio cut my pay. Serge went crazy. How dare they? He told me to refuse to sign the contract. But the studios wouldn't budge. Neither would Serge. I was a princess. I was too good for them. 'Don't sign, Pola,' he said. But where did he think my money came from? Serge would buy me gifts, acting as if he was so generous, but charging them to my account. At Cartier, he bought me an emerald necklace, 'to go with my eyes,' he said so charmingly. Then the bill came, and I saw he'd thrown in two rubies for himself. Two large rubies. He had them set as eyes in the snakehead horn on his Rolls-Royce! Oh, I bought the Rolls too."

My careful sip of vodka turned into a gulp. I'd helped Jojo pick out a ruby necklace for Roussi. I'd insisted he buy the most expensive one.

"Well, I told myself again, 'Pola, don't worry, it will all even out in the end, when his oil royalties come in.' Then I found out I was with child. As soon as I told him, he changed. He was so sweet, so doting. He said all that had happened with the studio was meant to be, that we should move to France, to the château. We would live peacefully there on returns from my investments and his when they came in, which would be any day. We would raise a family and make it a working farm. It would be profitable under his guidance, he said. I felt I was in love with him again. This was the Serge I'd first met. Protective. Caring. Always willing to listen to my concerns and comfort me. But Misia, there were no profits. Just more bills. He spent so much money on horses, on dinner parties night after night, as if he were the Sun King himself and I worried so much—"

She reached out a hand, gripping my wrist, squeezing, her orange nails digging into my skin.

"—I lost the baby. After that, the stock market crashed. I had to sell my beloved château to pay his bills. I could no longer support his lifestyle. So he found someone who could."

"The opera singer," I said.

She loosened her grip. "Yes. Mary McCormic. And then he brings in that man, his brother-in-law."

I froze. Huberich. A queasy feeling grew stronger.

She refilled her glass and mine. "Serge informed me he was filing for divorce. Huberich would take care of the paperwork. I'd known the marriage was over. The only reason I didn't file first was because I was trying to scrape up the money for a lawyer. That thieving mongrel son of a bitch. He told the press in that grand princely way of his, that manner that once made me think marrying him was a good idea, that—"

Here she mimicked a deep voice with a Georgian accent.

"'—Pola and I will each retain the goods and chattels we had at the time of our marriage.' Well, he had no goods or chattels at the time of our marriage. Everything he had, he bought with my money. A wardrobe worthy of the Prince of Wales. A convertible Rolls-Royce with ruby snake eyes that he drives around with that floozy Mary McCormic glued to his side. An apartment in Paris I stupidly put in his name and not mine."

I felt as if I might be sick but not from the vodka.

"He owned a string of polo ponies. I bought those too. Serge barely knows how to sit a horse but acts as if he's played all his life. This is something he thinks important. Evidence of a princely life. If one knows how to play polo, one must naturally be a prince. It's incontestable! At least Alexis has more of a natural aptitude for it."

"You mean Serge doesn't know how to play?" I said. "Roussi is always talking of playing polo with her brothers back in Georgia." Maybe this was one of Pola's exaggerations. Maybe all of this was an exaggeration. I was disoriented. She was speaking of people I thought I knew.

"Roussi," Pola said, and as she continued to speak, my stomach dropped. "I fell a little bit in love with her. So whimsical. So endearing. Her joie de vivre is infectious. She seemed genuinely warm. I trusted her. Well, she told a lot of stories, no? Before the wedding, I was ready to call off the engagement. Serge was too jealous. Whenever I spoke to another man, he raged. He said I was humiliating him. Making him a laughingstock. It was ridiculous. I said to myself, 'Pola, you should not go through with this, you cannot live like this.'"

She sat back in her chair and sighed. "But Roussi talked me out of it with that cooing voice of hers, the way she would put her cheek to mine, whispering that Serge never loved anybody as he loved me, and he would change after we were married."

I was mortified. Roussi had warned me Pola was an actress. To not believe a word she said. But Roussi was the actress. The cooing, the tender ministrations. I'd always thought it was strange. Now I knew why. It didn't come from the heart. It was a ploy. It was what she did when she wanted something.

"Yes," Pola went on. "Roussi and her stories. Of a childhood of wealth and privilege in the Republic of Georgia. Well, let me tell you, I've seen photographs from their youth. The Mdivanis could not be more unsophisticated. The photographs are common. Taken in a studio. You know the kind. A common backdrop. The boys in rented sailor suits. The girls in rented dresses. Anyone can have these kinds of photographs. Princes and princesses don't go to studios to have their photographs taken."

I was reeling. Studio photographs. Rented clothing. The version of Roussi I knew would mock such things. *Wouldn't it be hilarious if we went to a studio to have our photographs taken like the peasants . . .*

Pola shook her head. "I have worked since I was thirteen. I'm not naive. And yet . . . I allowed her to convince me. I was weak, still grieving after Valentino's death. Serge swooped in. The Mdivanis are opportunists. You should see what they did to Mae. Their oil interests? I thought they were investing my money in the Venice oil fields. Instead, they spent it all on themselves and convinced Mae to let them dig for oil in her front yard down the road in Venice Beach. They've dug it all up. She built her dream home right on the water, a horrid-looking place she painted pink. David and Serge turned it into a nightmare. They have yet to produce any oil." She leaned forward. "I should have known better. But Serge had unusual charm. Such charisma. I know true charm and charisma. I, Pola Negri, was adored by Charlie Chaplin, America's darling, and turned him down! I, Pola Negri, was to marry Rudolph Valentino! I am a discerning woman. And then, somehow, Serge." She leaned in farther. "He cast a spell on me."

Yes. Like Roussi. Like all of the Mdivanis. This was what they did to get what they wanted. A hex that caused people to suspend common sense.

Pola's story. It was my story.

She refilled my glass again. I thought of how Roussi said Pola drank vodka all day. Who could blame her after what she'd been through? I wondered how much I'd had. It didn't matter. It didn't affect me. I was too shocked by what I was hearing for the spirits to penetrate. She took my arm again, this time more gently.

"I didn't want to tell you this, Misia, my Polish sister. I beg your forgiveness for what I will say. But you are strong. And you should know. It has torn at me these few years."

She took a breath, and I tried to settle myself as she did. "What more could there be?" I said.

"Roussi came to visit me at the château after Serge and I were married. She burst in, laughing, smiling. She said she had exciting news as she danced about the room. 'Pola, Pola,' she said. 'It's happening. I'm going to be rich. I'm going to marry José María Sert.' I didn't believe her at first. 'But what about Misia?' I said. 'Oh,' she said, 'it's all very amicable.' Then she went on about not having to worry anymore. She said once she was married, she could afford anything she wanted. She could take care of Alexis too. She said nothing of love. Nothing of adoration. She spoke only of money."

Outside, the surf pounded the sand like small explosions. Everything Pola told me, I already knew in my depths. Yet I'd buried it there. I hadn't wanted to believe it. On the wall, a banjo clock ticked out time like an old woman saying "tsk, tsk, you should have known better."

"I want to warn you, Misia. They are scavengers. They are rotten. Bottom-feeders. They'll try to take everything you have. Roussi is the worst of them all."

What hidden strength the human heart must have for mine to keep beating, to keep pulsing blood through veins frozen with fear of what revelation would come next. My voice was low. "What do you mean, Roussi is the worst?"

Pola took a deep breath. "One night near the end of our marriage, after I'd lost the baby, after the stock market crash, when things were very, very bad, Serge was drunk. Blind drunk." There was an anguished look on Pola's face as she relived the experience. "We'd been arguing. It was dreadful. His shouting turned into a laugh. A vicious, cruel laugh. He stood over me, trying to intimidate me, and said, 'Who do you think you are, Pola? *Princess* Mdivani? You are no princess. You were never a princess. Because I am not a prince. We made it all up. Roussi made it up.'"

"What do you mean, made it up?" I said. "Are you certain he told you this? That you didn't dream or imagine it?"

Pola was famous for playing the femme fatale. The tragedienne. How desperately I wanted to hope that all of this was a lie to hurt Serge. I was in a daze. I knew Roussi and the Mdivanis were capable of great exaggeration. But to call themselves royalty when they had not even a sliver of a claim to it, to hold themselves out as that, was diabolical. I pushed away the image of Roussi crawling into the room in Venice while Jojo and I were making love. Wasn't that diabolical?

"I didn't dream it," Pola said.

"Serge was drunk," I said. "Could he have been lying to you?"

"No. I know him. That was the only time he wasn't lying."

She stood and went for a cigarette from a case on a nearby table. She gestured, offering me one. I took it.

"It is shocking to hear, I know," she said, sitting back in her chair. "You must believe me. Roussi deceived you as she did me. You are the only one I tell this to. No one will believe me against Serge. I'm a woman. I'm an actress. And I can't look like I've been taken in. I have to look like a movie star. Admired, not pitied. And there's Serge. All the Mdivanis. They are dangerous. Serge sued a journalist who implied the Mdivanis were lying about their titles. Oh, the outrage Serge is able to muster! How dare anyone question them! But you see, this is what they do. They overpower you. Then they ruin you."

She rested her cigarette in an ashtray, then picked up her glass, swirling the vodka around like an eddy.

"Protect yourself, Misia. I trusted the Mdivanis in part because of you. You are revered in Poland. Everyone knows who you are. Everyone admires you. You are part of the intelligentsia. I told myself, 'Pola, if

Misia Sert is so closely associated with the Mdivanis, with her Russian background, they must be who they say they are.' A woman such as you has standards. You don't let just anyone into your world. I ignored my suspicions in part because of you."

I realized with a sense of horror she was right. I was so single-mindedly intent on staying close to Jojo, on not driving him away, that I inadvertently gave the Mdivanis legitimacy.

"I don't blame you," she said. "I was taken in as well. I am the most despicable of all. I lied, Misia, to the press. I told them I had someone look into the Mdivanis, an expert on Russian aristocracy. I announced I'd verified their claims, that I had no doubt they were royalty. It was printed in newspapers everywhere." She drank the last of her vodka, then set down her glass so hard I was surprised it didn't break.

"You see, Misia, we have created our own monsters."

I'd arrived at Pola's believing the world was one way. I'd left realizing it was quite another. I was up against much more than I could have conceived.

Roussi was dangerous. The Mdivanis were dangerous.

My first thought, back at the hotel, was to wire Jojo, to warn him. But then I imagined Roussi coming upon the message first and reading it, of the possibility that she could destroy it or somehow twist it to make me look the villain. That, she would certainly do.

Pola Negri is an actress, Roussi would say to Jojo. *She makes things up. She's bitter Serge left her. Just as Misia is bitter you left her . . . Spurned wives, both of them.*

I had to be careful. I had to think.

I took the elevator down to the lobby. There was a grand piano there in a far corner. I approached, and with no one nearby, sat and tested the keys. The main part of the lobby was busy with people going about their lives. They paid no attention to me.

My thoughts, dark and swirling, ran a current straight to my hands. What to play? Something turbulent. Something difficult that I could conquer and wrestle to the ground like Roussi herself. Liszt. Yes. That was what I needed. Liszt's *Totentanz*, which meant "Dance of Death" in German. "Danse macabre" in French.

This was one of the most difficult pieces for even the most accomplished to interpret and play. Liszt wrote *Totentanz* as a symphony so that the pianist must create the illusion of a full orchestra. It required strength, endurance, finesse.

I began, the first notes explosions of fury, dark and commanding. Then ominous chords and octaves melded into intricate sequences representing a cast of changing characters, young, old, rich, poor, spinning in revels of doom from which there was no escape. It was true. Death, the equalizer, would come for all, the idea told via Liszt's composition with unpredictable twists, fast waltzes, and somber chorales. My hands slid in glissandos over the keys, my fingers pulsing in fluttering tremolo.

Roussadana Mdivani was nothing. A liar. A pretender. A thief.

I was fortissimo chords, deep and powerful.

I was rapid-fire arpeggios she could never keep up with.

Adrenaline surged through me as I played and played, the piano the one thing I could control. When the piece ended, I sat, breathless, my body tingling with exertion. That was when I heard rustling behind me. I turned, shocked to see a crowd had gathered. There must have been thirty or forty people, nodding, looking at me with expressions of awe on their faces, speaking in low voices.

I hadn't expected this. I rose to leave, and as I did, the onlookers began to clap, slow applause that picked up pace. It was strangely calming. These unknown people nodding and smiling at me with admiration reminded me of who I was, who I'd always been.

I could master Liszt's *Danse macabre*. I could master Roussi.

On the crossing back to France, I told Coco all I'd learned from Pola. We sat out on the ship's deck, woolen blankets covering our legs, the Atlantic spread out before us, gray, heaving iron as far as one could see.

"To think," I said. "I'd once thought that hapless little milkmaid was harmless."

"I never thought she was harmless," Coco said.

In Paris, Roussi was now considered one of the young reigning beauties. The magazines printed her photograph. She wore clothing not just from Chanel but, to Coco's annoyance, all the best couturiers. They wanted to dress her for publicity. Even her apartment, with its modern, soulless decor, had been photographed by magazines.

"Well," Coco went on, "we both knew that whatever their claims to aristocracy, the Mdivanis were low on the pecking order. No one had ever heard of them. The problem is the world would rather be entertained by questionable princes and princesses than bored by real ones. Including us. But Roussi and those brothers. Their self-promotion would be impressive if it wasn't so sinister. What are you going to do, Misia?"

"What can I do? I'm in the same position as Pola. Can't you just hear Roussi? *Why, Misia is simply jealous of our titles, that she doesn't have one too . . . It's so sad that Jojo doesn't love her anymore. It's natural she would tell lies . . .*"

Coco shook her head. "That sounds like her. There's got to be something that can be done."

I pulled the blanket closer. "It's too late. She's attached herself to me, Jojo, even you, like a barnacle on a hull. We are people known for our taste and discernment. If I come out and reveal her lies now, people will question our judgment. We are the arbiters of sophistication and style. Of quality. We *make* people. We don't get deceived by them. Jojo took Roussi in. I took her everywhere. You dressed her. Jojo married her. We gave her legitimacy. We didn't question her claim to a title. Because we didn't, others assumed it was true. Pola said it best. We created our own monster. Now, the monster is out of our control. She's become a personage. She stands on her own."

It was nauseating, truly.

"But what about Jojo?" Coco said. "You have to say something to him."

I took a deep breath. "Tell him his so-called wife isn't a real princess? I can't seem the scorned wife. Roussi will play right into that. I don't know what I'll do. Nothing, right away. I have to be cautious. It will require a great deal of finesse."

◆ ◆ ◆

Late morning the next day, the ship still steaming toward Europe, I joined Coco on her daily laps around the deck. She'd cajoled me into coming. "It will be good for you," she said. Exercise, whether through dance classes, walking around the Bois de Boulogne, or running up hills at Versailles was always her habit.

I begged her to slow to a more leisurely pace as she propelled forward, arms pumping at her sides. "Moving the body clears out the rubbish in the mind," she said.

"And that is what playing piano does for me. As an added bonus, one can sit on a bench while doing so."

"Speaking of piano," Coco said. "That reminds me. Listen, I have an idea. I came up with it last night when I was trying to sleep. It has nothing to do with Jojo and Roussi." She slowed so she was no longer a half step ahead of me. She wanted to make sure I was listening. "I heard you play that day in the hotel lobby. I was there. You were extraordinary. Instead of thinking always of those two, why don't you think of yourself for once? You are better than them. You have talent. Exceptional talent. I saw all those people gathered around the piano as you played. I heard their applause."

"That was nothing. A hotel lobby. A piece Americans aren't used to hearing. They stopped to listen for a moment and now they've forgotten all about it."

"But they stopped. Your playing moved them. If I can't convince you to perform for yourself, you could at least help Marcelle."

"Marcelle?" Marcelle Meyer had been in our circle for years. She played for Stravinsky and others, interpreting their pieces in ways they found divine. She was close with Jean and sometimes played piano with Les Six at the Boeuf. Yet her career as a virtuoso had never ignited. "I'm always willing to help her. But how?"

"You've often said that you don't understand why she has yet to make a name for herself. You should play a concert with her. The two of you, performing onstage. It would make her career."

"You know I don't want to be onstage."

"You're being selfish. Think of it. You, Misia of the Ballets Russes, Misia of Satie and Stravinsky, always behind the curtain but now in front of it. Everyone will come to hear you play. And in the process, they'll hear Marcelle, realize her talent, and voilà, she'll be on her way. All because of you. And it will be good for you to focus on what you love—music. And giving someone a leg up. That's when you're happiest."

"I want the best for Marcelle, but—"

"But what? You help struggling musicians. You launch them. That's what you do. Unlike the Mdivanis, Marcelle is quality. Instead of thinking of Roussi who has nothing to contribute, think of Marcelle, an artist. A woman. Why not put her forward? Is she not as deserving as a man?"

Coco, always so clever. She knew I would hear my father. *A shame she is not a boy . . .*

"You're right. I'll talk to Marcelle when we get back."

"Good," Coco said, picking up her pace again as I bowed out, settling in a nearby recliner. I did want to help Marcelle. And there was more. The feeling of power I'd had at the hotel. I'd moved people, Coco said. Maybe I could move Jojo right out of Roussi's arms. Maybe there, onstage, in front of all of Paris, he would break out of the spell.

◆ ◆ ◆

Marcelle was thrilled with the idea. We began planning, and I was glad to have something to feed my mind rather than deplete it. Soon, after we returned to Paris, the Mdivanis had secured their next victims. Just two weeks after Serge and Pola's divorce was final, Serge married his opera singer, Mary McCormic. Mdivanis certainly had no shame.

Then Louise Astor Van Alen was conquered, she and Alexis marrying in Newport, Rhode Island, and settling in Paris. Roussi wanted Alexis close so she could direct the pillage. In addition to a string of polo ponies, Louise bought an enormous mansion on the Place des États-Unis. It was lit up nearly every night with parties, orchestras, and laughter, a revolving door through which all of Paris entered so Alexis could show off and further the fantasy that he was a true prince.

I was invited to everything because I was part of the plan. It was so obvious now. Misia the Queen of Paris in attendance was further proof of the Mdivanis' standing. I wondered if it was Alexis's idea or Roussi's to stamp a crown motif with his initials on everything. The footmen's brass buttons, the linens, the tableware, the ashtrays, the upholstery, even the pâté.

Only frauds had so much to prove. This was an opening I'd been waiting for with Jojo. At one of these decadent fetes, I asked him to stroll about the home with me so we could take in the decor. Did he see how ostentatious it was? Bought purely to impress?

"Jojo, all of these crowns. They're everywhere!"

"Yes, yes. They certainly are. Well, Alejo doesn't know any better. He's young. Enthusiastic. Like Roussi. Proud of his heritage."

Jojo's reaction annoyed me. He knew as well as I did it was gaudy. Yet he always made excuses for "Alejo."

I didn't let up. "It's as if Alexis is afraid people will forget he's a prince. It reminds me of something odd. When I was in Hollywood, Pola Negri invited me to tea. She told me an interesting story."

"Did she? What was it?"

"She said that once, when Serge was drunk and angry with her, he shouted that he and his family weren't actual Georgian nobility. He laughed, viciously she said, and told her that Roussi had made it all up. 'You, Pola Negri,' he'd said, 'are nothing at all. You are not a princess. Because I am not a prince.'"

Jojo frowned slightly. "How strange. Do you believe Pola Negri was telling the truth?"

I looked him in the eye. "I found her convincing."

He scratched his beard and thought for a moment. "You know, Toscha, Russians, especially when they're drinking, say all sorts of things."

"But Roussi does like to make up stories, doesn't she?"

"Yes, yes. But Roussi's stories . . . they're all fanciful. Fairy tales."

I held his gaze. "Exactly."

I soon realized another motivation for the parties at the mansion on the Place des États-Unis. A young, pretty American named Barbara Hutton was at each one, Roussi at her side. "Poor little rich girl," people called her. A client of Coco's, she was an heiress of the Woolworth's department store through her grandfather and the EF Hutton brokerage company through her father and uncle. It was said her mother committed suicide at the Plaza Hotel when Barbara was five years old. Now, Barbara was worth $48 million. Just twenty years old, she had yet to be married.

"Do you know, Misia," Roussi said to me at one of these dinner parties, "when Barbara Hutton turned eighteen, she gave all of the guests at her debut—a thousand of them!—party favors of unset diamonds?"

"Remarkable," I said, eyeing her. Clearly, Roussi had plans in the works for Miss Hutton.

I noticed Alexis and Barbara were always seated together at the table, their bodies practically touching. It shocked me to see them so near to each other. It shouldn't have. Roussi was always on Barbara's other side, pressing her in, literally, figuratively. It didn't matter that Alexis was taken. It hadn't mattered that Jojo was either.

Déjà vu rippled through me. Everyone saw what was going on. So did Louise Astor Van Alen. Like me, Louise worked to keep up appearances. I understood. I knew her mind as if I were inside it. She was waiting, hoping infatuation would run its course, unaware of the extent of Roussi's maneuverings and greed.

◆　◆　◆

"There's nothing that can be done," Roussi confided to me one day at Fauchon where I'd invited her for tea, the two of us still playing cat and mouse, still keeping an eye on the other under the ruse of friendship. "I adore Louise. But Alexis loves Barbara. And Barbara loves Alexis. It can't be helped. It is only Louise who stands in the way."

Behind that serene smile, those glistening eyes, that effortless gleam of youth, I saw the devil. It was the same speech she'd given me in Berne. How ironic she sat before me eating a box of marzipan roses just as she had there.

"Louise is a lovely girl," Roussi said. "It's just that she's so simple. Alexis is complex. Complicated. He needs more."

"More?" I laughed. I couldn't contain myself. "Alexis needs more polo ponies? More mansions? More rings from Cartier? Another Rolls-Royce? Pola Negri told me that your brothers don't actually have oil interests. That it is all made up."

Roussi seemed to reel slightly from my bluntness. It was satisfying to put her off balance for once. But then she smiled. Her voice was as sweet as the sugar she devoured.

"Pola Negri, as you know, is a liar. She's simply upset that Serge fell out of love with her. As for Alexis and Barbara, when I say 'more,' I mean more of an intellectual challenge, that's all. Barbara is young, but she's had to grow up quickly. She's traveled. She's sophisticated. Like Alexis. Not sheltered, like Louise. Poor Barbara never really had a childhood, always being in the spotlight. She's never just had fun. She does now with Alexis. And me. In fact, darling Misia, I'm afraid I must dash. Alexis and I are taking Barbara to the marionette show at the Champ de Mars. Can you believe she's never been? She'll think it's absolutely hilarious."

She pushed the box of unfinished candies to me.

"I see," I said as Roussi stood and moved for the door. "A campaign of hilarity. But what to do with the current wife? You'll come up with something, I'm sure. You always do."

Roussi stopped for a split second, then went on without turning around.

◆ ◆ ◆

Jojo had just finished constructing a home on the Costa Brava in Spain from the ruins of an ancient building. He called it Mas Juny, a Catalan name, "Mas" for farmhouse, "Juny" for June. Roussi told me they intended to spend summers there where she could swim in the sea. She also made sure to tell me he'd built it as a gift to her.

How wonderful, I wanted to say back. From the fruits of the generous Waldorf-Astoria commission. It was I who had built her this lair.

I soon realized I would never see it. Over time, it became clear she had no intention of inviting me. Coco was invited. Lifar too. They described the house to me as sublime. Jojo had crumbling walls reinforced and repaired, the rusticity lending a charming air, especially as it was paired with tasteful extravagance. He filled the cool, low-ceilinged rooms with modern white sofas, comfortable for lounging. He brought in modern plumbing. Guests and servants dressed informally, wearing espadrilles or going barefoot. People wandered in and out from the beach or the ocean half clothed. There were flowers everywhere. Baskets of fruit. Plates of olives. Buckets of champagne. And for Roussi, animals. Donkeys. A huge dog. A collection of monkeys. I was told she spent most of her day riding about on one of the donkeys or in the sea swimming or paddling in a sports canoe, always active.

Jojo preferred solid ground. He took guests on excursions as he did in Italy, showing them all that Catalonia, of which he was so proud, had to offer. He took them to grape farms, olive farms, to meat curers to taste freshly carved Iberico hams, to stands along the road to sample

Spanish cheeses and little-known restaurants on the beach. The affront of me not being there at his side, as his wife, as his partner and cocreator, drove yet another nail into my hole-riddled heart. Yet that heart, forged now in part with metal, had toughened.

I knew what Roussi was doing. For Jojo, Mas Juny was a project. Something to create. For Roussi, Mas Juny was her marionette show. There, she could control the strings and maneuver people into the places she wanted them.

The first act was Louise.

I wasn't there to see it, but Coco was. She was a guest along with Barbara Hutton. One afternoon, Jojo was to take them to Barcelona for one of his grand tours. Barbara had begged off, claiming she was tired. The cars were waiting when Roussi insisted Coco, Louise, and Lifar go to Barbara's room to try to persuade her one last time to join them. Lifar knocked on the door only to find it wasn't latched. It sprung open to a panoramic view, there in the wilderness, of nature at work. Barbara and Alexis in bed, in flagrante delicto.

Louise ran off in tears. Everyone was embarrassed.

"You mean to tell me you had no idea?" I said to Roussi later.

"I had nothing to do with it. How was I to know they were together? Although to be honest, it didn't shock me. They're in love. Yet Louise refuses to step aside."

And this was Roussi's way of forcing it.

Separately, I brought the affair up with Jojo as the two of us made the rounds of our favorite Paris antique shops, digging for treasure as we used to do. Roussi didn't care for the old, cluttered places Jojo preferred. And she was always busy with Barbara.

"The thing is, Toscha," Jojo said, picking up a small, dark oil painting from a box of dust-covered canvases and studying it, "Alejo is a young man. Impulsive. Like all young men, he sometimes doesn't think. He acts."

Excuses, again. "He doesn't have to think," I said, planting what I hoped was another seed. "Roussi does all the thinking for him. For Alexis and all the Mdivanis."

Jojo turned to me, his eyes probing. "What are you saying, Misia? You don't think Roussi arranged it in some way, do you? No, no. I can't imagine she'd put Alejo in that position."

I wanted to shake him. As he wiped dust from the painting, I wanted to yell at him not to be so naive, to wipe the dust that covered his eyes. It frustrated me that Jojo still didn't see her for who she was. Did he not remember the afternoon in Venice when Roussi had come crawling into our room on all fours? The position she had put us in? At least there had been no spectators.

Strength, I reminded myself. Endurance. Finesse. That was how I got through a difficult piece of music. That was how I would get through this. Eventually Jojo would see. Deep, deep cruelty resided beneath Roussi's lighthearted exterior. She would do anything to get what she wanted, even devise a humiliating public spectacle.

And it worked. Louise had no choice but to agree to a divorce.

Huberich was brought in. He negotiated a generous one-million-dollar settlement from the Van Alens, bartered with a bribe: the Mdivanis would keep quiet about the indiscretion. A little over a year after their marriage, Alexis and Louise were divorced.

Massine, Balanchine, Lifar. They knew how to choreograph a ballet. Roussi knew how to choreograph a scandal.

Chapter Seventeen

Paris, 1932

Coco knew how to choreograph a sale.

"My love of all that glitters," Coco pronounced to a crowd gathered in her Faubourg home for her *Exposition de Bijoux de Diamants*, "is what has inspired this collection."

I'd taken a break from rehearsals with Marcelle to come, Coco's salon filled with press as well as notables there for the long-awaited reveal of her new diamond jewelry collection. The woman who had made fake jewelry fashionable during richer times was promoting diamonds in the midst of a depression. Coco was always a contrarian.

Milling about were Rothschilds. Polignacs. Beaumonts. Mrs. Cole Porter. Lady Juliet Duff. Diplomats like the ambassador to Great Britain. Collectors like the curator of the Louvre and the Musée des Beaux-Arts. Picasso was talking with Jean, who'd written the collection manifesto. Paul Iribe was talking with Jojo. Iribe was a decorator. An illustrator. A man with strong opinions and round, gold-rimmed spectacles. He was Coco's collaborator on the designs. I watched Coco closely, waiting for her to look over at him. When she did, her eyes softened. It had been a long time since I'd seen that.

She was in love again.

Iribe had been in Jojo and my circle years ago, before we knew Coco. It tugged at me to see him with Jojo now, like a glimpse of the past, of lost times. He had been our ambulance driver along with Jean to the Western Front, but we'd lost touch after. Iribe moved to California to work in Hollywood for the director Cecil B. DeMille, where he made a fortune and a name for himself. Iribe did costumes and sets. He drove a Cadillac he named Fifi. He had a Japanese butler. He had a beautiful American wife, an heiress. He had a talent for drawing, decoration, taste. He was the toast of the town, until rumor had it, he became too arrogant, arguing with DeMille.

He was fired. He came back to Paris with his wife and children and his gold-rimmed glasses. He opened a decorative shop on the Faubourg Saint-German, steps away from Coco's apartment. They became friends. And now more. The wife had since moved back to America.

Coco's salon, with its black and ivory Coromandel screens, the floor-to-ceiling antique mirrors, the pink quartz and rock crystals dangling from the chandeliers, all served as the backdrop for the exhibition. To further showcase her diamond pieces, Coco employed old store displays: waxen torsos of poised, posed ladies set on antique pedestals. These eerie creatures, just heads and shoulders in capes and now diamonds, gazed out with mirthful eyes and open smiles, captured forever in frozen delight.

Odd, but I understood. Coco chose these mannequins because they couldn't complain about low wages as the girls at her boutiques did. They couldn't run off with a pendant or a ring in their pocket. No one could run off with anything. There were armed guards with revolvers keeping watch. There were fifty million francs' worth of diamonds in Coco's salon, provided in partnership by the Diamond Corporation Limited of London. The busts wearing the most expensive pieces in the collection were encased in shatterproof vitrine cases.

I would have given fifty million francs to enclose Roussi in one of those cases, trap her inside for good.

Instead, she stood next to me. To the observer, she was stunning. An angular, lissome, iridescent beauty. The former Princess Mdivani.

Now, Mrs. José María Sert. Roussi the style maker. Only a few of us were aware of the rot behind the sheen.

As part of the show, Roussi wore one of Coco's spectacular diamond pieces around her long, smooth neck. It was a comet design, a large star shining on one bare shoulder, its glittering tails falling in a shower of much smaller stars across the other shoulder. Instead of closing at the base of the throat like a typical necklace, this piece was stiffly constructed to open, suggestively, to the chest, in her case, flat and desirably modern.

It was all so fitting.

"How well you wear a falling star," I said to Roussi in a low voice. "A momentary burst of light streaking through a night sky." I took a glass of champagne from a passing waiter. "From afar, comets are stunning, but do you know what scientists say comets are actually made of? Dust and ice."

Her eyelids lowered as she looked at me. She pushed her shoulders back, then nodded to the crescent moon in my hair, crossed at the top with a star, diamonds ablaze. "And look at you, Misia," she said. "Did you know that the moon is old? Scientists say it is very, very old."

Her words that tried to cut, didn't. I'd grown immune to her barbs. That was the blessing of time. Wounds covered over and turned to scars. Skin thickened like a shield so that now I no longer held back from throwing out barbs of my own.

I smiled. "Coco calls the piece I'm wearing *Lune Éternelle*. The moon is eternal. The moon always rises."

Roussi pursed her lips. I let my words sit for a moment before motioning toward Alexis and Barbara Hutton, who stood nearby. They were admiring an exquisite pin, diamonds set in platinum and arranged in the shape of a large, curved feather, light and airy, so that it gave the sensation of movement.

"There's something I don't understand," I said to Roussi. "Maybe you can explain. Serge married Mary McCormic two weeks after his divorce from Pola was final. Alexis's divorce has been final longer than that. What's taking so long?"

"Why, there's no rush," she said in her singsong voice. "He and Barbara are simply enjoying spending time together. As you can see, they're very attached. The attraction is undeniable."

Alexis had a hand on the small of Barbara's back. He leaned in to say something only she could hear, drawing a small, amused laugh from the debutante's pouty lips. He was appealing. More magnetic than his brothers. One might think the picture he presented to the world was really who Alexis was and not the result of Roussi's careful curation. The Cambridge bearing. The aristocratic British deportment and wardrobe. The appealing hint of Russian/Georgian recklessness. The underlying vitality of a polo player who controls large beasts with ease. The slight, tender, melancholic air of a prince with no country.

Roussi's medium wasn't clay. It was flesh and blood. Alexis was her most triumphant work. How carefully she'd sculpted him.

How did Jojo not see that?

But Alexis was still a work in progress. Roussi watched her brother and Barbara intently. That was what she did. Observing every move Alexis made and every reaction from Barbara. Measuring. Calculating. Tweaking. So she could advise Alexis later, temper his rogue instincts. I imagined the conversations. *Barbara was confiding in you, and you looked away, disinterested. You can't do that. Did you not see how she glowed when you were looking into her eyes, pretending to listen to her? Do more of that.*

Just like Roussi, Coco wanted to make a sale. She came up to Alexis and Barbara as they admired the feather pin, her voice projecting so that the reporters in the room would hear and take down the clever lines she and Iribe had crafted in advance to define the collection. "Just because we weren't born with wings," Coco pronounced, "doesn't mean we can't fly."

"Perfectly put," Alexis said, turning to Barbara. "There's no other way to live, is there, darling?"

"Unless you fly too close to the sun," I said in Roussi's ear.

Roussi turned to me and laughed, real merriment in her eyes as if she thought I was hilarious or hysterical. "Oh, Misia. Alexis is no Icarus. He can't fly too close to the sun. He *is* the sun."

She stepped away, moving toward the brother she loved so much. Barbara Hutton gazed at her with bright eyes, probably already considering Roussi a sister, probably already thinking of herself not as the Poor Little Rich Girl, but as the next Princess Mdivani.

◆ ◆ ◆

The night of the piano recital, I wore Coco's Lune Éternelle ornament in my hair.

At the Hotel Continental, from a long line of chauffeured cars, men in top hats and tuxedoes, women in furs and diamonds spilled out. The ballroom's colonnades stretched to the ceiling. The gold walls shimmered. Onstage, our instruments awaited, a pair of white Pleyels face-to-face. Their lids soared open like two enormous wings. The stage near the audience was covered with a bounty of flowers, tributes not yet earned. I was nervous, not accustomed to this side of the lights.

Walking out with Marcelle when the time came, I took my seat at the piano and scanned the crowd, the expectant faces, fearing I may have made a terrible decision. Playing in a drawing room among friends was different from performing in front of a packed ballroom. Here, there was no room for error. The program Marcelle and I had chosen was rigorous. Schumann's *Andante et Variations*. Chopin's *Rondo*. Rachmaninoff's *Valse*. Debussy's *En blanc et noir*. D'Infante's *Danses Andalouses*.

Instead of helping Marcelle, I could ruin her.

And then I saw Roussi in the front row, shoulder to shoulder with Jojo. Everyone saw her with him. The bewitching beauty who had displaced me, tossing her head, smiling, leaning toward Jojo and whispering in his ear. She wore over her white satin evening gown a scarf

I recognized from Lanvin. Draped low on her shoulders, it was made, appropriately, of fox.

I reached for the crescent moon affixed in my hair, touching it as if it had magical powers. Roussi was nothing. Nothing at all. Nothing compared to me. Would Jojo see that tonight? Perhaps there had been more to my agreeing to do this than simply helping Marcelle.

This performance had to be exceptional.

Poulenc stood at my side like a guardian angel, sweetly insisting that he be the one to turn the pages of the sheet music as I played. I remember the once shy, quiet young man who I'd worked with side by side at my piano at the Meurice, whose compositions I'd tweaked then played for Diaghilev and that eventually became the ballet *Les Biches*. As I'd predicted, everyone now knew the name Francois Poulenc.

Lifar beamed at me from the audience, on the edge of his seat, his black hair slicked back, his muscular form evident beneath the fine cloth of his tuxedo. Lifar, the once unknown Ukrainian who I, along with Coco and Picasso, had chosen from a lineup for Diaghilev ten years before. *That little Russian dancer is charming,* I'd said. *That's your dancer,* Coco added. *He has ideal proportions,* said Picasso.

Now, Lifar was here for me. He'd worked with me, teaching me how to bow to the audience with grace.

Jean was in the audience, fluttering about excitedly with an entourage that included the other members of Les Six. I saw Picasso with Olga. There was a large contingent of those who had been part of the Ballets Russes, former dancers, costumers, set designers, musicians. Coco was there, of course, with my old friend Iribe in his round glasses, his wide collar, his bearing of a man who had taste and knew it. There were society friends all in attendance. Political friends. Even British friends who'd come across the Channel. All these warm, familiar faces. This was simply a larger version of my drawing room. My nerves fell away.

Before playing commenced, Poulenc was to give a brief introduction. He welcomed the audience, then to my surprise called on Jojo. He rose from his seat and came onstage, taking a microphone. The audience fell silent as he spoke first of Marcelle, her talent, her promise. Then he began to speak of me.

"It would be a travesty," he said, his back to us, "if all that posterity were to know of Misia is the intense gaze of an anonymous muse captured in paintings on walls in museums and private collections. The muse, her brow furrowed, as she sits at her dressing table. The muse, her lips pursed, her eyes focused, as she sits at her piano in quiet concentration. Nameless. Her history forgotten. Painted by Renoir. Vuillard and Bonnard and Toulouse-Lautrec. But . . ."

His voice suddenly hitched with emotion. What was he going to say? I longed to see his face. I hadn't expected this.

He continued. "My friends, Misia is more than simply a muse. We must also know that she is the very reason these artists are revered today, are known today, are exhibited in the museums and private collections. It is Misia who sees and hears genius when others don't, who took these artists into her world and quelled their doubts and insecurities, who tended to their everyday needs so they could focus on their work, who nurtured their talent as no one else did. Always their fierce defender, she kept them from the clutches and obscurity of poverty. Misia's generosity is not limited to the visual arts. She, with her instinctive ear, takes the time to listen to unproven musicians and composers, to guide them. She has taught them to 'astonish'—Diaghilev's criteria—the impresario who only then saw the genius too."

Could a heart break and be full at the same time? Beneath the piano, my knees trembled. How would I play after this?

"Now, tonight," Jojo continued, "it is us, this fortunate audience, that will be astonished. Why? Because tonight, all of Paris will know that Misia, our Misia, the discoverer of geniuses, is in fact, a genius herself."

I could do nothing but stare at Jojo, stunned he was honoring me in this way, in front of so many people, in front of Roussi, who was trying not to frown and give herself away, that falling star, that comet that would blaze out, I hoped. He turned to me finally, as I sat at the piano, our eyes meeting, his soft yet intense. Proud. I thought I saw sadness in them. Was it regret? Mine were wet with tears.

And then he walked off the stage. He went back to Roussi, that piece of dust and ice, to sit beside her as her husband in the audience. The moment of euphoria was gone, replaced by fervid conflicting emotion. Love. Betrayal.

I nodded to Marcelle, and we began to play, and for me it came out as a torrent. Schumann was right when he said that music was the state of the composer's soul. Chopin and his mazurkas and nocturnes, preludes and études. They were intricate embroideries bloomed from the anguish of his romantic sufferings. It was the state of my soul that bloomed out of me, the anguish of my romantic sufferings. I felt my hands translating over the keys. I lived Schumann's melancholy and exaltation. Chopin's delicate nostalgia. Rachmaninoff's mental breakdowns. Debussy's dreamy rebellions. Infante's complex, frenetic tempos.

We finished, exhausted, exhilarated, and the crowd exploded with applause. Marcelle and I rose and stood together, our grasped hands still trembling from exertion. There were loud cheers and shouting as we received an extended standing ovation.

I looked out at Coco. She nodded to me, her smile broad, her hands clapping furiously. I heard her thoughts. *Revel in it, Misia. Wrap yourself up in it. Let yourself feel adored.*

That was what she'd said she would do if she could play as I did.

Marcelle and I left the stage to insistent calls for an encore. "Come," I said to Marcelle. "We'll play one more."

Instead of walking with me, she took a step back. She smiled graciously. "Misia, don't you hear it? They're chanting your name. You've done enough for me. Now you go out. You play. They want you."

I hesitated, unsure at first, but she nudged me forward. I walked back out, alone. I sat again at the piano. The crowd calmed, and I began to play. What came out was Beethoven's *Bagatelle in C Flat*, the piece Liszt had requested as I sat on his knees when I was seven years old at my grandparents' villa. This time, I played it for myself and for my father, and I hoped that wherever he was, heaven or hell, he heard it. I hoped he heard the applause afterward that didn't die out, that went on and on and on. For me. His *daughter*.

I'd achieved what my father said I couldn't.

I reveled in it. I wrapped myself up in it. I let myself feel adored.

◆ ◆ ◆

Marcelle and I were overwhelmed with requests for additional engagements. We gave one more performance together, just as successful as the first. After that, I had to step away. Instead of launching Marcelle, I feared I was overshadowing her, which was never my intention. All of Paris knew her name and her talent now. I had done what I'd set out to do.

And within it, the unexpected. Jojo. It was sadness I'd seen in his eyes. I was sure of it.

◆ ◆ ◆

I lifted people up. The Mdivanis consumed them.

There were headlines, appalling ones, coming from America. Aimée gathered them for me from the newsstands.

OPERA STAR MARY MCCORMIC SINGS NEW ARIA TO PRINCE SERGE: I WANT A DIVORCE!

GIRL WITH BEE-STUNG LIPS, MAE MURRAY, STINGS BACK, SUES PRINCE DAVID FOR DIVORCE

PRINCESS MARY TELLS ALL: WORLD'S BEST LOVER IS WORLD'S WORST HUSBAND

MAE MURRAY SAYS BEING A PRINCESS WAS SUPPOSED

TO BE HEAVEN BUT BEING MARRIED TO PRINCE
DAVID WAS HELL

Reporters wrote also of Alexis's marriage and abrupt divorce from Louise Astor Van Alen and his current pursuit of the much wealthier twenty-year-old debutante, Barbara Hutton.

They were calling the Mdivani brothers the "Marrying Mdivanis." Now *that* was hilarious.

"The American press loves a story," Roussi said when I confronted her about it. I'd come over early, when I knew she'd still be in bed after a late night going to parties with her friends. Jojo would have been at the studio for hours. She rolled her eyes with her usual insouciant denials. "They don't care if it's true or not. And these silly Hollywood actresses. They make everything up."

How ironic that statement was.

"Mae and Mary. They spend and spend," she continued, "then act as if my brothers are at fault. David and Serge have been more than generous. But they have to protect their assets. Do you know why Serge's bank account is empty? He had the funds transferred to a foreign account so Mae couldn't get her greedy hands on them. Serge has done the same."

"Is that right?" I said in a tone that clearly signaled I didn't believe a word of it.

She ignored my skepticism. "They have to protect the money for themselves and the oil company investors. Well, I don't have time, even a minute for Mae and Mary and their false accusations. They just want attention because their careers are over."

Careers over. Bank accounts emptied.

I saw now why she pursued Barbara Hutton with such intensity. The Mdivanis were out of money.

FEMME FATALE WIVES STICK IT TO 'EM: SAY MDIVANI PRINCES SPENT EVERYTHING ON CARS, HABERDASHERY, AND STICK PINS FROM CARTIER

MAE MURRAY LAWYERS DISCOVER PRINCE PAID
HIMSELF $500 PER MONTH FROM "OIL COMPANY"
MAE FUNDED; MONEY WENT OUT OF HER ACCOUNT
AND INTO HIS

INVESTORS IN MDIVANI BROTHERS' OIL SCHEME
DEMAND ANSWERS: WHERE ARE THE RETURNS?

These oil interests. It was as Pola said. There were none. It was as I'd told Jojo. Would he remember?

And where were Alexis and Barbara? I hadn't seen them out and about lately. When I asked Roussi, her voice rose an octave. Her face took on a heightened animation. Even her wavy blonde hair seemed more dense, more undulating. "Didn't I tell you? They're in Indonesia."

"How interesting," I said. "The Far East."

And deliberate. Far from the sordid revelations in Hollywood. I understood as if I were a devious, manipulating Mdivani myself. Alexis had to lock Barbara in before she saw the headlines and balked. No better place to do it than the opposite end of the world.

Roussi went on. "Barbara loves to travel to exotic places. She's very adventurous. Just like Alexis. They're perfectly suited. She simply adores him."

"All these headlines about the Mdivanis," I said to Jojo as we sipped tinto de verano, his favorite summer aperitif, during Sunday luncheon at a café. "Do they concern you?"

"Absolutamente," he said, leaning forward in his seat. "They are a disgrace. Who are these so-called men putting themselves in a position to be talked about in such a way in the papers?"

"What does Roussi say?"

"I've ordered Roussi not to speak to anyone of David and Serge. Particularly not the press. I can't have their mess reflect on me in any way. I work amongst the highest echelons. The King of Spain is a client!" He stabbed an olive with a toothpick. "This could affect my reputation."

I was relieved he saw this as I did. But there was something else that concerned me. "I fear there's more to it than just your reputation," I said.

"What do you mean, Toscha?"

"Do you remember I told you that Pola said there were no oil investments?"

"Yes, and at the time it seemed unbelievable. Absurd."

"I thought the same at first. But now, it sounds like a scheme. Deliberate. Investors are looking for their returns and David and Serge don't have them. They can't cover their debts." I wanted to bring up more. That Alexis was running through money too. That one-million-dollar settlement from Louise Astor Van Alen could only go so far when he was trying to impress the richest debutante in the world. "I don't mean to be accusatory. I'm just . . . concerned."

"Yes, yes . . . but why are you bringing this up?"

"Is Roussi asking you for money? To help her brothers?"

Jojo shot back in his chair. "No. No. Not at all. And if she did, I would say no. Absolutamente. David and Serge. They are vultures! Vulgar vultures!"

Jojo's voice was full of Spanish machismo, firm when he spoke. But so was the voice in my head. Was he capable of saying no to Roussi?

Even I hadn't been capable of saying no to her. I'd let her have Jojo.

While Roussi was distracted with Alexis, I gave Jojo the time and attention he was lacking. Since the musicale, we saw each other more often. He had a new commission that came in thanks in part to the Waldorf-Astoria grand dining room commission, with its Don Quixote–themed panels, that was such a success they called it the "Sert Room."

Now, because of that success, he'd been hired to paint a mural for 30 Rockefeller Center in New York. The Rockefeller family dismissed Diego Rivera for painting a scene with communist symbolism and chose Jojo as a replacement. Jojo and I discussed themes. I thought of my journey across America, that vast, unending space, where everything was new. We came up with "American Progress," an allegory of images over the nation's three short centuries. Nearly every night, we had dinner out, going to Maxim's as we used to. He told me Roussi said she would join us, but she didn't. Alexis and Barbara were her priority. For Jojo and I, it was like the old days. We drank wine. We laughed. We danced.

"I have fun with you, Toscha," Jojo would say on more than one occasion, and we did.

I didn't like to be aligned with Roussi. But this one time, our interests were the same.

If the Mdivani brothers needed money, Roussi would use whatever wiles she had to get Jojo to back them up. With Barbara Hutton's wealth in the Mdivani family coffers, Jojo's would be secure. I wanted this engagement as much as the Mdivanis did.

I didn't worry for Barbara Hutton as I did for Louise Astor Van Alen. In Barbara, I saw some of myself. A girl without a mother. Resilient. A quick learner. And she wasn't rushing into Alexis's arms. As much as Roussi and Alexis meant to use her, she could be using them. Roussi said she'd never really had fun. If Alexis was anything at all, he was fun.

I asked Roussi to lunch. The two lovers were still in the Far East, Alexis still hiding from the news about his brothers, the Marrying Mdivanis.

"Oh, Misia," Roussi said, beaming as if she hadn't a care. "Alexis had a driver take Barbara and him through Bangkok and you know Alexis, he's so spontaneous. He insisted on stopping at each flower stand they passed. He told her he was going to buy her all the flowers in Bangkok. And he did! He bought all of them out. The whole car was filled with the most exquisite blooms. Every flower in Bangkok for Barbara Hutton!"

"Quite the grand gesture," I said, wondering nervously how much of his divorce settlement from Louise Astor Van Alen that cost him. Maybe the settlement was already spent. Maybe Roussi—through Jojo—was already funding the costly pursuit of Barbara Hutton. And what if it didn't go through?

Roussi continued, her tone still filled with delight. "The next evening, they were out dancing until very early in the morning. Alexis. Barbara. A group of their friends. When the club closed, no one wanted to stop. Alexis hired the whole orchestra there on the spot. He had taxis bring them back to his hotel suite to play. They danced until dawn. Why not?"

Why not, indeed. The Mdivani brothers liked to gamble. Alexis was wagering everything on winning Barbara Hutton.

"And then, early the next day," Roussi said, "Alexis had the droll idea to send one of his men to a market to buy baby ducks—over one hundred of them! Alexis had the staff put them in Barbara's and her friends' bathtubs while they were still sleeping. What a surprise when they woke up, to find their baths drawn, little ducklings paddling about. Isn't that simply hilarious? Barbara was delighted."

"Absolutely comical," I said. These were the idle rich, people who weren't afraid to spend a fortune on trivialities. I'd used Edward's fortune to support Renoir, the Ballets Russes, Proust, Van Gogh, Picasso. Alexis spent money on ducks. On childish antics to please a child heiress. Nothing was spontaneous. Were these his ideas or Roussi's? Either way, they were all perfectly designed to amuse and distract the young Barbara Hutton.

◆ ◆ ◆

Each time Jojo and I dined together, we sat a little bit closer to one another. We reached out more and more with affectionate touches on the hand or arm when making a point. Even after all we'd been through, it felt natural. Our physical chemistry was still there. I recognized that piercing look he gave me at times, eyes hooded, taking me in. It surprised me. He still wanted me. I still appealed to him. With all that had happened, I forgot I could. I'd thought those days were gone. Now, I felt beautiful once again. Enticing. Sensual. At the evenings' end, I would almost forget we were going separate ways and not to our apartment at the Meurice, Mezzo waiting for us amid all of the furnishings and antiquities we'd collected on our travels, the cocoon of our life together.

One spring evening, after another long dinner at Maxim's, instead of calling Alphonse, Jojo walked me to my apartment at the Invalides, tucking my arm in his. The air was gentle, the streets quiet, lanterns flickering like earthen stars. We were in no hurry.

"Toscha," he said quietly as we crossed the river from Right Bank to Left. "Do you ever . . . think of me in an intimate way?"

Of course I did. But how to respond? I didn't want to say yes and give him the satisfaction. I didn't want to say no and lose the possibility that a door might be opening. Just hearing the question from his lips rendered a warmth in my depths. How did he still have such an effect on me?

I tilted my head and smiled.

"Maybe," I said.

He gave a little satisfied nod. I hadn't said no.

"I think of you," he said, turning to look at me. "Often."

We walked quietly after that, something new forged between us.

At my door, his eyes penetrated mine. Mon Dieu, the effect they had on me. "May I come in?" he said, vulnerability in his voice. We stood so close together. Was it my heartbeat thumping in my chest or his? I didn't answer his question immediately.

"It's all right to say no," he said. "After all that's happened, I understand if you do." He started to turn away.

"Yes," I said.

I craved his intimacy. Did he actually desire me when he had the youthful, glimmering Roussi back home?

"You understand me," he'd said. I did. She didn't. That, I realized, meant more to a man than anything.

In my apartment, he didn't hesitate. That was Jojo. He took my face in his hands and kissed me as he hadn't since Roussi had crawled into our room in Venice. I'd missed his kiss. It was enveloping, like being drawn into a special place, dark and sensual, a world of just the two of us, a world I didn't know existed, for me and this man who not only wanted to please me but enjoy me.

"How I've missed you," he said, kissing my breasts after releasing them from my dress. And how I'd missed the familiarity of the scruff of his beard tingling the soft fullness of my flesh. I was no Roussi, with a flat, boyish chest. A flash of anger tried to spoil the physical euphoria. *He left you for her, Misia. He discarded you.*

And now he wanted me.

Roussi wasn't enough for him. She couldn't fulfill him the way I could.

He threw off his tie. He unbuttoned his shirt. The pendant I'd given him so long ago dangled around his neck.

E pericoloso sporgersi.

It is dangerous to lean out.

I touched it. He looked up at me. "I've never taken it off," he said, a hand over his heart. "Never. We are connected, Misia."

I didn't know what would happen after this night, but I knew with certainty I would have no regrets. Jojo was my husband. We'd married in the church. Huberich couldn't void that. A false annulment couldn't either. But for the first time in so long, he was in my arms, and I was in his. He wanted me, and I needed to be wanted.

◆　◆　◆

Jojo came back again the next afternoon and then the next, both of us driven by the exhilaration of our renewed connection. The difficult part was the times in between, when we couldn't see each other because of our obligations. I would wonder when I would see him next. Would I see him again? Or would Roussi find out and try to stop it?

Then he'd phone. Just a few short words. "Can you? Today? I need you."

He needed me. I waited for him at my apartment, having Aimée set out tea, food for after when he was "famished," then sending her off. He arrived. We made love. Eventually, he went back to the home he shared with Roussi.

But we had a secret. A delicious secret. One Roussi didn't know.

Coco didn't either, at first. I was at the rue Cambon, considering my next season's wardrobe when she commented. "You have a new glow. You're slinking around like a cat. What's happened? Wait a minute. You're sleeping with someone. Is that it? Yes, that must be it. Who? You must tell me."

I didn't want her to know. I tried and failed to keep my lips from curving into a little smile.

She put a hand to her head. "Mon Dieu. It's Jojo. Jojo! After everything. Misia, what are you doing?"

"I'm doing something I haven't in a long time. I'm allowing myself some pleasure."

"Oh no, no, no. I'm worried. This cannot be good. I know I told you to take a lover, but I didn't mean Jojo. What is your plan?"

"I have no plan. When it doesn't make me happy, I'll stop. Until then, I'll keep going. All I can do is piece together moments of joy as best I can."

Chapter Eighteen

Paris, 1933

The high jinks in the Orient worked, the campaign of hilarity a success. Barbara Hutton succumbed. Roussi, visiting me at my apartment as if to do a victory lap, showed me the telegram from Alexis.

BANGKOK. APRIL 14, 1933. HAVE WON THE PRIZE. ANNOUNCE BETROTHAL.

"The prize?" I said, eyebrows raised.

"Love," Roussi said, lying with her usual nonchalance and sashaying toward my divan with Poki on her shoulder. "Love is the prize." Her chin was lifted. She wore an expensive suit from Lanvin. So did Poki in miniature version. "Don't be so jaded, Misia."

Love. And forty-eight million American dollars.

Roussi exuded relief. She exhaled it. All of her nervous energy had burst, cascading into a victorious serenity. She was like the bubbles in the coupes of champagne I'd had Aimée pour to celebrate, an endless stream floating up and up, lighter than I'd ever seen her. She sat down and teased the little monkey, nuzzling him, offering him sips from her glass, asking him what he wanted to wear to the wedding. "You know, Poki," she said in a baby voice. "Miss Hutton will insist on having you as an attendant." She turned to me. "Barbara adores my monkeys."

How could Jojo stand it? I smiled with gritted teeth. "Of course she does."

Alexis, Roussi told me, gave Barbara the most exquisite engagement ring, platinum with a black pearl from the China Seas. "Isn't that romantic?" Roussi said. "The place where they declared their love."

That ring. Who paid for it?

The Mdivani-Hutton engagement. I couldn't help but feel relief myself. This wedding had to happen quickly—as all Mdivani brothers' weddings did—before the bride could change her mind.

◆ ◆ ◆

Though I despised him, I was glad when Huberich swooped in. I was glad when he took charge of negotiating a prenuptial agreement, an arrangement insisted upon by Barbara's wary father. *He* had seen the newspaper accounts of the Marrying Mdivanis.

Coco took charge of Barbara's trousseau. I took charge of pulling strings at the Russian Orthodox Church, where Alexis insisted a ceremony fit for a prince be held. I'd arranged for him to be baptized, the only way the high priest would allow it.

The Hutton-Mdivani union was picking up speed, growing momentum squeezing out room for doubts in Barbara's pretty head. Gifts came in by the hour. From Serge Mdivani, gold cuff links for Alexis and a gold vanity case with rubies for Barbara. From David Mdivani, a diamond-encrusted Cartier clock. All of these, I was certain, were carefully chosen by Roussi and paid for on Jojo's account. It sickened me to think of it.

Barbara's father gave her a pearl necklace that once belonged to Marie Antoinette. He gifted Alexis a powerful, top-of-the-line speedboat he christened the *Ali Baba*, a combination of "Alexis" and "Barbara." It was delivered to the Lido in Venice, a future stop along the honeymoon trail. Barbara gave Alexis shirt studs made of pearl from the Far East, a sentimental token. She also gave him a string of Argentinian polo ponies, a required bequest for anyone marrying a Mdivani brother.

When Barbara learned Louise Astor Van Alen had given Alexis a string of polo ponies as a wedding gift as well, Barbara gave him two.

The newspapers now devoted pages to describing Barbara's trousseau of eighty ensembles, the extra suite at the Ritz Barbara had to take for all of the wedding gifts, predictions as to the wedding decor and what type of lace would be used for the bridal gown. In America, some journalists criticized the excess. Yet in a time of scarcity, people loved reading about the dream of a motherless American girl becoming a princess, so much so they ignored the fact that the prince might not really be a prince.

As if to quell any doubts, Alexis ordered a new set of luggage for the honeymoon, seventy trunks and suitcases, all embossed in large script with the Mdivani crown and initials.

Coco and I traveled by limousine to the city hall in Passy for the civil ceremony required by French law. Outside on the street, crowds gathered. Inside the marriage room, along with Mdivani and Hutton family members and close friends, the ceremony proceeded.

Coco had dressed Barbara for the occasion in a demure pearl-gray print dress with matching cape, a picture hat in gray organdy, and a sable stole for her shoulders. In my own Chanel ensemble, I watched from my seat as Barbara and Alexis agreed to be man and wife. Outside in the antechamber, Barbara took a seat in front of several dozen photographers. Alexis stood behind her like a watchman, a hand on the chair back. She picked up a pen. She smiled. And then she signed the marriage contract, flashes from two hundred cameras exploding.

The next day was the religious ceremony.

Inside, the church brimmed with lilies and chrysanthemums in yellow and white, enormous palm fronds, thousands of candles flickering from tall, gilded candelabras. There were eight hundred guests in the finest of formal wear, all of them standing for a full mass because there were no pews.

Alexis had fourteen attendants he called "royal guards." Barbara had only one attendant to hold her train. Roussi's chimps were not present. It was Jojo, who had played the part of Alexis's witness at the civil ceremony, who stood beside him again. Alexis's father, the general as they called him, had passed several months before. Jojo was wisely cast to bring a legitimacy to Alexis his brothers could only corrupt. From my place in the front row, beside Coco and Iribe, I looked at Jojo with a mix of tenderness and fury, thinking of our own wedding years ago, the vows we'd made before a priest that in my heart remained. The proud expression on Jojo's face—he thought of "Alejo" almost as a son—made me feel weak.

How had life turned so completely unrecognizable?

Alexis appeared bored and impatient. Barbara radiated the perfect bridal glow at the altar in an ivory satin gown by Jean Patou that, Coco whispered to me, was ill fitting.

"Patou doesn't understand how to dress a woman with a bosom," Coco said. Beneath the satin top pulled tight across her chest, the two bulges were askew, one high, one low. "That tailoring is a crime."

So was what came next.

When the priest asked if either bride or groom had promised their love to anyone else before, Alexis didn't hesitate. In his deep, swaggering voice, he loudly proclaimed, "No." And just as her settlement money had disappeared from the ledger books, so did Louise Astor Van Alen.

Barbara in this moment didn't flinch. She knew Alexis was lying, everyone did, yet no one snickered or objected or even choked back a laugh. Everyone was too entranced by the pomp and the circumstance, the crowds and the cameras, the fields of flowers, the smell of money, the lure of decadence. And the bold, steadfast brazenness of the Mdivanis, their ease at crossing lines most would never cross to get what they wanted. It was almost to be admired if it weren't so destructive.

And Roussi, there with smug Nina, lackluster Huberich. Roussi beamed pure exaltation, this the consummation of the fairy tales she'd been telling for years. The handsome prince, her younger brother, who deserved everything and now would have it. Alexis was the true golden child. I saw radiating out of them both an unholy confidence that they could do whatever they wanted, the world their playground, so certain their wings were not made of wax.

A few weeks later, a new headline appeared in the papers.

> Prince Mdivani Too Happy to Pay for Church Wedding—
> Barbara Hutton's Husband Said to Ignore Repeated
> Bills for Ceremony

Same story, different prince. He was Barbara's problem now.

Seventy bags and a retinue of attendants, chauffeurs, and secretaries, a Swedish masseuse, a French maid, and an entourage of Barbara's friends all set out on the royal honeymoon to its initial stop, Lake Como. There, Barbara phoned Coco in distress.

Alexis, on the first night of the wedding trip, had told Barbara she was too fat.

What man would say such a thing? What man wouldn't enjoy the voluptuousness of his new wife's figure?

On our honeymoon, Jojo derived unbounded joy in feeding me from his own fingers, morsels of cheeses and meats and pastas. "You must try this, Toscha," he would say, choosing the most delectable piece, describing in the most eloquent of terms the combination of flavors, putting it to my lips, watching me closely for my reaction. Jojo adored my voluptuousness.

And now in the quiet of my apartment from time to time, Jojo and I relived those days with an intimate decadence of our own. Taste. Touch. To him, every part of the female essence was delectable. How my lion roared, and when he did, I thought with deep satisfaction of Roussi, how it was me who brought Jojo such pleasure.

Poor Barbara. Coco, who worshipped at the altar of slenderness, rendered her usual advice when clients asked how to slim down. Three cups of black coffee a day and nothing else until you reach your desired goal. It always did the trick.

I didn't have such fortitude. And to restrict oneself in Italy of all places. What cruel torture. I wondered if Barbara wanted to please Alexis that much.

The Italian tour continued to Venice. As Barbara drank coffee, Alexis tore up and down the Grand Canal in the *Ali Baba*, creating obnoxious wakes and annoying all, Italians, tourists, and especially the vaporetto drivers.

Coco, for publicity, threw an enormous dinner party for them at the Grand Hôtel des Bains. I helped, behind the scenes as always. Iribe was in charge of decor, the exquisite touches. He was a penguin of a man, yet he exuded confidence, swagger. He was proprietary of Coco. I was surprised to see her give way to him, to allow him such influence over her. They lived together. They worked together. Sometimes tempestuous. Other times, easy. I didn't know what would happen between them. He wasn't her usual type. Yet her eyes still softened when she looked at him.

Coco brought in seamstresses to alter the newly slimmed down Princess Mdivani's many ensembles. Roussi was there too, commenting on Barbara's new silhouette beneath her breath.

"You know, Misia, it simply had to be said. Alexis was being kind by telling Barbara she was too fat. Look at her now. So sleek. So slender. It was just baby fat anyway. She's much happier this way."

Barbara did have a different polish about her, but happy? No. Hungry.

From Venice, the wedding party progressed to Florence, then Rome, then Capri. The last stop was Biarritz in September where Alexis, Roussi told me, competed in the Prince of Wales Cup polo competition, leading his team to the championship, naturally. The name he chose for his team? Los Diablos. The Devils.

What a vapid journey. Barbara drinking coffee. Alexis making waves, rocking boats. At least he was entertained. Barbara was so rich even he couldn't spend all of her money. Not in his lifetime. He could never get bored. Which meant the marriage might last.

"Paul asked me to marry him," Coco announced one evening at the Ritz Bar where we met for a late dinner. My heart fell to my feet. It was selfish, but I feared losing my dearest friend.

"I said yes. Are you surprised?" she asked.

"Not that he asked," I said. "But that you accepted."

"Why?"

"I assumed at some point you'd grow tired of him. You don't like to be controlled or told what to do."

She sighed and looked away.

"You're not the beaming bride-to-be," I said.

She turned to me with a shrug. "I'm forty-nine. I know he's not my usual type, but I'm tired. Paul takes care of me. Best of all, he manages parts of my business, the ones that drive me crazy. He makes things easier for me. He's in the same profession. I respect his taste, his eye for luxury, and you know there are very few people in this world I will say that about. We have fun together when we're not fighting." She laughed.

"He has faults, yes. But who doesn't? We're friends. We're lovers. I can rely on him."

"Rely on him? Coco, you have many rules and first among them is to never rely on a man."

When it came to her business, she'd had financial help along the way, but the urge to take care of herself was what drove her. She'd paid Boy Capel back all he'd given her to open her first boutiques. It took time, but she did it. It was a matter of pride. And perhaps fear. Her background was murky. Her father had left her as a young girl, after her mother died. She told people he went to America to make his fortune, leaving her with her aunts. He never came back. What a grave hurt that must have been. She'd learned she could rely only on herself.

Somehow Paul Iribe had pried open the door. He had gone to America to make his fortune. After it went sour, he'd returned to France. Maybe in some crevice of her mind, Coco saw Paul as a kind of redemption. The father figure returned at long last. Maybe that why she listened to him. Whatever it was, she was compromising. Growing soft. That was not like Coco.

"With age, comes reckoning," she said. "I'm lonely, Misia."

My heart splintered. I understood. These last years, I had handed over everything in the faint hope of keeping Jojo's love, even accepting Roussi for him. That to me was better than being alone. I took her hand and squeezed it. "I'm ecstatic for you," I said. "You deserve to be happy. You deserve to rest."

"It's nothing," Roussi said when I asked her about the latest spectacle in the chronicle of the Marrying Mdivanis. "False allegations that will soon be sorted out."

David and Serge had been indicted by a court in Los Angeles. Fourteen counts of grand larceny. The accusation was mismanagement of the so-called oil investments. If convicted, they could go to prison.

Meanwhile, there were bonds and lawyers to pay. David and Serge didn't have money. Nor did Alexis. His money was Barbara's money, and he didn't dare ask her. She'd been the subject of harsh criticism in American newspapers, opinion pieces saying the Mdivanis had developed in her the dangerous trait of extravagance, that she'd become decadent and reckless, like her foreign husband all at a time when Americans were suffering.

Roussi turned to Jojo for money.

"She's making my life miserable," he said to me at luncheon, stabbing olives left and right and popping them in his mouth. He refused to give her the money. The headlines were embarrassing. The divorces were nasty, but this was criminal. He was furious with the Mdivani brothers. "But I will not get involved."

Making him miserable? This was music to my well-tuned ears. An opening.

"What a terrible thing for her to ask of you," I said. "To expect you to pay for her brothers' crimes. You can't be involved in that. You're a man of principle and high ideals. A man working on panels for the League of Nations can't soil his reputation for them."

"Exactamente," he said, piercing the last olive aggressively. "I cannot be dragged down into their mud."

"Certainly not. They're grown men," I said, repeating what he often said about them. "They must take care of themselves. Why would Roussi even ask such a thing of you?"

"She cries and pleads. My only escape is my studio. And you, Toscha."

And me. How happy it made me to hear that. "You're right about this, Jojo. Stand your ground."

"Yes, yes. That is my instinct." He took my hand under the table. "You understand me. You've always understood me. You and only you."

I reveled as always in the sentiment, but one thought upset me. It was not true. I hadn't always understood him. I hadn't told him he was the man of my life as he'd needed. I hadn't even understood myself

287

and how much pride I'd had. I'd handed him over to Roussi. I'd made a mistake of great consequence.

But now it seemed more and more I could fix it.

"Alexis and Barbara, they're so much in love, they're going on a second honeymoon back to the Orient," Roussi said in her false cheery voice.

Second honeymoon? I didn't believe it for a second. The newspapers had revealed that Barbara Hutton Mdivani paid the bonds to release David and Serge Mdivani. Americans were furious, wild with condemnation that her Woolworth inheritance, money from hardworking Americans, was going to men who had fleeced Americans. This trip was an escape, another voyage to the Far East in order to be far, far away from the ugliness the Mdivanis were always conjuring. Barbara was seen in Shanghai wearing a necklace made of luminous jadeite beads with a red ruby art deco clasp fashioned by Cartier. Surely that helped keep ugliness at bay.

At my apartment. At dinner or lunch. I was Jojo's escape. He said so himself.

Barbara and Alexis returned from their "second honeymoon" separately. They were rarely seen together. Barbara spent most of her time in London. Alexis went from Paris to India to play polo with the Maharaja of Kashmir. When summer came, he went to Mas Juny with Roussi.

To my disappointment, Jojo did too.

At La Pausa, I was miserable. I missed Jojo and our renewed connection. What if Roussi was enchanting him again? David's and Serge's indictments had ended on a lesser charge and a small fine. I was relieved they were out of the headlines but infuriated they got away with something once again. I sat outside, distracted, watching Coco and Iribe bat a tennis ball about, Coco complaining he was hitting the ball too hard. In the afternoons, I took walks with Coco through the lavender, Coco still asking me what my plan was with Jojo. I still insisted I didn't have one.

Was Jojo missing me? I told myself he was.

After two weeks, he returned to Paris to work. I went back to Paris too, to our intimate rendezvous.

I was biding my time, that was my plan. Huberich managed divorces in record speed. He could manage one more for Jojo and Roussi.

By August, we were all in Venice for the social season, the Venetian lions everywhere. On door knockers, flags, and bell towers. On the column next to Doge's Palace. In Saint Mark's Square.

And, some afternoons, Jojo in my hotel room. Now we were always sure to turn the lock.

Alexis and Barbara were in Venice too, Alexis careening up and down the canals in the *Ali Baba*, the vaporetto drivers shaking their fists as they nearly capsized in his wake.

"I won't get in that horrid thing," Barbara said one afternoon when Coco and I joined her at an outdoor café table at Florian. "He goes so fast, like a maniac."

Barbara preferred a quieter life. She wrote poems that she kept beside her in a Vuitton suitcase. She read a few of them to us, stanzas of Venetian scenes, rose palaces, drowsy mermaids, of disenchantment and love, "a simple lovely thing" that had turned "ashen, cold, and gray."

To keep Alexis out of her hair and the canals, Barbara told him she wanted to purchase a residence in Venice. She gave him a blank check to buy a palazzo of his choosing. Alexis bounded at the chance, already envisioning Mdivani crowns on doors and gates. He asked Jojo, perfect for the task, to help him find one "suitable for a prince."

Barbara Hutton, the plump debutante from just one year ago, so taken in by Prince Alexis Mdivani, had changed. She had been a child then. Now, she treated him as if he were.

She was tired of him.

Roussi knew it. I noticed Roussi and Alexis drank too much. She ate too little. He was loud. Overly boisterous, surely wondering along with his sister what had happened. It was the Mdivanis who tired of people, not the other way around.

Did Roussi see Jojo was tiring of her?

◆ ◆ ◆

In November, Alexis threw an extravaganza for Barbara's twenty-second birthday, his attempt to win back her favor. He rented out the Ritz in Paris. The theme was "A Street in Casablanca." There was a sit-down dinner for 150, then a ball for two thousand.

Everyone was there. Paris society, English society, notable Americans, European aristocrats. And a Prussian-born Danish count who lived in London, where Barbara had been spending so much of her time. Count Reventlow was tall, athletic, well mannered. He was seated, curiously, at the table of honor, to Barbara's immediate right. The orchestra played. Barbara danced first with Alexis. She danced with a few others. Then she danced with Count Reventlow. Again and again and again until the evening was over. Everyone noticed. Including Alexis, fuming on the sidelines.

Roussi was too busy trying to calm Alexis to notice Jojo danced every dance with me.

Six months later, Barbara traveled from London to Nevada. Roussi had tried to stop her, but Barbara wouldn't listen. In Reno, a quick divorce was followed less than twenty-four hours later by a quick marriage. A new Countess Reventlow was introduced to the world.

Barbara had out-Mdivani-ed the Mdivanis.

The headlines, as usual, were characteristically brutal.

The Prince is Dead. Long Live the Count!

Chapter Nineteen

Paris, 1935

Alexis was untamed. He drank incessantly. He drove too fast. He was arrested in London for disorderly conduct, Huberich sorting that out. In Paris, he bought an expensive apartment near Roussi and Jojo. To console him, Jojo offered to decorate it. Alexis wanted an Indian theme. He hired two Indian men to serve as butler and valet, dressing them in a uniform of silk Indian-style tunics with bright red sashes and turbans. He entertained nightly. Jojo helped him choose the wines and the menus, attempting to teach him to be a man of taste rather than ostentation.

Barbara had given Alexis a few more million dollars, thanks to her desire to expedite the divorce. That sum wouldn't last long. Alexis would tear through it, and when he did, he'd turn to Jojo, who had a soft spot for him but not enough money to support his maharaja lifestyle. I realized with great frustration it could be more difficult than I'd hoped to extricate Jojo from the grip of Alexis and Roussi. Twenty-two-year-old Barbara Hutton had seen through their ways at the speed of light. How was it Jojo didn't?

Roussi seemed shaken by the divorce. For the first time, her charm hadn't worked. At parties, I saw her sniffing Jojo's cocaine and anyone else's. Sometimes, she let her guard down and confessed to me her frustration. "Alexis and Barbara were perfect for each other," or "Barbara always listened to me before." Roussi thought she could control anything. Up until then, she had.

In addition to the few million dollars, Alexis also got the palazzo in Venice.

"Do you remember when Barbara gave him a check and carte blanche to choose a place?" I said to Coco over tea. "When he purchased it, he put the deed in his name alone. It's fourteenth century, the Abbazia di San Gregorio. It's stunning."

"Naturally," Coco said. "Jojo chose it."

"And now that's where Jojo spends all of his time," I said with dismay. He'd left a few weeks before. "Alexis has commissioned him to paint murals on the walls." Jojo's theme, he'd told me, was an "Oriental Mediterranean fantasy." It would feature Cossacks, a nod toward the Mdivanis' origins, in transparent colors over a silver background.

Cossacks? I almost said. *You mean sheepherders.*

I feared Jojo was in retreat, hiding in the fantasy worlds of his frescoes, hiding from making a decision. He sensed what I wanted. Once again, he was caught in the middle, called to make a choice, a man stuck between the Old World and the New.

Just weeks after the divorce, there was a new conquest on Alexis's arm. A beautiful German woman, blonde, tall, and lean, cut from the same mold as Roussi. Coco knew her. She'd dressed her. Maud von Thyssen, Coco said, was a model from the Berlin fashion houses, the twenty-three-year-old wife of Baron Heinrich von Thyssen, an industrialist forty years her senior. How boring that must have been to young Maud. The newly single Prince Alexis Mdivani was anything but boring.

Alexis and Maud became part of the regular crowd at Mas Juny, with people like Salvador and Gala Dalí and Roussi's running-around pal Bettina, third wife of French politician Gaston Bergery. Bettina had been a model in New York and now worked for Coco's rival Elsa Schiaparelli, a rising young Italian fashion designer Coco despised.

Like Roussi, Bettina was tall, blonde, fashionably slim, the two always in search of the hilarious.

"You would be bored at Mas Juny, Misia," Roussi said. "There's no art. No culture. Mas Juny is for those who like the outdoors. Nature."

Roussi's skin was brown, her hair streaked with light. She was still that star. Bright, but burning harder. Still devastated Barbara divorced her darling Alexis and realizing she didn't have all the power she thought she had.

Mdivanis were always late. That was part of the charm. The mystique. People were only early or on time because they weren't happy with where they were. But the Mdivanis were perpetually happy where they were, peeling themselves away from some princely event to head to the next princely event. Only commoners conformed to the strictures of the clock and time. When you were a Mdivani, time was irrelevant.

Alexis indulged himself for too long that afternoon at Mas Juny. This was what I was told later, because of course I wasn't there.

A call came in for Maud, alerting her that her husband the baron was to unexpectedly return to their marital home in Paris. Her absence could lead to suspicions of infidelity. She had to get back before him.

Alexis, in his laissez-faire way, told her not to worry. They would make the train.

I imagined the warm caress of the Spanish sun on bare skin. The easy breeze of the Costa Brava. A little more food. A little more wine. Were the women walking about with bare breasts as the locals, who peered over the walls, claimed? Were there orgies the gossips talked about? I doubted that. Roussi and Bettina and Maud would have been wearing espadrilles and shorts and Roussi would have had a monkey or two on her shoulder or taking one of her larger ones by the hand. The clock, ignored, ticked on, melting as if in a Dalí painting. Fruit softened in the heat. After siesta, cocaine was sniffed to wake up.

Maud and Alexis set off finally in an exciting romantic dash for Figueras, where Maud would catch the night express train to Paris. He drove a gold Rolls-Royce Phantom II Continental that Barbara had custom made for him shortly after their wedding. It was a magical chariot, like the *Ali Baba*, capable in Alexis's deft hands of defying time and space that constricts only mortals. Alexis was not a mortal. He was Icarus, with wings.

Maud must have reveled in the romance of it. Barely making the train, her lover bidding her sweet adieu, breathless as she felt the press of his athletic, rugged body against her slim model frame.

But that would never happen.

Halfway to Figueras, speeding along the narrow country roads climbing the foothills of the Pyrenees, Alexis lost control. The Rolls hit a banana tree. It rolled over several times before landing upside down in a ditch. Villagers heard the shattering, metallic noise. The horrid crunch. They came running out to find a disturbing sight. A woman, blonde, well dressed, except without panties, half naked in the road, gravely injured but alive.

The only noise was the hissing of the fluids in the car. The sighing of the crumpled metal as it settled into ruin.

Was there anyone else? There must have been. They looked to the remnants of the spent vehicle. They sensed someone under it. Villagers worked together as they always do in crisis, young, old, straining to lift the smoking carcass, sighting underneath what they slowly recognized as a person. Golf pants, a blue shirt, white shoes, a pool of blood. Alexis. Nearly decapitated by the windshield, slaughtered by the glass.

Jojo had been in Venice, still painting Cossacks on Alexis's walls, unaware. It was Lifar and Dalí, guests at Mas Juny, who told me the details of the accident, all that they'd heard from the villagers and what they'd both seen firsthand.

I could only imagine when the phone call came, Roussi in disbelief. Then shock when they arrived at the village, and she saw with her own eyes Alexis's body maimed and unmoving atop an old mattress on a donkey cart. He was dead, definitively.

Dalí said Roussi screamed and flung herself on Alexis. She begged those around to fix him, sobbing, crying, soaked in Alexis's blood and running up to people, farmers, their wives, their children, shaking them. "Do something," she cried. "Can't you do something?" She called out for Jojo to fix him, as if Jojo could magically appear.

Maud, in critical condition, had already been taken off to a nearby clinic. Villagers described her face as horribly mutilated. A crushed cheekbone. An eye popped out of its socket. She had lost teeth. Part of her tongue was cut off. The fact that she wore no panties mystified them.

The coroner arrived. It began to rain as he examined the body, everyone motionless, water running over them as if unnoticed. Dalí signed the death certificate. They moved Alexis's body into a nearby chapel. Roussi went too. She refused to leave, Lifar said, spending the night with the corpse, waiting for Jojo to come from Venice. Roussi was certain he could bring Alexis back to life.

The next day, the body was transported to Palamós, the village closest to Mas Juny. Jojo arrived, and they buried Alexis in the cemetery there. It was a small ceremony. My instinct was to go to Spain, to Palamós. In spite of my feelings toward her, I wanted to comfort Roussi. It was a terrible thing to go through. I wanted to help Jojo, but I was told there was no place for me to stay. I would have to find a hotel. Jojo didn't return my messages. He was lost in consoling her and himself. He too had loved Alexis.

I stayed in Paris, in the silence of my apartment. The doctors would medicate Roussi to calm her. I medicated myself, jamming the needle in my thigh.

I felt terrible for thinking of myself at such a time but I did. Jojo wouldn't divorce Roussi now. It would be too cruel.

Tragedy struck again in September, just one month later. Another horrible shock.

Paul Iribe was dead.

It was impossible, but true. Coco's fiancé. The man she was to marry. Coco's maid phoned from La Pausa, crying. "A heart attack," she said.

I left immediately for the Riviera. When I arrived at the house, all was eerily silent. Coco had sent her guests away. She was in her room, alone in the large bed. She wasn't crying, yet I'd never seen her more distraught.

"It's my fault," she said, her voice low and weak. "Paul is dead, and I killed him."

"Coco, you didn't kill him. He had a heart attack."

She shook her head. "No, Misia. I killed him. We were playing tennis. He said he was tired. He wanted to stop. I didn't. 'Just a little longer,' I said. I made him keep playing. He wasn't feeling well, and I pushed him. I didn't listen. And then . . . he collapsed, right there in front of me. I killed him."

There was nothing I could say to soothe her. Coco was alone again. She had finally decided to rely on a man, and he died on her.

I stayed with her at La Pausa through the autumn. She had never left her business to run itself before, but she was too distressed to return to Paris and all that she had to face alone. We had always been stoic companions through the process of absorbing wounds. We didn't cry or moan or wail. We were women who endured.

We took our walks among the lavender and the olive trees, all that were planted at Coco's direction, this paradise she created that was to be a home for her and Bendor, then her and Iribe.

"You will get over this," I said to her.

"I will," she said. "But I'll be bitter to the end of my days. Time and again, fate has decreed I'm unworthy of love. Happiness doesn't exist. It's an illusion."

"You have been loved. Many times. It's marriage that has eluded you. And marriage doesn't always equate to love. Or respectability. Look at me. I've been married three times and no one thinks I'm respectable."

We both laughed at the truth of that.

The blue sea sparkled in the distance like one of her gowns, navy with sequins. Would she go back to Paris? Would she have another collection?

That sea. It held secrets. Mysteries. It held the deep, unfathomable darkness.

Coco was living that darkness. I was too. At night, I helped Coco inject herself with Sedol, a prescription sleeping drug. Then I injected my morphine.

Eventually, as the months passed, the old Coco stirred, that essential part of her that was a survivor. She phoned the rue Cambon. She began giving orders, little by little. Work had always been her cure, and it would be again, even if from afar.

Time slithered on. Over these months, Jojo apprised me of Roussi's state. She was not doing well. I'd written her several times, but she didn't respond. Jojo said it agitated her to hear my name, that his presence agitated her as well.

Why? She had gotten everything she wanted out of us. Because it had turned to tragedy?

Jojo spent most of his time in Paris at his studio to complete the League of Nations commission. Roussi's look-alike friend, Bettina Bergery, stayed with her at Mas Juny. Roussi refused to leave Spain, convinced there was a chance Alexis could magically return in his Rolls-Royce after dropping off Maud, as if it all had been a dream.

Chapter Twenty

Paris, 1936

Coco and I were back in Paris the next March when Jojo phoned me in distress. "Misia," he said. "It's too much."

Serge Mdivani had fallen from his horse during a polo match in Palm Beach. As he landed, the horse kicked him in the head and crushed his skull. He was dead. Louise Astor Van Alen was there. She and Serge had married after his divorce from Mary McCormic. Louise had the distinction of being a Mdivani princess twice over. Now both Alexis and Serge were gone within the span of six months.

I sat at my piano. What was happening? *Danse macabre.* Liszt's composition unfurled in my head. I played a bit, not much. I couldn't. My mind whirled.

I remembered that Pola said Serge didn't know how to play polo, that he could barely sit a horse. That it was all an act. That he wasn't as athletic as Alexis.

I had hoped for so long for the Mdivanis' demise. But not like this.

I tried to reach Roussi. I left messages, but still she didn't return them. She didn't want to talk to me. She was averse to my company.

Two brothers, dead too early.

A family of Icaruses.

◆　◆　◆

Worker strikes were taking over France. In the textile industry. At the department stores. At the hotels in Paris and the Riviera. Just when Coco needed work the most to settle herself, her own employees went on strike.

"Who do they think they are?" Coco said. She complained it wasn't ladylike.

I understood her frustration but had to laugh. "You, who put women in men's sweaters and trousers?"

She half smiled, half scowled. "That's different."

When they locked her out of her own boutique, she railed. "How dare they do this to me?"

I hated to see her agitated, but sometimes she could only see her side. "It's not personal, Coco. It's the economy. They're suffering."

She snapped. "So am I! Whose side are you on?"

"Yours, but—"

"But? If it weren't for me, they'd have no money at all! I've given them a trade, a craft. Have you seen what they're doing? Dancing and playing music inside the showroom, cavorting around as if they're having a grand time. Isn't that a fine thing? It's theft, I tell you! Trespass! They should be locked up! They complain about the hours I have them work, and now they won't leave. It makes no sense. So do you know what I did? I told them—through a negotiator, they won't talk to me— that I will sell them my entire business. If they're so smart, if they know better than me, they can take it over."

"That's your offer?" I said.

"Yes."

"But obviously they don't have money for that, Coco. They barely have money for food."

"As I said, if they're so smart, if they think they know how to run a business in a time like this . . ."

"But Coco. It's outlandish. You know it is. What are you going to do with yourself now?"

"Wait for their answer," she said, crossing her arms in front of her.

It was a standoff. And Coco was not good at waiting. Especially now with the loss of Iribe.

Days passed, and Jean swept in with ideas to keep her busy, knowing activity was her cure and he owed her. He had a new play he was writing. "Coco," he said, "only you can do the costumes." And he had a new friend he'd picked up in an opium den. Panama Al Brown. A flamboyant former world boxing champion, the grandson of an American slave, who drank champagne day and night, now, as a result, down and out. Jean made a compelling presentation, and Coco agreed to finance his comeback.

"A fighter," she said. "I like that. If he puts in the work, I'll support him."

I had an idea to keep her busy as well. Soon it would be a year since Alexis's death, and Roussi still refused to reply to my messages. Jojo said she was still taking the loss hard. The usually energetic Roussi was listless. Seeking vigor, Jojo spent most of his time at his Paris studio, plotting scenes for Rockefeller Center of half-naked, muscular men building skyscrapers, hefting large stones and straddling heavy beams.

What did it mean for me that he wasn't living with her? We spoke nearly every day, but he didn't come to my bedroom. I understood. The idea of it, in the circumstances, felt unseemly.

If I couldn't meddle myself, Coco could do it for me. I suggested she visit Roussi at Mas Juny. Coco sympathized with her. Few knew that Coco had lost two sisters earlier in life to the tuberculosis that also took her mother. Coco understood the grievous hurt of losing those who knew you earliest and knew you best. The person you really were. The secrets you covered up.

Which was exactly what I wanted to know about Roussi.

Coco stayed at Mas Juny for two weeks. When her workers admitted they couldn't come up with the capital to buy her out, she gave them forty-eight hours to leave the premises. They did. She came back and hired new workers. The store reopened. But neither side "won."

"Roussi hardly eats," Coco said when I saw her after she returned. "She can't sleep. She goes to the beach and swims for hours. I watched like an eagle, terrified she'd sink beneath the surface. After all this time, she's still in an awful state."

Roussi doodled on scraps of paper, drawings that were disturbing. Sketches of gallows. Of a priest who looked similar to Jojo hanging from a hangman's noose, a wood fire burning beneath him. I was shocked and surprised to learn Roussi wrote my name here and there too. She wrote "Misia Pisia."

How strange. Jojo in the gallows? Horrifying. Despicable. *Pisia.* A derogatory word in Polish, a vulgar term for "vagina."

"What does all this mean?" I said. "Is the priest Jojo? Why the hangman's noose?"

"I asked but Roussi claimed they were just silly scribblings. Isn't that a thing to say? Morbid is what I would call them. There was one sketch that from what I could tell was of a priest pouring water over her like a baptism, angels crying, a small, ominous winged creature with Jojo's face in a demonical expression flying above like a bat or an insect. She's angry with Jojo, to say the least. She seems to think he should have been able to do something to save Alexis. She's delusional."

She blamed Jojo for not being able to bring Alexis back from the dead? It was fantasy, but that was Roussi and the world she created. Jojo spent a lifetime turning bare walls into epic triumphs and resurrections. But he couldn't resurrect Alexis.

When he first started building Mas Juny, Jojo bought an old Venetian merchant ship with plans to remodel it into a sailing yacht. To date, he'd been so busy with commissions, it sat untouched, docked at Mas Juny.

When there, Coco suggested Roussi urge Jojo to begin the transformation. It would be a way to give her "work," Coco's proven cure-all. Coco told me Roussi roused slightly at the proposition. She went out for a swim. When she returned, it was with an idea. A name. The yacht, she said, would be christened the *Saint Alexis*. If Alexis could not return in the flesh, he could at least be canonized.

Roussi eventually came back to Paris. She would see friends. Go here. Go there. But she never lasted long. Her heart wasn't in it. Did she have a heart? Did any of the Mdivanis? Nina had just divorced Huberich. The man who had facilitated so many divorces in The Hague had facilitated his own. Nina had traded him in for the son of Sir Arthur Conan Doyle and a steady stream of lucrative Sherlock Holmes royalties. David Mdivani needed a new wife. That could keep Roussi busy. She tried to come up with candidates, but her heart wasn't in that either. Besides, it was too late. He was known as one of the Marrying Mdivanis now. He was considered absurd.

Roussi still refused to speak to or see me. Then suddenly, she started calling me very late at night when she was alone. Jojo was away in Geneva, working on the League of Nations installment. She was nonsensical, in a sort of delirium. *Misia, you know how much I loved Alexis. I've lost the only thing I cared about. Why couldn't Jojo do something? Why couldn't he stop it? And you, why couldn't you fix it? You fix everything for everyone. Why not for me? Instead, you called him Icarus. You cursed him. You did!*

I reeled at that. So this was what angered her? I had referred to Alexis as Icarus, but if I had the power to curse anyone, she would have been gone long ago. Surely she realized if I had known it would end as it did for Alexis, I would never have said it. I never meant anyone physical harm.

It was Roussi who came up with the plan that her brothers declare themselves princes. Roussi who encouraged them to believe they were gods, not subject to force and gravity like everyone else.

Once, she laughed, deep and sarcastic. "I've never understood you, Misia. You love Jojo too much. He isn't worth it."

Some nights she was so distraught she begged me to come over when she was home alone, her friends gone, Jojo in Geneva, distracted with his commissions and growing political upheaval in Spain that he worried could lead to civil war. I was the only one left. I went over and saw her for the first time since Alexis's death. She was in bed, a cigarette in her hand. She reeked of vodka. She was thinner than she should be. Her cheekbones sharp. Her eyes sad. All the merriment was gone. The mischievousness. The plotting.

I never thought I'd be sorry to see that.

In its place, she complained and wept. I didn't know this Roussi. Sometimes, familiar parts of her would come out. She told me she loved me. She would always love me. Those rote, manipulative declarations I knew were false. Yet I was torn. She looked so helpless. My natural instinct was to fix. If she was better, Jojo could divorce her. I watched as she would doze off, a cigarette between her fingers, ash dripping to the sheet, burning holes so that I was afraid to leave, afraid she would set her bed and herself on fire.

If she was dead . . .

How I wanted to be rid of her. But that was unthinkable.

She needed to sleep. I of all people understood the medicinal effects of letting time pass in an unconscious state. When she summoned me again, I brought morphine. When she was dozing, I administered the dose. I didn't want her to burn to death. It was for her own safety. I would wait for the drug to take effect, then creep off as the sun began to rise, feeling as if I was in purgatory, somewhere between heaven and hell myself.

Late one night, another telephone call. I expected it to be Roussi summoning me. Instead, it was Jojo from Geneva. "It's gone, Misia. All of it. Burned to the ground."

I thought with horror of Roussi and her cigarettes in bed. "Jojo, what are you saying?"

"Spain, mi amor. I've just received word from Barcelona. The war is in earnest. The socialists set fire to Vic Cathedral. Most of it has burned, my panels engulfed in flames."

"Oh, Jojo."

"I can't blame the people, Toscha. They've suffered from hunger, from false leaders, for too long. They blame the church for their oppression. They're not entirely wrong. They're vandalizing all of them. They're murdering the priests! Franco has come in to brutally seize power from the socialists, to impose dictatorship and force all of Spain under one rule, and they see the church as his ally. There are reports his army is lining up and shooting men and boys in Barcelona just for speaking Catalan." I heard a crack in his voice. "It's unimaginable."

"It's horrific."

I felt his agony through the line. How sadly ironic he called to deliver this message from Geneva where he was installing a mural he'd titled *That Which Unites and Separates Men*.

"I can paint new panels if and when the time comes," he said, "but I thought you should know, Toscha. The panels, they were as much yours as mine. For now, I must figure out what I can do for Spain. For Catalonia."

Roussi couldn't go back to Spain now. If the ghost of Alexis showed up at Mas Juny, she wouldn't be there to greet him.

Coco had confided in me that when she was a young girl, she was so lonely she played in graveyards with her rag dolls. She pretended the people whose names were on the tombstones were her friends. Now, Roussi was her rag doll, the two of them living among the tombs in their minds.

All Roussi had suffered had given her an ethereal appeal, so much so that Coco had her photographed for an advertisement in *Vogue* in a gown covered in mother-of-pearl colored sequins with a matching jacket. Roussi's head was tossed back, her chin lifted. Her hips tilted forward as she leaned against a wall, her stomach flat, almost concave. She appeared to be the peak of elegance, unless you knew that the wall was actually holding her up, her large, forlorn eyes rolled toward the heavens, toward Alexis.

Chapter Twenty-One

La Pausa, 1937

A second year passed since Alexis's death, and Roussi grew worse. Jojo felt powerless. He spent nights at his studio, single-mindedly immersing himself in panels for Rockefeller Center, escaping to the world of American Progress while Roussi was uninterested in making any kind of progress whatsoever and his country fell further into chaos.

All over Europe, socialists and traditionalists battled, complete with riots and assassination attempts. We listened to the radio at La Pausa as the world seemed to be slowly igniting. There were reports from Spain that Adolf Hitler was fortifying Franco's side and testing his new modern war equipment on helpless citizens. In Germany, he passed laws that said Jews were an inferior race, that they were not "real" Germans. It was appalling. My Russian grandmother was of Jewish descent. She was certainly not inferior to anyone. I carried her blood. What would he say about me? Hitler ranted about uniting Austria with its "German motherland." I'd heard he was born there. It was a mystery how such a vile man could come from the same land as Mozart, Schubert, and Strauss.

I feared another war was coming. Coco did as well. She worried about her nephew André, whose health had always been frail. He was just the right age to be called up by the army.

"Now everyone's listening to Winston when no one did before," Coco said. "But it may be too late."

Winston Churchill was Bendor's friend. He'd been ridiculed for years for constantly warning about the evil of Hitler. At Bendor's country house, Coco used to fly-fish with Churchill. She'd had him recently to lunch at her apartment at the Ritz. She said he was like "one of those big dolls with weights in their feet. The harder you knock them down, the quicker they bob up again."

I, like Churchill, had become skeptical of humanity. I spent my life supporting those who wanted only to create. Now, I was seeing firsthand there were those born to destroy.

Because of the civil war, Jojo and Roussi had moved the *Saint Alexis* from Spain to Monte Carlo. From there, Jojo hoped to embark on a Mediterranean cruise that might revive Roussi once and for all.

Coco and I drove down from La Pausa to see the newly refurbished yacht. Among all the exceptional vessels in the marina, the *Saint Alexis* stood out. The yacht was superb, as was anything touched by Jojo. An original. An artist's vision. Who else would keep the patina of the black hull and sets of long, wooden oars, once essential, now decorative? The sails were red, the interior made of fine woods, and the furniture upholstered in a vibrant green. There were four double cabins and luxurious bathrooms with solid silver faucets.

Roussi seemed disengaged from all of it except the crew she'd hand chosen: six young men, the closer the resemblance to Alexis, the better. She had them wear uniforms, white trousers and sweaters with "Saint Alexis" stretched across their chests. She wore the uniform too. "Isn't it hilarious?" she said with strained enthusiasm.

No. It was unsettling. I was shocked by Roussi's appearance and how she'd continued to decline. She was withered, hollow-eyed, sinewy, more bones than flesh. It was as if she and the *Saint Alexis* were caught between two worlds, the living and the dead, an ancient Egyptian funerary boat conveying the deceased into the afterlife. Maybe that was what Roussi was trying to do. Maybe once this cruise was over, she could release Alexis and heal.

Roussi wouldn't leave the yacht. Coco stayed with her on board. Jojo and I went to the Hôtel de Paris for luncheon on the sunny terrace. Those on their way to the casino next door passed through the hotel lobby to touch the knee of the Louis XIV horse statue for good fortune. Jojo sat across from me in his usual white summer suit and sombrero. We drank cocktails, a mix of prosecco with juice from fresh white peaches. Jojo called them "Bellinis" because they reminded him of the pink hues in the fifteenth-century paintings by Venetian Giovanni Bellini. I hoped they would relax him. He was tense.

"It's been two years since the accident, Toscha. Two years! I understand it was a tremendous loss. I am not callous. But still, one must go on. I've done all I can. Anything she wants, I give her. I have built this magnificent yacht. I've spared no expense. Yet she remains indifferent to everything. Indifferent to herself. To life. And she does this to herself. Day after day, she sleeps or sits listless on the deck. I try to coax her to eat. I ask her to drink something other than the vodka. She doesn't listen. She speaks to me only in angry tones. She glares at me as if I am the cause of her misery."

"It's terrible, I know," I said. "She needs someone to blame. She's incapable of believing Alexis could ever be at fault."

"It's delusional."

"It's Roussi. She created a world of delusions all around her."

"Yes. And there is nothing I can do. Nothing. Not if she refuses to try to get better. Meanwhile, Spain is a bloodbath. There are important matters there I need to attend to."

In Spain, more churches were set ablaze. Museums too were threatened. Jojo had determined to use his vast connections to try to rescue the precious art collections at the Prado Museum and the homes of wealthy madrileños, to secretly transport them out of Madrid where battles raged. He knew of places near Barcelona where they could be hidden. If necessary, he could have them moved to Geneva, to the League of Nations. But to accomplish this, he had to use connections on Franco's side.

I was stunned. "But Franco and his generals. They're fascists, Jojo. You said yourself, they're trying to erase Catalonia. How can you be loyal to them?"

"I'm not loyal to them, Toscha. I'm loyal to Velàzquez, to Goya, to El Greco. I can rebuild Vic, but if the works of these great masters are lost, they're lost forever. Their value is incalculable. I have to ensure Franco doesn't bomb the roads as we transport them out. How can I do that if I don't appear to be on his side? If they go to Geneva, I have to make sure they agree that the art still belongs to Spain. I'm fighting for the survival of the Spanish culture. So that when this all ends, there will be some of it that still exists."

He reached across the table and took my hand. "I hope that when the time comes that I can go back to Vic and work again, you'll help me."

"I will," I said, squeezing his hand. "You know I will."

We were the Vic Cathedral. It was what first brought us together. I would never have conceived it could be destroyed. I would never have conceived Jojo and I would divorce. Could we rebuild? That world we knew and thought would last forever, built on dreams of art and creating and expressions of the soul, was slowly being wiped out by those who had no soul.

I knew in the back of her mind, Coco had many fears. Fear for André, her business, France. And she was lonely. Since Iribe's death, she had a new method of coping, turning discussions into monologues on more frivolous subjects that couldn't be stopped.

A recent headline set her off.

Schiaparelli Announces Coco Chanel Dethroned!

During a dinner party at La Pausa, Coco fumed. "That horrid Italian woman! How dare she!"

Jean, "that traitor," had collaborated with Schiap by designing a brooch in the shape of an eye with a pearl as a teardrop. "He's supposed to be helping that boxer I'm supporting," Coco said. "Not working against me by helping my enemy."

Dalí too was collaborating with Schiap. Dalí, who had once made a portrait of his wife, Gala, with a raw lamb chop on each shoulder. Why?

"I love my wife," he said, "and she is raw. I love lamb chops too. Why not?"

It was all nonsense. "Nonsense, I tell you!" Coco said. She raged because she was sad. She was angry. She feared Iribe had been her last chance at happiness.

Coco went on about Schiap's latest evening gown.

"A dinner dress with a lobster on the front? Ridiculous! Dalí, my friend. Thank you for allowing that Italian woman to use your drawing. It's obvious she has no future in fashion with that gimmick. Wouldn't that be a fine thing if we all wore main courses and appetizers on our clothing? That is costume, not fashion. This is what those who are always seeking attention wear. Because otherwise they'll be overlooked—like that plain Italian woman. Gimmicks. She tries to shock to be relevant."

Coco only took a break to inhale from her cigarette.

"Now, Wallis Simpson has herself photographed in that lobster dress for *Vogue*. As if she hasn't shocked the world enough turning a king into a duke. She's another plain woman, I tell you. I suppose she needs to find new ways to shock too."

Dalí told Coco the lobster was sexual. The way it was positioned on the dress below the waist. The long, thick body. The two pincers at the end. "Don't you see it, Coco?"

She dissolved into laughter. "A lobster isn't sexual. A lobster is a lobster. I adore eating lobster. Now I must think of this? Why must you and that breed of Italian have to ruin lobster for everyone?"

The farce of Schiap's designs reminded me with foreboding of the last war, when Jean and Iribe had dressed themselves in absurd costumes as our ambulance drivers. Did the world always unconsciously teeter toward the absurd before all hell broke loose?

"Did you see the photographs of Mrs. Simpson and the duke visiting Hitler in Germany?" I asked the group. The images were in all the papers. "That photograph of Hitler bending over to kiss Mrs. Simpson's hand? It was disgusting. She looked so pleased."

"Another way to shock," Coco said. "I'll tell you what. If we go to war, I'm closing my shop. War isn't a time for fashion."

"Would you really shut down your business?" I said. "It was your practical ideas of fashion that got us all through the last war."

She waved a hand dismissively. "That was different. And no one's afraid to wear jersey anymore. Or rabbit fur. I simply can't imagine putting together two collections a year with bombs going off. The Wertheimers take everything from me anyway."

"But what about your employees, Coco? You would close just when people are desperate to make a living? Especially women?"

"I have a thousand worries, Misia. Right now, I can't take on anyone else's."

Back in Paris, at a forest-themed costume ball, Coco pushed Schiap into a candelabra. "It was an accident," Coco said to me as I chided her, her driver whisking us away from the party. "I stumbled."

Coco had come as a tree. Schiap had come as the Queen of the Ants with long, swinging feelers that had brushed against the flames and caught fire when Coco shoved her. Once Schiap realized, she screamed in terror. I and other onlookers doused her with seltzer water, averting tragedy. Now, it was me scolding Coco and not the other way around. "It was no accident," I said. "What were you thinking?"

She put her head down. "I wasn't thinking at all. I shouldn't have done it, I know, but it just came out of me. All I have left is work, and she's threatening to take that away from me. She's going around telling people I'm finished. She's taking my friends. She's taking my customers. I didn't intend to hurt her. I just, in a moment of passion, wanted her to go away."

I understood wanting someone to go away.

The only thing that quieted Coco was Sedol. Now, she said nothing about my use of morphine. We often took our doses together in the evening, like digestifs.

Coco had changed since I first met her, from the shy dressmaker to the sophisticated couturiere to . . . what next? I worried she would become too hard. Successful in business but not in love, yet being loved was how she judged herself. She was generous to those she cared about, helping Jean through his struggles with opium. Helping Stravinsky and his family when they were in financial distress, sending a regular allowance, giving them a home. Helping the poet Reverdy, whose books she paid publishers to print without him knowing it because she believed in his poems and wanted him to feel successful. All the checks she wrote to Diaghilev and the Ballets Russes. All the funerals she arranged and paid for. But there had always been a selfish side to her. A survivor's instinct. If there was a war with Germany, she told me she intended to survive it. She even mentioned the Wertheimers. That maybe she could get her company back.

"But how?" I asked.

She shook her head, but I could see her mind was working. "I don't know. Maybe there will be a way . . . can we talk about lunatic Schiap? Did you see she claims to have invented a color? Shocking pink, she calls it. It's shocking all right . . ."

She went on talking. I tuned her out, remembering a set of Russian nesting dolls my grandmother had given me when I was young. It fascinated me how one doll opened up to another. Now, I imagined the last one, the smallest one buried inside, as the child, innocent. Then with each hurt, a new doll grew over her, to protect her like a new skin. A girl hurt by her father. And loss after loss after loss.

In Venice, a private gondola Alexis had customized during his marriage to Barbara Hutton sat forgotten against a dock. The Italian government requisitioned it and put it up for auction. It was Roussi who bought it, outbidding a gondolier who wanted to use it as a taxi. Then she took it out in the water, alone.

I didn't see her until the crowds formed on the Piazza di San Marco along the waterway, drawing my attention as I took a stroll. People said a boat had capsized. That there had been a woman steering it alone, her feet unsteady. I made my way to the front just as firemen pulled a bedraggled Roussi out of the water. I recognized the leopard fur coat, one Coco had given to her.

It was a disturbing sight. Roussi was far too weak to take that boat out into the busy canal alone. Afterward, I tried to see her at her hotel, but she wouldn't let me up. Why had she done it? Surely she knew she hadn't the strength. Perhaps she thought to sink beneath the waters in the canal where her brother so notoriously raced the *Ali Baba*. Perhaps she thought that might be the portal back to Alexis.

Instead, she was fished out. It wasn't her time.

Chapter Twenty-Two

Paris, 1938

Three years since Alexis's death, and Roussi was no better. Still feverish, she was wrapped in fur on warm days, shivering beneath. She developed a hoarse cough that was painful to hear. Her once golden blonde hair was thinning and dull. She was only thirty-two. Roussi's natural vitality had been her charm. Now it was gone. The ethereal aura had passed. She'd lost her mask of beauty. Jean said she was a vampire slowly revealing her true self. A person who fed on the essence of others so she could live.

Jojo stubbornly kept his eyes closed to her health. He didn't believe she was ill. He believed it was in her head and she still wasn't trying. Just as he had disappointed her, she had disappointed him. She wasn't lively anymore. She wasn't exciting. Instead of distracting him from his own mortality—the basis of their relationship—she reminded him of it.

All Coco saw in Roussi lately was her mother. Coco was certain it was the consumption—now called tuberculosis—the same illness her mother succumbed to when Coco was eleven. Coco had watched in their drafty, cheap rented room as the overworked, abandoned laundress faded year after year. Coco's father had long before run off. Coco hated talking about her past. But in unguarded moments, she still talked to me.

"I know the sound of that breathing," Coco said with urgency. "I know the timbre of that cough. We have to do something, Misia. I feel like I'm in that room again, eleven years old, alone, watching my mother die."

That dreaded feeling of helplessness. It was an anathema to Coco. She had trained herself to be a survivor out of will and necessity.

"I'll help," I said, "but what can I do? Roussi still rarely speaks to me, and only when she's desperate or out of morphine."

Coco took it upon herself to convince Roussi to see a lung specialist in Paris. Where was Nina? Where was David? Just like Jojo, Roussi's own family ignored her or were in denial as to the seriousness of her condition. That or they were too busy living their own lives to care. They hadn't gone to Alexis's funeral. Nor had they gone to Serge's.

At the specialist, X-rays confirmed what Coco already knew. Advanced tuberculosis.

"She must go to a clinic," Coco told me when as we walked through the Luxembourg Gardens. "They can't cure her, but they can ease her suffering. But she won't. She refuses."

"What if you tell her it's you who needs to go?" I said. "That you don't want to go alone? That was how Roussi convinced me to go with her to Berne all those years ago. Remember? Back when you thought she would push me off a cliff? Well, she did in a way, didn't she? Telling me she and Jojo wanted to marry. What if you told her you've been diagnosed with tuberculosis too?"

Coco nodded. "It could work. She listens to me. I'll tell her I'm taking her to Saint Moritz, she and I, for a holiday. I always go this time of year. You tell Jojo about the diagnosis. He has to face facts. He needs to say goodbye, although we must take care she doesn't know that's what it is. Tell him he'll meet Roussi and me in Saint Moritz. It will be brief, so she doesn't get upset as she always does around him. Later, I'll tell her I need to go to the clinic, it's just a short train ride away, just the two of us. There will be people to watch over her there. To try to make her eat. Help her sleep. Keep her from doing anything dangerous."

Like taking a gondola out by herself in the Grand Canal in rough waters.

Like swimming for hours on end with a high fever.

"They'll make her comfortable," I said.

"As much as they can. It's not a comfortable illness. It's agony, I tell you. Chills. Fever. Night sweats. Coughing up blood. Oh, Misia. It gets everywhere. She doesn't have long, maybe a week or two, but every second is excruciating when you're being consumed by a disease that eats you from the inside out. And you are helpless. Helpless against it."

I didn't like to think of it. Even for Roussi. Even after all of the pain and suffering she and her family had caused. She'd had so much promise. She could have had anything she wanted. And she chose Jojo. She chose to take a man who belonged to someone else. In Berne, as she'd recovered from that cough, when she knew she was soon to make her declaration that she and Jojo were in love, she'd chattered on about her brothers. Now two of them were dead. There was no joy for me in her suffering. The damage was done. The comet had blazed out. Her death would give me no peace. Instead, it compounded an overwhelming sense of futility and loss. When someone takes everything from you, even if in the end they suffer, you've still lost everything.

I asked Jojo to meet me for dinner at Maxim's. Instead of our usual table in the thick of things, I requested a quiet spot in a corner. There, I told him about Roussi's diagnosis.

He was upset. "Tuberculosis? And they say there's no cure?"

"No."

"I don't understand. Roussi was so full of life. Then, these last three years, all she thinks of is death. She's become someone I don't know."

"You never knew her," I said. "None of us did. We still don't."

He thought for a while, a pained expression on his face. "I suppose not. I don't want her to suffer. I never wanted you to suffer. But . . .

here we are. Standing among the ruins. There is one thing, Toscha, one very important thing I've never understood." He paused again, looking down at his hands and then finally up at me again. "If you really loved me, why did you let me go?"

This was a knife in my heart. "Let you go? If you really loved me, you wouldn't have gone."

"But I did love you."

"But you never said it. You wanted her. You did. And I let you have her. *That* was how much I loved you."

"But not enough to tell me I was the man of your life."

"You knew you were."

"And I thought you knew I loved you."

I shook my head. Why was loving someone so hard? Shouldn't it be easy? It was love. This was the human condition, fate making us work against ourselves.

"Oh, Jojo," I said. "What have we done?"

Jojo went to Saint Moritz. Then, Coco and Roussi traveled under false pretenses to the clinic. Roussi was too weak to fight. Coco saw to it that she was settled in, then went back to Saint Moritz ostensibly to ski and spend the Christmas holiday. The truth was she wanted to be nearby because she knew the end was near.

A week later, in Paris, a letter came to me on the clinic's stationery addressed simply to "Misia." It felt like seeing a ghost. The old Roussi.

> Dearest Misia, I wanted the sea to swallow me up.
> I wanted vodka or morphine to stop my heart. None
> of it worked. Now here I am. Trapped in this clinic. I
> think of throwing myself out the window, but I don't
> have the strength. I see Alexis there, on the other side,
> but I can't reach him. Darling Misia, I will tell you one

truth in all of the lies. I went to Jojo's studio because
of you. I wanted to be you. The Queen of Paris. I took
everything from you and look where it got me. Now,
the last person you would want to help implores you.
I'm afraid, Misia, and you always know what to do.
Can you fix this for me? I don't blame you if you want
me to suffer. I would. Your Roussi.

I read it again and again. "Fix" this. The import of the letter was
clear. She didn't want to recover. She wanted to be with Alexis, whom
she believed was there on the "other side." Waiting was suffering.

You could wish a person dead, but that didn't mean you wanted to
have a hand in it. But what if they wanted to die? What if they had a
mortal illness? Would it be wrong to end their suffering, even though it
was something you might benefit from? What if they asked you to do it?

If Jojo had never opened the door to his studio, if Roussi had never
knocked upon it, I would not be faced with this choice. But it was my
fault too. I let her in just as much as Jojo had.

I contemplated what to do for days. I phoned Coco in Saint Moritz
and read Roussi's letter. "We don't have to be helpless," I said. "We can
do what you couldn't do for your mother." I told her my plan. She was
quiet for a moment and then agreed.

"We have to be careful," she said. "Subtle. And Misia, you must
not stay long. You must leave before it's over. No one will suspect me.
But you . . ."

I understood. The next day, I went to Fauchon as if it were any
other day. I bought a tin of marzipan roses.

At home, I took the needle from my kit. I filled it and injected each
rose until my bottle was nearly empty. Then I went to dress. I heard
Coco in my head, how she always said one must be presentable. What
was presentable in a situation like this?

I chose a black velvet Chanel suit with a cinched waist. I was thinner
than I'd ever been. The morphine had its effects on me too over the

years. Beneath the suit, I wore a white silk blouse with a pointed collar and cuffs, softened with delicate embroidery. Then I chose the fur Jojo bought me after I'd given Roussi mine, when she'd gone to America, and I thought she'd never come back.

At the station, I boarded the train, closing my eyes as it hurled forward. I switched lines in Italy, the trains with their same warnings on the windows. E pericoloso sporgersi.

When I arrived in Lausanne, a driver took me to the clinic. Coco was there waiting just outside Roussi's room. She embraced me, then reached for the tin from Fauchon. "You've done your part. I'll do the rest," she said. Together we walked in the room.

Roussi. My god. My first sight of her. I took a step back. I saw death at work, Jean's bees buzzing around her.

The face that had been famous as one of the most beautiful in Paris was now ghastly, ghostly, skin pulled tight as if the skull was already absorbing the flesh. Her hands, unmoving on the coverlet, resembled the feet of a bird, curled and stiff as if they'd been clenched into fists for long periods of time. She was breathing but seemed as if she was no longer there. Coco gently rearranged pillows beneath Roussi's head, then took a seat next to her. In a fur-trimmed coat, Coco had a feral aspect, her dark eyes anxious, her wide mouth set, her hands, as always, capable. Her nails were enameled in glossy blood red. Two matching cuffs with a Maltese cross embraced her thin wrists. She wore a black ribbon in her hair, pulling loose curls away from her face, tied in a bow at the top.

"Are you sure?" I said to Coco, suddenly full of doubt.

She nodded with grim surety. "It's too cruel to let her suffer a minute longer."

Carefully, she took a rose from the tin. She unfurled a petal as if pulling out a seam.

"Darling," she said to Roussi in a soft, coaxing voice as she held the candy between index finger and thumb. "Take this. It will make everything better."

Coco put the petals to Roussi's open lips. Roussi took them in, letting them dissolve in her mouth. When half of them were gone, Coco gave me a look to tell me it was time. I had to leave. My presence there, the spurned wife, could arouse suspicion. I moved toward the door, twisting my gloves in my hands as I took one last look at Roussi, there against the backdrop of the Alps out the window. Their steepled peaks seemed as if from a fairy tale, the kind not with a happy ending. A thick coating of snow, pure and white, disguised the jagged ridges, the perilous slopes, the icy shears beneath, the soft, treacherous, illusory mask of beauty.

Author's Note

Who was Misia Sert, and why had I never heard of her?

Misia Sert first caught my attention when I was researching the life of Coco Chanel's sister, Antoinette Chanel, for my novel *The Chanel Sisters*. I was intrigued by this woman I'd never heard of who swooped in when Coco was suffering after the tragic death of a lover and took Coco under her wing. Coco Chanel had always seemed to me to be a solitary figure, so it surprised me that, as I read more, I realized Coco had not just a friend in Misia but a best friend. This relationship was too tantalizing not to dive into, especially when I learned that Misia was known as the Queen of Paris and was much more famous than Coco when they met. Then, when I read about the strange love triangle with Jojo and Roussi, I knew I had to tell Misia's story.

Misia was never conventional, but her choices when Roussi came on the scene were shocking. She allowed her husband to have a mistress—not uncommon in France at that time—but she helped him marry the mistress in order to try to keep him. Was she delusional? Unhinged? Her actions are difficult for modern readers to understand. They were difficult for people at the time to understand. But it happened, all of it documented, including by Misia herself in her memoir. Cocteau wrote a play about it called *Les Monstres Sacrés* (*Sacred Monsters*) in which Esther, the fictional Misia, says, "It's perfectly normal that extraordinary things happen to me. I'm an exceptional person. Oh, don't think I'm boasting. I mean to say that, unfortunately, I'm exceptional and that, unfortunately, I can't live by the rules. I must make my own." I imagine these words came straight from Misia's mouth.

As part of my research for *Glorious Ruins*, I went to Paris. I visited the stunning Musée Carnavalet, the museum for the city of Paris, where the panels for Jojo's ballroom at the Hotel Wendel are. After taking them in, I went to the museum bookstore, hoping to find materials on Misia. There were books on Proust, Cocteau, Apollinaire, Renoir, Toulouse-Lautrec, and more—yet to my surprise nothing on Misia or even Jojo, who has also faded into obscurity.

The more I researched, the more it seemed that Misia had been erased.

For example, in Jojo's obituary published in the *New York Times*, Misia isn't mentioned. But Roussi and the Mdivanis are—over and over again. It seems outrageous. Was Nina Mdivani the author? Or did she put her second husband, the son of the famed fiction writer Sir Arthur Conan Doyle, up to it?

Even Coco, in a fit of anger, attempted to erase Misia by insisting she leave any mention of Coco, her closest confidante for over twenty years, out of her memoir. Misia was the Queen of Paris, but Coco was Queen of Controlling Her Own Narrative.

If Misia wasn't completely erased, she was diminished or unfairly judged. Many of the biographers of the famous men Misia advised gave her little to no credit. Some intimated—as a few of the famous men had as well—that instead of helping them, Misia only interfered with their genius.

And what of all those hundreds of paintings, drawings, and photographs of Misia? Renoir's most famous portrait of her, titled simply *Misia Sert*, is on display at the National Gallery in London. You can find *À table chez M. et Mme Thadée Natanson* at the Museum of Fine Arts in Houston. This is the portrait in which Toulouse-Lautrec purposely made Misia look like a whore. Others are spread about, with many in private collections or relegated to a museum storage closet, a number on a well-packed box.

Misia's story didn't end with Roussi, though it took another trajectory. The day of Roussi's death, Misia suffered a medical episode that caused her to lose a portion of her eyesight. In her mind, this crisis and the demise of Roussi were connected. The next year, she had a heart attack. Her eye for art and her heart for struggling artists for the first time were failing her. Perhaps they were just worn out.

It is possible that Misia and Jojo remarried after Roussi's death. An article published in a British newspaper in July 1940 announced that they were remarried in Biarritz. One of Coco's best-known biographers and contemporaries, Edmonde Charles-Roux, also stated that they were remarried. According to Misia's biographers, however, they remained divorced. Official or not, the close relationship between Jojo and Misia continued, but although they were still inextricably involved in each other's lives, they would never be as happy as they were before Roussi.

During World War II, Misia was one of the few among her friends who expressed outward disdain for the Nazis and vocally supported the Resistance. Serge Lifar and Jean Cocteau were accused of collaborating. Lifar, who had taken over as Ballet Master of the Paris Opera, openly socialized with Nazi patrons. Jean Cocteau had befriended an official Nazi sculptor as well as continued to put on plays that required Nazi approval in order to be performed.

The person most closely aligned with Misia was Picasso. One of his most famous paintings, *Guernica*, was finished in 1937 during the Spanish Civil War. An anti-war piece, the work depicts the aerial bombing of the civilian population in the Spanish village of Guernica by the Nazis "practicing" for the next war. During the Occupation, Picasso remained in Paris, self-isolating in his studio. He was considered a degenerate artist by the Nazis, who did not permit him to exhibit his work.

The most notorious collaborator was Coco. She stayed true to her word and shut down her business. She took a Nazi officer as a lover. A whole thirteen years her junior, it's possible he "took" her as well as a deliberate Nazi ploy for entry into closed Parisian circles. As she feared, her nephew, André, was called up by the French army and ended up in a German prison camp ill with consumption. Coco used her Nazi connections to eventually get him released. She also hoped to use Nazi laws that prohibited Jews from owning businesses to wrest the Chanel company back from the Wertheimers but was outsmarted when the brothers transferred the business to a relative in America. The brothers' descendants still own the company today.

Though he was strongly anti-German, Jojo maintained ties with Franco's Spanish government during the Occupation. As such, he had access to food and other luxuries those in Paris did not, which he certainly enjoyed himself but also shared with his friends, including Misia. He was able to use his influence with the Spanish embassy to to save Colette's husband, Maurice Goudeket, from a German deportation camp, and according to Misia, to save many others. At Misia's behest, he attempted to rescue Max Jacob, a Jewish poet who had written poems to Misia when she was younger. By the time Sert obtained the release, Jacob had already perished in the Drancy internment camp.

In November 1945, Jojo collapsed and passed away at the age of seventy. He was in Spain, at the Vic Cathedral, still perfecting the panels despite poor health and doctors' warnings. It's there at the cathedral that meant so much to him that he is buried. In her memoir, Misia wrote that "with him disappeared all my reasons to exist."

There is evidence that at least in one way, Misia, who knew no other way than to follow her heart, was ultimately vindicated. I like to think that it was her, from the heavens, who dropped the link to a little newspaper article from 1950 in the search results box of the online archives of the French National Library while I was researching. When I first read the article, I couldn't believe it. According to the reporter, Alexis Mdivani had bequeathed his property to Roussi so that when he died, his remaining fortune from the divorce settlement with Barbara Hutton went to Roussi. Because Roussi died before Jojo and they were married, the Hutton settlement then passed to him. Upon Jojo's death, however, it was determined that Jojo's divorce from Misia was not valid according to Francoist law and that, as she so often asserted, Misia legally remained his only wife. All those times Misia insisted that she and Jojo were still validly married, she had been right all along. And as a consequence, the Hutton settlement Roussi so desperately sought for Alexis came to rest with Misia, who was deemed Jojo's legitimate heir.

By that time, Misia's dependence on morphine had deepened to the extent that she would jab herself with a needle through her skirt at restaurants and other public places, much to Coco's horror. It had also become much harder to obtain. In 1949, French police discovered Misia's name on a drug dealer's list. She was arrested and spent a humiliating night in prison.

On October 15, 1950, at the age of seventy-eight, Misia died in her bed at home. She had had one last request of Coco for after she passed: Make me beautiful again. As Coco had for Diaghilev, she stepped in. She brushed and arranged Misia's hair. She applied touches of color to her cheeks, temples, and lips. She filed and painted her nails. She dressed Misia in white and surrounded her where she lay with an abundance of white flowers. With a straight pin, she secured a pink rose to a ribbon on the front of Misia's gown. Then with more straight pins, she attached the loose skin of Misia's jowls behind her ears. It was said that at her funeral, Misia, the Queen of Paris, appeared once again in all the magnificence that had inspired the great painters.

Acknowledgments

My first thanks goes, as always, to my amazing agent, Kimberley Cameron, who picked me up out of the slush pile years ago. Thanks to her eternal patience and optimism and belief that you should never be afraid to ask for what you want and more, here we are three books later. Cheers!

Many, many thanks to everyone at Lake Union Publishing for taking on this project and making it the best it can be, especially to Ali Castleman for calmly and wisely guiding me through edits and having the vision to see the overall picture, to Carissa Bluestone and Megan McKeever for their very helpful insights and suggestions, and to Danielle Marshall for taking a chance on *Glorious Ruins* in the first place. And for all the people behind the scenes who worked so hard to pull *Glorious Ruins* through the "dogfights" of production and out into the world, my sincerest thank-you to each and every one.

Since *Glorious Ruins* is a story of unwavering friendship through ups and a lot of downs, an enormous hug to the best writers, editors, cheerleaders, therapists, and party-throwers anyone can ask for: Ann Weisgarber, Julie Kemper, Lois Stark, Rachel Gillett, and Laura Calaway. This wouldn't exist without you. I might not either.

And, of course, much appreciation and love to the community of passionate readers, book clubs, Bookstagrammers, and others who have supported my books over the years and invited me into their homes or on their social media. You know where to find me!

Lastly, to my family, Les, Scott, Lindsey, and Olivia, for your love, your immense patience, and just being who you are. As Diaghilev would say, you astonish me.

About the Author

Photo © 2024 Traci Ling

Judithe Little is the *USA Today* bestselling author of *The Chanel Sisters*, an Amazon Editors' Pick, and *Wickwythe Hall*. She grew up surrounded by history in Virginia, where she attended the University of Virginia and the University of Virginia School of Law. She also spent a semester at the Institut Catholique in Paris, France, where she fell in love with everything French. A writer of historical fiction, Judithe has a passion to bring forgotten but significant events or people from the past to light in the hopes of helping understand where we are today.

Printed in Dunstable, United Kingdom